An exceptional, futuristic landmark among colorful, greatly diverse beings of land and sea, human and otherwise. A fight for justice, for the best quality of life through all creation. Action packed with vivid visualizations. Greatly enjoyable.
~ *Andrea Roth, memoir and childrens book author.*

Morphers and Mayhem is an irresistible roller-coaster ride of action and humor. Prepare to love this hell-raising gang of morphers in their no-holds-barred battle to keep earth-hating uber-villain Venamir from destroying all efforts for diplomacy between worlds. Action is your meat and milk.
~ *Cathy McGreevy, fantasy and historical romance writer.*

I have worked with Bert on her wondrous book of fantasy, action, and suspense. Prepare yourself for the ride of a lifetime, or perhaps spacetime, along with the ensuing adventure, and the thrill of the hunt.
~*Tony Marcolongo, Author & Vietnam Vet*

Morphers and Mayhem,

A Werefolk Tale

Morphers and Mayhem
A Werefolk Tale

Berta Davis

Samati Press

Sacramento, California

ISBN-13 — 978-1-949125-30-6 (Print Version)
ISBN-13 — 978-1-949125-31-3 (Digital versions)
ISBN-13 — 978-1-949125-32-0 (Audio version)

Library of Congress Control Number: 2021924561

Front Cover design by Jeff Brown,
of Jeff Brown Graphics

Publisher: Samati Press
Sacramento, California

Manufactured in the United States of America

Table of Contents:

List of Characters and Technology

Notes: Most characters in this century have some piloting skill. It's as common to us as driving a car.

Each person is a land humanoid unless specified otherwise.

Atlean   Most of the protagonist's species are land Atleans, the primary population. Atleans are humanoid, with various earthy tones for skin color. Most can morph to other humanoid forms. Exceptionally skilled Atleans can morph into limited animal shapes with reasonable differences of body mass. All Atleans possess at least some level of empath or telepathic talent. The primary characters have stronger abilities than much of their population. Atleans resemble humanoid elves with feline or canine-like eyes, animalistic stripes or spots, various earthy hues for skin color, and yes, pointy ears.

Atleans have evolved into three primary species: 1: Landwalkers,the most humanoid in appearance. They have pointed ears, eyes similar to canine or feline, and some dragonlike eyes, varying skin tones, and skin stripes or spots on the edges of their face and down their bodies, consistent with fur colors when morphed. Slade and most of his closest allies are from the forest-dwelling Druwen clan. 2: A feline race of Draolith cats. These felines morph little to none, but have exceptional stealth and dexterity. 3: Aquatics or "Merfins" who are water-breathers.

Atlearon   The homeworld of Atleans. Somewhat comparable to Earth except with more water and more vast, ancient forests.

Axehat   Atlean mix, cyborg hitman who works for Venamir.

Birds, Fat Bird and Skinny Bird   Hrokas that resemble seven-foot tall crows. These two have difficult names to pronounce outside their race, thus the nicknames. They are opportunists and their broken speech makes them sound like idiots, but they are intelligent, cunning, scavengers and repairmen.

Berku (Berkiru)   Atlean. Slade's big brother. "Pack leader" aka primary trainer of Druwens. Dresses something like Earth bikers.

Body Shield   A portable force field with a small operator mechanism adapted to clothing. B-Shields can be adapted to bracers, belt buckles, or other pieces of attire.

Caitlin Foster, Ambassador   Full Human, European ambassador rumored to also be nobility, even a princess.

Comm Bracers, or "Bracers"   Serves for communication, can cast limited holographic images, and help protect the wearer.

Coveness   Title of female clan leaders.

Crawshen   Homeworld to the bird people, the Hrokahs. Crawshen in the same star system as Atlearon. Crawshen is famous for their huge trading hubs and multiple species onworld. The Draolith cats and Humans have settlements here, as well as other species.

Comm   Derived from Earth slang for military communication equipment.

Cruentin   Dr. Cruen is Venamir's most long time and closest friend. He's a Deeps Merfin, a highly skilled surgeon who specializes in DNA manipulation, and is infamous for experimentation on different species, usually with high success. A strong telepath and devious and skilled doctor, he is one of few who will challenge Venamir's decisions. Slade and his crew call him "Cretin."

Deeps   A subspecies of aquatic Atleans. The Deeps are known for their reclusiveness, ability to thrive in the ocean depths, and mastery of medicine. Their medical knowledge and expertise surpasses most Atlean medics on land.

Diser   Named for the disdain they cause, Infamous weapon, outlawed in most civilized cultures. Energy rifles capable of melting most surfaces and causing damage over time. Medics are hard pressed to save a person from one mere diser blast.

Dopp or dopps   Slang for doppelganger, clone, or cyborg made in the likeness of another.

Drakir   Equivalent to dragons from Earth. Perhaps the dragons on Earth were from Atleareon. Size ranges from the mass and height of an elk or mythical Griffin, up to three and rarely, four times that size. Drakirs have winged species who tend to live in caverns, and sea species. They have intelligence enough to speak numerous languages.

Draolith Cat   Atlean, feline race who evolved on Atlearon but are more known for colonizing other worlds. Their morphing skills are limited, perhaps because they feel what species is better than cats. The term "feline" is slang for this species.

Druwens   Land walking morphers who primarily guard and care for the forest. They are of Slade's clan and are mostly Atlean. Primary morpher forms are wolf, bear, and some flying beasts. Druwens are know for their battle skills, stealth, and love of nature. They will hunt bounty depending on the crime, and almost always bring their targets in alive.

Elowren   Atlean. Originally on Zared's crew. Science officer and doctor. Morpher forms, panther and draker. Slade's love interest.

Faron   Vanysa's sexy Merfin-landwalker mix bodyguard.

Ferally Station   An outpost run by felines, Draolith cats.

Firgun   Laser gun of Atlean design. Filgean is the inventor. Furgun is a nickname of this gun because it is commonly used by morphers who have furry alternate forms.

Fish   Slang for aquatics people or Merfins.

Fiske and Chippen   Two Deeps Aquatic (Merfin) surgeons who act as Ambassadors between landwalkers and aquatic Atleans. Rhoan nicknamed them "Fish n Chips."

Flocker Casino   Casino on Hrokah, where multi-species trade, gamble, and bet on combat games. Guards are often women. Serica and Delphi work for the local Mayor.

Freak   Freak is a dirty insult to Atleans, a means of ridicule for being morphers or telepaths.

General Barrow   Human, Earth General who works closely with the President McGreffor.

Griffa   Telari's large Atlean cat, size and appearance of a long-haired Bobcat/Puma mix with more vivid coloring. She will defend her owners but is trained in search and rescue. Her breed is Atlean Fiersa, able to detect morphers.

Gus MacCabe   The only full human on Slade's crew, a mechanic and munitions expert.

Herja   Not used much anymore, were common on Atlean starships during times of war. When a crew person is dedicated as the last resort guardian, they are called a Herja, and may go into deep sleep within a guardian chamber which is heavily shielded to scans and psy senses.

Hrokah   Birdlike creatures who resemble birds more than humanoids. Most have nimble hands with clawlike fingers, can speak multiple languages, and can fly. They are allied with Atleans but their alliance has been shaken since Venamir killed their ambassadors in a crucial morpher conference.

Huvster   Any vehicle capable of carrying multiple passengers that can hover over land and water. Some like Scruffy's vehicle, have the option of wheels or all terrain treads.

Jasko   Draolith cat, tall, black and silver-furred feline, more feline than humanoid, with swirly dark blue spots. He works for Slade, is a munitions specialist among other talents, of which he is rather secretive. Jasko does not like Motley, for Motley's mysterious disappearance and personality is shady to him. He has a congenial personality toward friends and humans.

Jetbike or Jetrig   Hover-capable motorcycles. Shocks and his gang's jetbikes are geared for combat.

Kestral   Atlean, tactician and weapons expert of Slade's ship.

Kilter   Fist and cuff weapons, a favorite of Slade's crew. Gloves can be modified to cast lights or thicken around the wrists and knuckles for combat, and other enhancements.

Krizer   Hrokah bird species, owlish features, Mayor of major trading hub on Crawshen.

Leifur   Motley's cub, grey and brown-furred, young Draolith cat, twelve human years old. He is crafty, intelligent, shares his father's talent for computing.

Lizard   Slang for Rezoan, lizard-like people and other amphibious species.

LuvHuv   Joking nickname of Scruffy's versatile land/hover truck.

Lyriad   Wulvur's brother, a more light-hearted spy who engages in combat when he has to but would rather remain a peaceful musician.

Maska   Atlean mixed with who knows what. He is cunning, cowardly, and a competent morpher with forms of humanoid, hyena faced wolfish man, and giant bat. Maska is loyal to Venamir thus far.

Merfin   Atlean water-breathing race, known for reclusiveness and highest skill as doctors. The irony is, they are the best merchant-traders on their homeworld, Atlearon. Merfin eyes are pearlescent. Merfins can morph, but few choose to. They can breathe water or air but prefer the ocean.

Moradin   Atlean who lost her morphing and most of her telepathic abilities when she became cyborg. Part land-walker, part

Merfin, she works for Venamir. She has inner conflicts and debatable loyalty.

Mora-dopp   Replicas of Moradin, infiltrator doppelgangers. They look like her, but quality and capability varies. Mora-dee and Mora-da are two dopps reprogrammed by Gus.

Morph   Alter one's body at will, no moon needed. Advanced morphers like on Slade's crew have three levels of morphing: to another humanoid or human form, to a furred humanoid form similar to a lycrnthrope, and to a full beast with four legs and a tail. Some morphers, rare, can grow wings.

Motley   Draolith cat, talented in computer technology and spying. He is a grey, disheveled, long furred feline who is not hesitant to admit that he is tired of spying and wants to settle with family.

Mushier   Merfin, may be part land Atlean, beast trainer on Crawshen. His nickname is Mushy.

Mutirian Caller   These beautiful creatures are small enough to sit on your shoulder. Normally, they look like tiny mermaids. Venamir has a female hybrid who can fly and swim. A caller's song is similar to a siren's song. She can hypnotize and dull the telepathic abilities of those around her.

Nelzyr   Atlean, Slade's chief surgeon. Nelzyr goes by "Doc" and is one of Slade's confidants. Doc is Rhoan's primary trainer in the skills of medicine.

Noxus   Atlean mix with some reptilian blood, brother of sorts to Axehat, Venamir's top hitman. Noxus is a scumbag. He has the most cybernetic body components of Venamir's crew, is limber despite his enhancements, excels in weaponry, infamous for poison use.

Orion Spaceport   Earth's latest, greatest spaceport near Earth, the first built by humans and their Atlean allies.

Parleigh   Deeps Aquatic Merfin, dark blue skin with spots, Magistrate of the Morpher Council. Decent guy, open-minded to Atleans of land and sea.

Pteram   Merfin scientist and psychiatrist. Loyal to Venamir's cause to put the Deeps in power.

Portal   Nickname for teleportal entry.

Psy   Telepathic activity of transferring imagery or conversation. Psy talk, release one's psy are examples of psy use. Psy can be used by advanced individuals to interrogate or dominate another person's actions whether the recipient is a telepath or not. Rare telepaths can project their voices or hear many people for long distances, such as to nearby ships. To use one's psy is distracting and tiring. The more familiar both parties are with each other, the easier it is to psy.

Raaker, Talen   Hrokah hawklike bird person, Ambassador for his feathery species on Crawshen.

Rezoan   Lizard race, formerly engaged in war against Atlean, now part of a shaky peace agreement.

Rhoan   Atlean and a quarter human. Rhoan is handsome with a boyish grin and quick humor, a young combat medic and fighter pilot. In his early twenties, he can change to humanoid forms but no animal forms, yet. Works for Slade.

Scruffy   Doctor Scrufius prefers to be called Scruffy, as it matches his appearance and demeanor. The crazy professor of the bunch, Scruffy has doctorates in neurobotanical science and botany of near-sentient species of plants. He creates wondrous goos, teas, and other medicinal marvels using plants from Atlearon and surrounding worlds.

Shanto   Atlean and some human. He works for Zared as engineer and spy. He serves as a double agent between the Morpher Council and Slade's crew.

Shocks, Jr   Young John Shockinzo, American biker, aviator, and fighter pilot. He served with Atlean morphers to help initiate Earth colonies on other worlds. John goes by the name "Shocks."

Starship *Jacobyte*   Slade's ship, a prototype with greater stealth than any in the fleet, and infamous "main guns" which are plasma cannons.

Starship *Mythos*   Zared's ship, a sleek sports car of ships compared to the other ships. Zared was primarily a professor and diplomat, until Venamir busted out of prison.

Starship *Sorsia*   Vanysa's ship, small, scout class.

Starship *Spectre*   Venamir used to captain this ship with Slade next in command. It crashed during the war against Rezoans and other species. The Morpher Council was turning it into a museum piece.

Starship *Vernacular*   Scruffy's ship, a bulky, old starship modified from many sources to become a flying tank famous for her survivability in battle.

Starship Graveyard   Where old ships are put as humans would say, "into mothball."

Shocks, Sr   Max Shockinzo, John's dad. Shocks senior goes by Max. He is also prior Earth military.

Stealth Gear   Advanced morpher gear, clothing and often armor that adjusts when a morpher shape-changes.

Steely   Atlean cat, large silvery leopard type of cat rescued from being a guard animal at the prison. He is named for his silver coat and steely eyes.

Submarine ship *Wandering Fortress*   Deeps Atlean submarine, octagonal shape, large and sturdy enough to serve as compact floating landing for small ships.

Tatts   Young son of Shocks Jr, age fourteen, looks older, nicknamed Tatts for his talent in tattoo art.

Telari   Atlean and slight human, spent a decade on Earth with Rhoan, works for Slade, and is a talented mechanic, exotic animal trainer, and fighter pilot. She can morph into a human and is exploring feline forms. Nickname is "Tel."

Telepath   Most Atleans have some level of empathic or telepathic abilities. Many people have minor levels of ability, while some become powerful. Atlean laws against abusing mental powers are strict.

Teleportal Chamber   Atleans and allied species use these platforms and similar technology to teleport people and items. The portals can be used as far as planetside to an orbiting ship.

Thiun   Merfin, more of an alchemist then a medic. He specializes in alchemy of poisons, cures, and body and mind enhancement.

Toybot   Usually small enough to carry a dozen in a pocket, smart combat toys. They are typically fighter planes, land or water animals, and sometimes, weapons.

Vanysa   Atlean Merfin, Ambassador for the Morpher Council. She is a strong telepath, distant niece of Venamir, and competent morpher. She can control drakirs, ("Dragons") from her planet.

Venamir   Deeps Atlean, believes he is the rightful leader of the entire Morpher Council that loosely governs the clans of landwalkers and water-breathers. He is a masterful scientist, good in combat, and one of the council's most powerful telepaths. Formerly a Prime Inquisitor, he was ousted from the councils when he led an uprising to take over and dictate what species could be allowed on Atlearon.

Watchers   Guardians of the drakirs and their young. These people are usually Merfin.

Werefolk   A pun on Earth's werewolves, a term used by Atlean morphers.

Wild Paint Gang   Humans, former flight crews gone into semi-retirement. More known as bikers and tattoo artists who sometimes do vigilante work to protect their colony.

Wulvur   Atlean, Druwen clan, the Morpher Council's best hunter of enemies, Wulvur is of the "Rangers" who are weapon masters and protectors of their people. He can design, modify, and craft weapons, witty prankster. Wulvur has the most forms of the group, from wolfish man, to human, several Atlean landwalker aliases, Earth dog and wolf shapes. He is an Energy Channeler. He can transfer plant life to people to heal them, an exhausting, but virtuous talent.

Wyatt Gray   Human, Earth Ambassador "Lady" Caitlin's bodyguard.

Xerat   Human, defense flight leader on Crawshen, of questionable loyalty.

Yeti, "Junior"   Zared has more sophisticated names, but this stocky humanoid has thick, various types of horns, and resembles a yeti. Adults are nine to ten feet tall. They have their own language.

Zared   Atlean Druwen, morpher, middle aged hunter-spy who is tired of his work. Zared is a natural diplomat and powerful telepath, capable of communicating with large numbers over significant distance. He was quite happy teaching as a professor on Atlearon, and later, Earth.

Zephyr   Search and rescue fighter ship, small, two or four man vessels used by Atleans.

PROLOGUE
We Are Wereworlds

Generations ahead of Earth's technology, the starship *Jacobyte* waited in the refuge of a brand new docking bay. Inside her cockpit, in the comfort of a reclined captain's chair, a pointy-eared humanoid with wolfish eyes set a barely touched glass of wine aside. He activated his personal data pad.

"Captain's Log, Consul Slade, Earth date March first, 2250. We've finally made real progress. First contact with humans was shaky at best. It's been a few decades, but tonight, our first joint space station is about to open. Whew, humans in the galactic community. We weren't expecting them this soon. The councils of Atlearon were almost as reluctant to intake human colonists as humans were to let us aliens live on Earth. I understand their concern. We're shape-changing telepaths. Besides, we were hoping for a few more generations to go by, but the lizards, I mean, Rezoans pushed our hand. The lizards wanted Earth first. Humans make better neighbors than Rezoans."

Slade frowned and sipped his wine. "Venamir nearly destroyed our alliance. Our aquatic people prefer solitude, but we didn't know how badly until their lead diplomat threw a damned uprising. I hope he is the worst challenge our Morpher Council will have to face."

He eyed a flight jacket that laid across the copilot's chair. The patch over the left top pocket bore a patch of two worlds swirled together, with claw marks around the edges. Earth and Atlean, held together by morpher claws.

"So now I'm a diplomat. I rather be schooling cadet Rangers." He chuckled, shaking his head. "I do have a knack for dealing with humans, though. Now if we can keep this alliance going, it'll be good for Earth, and my people, in the long run."

Chapter 1
Nemesis

Nothing thrilled him more than to clench a life in his grip.

Tonight, he would prove that his brethren, the aquatic morphers, would rule again, for he was Venamir, the true heir and leader of his people, the Deepwater Aquatics. None would keep him from his rightful command. From the darkness beneath a regal hood, his pearlescent, yellowish eyes gleamed with spite and deep intelligence.

He strode down a corridor to where a holographic map of Orion Space Station hovered by the wall, with a small image of Earth against a starry background. The heart of the space station pulsated with music, festive with people from Earth, and his world. Humans, Atleans, catlike and other species of humanoids were all celebrating Earth's first truly modern intergalactic hub, one with real artificial gravity. Venamir scowled, knowing that every deck revealed exotic handiwork of his people, Atleans. He fumed at the thought of his world allying with humans, a problem he would solve.

Venamir dismissed the space station noise to the recesses of his mind. The only sounds that mattered to him were the voices of two guards up ahead. He sent his psy adrift, a wisp of his presence, searching. Whispers of other voices drifted through his mind, useless chatter, until he felt a voice. It was all he needed, a glimpse of familiar memories and nervous emotions. He sensed another mind, a naive young man whose daydreams reeked of bravado.

His face a calm mask, Venamir strolled toward two guards blocking the doors to a docking bay. Eying the nonchalant dignitary, they stood at ease.

"Good evening, Magistrate Parleigh," the youth greeted in good cheer.

The older guard's eyes shifted as he glanced around. "Sir, show your badge."

"Now, Maska, you know who I am," Venamir said with a mirthless smile.

Maska began morphing, his face and ears elongated, yellowish teeth formed canine points. His face and body sprouted

18

coarse, mud-colored fur. Clothing and boots adjusted to fit his shape.

Eyes wide, the younger guard jerked his rifle up to fire as Maska knocked it aside and slammed him against the wall.

Venamir focused his psy on the young guard, forcing the man's gun hand to relax. The guard stiffened, his eyes flashed with panic and rage as he tried to move and call for help.

"Aw, Captain," Maska groaned, his ears drooping, "I had him."

Venamir grasped the young human by the collar. "Poor boy, no heroics?"

Maska stood guard while Venamir hypnotized their prey into a deep sleep and then dropped the youth into a comatose heap.

"Resume your human form or Slade will spot you blindfolded."

"He's probably drunk," Maska started. One sharp glance from his captain silenced him, so he morphed into a human guard again. "I'm not Noxus. I don't kill for fun," he grumbled. "Captain, drunk or not, well, Slade's tough. He's of the Druwen clan. They're infamous Rangers, the best combat spies in the Morpher Council."

Venamir waved him off. "I know all about the Druwens. We used to work with them, remember?"

"Humans think he's only a diplomat."

"Pfft, Slade, a diplomat," Venamir sneered. "The Morpher Council must have been desperate to appoint him." He turned and listened to the quiet corridor. The muffled hum of generators whispered to his sharp senses. No other noise, simply a peaceful docking bay up ahead. He muttered into his wrist comm, "Noxus, report. Mind you, no deaths."

Noxus replied in a heated voice, "Station security's down, almost done here."

"Moradin would have been ready by now," Venamir retorted. "Stop toying with them." He heard Noxus snarl amidst scuffling and thuds.

"Command center's ours," Noxus said at length. "The space station's shields are down. Our troops await your order."

"Teleport them onboard. Docking bays locked down?"

"All bays locked except for Slade's. I hope her new stealth mode is as good as the spies bragged," Noxus stated. "There are Atlean fighters patrolling Earth."

"We only need a few minutes," Venamir assured in a lofty voice. "Tell the patrols to hold their fire, or they will taste fire from the *Jacobyte*'s plasma guns, and you will blow up the station."

"Aye, Sir," Noxus said.

Venamir entered the pass codes on a small control panel on the wall. The door slid open, and he strode down a short hall to another heavy door with a small, thick window. One glimpse through the window revealed a large, sleek, winged form inside. He opened the door to a huge docking bay reserved for elites, where she waited.

Venamir's hopes lifted at the sight of her. There she is, my jewel, so winsome. For a swift moment, he forgot all else, his eyes locked upon a sleek starship of cliff grays and ocean blues, the newest prototype from his world. The ship gazed back at him with her shimmering cockpit windows, her wings casting shadows of a predator ready to escape her confines. His heart ached to command this craft once again, and tonight, he would. He recalled that she could house a crew of ten with fair comfort, more if he used the cargo bay. Her original artwork depicted an armored woman painted on the bow. Scrolled out above her flaming spear was the name, *Jacobyte*. Her wings and tail bore the graceful paint scheme of the old Atlean fleet, painted with waves of blue and green with shadowy claw marks for each of her victories. Venamir smirked at her blackened gun turrets capped by red covers, blinded to incoming combat like a hooded falcon.

He murmured, "*Jacobyte*, I will free you from this piteous cage."

Venamir panned his smoldering gaze around the large docking bay. Along the walls and ceiling, robotic eyes made their relentless scans of the area. He noticed one man walking around the aft landing gear, and a second man near the entrance ramp. How convenient, he mused, hiding in the confines of his own sanctuary.

20

Venamir glanced at his hands. His skin was coppery in hue, common for land-walking Atleans. He morphed into a blue-skinned, aquatic man with greenish spots and thick, blue-green hair. His shoes widened to allow for webbed feet. A hooded greatcoat shrouded his face and body profile, and his epaulettes boasted the clout of an Atlean dignitary.

His eyes took on an eerie gleam while he sent out his psy. As a ghost freed from its prison, his consciousness roamed adrift from his mind, leaving his body standing in a dazed state. His psy brushed past the minds of four people, two inside, and two near the ramps. Telepaths inside the ship, strong shields—Slade and that miserable ship's doctor. Venamir's psy returned to his body. He saw a faint distortion around the ship, a translucent barrier that whispered with energy. "The ship's infamous doctor," he fumed.

Maska whispered, "You mean Doc Nelzyr's in there? He helped put you in prison."

"Yes," Venamir muttered. "I'd like to kill him, but even with security down, the life count would drop and every fool onboard this space station would be onto us. Keep to the plan."

A man walked down the *Jacobyte*'s open ramp, carrying a compact laser rifle. He wore segments of Atlean morpher gear over his clothes, typical of Slade's crew of shapeshifters.

Venamir noted the minor setback with amusement as he strolled toward the ship's guard.

Shanto strode up to the shield. "Down with the hood, fellah. Why are you wearing it like that? It's not raining in here."

Venamir smiled a bit. "Good eve, Shanto." He nudged his hood back just enough to reveal his form as an aged blue-haired man, one of the Atlean emissaries. "These infernal lights are so glaring. Why do humans need the light of midday? Are they blind?"

Shanto eyed him, one hand resting on his belt. "Magistrate, we weren't expecting you."

Venamir conjured a friendly voice. "Slade should be at the grand opening. Is he not our Consul? Tis not every year our people build a space station with humans."

"Times are changing."

Venamir kept a smooth mask. "Pity," he replied, "our councils not letting humans evolve further." He smiled at Shanto's perceptive frown. "Go fetch Slade."

"They're workaholics," Shanto drawled. "They'll be along. Say, where are your bodyguards?"

"Are we not among friends? Besides, Elowren sent me. How could I disappoint a member of the elite High Council?" Venamir's tone darkened with the last few words. He sensed Shanto's mental shields reinforce, reminding him of primitive warriors barring the castle doors and knew something he said gave him away. No matter. His eyes turned serpentine, glowing with a surge of energy as he focused on his prey. "This is urgent, so drop the force field."

Shanto leveled the rifle at the intruder. "Stand down! Where's the real magistrate? Slade!"

Venamir locked gazes with him. Shanto stiffened, hands shaking as he tried to reclaim control over his body. He flinched, startled when Venamir's voice dominated his mind and forced his unwilling hands to lower the rifle.

"He can't hear you," Venamir said with clear scorn. "Alas, your comms are being jammed. I remember you, Shanto, a human hybrid chump. Be a good mutt and lower the energy shield." Venamir's mind linked with his as a shark would snatch bloody prey.

Ghostly shapes and subdued colors replaced Shanto's field of sight, the beginning of mental combat where only wit and telepathic barriers could protect him. A virtual fortress formed inside Shanto's mind, protecting his thoughts and memories with formidable defenses, much like ancient strongholds.

Venamir's psy lurked around the fortress, creating nightmarish creatures within his target's mind. He found a few tiny weaknesses in Shanto's thoughts, then a few more, and more. Within seconds, Shanto's psychic fortress crumbled, leaving both telepaths facing each other as dreamlike images surrounded by illusions of reality.

Venamir's tyrannical voice chortled within their minds, "Is this your best psychic defense, an imaginary castle?"

Shanto grimaced from shock as his body obeyed commands of a stronger mind, forcing him to tap the controls at his belt. A hole formed in the energy shield between their physical bodies. Venamir stepped inside the barrier, his greatcoat barely missing the edges of the high-powered shield. Wisps of smoke curled from the hem of his coat, and then dispersed. The protective shield dissipated, leaving the ship vulnerable.

Hands shaking, Shanto surrendered his rifle. He panted with exertion against an irresistible control, and could only stand there, every attempt to move sending jolts of pain through his rebellious mind. His attempts to use telepathy to warn his friends failed because he couldn't reach their minds. He tried again, "Slade!" No luck.

Venamir kept the psy-link while grabbing the rifle and cracking the handle across the vanquished guard's head. Shanto dropped to his knees, dazed. Realizing he and his prey were not alone, Venamir kept one hand on the back of Shanto's combat vest as he found Gus, the other guard's mind, the mind of a human full of primal anger. "A full human? What are you, their mascot?"

Gus snuck around the ship and aimed his rifle at Venamir's head. "Get your meat hooks off 'im." He tried to fire, but his hands couldn't obey.

Venamir's psy engulfed the guard's senses with a dizzying intensity, his seething voice speaking over the human's thoughts, "Trying to shoot me, human?"

Gus tried to shoot again, but his hands refused to work. His mind fogged over, as if he were falling into a dream. Gus struggled to shield his mind, picturing himself in a war game where he was invulnerable. It worked, but only for a few seconds. He raised his weapon to aim when he heard Venamir's snide, mocking voice in his head again. "Oh, you can shield your mind. Not bad. You like war games? Good. Meet Maska."

Gus heard a low snarl behind him and felt a crushing force slam into his kidneys, stunning him even through his riot gear. He turned, starting a grappling match with Maska.

Maska morphed into his hyena-like shape, growling and baring his yellowish teeth at the wide-eyed human. He slashed with his claws and sank his teeth into Gus's gun arm. Maska started to morph into a tall, batlike creature. He buffeted Gus with his wings as they grappled. Pulling his teeth free, Maska knocked out his hardheaded prey. He stole Gus's weapon, then reverted to his normal, half-Merfin form. "Happy nightmares, little caveman."

Freed by the distraction, Shanto snatched the fallen rifle and slammed his foe against the wall.

Venamir's psy bored into Shanto's mind. Memories, random thoughts, useless, chaotic tidbits swept through his mind like phantoms until the maze of images and whispers from Shanto's recent memories revealed what Venamir needed. "Captain's onboard. Crew's on shore leave. Guardian program on standby. Oh, they have a Herja program. Sleep, Shanto. Dream of war."

Despite his fury and experience in telepathic combat, Shanto slumped to the floor in an unconscious heap.

Venamir turned away, sighing, "Am I the only intelligent species left?"

Maska plodded over, staying very close to the ship as he dragged Gus along. He took Shanto by the collar in his spare hand.

"Leave Slade to me," Venamir ordered. "Put our captives in Slade's flyer so they can't escape. He should have a shuttle in the lower bay." He withdrew a small orb-shaped cage from a deep coat pocket. "Earplugs in, I can resist her."

Maska dropped his inert baggage where he stood, grinning when the limp bodies thumped against the deck. He stuffed earplugs into his ears.

Venamir moved up the secluded ramp. Shadows crawled over his body as he passed amber lights until he halted, eyes glinting as he felt the presence of his primary target on the upper deck. Once past the ramp's peak, Venamir located a computer access port on the wall and pressed a pair of data chips from his pocket against Shanto's ID cards. The data chips molded to the ID cards, which Venamir held up. "Herja, pass code Spectral drakir. Scan me."

A few long seconds passed before the ship's computer emitted a hologram of Venamir in his authentic form, a Merfin with green skin and yellow eyes, dressed in regal attire. A computerized voice greeted him, "Welcome, Grand Inquisitor Venamir."

Chapter 2
Grand Opening

Orion Space Station sizzled with activity. Humans and their closest allied species congregated throughout the day to explore Earth's most advanced space station—one with real artificial gravity. At last, humans joined other galactic space travelers.

News stories lit up along walls of bars and lounges, where many humans looked at holograms of Atleans and tidbits about the race. Humans debated and joked over space alien theories.

"They've been here for centuries," an elegant lady told her bodyguard. "The Atleans have only been visible for a couple decades."

Her bodyguard nodded. "They look like elves to me. Trouble is, we still don't know much about them, except they build a good space station."

"Oh, there's that Drao cat. I hear their fur changes color, but they don't morph. His name's Jaskuro." She waved. "Jasko, over here!"

A tall, upright feline strolled up to them. The catman's coat was thick and dark, midnight blue in the light, with swirly, lighter silver and blue spots. "Hello, Lady Caitlin. Nice to meet you in person. Yeah, we call them elves."

He extended a pawlike hand toward her friend. "Bodyguard, yes?"

Wyatt shook his paw. "Wyatt Gray. You're perceptive."

Caitlin petted his paw. "I was telling Wyatt you're a Draolith cat. My children want one."

The feline chuckled. "Human cubs are cute too." He gestured to the pointy-eared Atleans nearby. "Have your cubs ask the 'elves' over there if they make toys?"

"They've asked, but no luck." She dug her comm out of a satchel. "Can we get a selfie?"

"Sure." Jasko grinned.

Caitlin beckoned some of her reluctant friends over. Her bodyguard stayed close to her, smirking.

Jasko posed with pizazz for pictures, a scary sight with his large, sharp, white teeth and menacing claws. His demeanor sent comforting vibes to those nearby, earning the nickname of overgrown lap cat. He ended up answering their questions about other races.

"My people evolved on Atlearon," Jasko explained. "So did fish and werefolk." As he rambled, he watched the crowd, ever vigilant for trouble. "Lizards are from Rezzo and birds are from Crawshen. The land tribes, werefolk, they're more open to other species than Merfins are, I mean aquatic folk."

"What do you really look like?" Caitlin said.

"We cats don't morph. Why mess up a sexy body?" Jasko gestured toward his Atlean friends. Most humans didn't notice, but their attire revealed discreet signs of being pieced together, typical of clothes worn by shape-changers. "Professor Zared taught Atlean history on Earth, and Scruffy taught plant medicine. The lady in the slinky dress, well, you've met her. She's a doctor and scientist."

"Yes, Ambassador Elowren," Caitlin nodded. "She's been most helpful. Who's the young Atlean man wearing the medic's emblems?"

Jasko chuckled, making her blush. "You like him? That's Rhoan. He's a combat rescue medic. The gal with him is Telari, Scruffy's mechanic."

Rhoan easily drew attention of women, with his almost human-like hair of deep umber, a quick, handsome grin and strong physique. He wore a medical pouch on his belt. Telari was toying with her comm as she gazed around. Her hair was long and wavy, streaked with deep purple through brown, with hints of dark green, like wild vines.

"We've had some human colonies on our worlds," Caitlin said, "for over twenty years now. Yet, people here are still getting used to offworlders."

"Takes time," her bodyguard commented.

The grand opening party carried on. People bought trinkets from vendors as others explored a plethora of flights to the nearest planets. Images of newscasters floated around, telling ambitious stories of humans settling on Atlearon, and Atleans living on Earth.

Most Atleans looked quite humanoid, with skin ranging from coppery near-human tints to mythical shades of brown, silver, or green. Pointy ears earned nicknames from human legends, while natural spots or striping on their skin hinted at animalistic bloodlines.

A handful of Merfin partook in festivities. While Merfins were Atlean, their feet were somewhat broader at the toes, and their skin ranged in shades of teal, blue, or green. Merfin eyes were pearlescent, and their leafy ears feathered out like fins along hair that flowed like thin strands of seaweed.

One Atlean stood out in the crowd. Doctor Scrufius behaved like a happily retired guy trying to make it to every party he could. Middle-aged human women gravitated toward his mythical image and pointed ears, paying special attention to the ear with an intricately carved silver and jade cap contoured over the top half. Scruffy, who dressed barely formal enough for any occasion, wore an open sports jacket that complimented his forest green shirt patterned with vines. Young humans often asked if he made toys, or was half plant due to his crazy green hair. Clearly enjoying the part by his smile and candor, he kept reminding people to call him Scruffy.

Professor Zared, a sophisticated, middle-aged Atlean lectured about his home world to a cluster of patrons. His elaborate wristbands depicted alien cities surrounded by vivid forests and strange creatures. The scenery changed to floating towns near spaceports, and homes built amongst great trees, their mostly round-roofed buildings linked by flexible bridges to adjust their configuration as the trees grew. His pewter hair matched his slightly pearlescent eyes, and his demeanor was patient and amicable.

Elegant in her silvery party dress and pointed ears, Elowren set her champagne on a nearby platter. She psyd to other telepaths in the room, "*Our Magistrate's running late. I can't sense him nearby.*" She sensed concern from multiple telepaths of her crew and clan.

Zared replied, "*Call him.*"

"*I did. His comm screen showed an empty lounge.*"

Now Scruffy shared her concern. "*That sounds like a prank. He doesn't do pranks. We better stall the crowd.*"

Elowren glanced around. *"Go charm the audience. I'll introduce you."*

Scruffy sighed, "Fine, I'll wing it," he grumbled.

Professor Zared switched off his holograms and excused himself. He sauntered off to join the door guards.

Elowren moved to the podium, all elegance and grace as she initiated the ceremony. "Ladies and gents, I give you our favorite eccentric Ambassador of science, wiser than wise, Professor and Founder of Neurobotanical Science, Doctor Scrufius."

Scruffy trotted up the steps to center stage, energetic despite his age. "Ladies and Gents, thank you and welcome. We are here in pursuit of dreams, dreams we make into reality. When we roam from across the stars to home shores, certain puzzles remain. I'm here to answer your questions about offworlders, and whatever else you dream up."

"I've got one," a fellow spoke up. "How long have you all been hiding on Earth?" His question brought echoes of agreement, curiosity, and suspicion.

"Spacers have visited Earth since the dark ages. We waited until the Renaissance era. Well, my people did. I'm not *that ancient*. I'm only older than barnacles." Seeing a number of amused faces, he grinned. "So let's see, what are the most popular questions? We don't brain blast people, and we're not always reading everyone's minds." Scruffy gestured to a pair of glittery fake Martian antennas atop a young lady's head. "We don't have antennas."

One woman waved for attention. "Why do most aliens have pointy ears?"

"Most intelligent species evolve longer tips. We're pleased that your race is doing this well."

Questions ground to a halt as several humans glanced at each other, as if sensing an insult.

Another person queried, "Why Earth?"

"We started out just wanting to observe, but oh boy, let someone get too cozy with the farmer's daughter, or one lucky shot hits a morpher and bam, it's on." Scruffy threw up his arms. "Next thing you know, there's mythology explosions, angry mobs and silver bullets."

Elowren moved to the far end of the stage, where she could observe the crowd. She activated her comm, conjuring little holograms over her wrist. "All hands, where is our magistrate? He's late and his tracker is off."

Two muscular Atleans in the crowd glanced over at her and nodded. Berkiru, the burlier one, wore a neatly braided beard that accented his thick, graying, furlike mane. Across the room, watching from a balcony, Wulvur had more of an acrobat's build, with roguish charisma and shoulder-length, rebellious hair of brown and black.

Berku spoke quietly into his comm, "All hands, our magistrate is missing. I want a status on him. Shanto was guarding him." Several lead voices confirmed his order, except for Shanto. Berku ordered. "Slade, you hear me?" No reply. Berku muttered, "Slade's not answering his comm."

"I noticed," Wulvur replied, watching his comm beep red. "Command post is silent too."

"Shit," Berku fumed. *"Psy talk only. Comms might be monitored."*

Scruffy kept a cheerful demeanor. "We're not the only species to visit Earth, but we may have been the only morphers. We had to be good infiltrators during the renaissance days. This is a fun world to spy on, so much diversity on your planet. Our mythologies have influenced each other. In the past three or so generations, some humans have become true clairvoyants with almost no alien genes. You're living older and healthier, and there's Human-Atlean hybrids. Our worlds are evolving, our people changing at inspiring rates. One thing is sure: due to our mixed blood, we are *wereworlds*."

Elowren stayed near the podium, elegant in her party gown of Atlean design. No human would guess that if she morphed into animal form, her shimmering attire would change with her. Slade would normally be here ogling her. She met Scruffy's gaze as she touched minds with him. *"Slade's still at his ship. The magistrate hasn't spoken to him, either."*

Scruffy restrained a frown as he continued, "Tonight, ladies and gents, we open our docks to intra-galactic species on the first star-class, multi-terrestrial space station allied with Earth." Scruffy raised a nearly full wine glass. "I think we should have celebrated

29

this on Hallows Eve; then we could've worn each other's getups."
Scattered laughter rewarded his comedy. "It's almost time to cut the
red ribbon. Party on." He smiled as they toasted, cheered, and
applauded, but Scruffy's smile faded once he turned away from the
crowd.

Wulvur leaned over the balcony's rail as he studied his
surroundings. His eyes fixated on a ceiling vent. Something felt
wrong. He heard odd noises from the next level, a sudden increase
in foot traffic.

Wulvur hopped over the balcony rail, landing in an acrobat's
crouch. He startled the nearest partiers, ignoring their protests as he
brushed past them. He flipped off his firgun's safety and joined his
friends, "Smells smoky up there, and noisy above the ceiling,
sounds like rats on a roof."

Scruffy grabbed the mic. "Everyone, listen up! There's a
security breach. I need you to return to your quarters." He waved off
protests from the audience and turned up the mic as he headed for
the door. "No arguing! Get out of here, now!"

Most of the crowd obeyed, starting through the exits. Scruffy,
Elowren, and their guards had led the way almost out of the hall
when wisps of smoke curled from the ceiling. The lights flickered,
drawing glances and murmurs.

Zared switched his comm to scan mode, revealing images of
numerous red life forms on the decks above and below them. The
images multiplied, appearing out of nowhere. "The station's being
boarded. They're Merfins and Rezoans." To the humans, he
clarified, "Fish and Lizards. They weren't invited."

One man started to argue that he'd met a few Rezoans at the
station. They seemed friendly.

Zared cut him off with, "Return to your quarters." He waved
Berku and Wulvur over. "Evacuate the main deck!" He shouted.
"Civilians, go to your quarters. Your living area's more protected."
His outburst caused a clamor among the startled crowd. Some
obeyed and ran, while others argued.

Elowren tried her comm. "Command Post, come in." She
shook her head at her friends. "No good, station security's down."

Zared opened his elite greatcoat, pulling out thick gloves from the coat's deep inner pockets. When he pulled the gloves on, the knuckles opened up and miniature firgun barrels poked out. "The intruders are wearing armor but what's freaky is, some of them look like Venamir."

"Probably clone dopps," Scruffy said.

Berku turned to some men who'd joined them, demanding answers. "We're in deep shit. That's your answer," he replied, pushing them toward the door. "Everyone head back to your ships or mid-deck below us. Go!"

High-pitched zaps from firgun fire pierced the air and burned into guards, followed by thuds of falling bodies and the clattering of weapons hitting the floor. Heavy footfalls drew closer, louder.

Wulvur and Berku morphed into their beast forms, their black and grey leathery attire adjusting to form thickened body armor, loose around the limbs to allow full movement. Startled guests shied away from them, some with shrieks or yelps. Other morphers followed suit, changing into their forest beast man shapes, spurring someone to yell, "Werewolf!"

"We're not werewolves," Scruffy defended, his voice rough as he morphed into a wolfish creature with elongated ears and stripes across his shoulders.

Explosions boomed from the next rooms, blasting open doors and knocking over the nearest bystanders. Smoke poured in while a high-pitched wailing emitted through the surround-sound. Atleans winced, fighting a wave of instant headaches from the noise. Berku, Wulvur, and their other morpher bodyguards joined forces to defend the partiers.

"I can't read your minds. They're using psy blockers," Elowren warned.

"Get to the ships. Knock out those speakers," Scruffy yelled.

"We'll cover you," Wulvur replied. "Go on."

"Just like old times," Scruffy replied.

Humanoids and lizard-like humanoids wearing riot armor and helmets stormed in through emergency exits. They shoved their way past humans, targeting the Atleans. Elowren whipped off her cloak and flung it toward the overconfident attackers. The cloak flashed

31

with electricity and bright lights as it spread out into an electric net. Several of her closest targets backpedaled, helping the net catch yet another. Elowren and her fellow morphers began mangling the attackers with Tasers, claws, and teeth.

Chapter 3
Old Enemies

Captain Slade lounged in the *Jacobyte*'s cockpit, leaning back in the pilot's chair. Earth's rock music played over the speakers. "Captain's Log, March 1st, 2250. Earth people have their first modern space station. My first job as Consul is bizarre. I get along with humans, but I'm not much of a diplomat. The grand opening party is tonight, and most of the crew are on shore leave. Why am I still working?"

Considered young by Atleans, 170 Earth years endowed him with the look of a man in his prime. His hair was like a forest, dark, earthy brown and green streaks. His beast-morpher bloodline gave a canine hint to his ears. Animalistic stripes started at his neckline and snuck beneath his flight jacket. His lupine eyes narrowed at the tactical surveillance screen beside him when the data flickered. His crew guarded the *Jacobyte*. Their onboard security readings showed a shield at full power, and they were docked onboard Earth's first multi-species space station. Still, something didn't feel right.

He rubbed his temples, trying to ignore a growing headache. Over the ship's quiet hums of power came an eerie, but familiar, melody. "Weird," he muttered. Giving his almost empty wine glass a suspicious look, he settled for trolling through his messages.

The first image rose from the screen as if a ghost had pushed a holographic cake into the air before him. The cake was shaped like a house, with each shingle holding a flaming candle. Voices sang out, "How old are you, a century and holding? Happy birthday, you old cuss." Catcalls and lewd sounds followed. The cake melted while the voices moaned with intensifying drama, "I'm melting! If only Slade weren't so old, it wouldn't melt." The house fizzled into a mess of melted candles before fading.

He rolled his eyes. "For the love of black holes."

"I can't believe you're still in there," said a voice from the next room. A light-haired Atlean strolled in from the adjoining ready room. He was either older than Slade, or mileage of life made him appear more weathered. "It's opening night. We're all supposed to be diplomats, now."

Slade grunted.

"You'd rather be a ranger, hunting fugitives and teaching combat."

"Beats sitting at tea parties with a bunch of windbags. The council should have made Zared their main diplomat, not me." Slade rose with a stretch. "You're right, Doc. Let's go party."

"About time," Nelzyr said, walking off.

Once the older man was out of sight, Slade rubbed his temples against the annoying headache. A subtle melody kept repeating itself in his head. Casting a suspicious look at his empty beer mug, he shrugged it off. He tried to psy to his copilot, "Shanto, report." His headache intensified, blurring his vision for several long seconds. Slade leaned against the pilot's window, peering outside. He saw nobody. He tapped his comm. "Ground crew, report."

Neither crewman replied.

The lights flickered throughout the cockpit for several long seconds before power stabilized again. He heard quiet footsteps, along with the almost silent sound of something sliding along the floor.

"Nelzyr, don't mess around," Slade replied. No answer. "Doc?"

Only silence answered.

Snapping out of his mirth, Slade grabbed his holster from the next chair and buckled it on. Only then did he realize that the sing-song noise in his head was getting louder. He reached into an overhead cabinet and grabbed his kilters, a set of combat gloves with armored cuffs. The gloves glowed around the knuckles and wrists when he donned them, then went dark. The cuffs extended to protect his forearms, and the material thickened above the knuckles.

A hushed voice whispered, "Slade, we're under attack. Come in. Put the ship on defensive!"

Slade turned to his ship's comm. He saw a holovid of swirling smoke and eerie beams panning like searchlights trying to cut through a stormy night. He wished it were another prank message, but his instincts knew better. An image of a shaggy Atlean werefolk came into view, a creature many humans would call werewolf because of his posture and nimble, paw-like hands. His clothes fit like combat gear, and one ear tip wore a green, ornate cover. His eyes glinted with cunning intelligence as he grabbed a rifle from a fallen guard.

Slade leaned over the comm. "Scruffy, what's going on? No alarms sounded."

Between coughs, the wolf's rough voice barked over an uproar of alarms and harried voices, "We tried to psy you, but got nothing. Get out of there!" Scruffy's voice cracked as his image faded.

Zaps from overloading circuits and power shutdowns resounded throughout the ship. Blackness enveloped every screen in the cockpit, silencing the smoky hologram and every other hum of power throughout his beloved ship. He whapped the emergency alert.

Nothing activated.

Slade sought out his friend's minds, "All hands, code red!" He could barely sense his friends' minds nearby. Now he recognized the noise in his head, a familiar humming in his mind. He tapped his comm. "Doc, intruder alert. Someone's using our psy blockers. Get off the ship!" Nobody answered. He barged into the adjoining ready room. "Doc, report."

Then it hit him. Fury engulfed his senses. Emotions from another mind flooded his thoughts, a concerto of passions livid with treachery, pangs of loss and yearning, all surpassed by a primal craving for vengeance. When the firestorm of emotions receded, his mind tingled with a sedative effect. Slade tried using his psy to find his friends. He glimpsed imagery from his friend's minds, garbled visions of the medbay swirling into darkness. "My crew's down," he fumed. *Another telepath, a strong one.*

The ship's power shut off with a series of resentful crackles from its systems. Main lighting shut down throughout the ship, leaving only light shining through his cockpit windows from the docking bay, and scattered backup lights.

An icy voice growled in his head. "Tonight, your rotten morphers will pay and it all begins with you, Slade!"

Slade conjured his mental shields, images of wild animals snapping at any telepath who dared enter his mind. He heard footsteps clopping from the entry passage, as if both feet were sore. "Merfin," Slade fumed. He moved into the equipment storage room, firgun raised and panning. Across the room, by the stairs, he spied a hooded man in the darkness. Pearlescent, yellow-gold eyes gleamed at him. The silhouette matched Slade's size and build with uncanny accuracy. Then the intruder vanished, and Slade realized it had been a psychic illusion.

In the next room, Venamir stepped over an unconscious Doc Nelzyr. Maska followed, then hefted Nelzyr over one shoulder and moved deeper into the ship.

Slade yelled, "Well, come on in here! Afraid to show yourself?"

Venamir's anger ran hotter, memories of imprisonment feeding his strength. He knew Slade's defenses well enough to invade his prey's mind like a stealth soldier sneaking through an enemy camp. Venamir attacked with his psy, unleashing his fury into Slade's mind like raging storm-fronts.

Slade's mind wandered into a world of blurry shadows. The air felt thick with smoke as flames took shape around him, searing the walls and blocking escape. Starship cannons and small arms fire thundered all around him over harried voices, his old crew. He spun to see a cockpit from his worst memories. Rezoans worked their way through the nearest hall, exchanging firgun-fire with Atleans. Flames around him fizzled out as the air turned damp and cold.

Slade reinforced his psy shields, creating a perimeter of wild beasts. The guards clawed at him as they vanished, leaving him in his natural form, onboard the *Jacobyte*. "No, it can't be him," Slade muttered. He raised his firgun and panned for a target.

An eerie voice taunted him from the darkness, "Nothing like old memories, eh, Slade?"

"Surrender now, or be carried out," Slade retorted.

The intruder strode into the room, holding a tiny glass orb that contained a small creature, a tiny mermaid of sorts, with fins on her arms and eyes like pearls. Wings fluttered from her back, lifting her out of Venamir's hand. She stared at Slade, flicked her delicate, glowing fins, and sang louder, an old Merfin chant meant to lull targets to sleep. Before, it had only sounded like a distant whine, but in proximity, the tiny, exquisite voice sang and cast images.

Slade scowled. "A mutirian caller. How d'you get one?"

The intruder smiled. "I've always had them."

Slade understood why he couldn't psy to his friends. Despite his mental shields, the tiny voice trickled into his mind. Glistening, spectral images of merfolk emerged from the creature's cage. The beings grew to life size, beckoning to Slade, baring sharp teeth when they smiled, their tail spikes flexing between softly glowing fins.

"Recognize this?" Venamir taunted, "The mutirian callers never went extinct. They thrive in deep water. These creatures dwarf the mind control your council tried on me. The members tried to brainwash me. It didn't work. I was raised around these creatures. The Callers can dull even the most primal thoughts of your Neanderthal human allies. Funny thing, their song works just as well on you." He held the small cage against his body. The creature emitted a hiss, her tiny eyes shifting from Slade to Venamir. "I'd rather not hinder our discussion."

The fogginess cleared from Slade's mind. He pried into the intruder's mind, to find Venamir thinking in the ancient Deeps language. He saw visions of dark caves with sleep tubes. An ocean's roar filled his ears, and he pictured himself trapped within a furious whirlpool. Salty spray stung his eyes, and soaked clothes clung to his body. Pressure squeezed air from his lungs as he sank into the whirlpool's dark abyss. Slade released his defenses—his wild kin, morphing beasts from his psy shields—water creatures, more beastlike than aquatic took form around him. His defenders deflected the virtual water attack with their flippers and tails. Slade morphed his image into an alien, bear-like being with claws that extended as he slashed at the creatures. He roared, overpowering their song. The attacking water beasts fled, with Slade's defenders close behind. The whirlpool and animals dissipated as Slade escaped from the psy link. He felt drenched as he breathed in air.

"You will pay for locking me in that torturous death-sleep," the intruder promised.

Very few had given him such a challenge. Could it be him? Slade refused to believe it. "I've caught scumbags for over a century. Who are you and what do you want?"

Venamir's coppery hands brushed back the hood. He looked like Slade's twin. "Why, I am here to replace you. This is my ship."

Slade chortled, "What are you, insane and stupid?"

"You would challenge your High Inquisitor Venamir?" Venamir scoffed as he stroked the orb. "I warned all of you about allying with humans, but you chose to bond with them and build a space station. We could still abandon the humans. Join me, Slade, for all our ancestors fought for, leave the Earth people alone. Those degenerates need a millennium to evolve. The councils are so worried about Earth being invaded, and for what? Not even our enemies want them."

Slade's blood chilled. Those baleful memories brought him back to the worst meeting the High Council ever had—a night of duels between brethren.

Venamir sneered, "Oh, you do remember my testimony. You almost listened. So did my dear niece, Vanysa. Too bad the Morpher Councils were blind. Our brethren had already lost their ability to foresee doom. That is all humans will bring us." He morphed, eyes turning a bloodshot gold, skin to a mottled green, webbing spreading between his fingers. "After serving in war together, you put me in prison, and yes, I am Venamir." He shrugged off the greatcoat, to show a body-hugging suit open at the ribs, exposing his gills. He was a Merfin of the most reclusive tribes. They had the most pearlescent eyes of water folk, along with the widest gills, low on the torso.

Slade stared in shock. There was no mistaking this Merfin, the traits and tone, nor the way the pearlescent, golden eyes looked right through him. Still, he was baffled. Venamir was back from the Prison of Comas. "You had to have help. Who broke your fishbowl and let you out?"

"A fishbowl," Venamir hissed. "It was a death trap! You and your bloodthirsty mongrels put me there!"

Slade cut in, "You're alive because our councils pitied you—after you killed a bunch of them!"

Venamir snarled back, "Pitied? They betrayed our world." Catching himself, he smirked. "You are stalling, Slade, hoping for a rescue by your pack of hounds. I'll give you one chance. Join me, because willing or not, you work for me, now."

Slade guffawed. "That deep sleep killed your brain cells. I'll drag you in by your slimy fins."

"Do you even remember how to fight?"

Slade's eyes narrowed. "Were you ever a good fighter?"

Venamir jiggled the orb, causing the tiny creature to sing again.

Slade's mind fogged over again. He stood in a dreamlike trance while his mind raged on, commanding his body to move. *Shoot him, shoot dammit!*

Chapter 4
My Ship

Two old rivals faced off inside the *Jacobyte*. Slade matched his will against Venamir, as he had in the past. Long, excruciating moments crept by as Slade and Venamir sought to control each other. Venamir stood in a perfect line of fire while Slade tried to shoot him. Slade kept trying to pull the trigger but couldn't move his hand. *He's stronger now. Whatever. I can still take him.* "Figures you had to steal our psy *callers*. Let it go. They're not bred for combat."

Venamir smiled, a sinister look. "This one is." He plucked the gun from Slade's numb grip. "You should talk, carrying laser toys like these. You want the little caller released? Very well." He twisted the top of his pouch, unlocking the globe. The creature flew onto Venamir's shoulder, its delicate body fins serving as wings.

Slade eyed the creature as he shook the feeling back into his hands. Already, sensations of countless needles shot through his fingers. *Good.* "Thought you didn't need a firgun to steal my ship," he taunted. "She won't obey you. This ship was never yours. Neither was the old *Spectre* that we crewed on."

Venamir's body tightened from toes to earfins. "The *Jacobyte* is my ship. Your conniving pack took her. You turned our council against me."

"You betrayed the council when you killed your colleagues, even your own kin!"

"Not all of them, but we digress."

"What about our dead crewmates? Their blood is on you!"

Venamir chuckled, "Is it? Still wondering which of us crashed the *Spectre*. You never solved the mystery."

"You crashed her."

"Did I? Are you sure? Haunts you, doesn't it? Let it go. Join my crew."

Incredulous, Slade queried, "How the freak did you breed a mutirian caller that can fly? Why are you trying to recruit me?"

"Before my alchemist, Doctor Cruentin was incarcerated, his genetic team had access to drakir DNA. He started the bloodline of flying, water-breathing, mutirian callers. And as for my prison, your miserable crew put me in that chamber of living death. Yet, despite our vast differences, you could prove useful." His finger twitched on the trigger until, slowly, he relaxed his grip. "Oh, bravo, Slade, stalling like a frightened whelp, hoping to be rescued. Flight bay, go. I know you keep a derelict flyer in there."

The *Jacobyte's* windows flashed between light and darkness as if a lightning storm were brewing inside her. The starship's power systems reset twice more. A static-filled voice announced, "Warning. Overload imminent. Security breach. Power failure." The ship's power fell into sporadic overload. Smoke wafted from deck to deck while generators whined as they wound down. This time, only dim emergency lights illuminated the ship.

"Last chance, Slade, flight bay, go," Venamir ordered. He smiled, eyes gleaming in the near darkness of emergency lights.

Slade raised his hands, still wincing and wiggling his fingers. He could feel his hands again, good enough to fight. He lunged for the firgun. One shot fired, burning through Slade's leather jacket, singeing his arm, and searing the nearest wall. The fiery pain only fed his anger, and the grappling match was on. Slade kept the barrel misdirected as he used a leg sweep to maneuver Venamir off balance, then jockeyed him down onto the floor. Erratic shots destroyed random panels until Slade bashed Venamir's weapon hand against a wall and sent the firgun skittering across the floor. He discovered that Venamir's rings and wristbands were weapons when the fancy adornments grew spikes that cut his arms and hands.

"Give up," Venamir smirked.

"No, we'll settle this the old-fashioned way," Slade said.

The little caller swooped onto Slade's back, scraping his shoulder with claws and teeth. When Slade let out a startled curse, the creature darted away before being swatted or squished beneath the grappling pair.

Venamir realized that Slade was neither drunk nor out of practice. Angered yet exhilarated, he fell back on his old school defense to twist and break free, using brief bursts of mental energy to cause pain in response to Slade's merciless hold on pressure points. Bodies alive with adrenalin, they broke free and squared off.

Venamir morphed into an amphibious creature, a fierce mix of a Merfin man with scales that grew over his skin like ancient armor. Thick claws grew from his fingertips while a long tail lashed with fervor. Venamir beckoned Slade. "Very well, one last sparring match for the ship."

"Good." Slade morphed from his humanoid form, his formal shirt ripping to reveal the markings on his upper body that matched the stripes of the fur sprouting from his skin. His face and body transformed to a wolf-like beast with traits of something burlier. Usually morphing felt natural, a mere rush of energy, but this time, his head swam, joints ached, and he couldn't hold the form. He heard Venamir laughing as his body reverted to his normal, near-human form. Only then, Slade noticed parallel slices on his arm. He glanced at bits of reddish algae clinging to his skin. "What the hell—I can't morph?"

Venamir replied with a nasty grin, "It's a new venom, made for *your kind,* you and your animal morphing pack. The serum on my claws and weapons negates your ability to morph. 'Tis long overdue. You always did need a muzzle."

Slade snarled like a wild beast, "You stuck me with the caller's venom so I can't morph?"

"Not just any mutarian caller. My little pets can fly and breathe water. Their venom is unique. The cure needs more than a mere serum. You will forget how to morph when I'm done with you."

Slade's eyes narrowed. "I don't believe it."

"You'll learn the hard way, as usual."

Slade tried to morph again. All he gained was a splitting headache, a fleeting bulging of muscles and lengthening of teeth, only to return to normal. He clenched his fists. "I don't need to shape change to beat you."

They charged again, crashed against a wall, then onto the floor. Slade bore into Venamir's mind again with the vengeance of a merciless recurring nightmare, locking their thoughts together, his raging will shattering down all defenses. Using his telepathy was painful now, uncontrollable. Slade locked his psy with Venamir's mind anyway. He heard thunderous explosions and firefights. And he saw bits of Venamir's memories, flight from prison, and the ocean rushing around him.

Slade's voice took on an eerie, hypnotic tone as he locked gazes with the fishman. "True form, true form is your power, only thus can you best me. Show your true power."

The mental strain forced Venamir to resume his true shape, a green Merfin, humanoid, less brawny than his opponent. "Out of my head, you rabid cretin," Venamir hissed, breaking free.

Slade tackled him and dug his fingers into Venamir's shirt, just below the ribs, finding the gills. He clenched the gills, reveling in his opponent's yelps of pain and panicked struggles. Venamir elbowed and clawed him, unable to twist free.

"You never could top me in a fight," Slade gloated. "I should just finish you off." Only then did he notice heavy footsteps approaching and a pair of shadows that lurked over his body.

"No, you won't," growled a bloodcurdling voice, "We want the captain alive."

Slade felt the fire in his veins ice over. He glanced up at a woman holding a diser rifle at his head. A sinister-eyed man stood beside her, a life of anger etched into his face. They were hybrid Merfins. Slade he didn't recognize the female one, his eyes narrowed at the man. "Noxus? Who dug you up? You're supposed to be dead."

"Get off the captain," Noxus ordered.

Slade clenched Venamir's gills, making his prey writhe in pain. "Back off or he dies."

Noxus pummeled Slade to the floor, denting the floor with a missed punch and not even wincing from the impact. Behind them, Moradin stepped over Venamir, her face a tightly controlled mask as she watched the two fight until Noxus reached for his daggers. Only then did she grab Noxus and pull him back with surprising strength.

"Let go," Noxus snarled.

Moradin shoved him aside. "The captain said alive."

* * *

Secluded within the hearth of the ship, powered by trickles of core energy from the engine stores, the Herja program activated. Life signs splayed across the main screen of a computer nestled between two hibernation tubes positioned in line with round, closed access doors.

A power surge swept through the ship's systems, causing emergency shutdown and restart. The main two computers linked to the cockpit, engine room, and other vital stations shut down and began a slow reset while multiple power cells throughout the ship overloaded. Shipwide, systems fell into backup mode, summoning what energy they could in respective order of importance.

A catwalk surrounded the tubes and computer, and racks of combat gear hung on the walls. Sustained by isolated power cells, the Herja computer struggled to compensate against repeated energy surges that threatened to fry everything in the chamber. Across the main screen flashed the warning, "Security compromised. Awaken guardian Herjas. Waking process failure. Activating Herja program."

A holographic Atlean woman wearing riot gear materialized, hovering in the center of the room. Her gleaming eyes widened at the sight of the hibernation bed. One sleep tube sparked inside like lightning. Seconds later, the tube's life support panel faded to black. The other sleep tube contained a female Herja, an exact double of the hologram. Sparks lit up the tube's interior while smoke clouded the small room. The woman whispered, "Wake us."

The computer replied, "Med-bots treating and analyzing injuries. Herja Kestral is in shock from electrocution."

"Evacuate her to medbay," the hologram ordered.

"Egress down. Doors locked. Transport actuators seized."

"Alert the doctor."

"Doc Nelzyr's bio readings show he's unconscious."

"Wake the real Herja," said the hologram, pointing to the woman in the tube.

"The power surges interrupted her waking process. Herja Kestral has suffered electrocution. Without the medbots, she may go into shock. Chances of survival would drop to twenty percent. Medbots are sedating the Herja until she is out of danger."

As the Herja in the sleep tube fell back into a deep sleep, the hologram of her gained power. The hologram appeared less ghostly as her program took control. "Let the medbots work. Keep psy shields up so nobody can detect her. Restore power to the other Herja, Quishen."

"Herja Quishen will die without stasis," the computer replied in a stoic voice. "His chamber is locked in full deep sleep mode. Medbots are converging on the living Herja, Kestral."

"Can Kestral be healed?"

"Yes."

The hologram paused. "Where's the crew?"

"Disabled."

"Divert all security protocols to my program. Lock down the ship's weapon protocols. Engage defense lockdown of our database."

"Complete. The Herja Kestral avatar is now in command of security and main guns." She shot a glare at the computer, to see it flashing every warning light it had, and making strained, whirring noises. "Who is the intruder?"

The computer's reply of "Override by Veeenaa-mm-r" crackled and with its shutdown, the holo-woman started to grow dim as the ship's systems reset yet again.

"No! Don't lose power! Keep me online!" Her words faded into incoherent static and she faded, still reaching with open hands toward sensors on the ceiling. Only dim lights remained from tiny, glowing med bots working inside the hibernation tubes.

* * *

Noxus and Moradin wrestled Slade against the nearest wall. Exhausted, Slade still fought back, but couldn't break free. Noxus was masterful at manipulating joints, and Moradin's unyielding hands clamped around one arm.

"You're only delaying your fates," Slade snarled.

"Captain," Moradin said, "looks like you needed help."

Little by little, Venamir sat up and groped for the navigator's chair. With pained efforts, he climbed to his feet, his voice weak. "Not true."

Slade studied the cyborg. Something about those facial features and her voice teased his memories. She refused to meet his eyes.

Venamir touched fingers to his forehead in a salute, the closest he ever came to giving anyone a true compliment. He massaged his gills. "Bravo, Slade, that was a dirty trick."

Slade scoffed in fearless defiance, "You're pathetic, need a thug squad to have a chance against me. Can't show weakness in front of them, can you?"

Ignoring the questioning, surprised looks from his henchmen, Venamir morphed more slowly than usual to Atlean shape, his natural Merfin form, and once again, an air breather. He held his vest open to let Slade notice how each body transformation negated the handiwork to gills. While bruised and scraped, the ragged gills smoothed out enough to lay flat between breaths.

Slade's eyes narrowed as he watched the accelerated healing. "So what? You're using black market serums."

"No, my energy healing has evolved," Venamir said, smiling.

"Inbred freak, you should have stayed in the fishbowl. By the time I hunt you down, you'll be nothing more than fish food!" *That's it, I just blew my stall time.*

Venamir's scowl twisted with dark pondering as the word *freak* settled in, the most hated of human words to morphers. He responded with a sinister grin and laid a webbed hand on Slade's chest. "You of all people to debate breeding, you wish to feel true weakness?"

Slade's energy leeched from his body as if his very arteries were draining. His thoughts and vision swirled with endless fog.

"Much better," Venamir said and bore into Slade's thoughts with everything he had, pawing through as if tearing pages from a book. He immersed his psy so deeply that they could feel each other's injuries. His voice blazed through Slade's thoughts as they viewed memories and visions of a shared past. Images formed in their joined psy link, glimpses of years ago, back when they crewed together on a heavily armed scout ship with *The Spectre* painted below her cockpit. "*I see your forgotten secrets. Your weakness is here somewhere, something you deny even remembering, a failure.*" When at last Venamir felt Slade's fear, he latched onto that weak point, a deeply hidden past experience they shared in battle that left a foul taste of failure and hindsight.

Venamir's mental words again overrode Slade's thoughts. *"Ah, here it is, our ship that crashed long ago. Your memories of failure will feel vibrant again, whenever you try to use your powers, or whenever you dare challenge me. May you drown in the depths of your worst nightmares. You shall find that forgetfulness is blissful. Say goodbye to your memory of tonight's fight."*

In fleeting seconds that felt like hours of confusion, Slade swayed in the grips of his captors, lost in illusions like a haunted sleepwalker. When he eventually looked up, all traces of anger had vanished. He gazed around, lost and disoriented. "Who are you? What happened?"

"Karma," Venamir chortled. "Moradin, help Maska secure our prisoners. Put them in Slade's puny transport. Disable the controls, and seal them in. Unlock the landing gear clamps. Go, before the hypnosis fades."

The two grabbed Slade and shoved him along.

"We still had to save you," Noxus fumed as he moved off with their prisoner.

"Move along," Venamir warned.

Once alone, Venamir sagged into the once familiar pilot's chair, where he belonged. Body still aching, he morphed a few more times with leisure, further aiding the healing process as only morphers could do. Bruises around his gills healed into the next stage of colors, mottled green and burnt orange. Not much relief, but enough to function. One glance through the cockpit windows reminded him of their predicament. They were still onboard the space station. His clones could only hold off defense troops for so long, and the stunned celebrants outside the docking bays would recover soon. He had to get out of here, fast.

Fire alarm systems spewed foam throughout most of the space station, most heavily in docking bays, with their highly explosive cargo of star ships and power units. The crazed blizzard of white foam smothered everything.

Venamir knew this digital snowstorm would die soon, so he sat back, muttering into his lapel pin. "Captain's log, add to research topics: How could Slade make me expose my gills? He must have mind-controlled me, for a whole second or two." Venamir activated hover mode. The *Jacobyte* cruised out of the docking bay, all systems go, landing gear retracting, and shields activating. Once clear, the ship lurched into open space; her blast sent servicing equipment in the bay tumbling into the sea of foam before the space station doors closed behind them.

"The ship is mine." Venamir laughed with glee, a rarity for him. He heard a tumble and Noxus swearing, which only fed his celebratory mood. He tested weapons controls so that two sets of gun turrets emerged from the *Jacobyte's* wing bases.

Maska trotted up from behind and settled into the co-pilot's seat. He was still brushing clumps of foam off mud-colored fur that accented his yellow ravenous teeth, his face shape a crude mix of predators that made up his ancestry.

Venamir left the space station behind, still glancing at scanners. "You completely trashed their defense system. Good work, you *can* be useful."

Maska sat tall and proud from the rare praise. "Thanks, Captain. The prisoners are in the transport. Slade's flyer is a search and rescue Zephyr, with an extra cargo room. It's a great rig. Can't I keep it?"

"Pfft, a Zephyr," Venamir sighed. "Are there any other vessels in the docking bay?"

"No," Maska grumbled, averting his face.

"Then we must jettison the Zephyr." In peripheral vision, Venamir couldn't ignore the highly unnatural shape sitting in the copilot's chair beside him. "What in the depths are you supposed to be? You look like a frothing, patchwork, mutant hound."

"You should have seen the look on Slade's face when I bit him." Maska gloated as he wiped at his dark, red stained fur and lips.

"I said keep him alive."

"It's just a scratch."

Venamir returned his attention to flying. "You have such a perverted flare for morphing, you should be female for your next assignment. That would feel natural."

Maska scowled in silence.

"Fly, while I go chat with our guest." Venamir rose and loped away in his odd gait, something akin to a human trying to run while wearing swimmer's fins.

Noxus caught up to Venamir in the corridor, all scowls. "Why can't I kill Slade? You hate him."

Hardly breaking stride, Venamir released a taste of his energy that made Noxus shrink back from a thumping, burning headache. "Because I have plans, you imbecile."

Chapter 5
Mine Oh Mine

Despite orders for combat, no docking bays opened on the crippled space station. Ships and fighters remained trapped in their foam-splattered docking bays. One old ship, built like a fat, mantling buzzard, sat with engines firing up as her crew ran onboard. Elowren stormed onboard, throwing her wet shoes aside. Her party dress clung to her body, drenched with fire foam. Her burgundy hair matched her fiery temper as she swore between orders. "Freaking psychotic-ass fish! I knew he'd escape sooner or later."

"Scruffy dropped into the captain's chair and powered up all systems. "I need Telari with Rhoan in the fighters. We're blasting off," he said as he ran scanners. "Command post's down, no wonder dopps could teleport onboard without alarms going off. I bet the hijackers hacked the whole damned station's defenses."

Elowren focused her psy to search for Slade so hard it made her head swim. *Slade, answer me. Slade?* "I can't reach him," she confessed.

Scruffy fumed, rubbing some green goo onto his leg. The goo moved on its own, forming a barrier over the cuts. Having to fight their way through a space station full of chaos and infiltrators, he was the biggest mess. "Dammit, it's my fault. My fault, I shouldn't 'a let him linger there."

Elowren grumbled, "No, if anything, it's all our faults for listening to the councils. No heavy patrols, ridiculous! They didn't want to scare the Earth people. This assault stinks of our own allies. There must be rogue morphers here, or spies."

"How else could Rezoans crash our party?" Scruffy remarked.

Two more young Atleans ran onboard and skidded to a halt in the cockpit. They wore flight suits donned on the run. Their crew chief, Telari, twisted her long hair behind her neck while search and rescue medic, Rhoan, grabbed their helmets from the cockpit's aft locker.

"The ship's ready to fly," Tel reported, panting. "What's going on?"

Scruffy turned in his chair, his gaze contemplative. "The *Jacobyte's* been hijacked. Slade's missing, and not sure how many others. Get the two Zephyrs ready to fly and stand by."

Telari and Rhoan ran through the ready room, past medbay, and down steps to the lower bays. A docking bay awaited them, where two compact fighters waited. The Zephyrs, nicknamed Medbirds, could carry four people, two in front, two patients in the back. They were tucked close, wings folded tight against their sleek bodies. The two unfastened the landing gear clamps, did a rapid inspection of the ships, and climbed into the cockpits.

"How the crap could someone steal that ship?" Rhoan asked as he strapped into the pilot's seat of the forward Zephyr.

"Had to be an insider," Tel panted as each lowered their canopy. "Comm check," she stated.

"Comm check two," Rhoan said.

"You're loud and clear," Scruffy's voice replied over their headsets. "Slade's ship has left the dock, and crew's not responding."

"*Jacobyte's* main guns are badass," Rhoan muttered as he hit the codes to open the dock.

"*Vernacular* has better armor," Tel replied, "but we don't, not in these little Zephyrs."

"Launch when I say," Scruffy ordered over the ship's comm, "and go in stealth. Let my ship draw any fire."

Telari reported, "I'm scanning the area. There's Slade's Zephyr surrounded by mines, and the *Jacobyte's* out there. Nobody's coming to help." Rhoan and Tel started engines and ran scanners, scraping for more information.

Rhoan keyed only Telari's comm. "Tel, patrol ships are launching from Earth, veering off. There's another ship approaching, no, they're beefed-up shuttles. Station's just beyond Earth's moon. Looks like a standoff there."

Scruffy hailed the station's control center. A frazzled control officer appeared on the holo-vid. The Command Post was in shambles around him. Behind the officer, response crews were putting out residual fires and helping the injured. Smoke lingered in

51

the air, and there were charred burns in the walls from earlier laser fire.

"I'm Doctor Scruffius on the *Vernacular*. Open our docking bay doors."

"We're in emergency lockdown," the angry controller replied. "We can't open the doors, anyway. Whoever hacked us made sure of that."

"But the *Jacobyte* was able to launch," Elowren argued.

The station officer's voice sounded curt. "Yes, whoever hit this station overrode all the other docking bay doors. You have to wait." He reached for the off switch.

Elowren barked, "No waiting. The *Jacobyte's* been stolen. We have to go after them!"

"We're aware of the breach. Reinforcements are on their way, but some psycho is threatening to kill Slade and three others onboard, and open fire on this space station."

"Screw this," Scruffy huffed. He put the ship in hover mode and retracted her landing gear.

"What are you doing?" the officer growled. "Shut down your engines!"

Scruffy asked, "There's nobody in our docking bay but us onboard my ship. I trust you can secure the emergency doors to this bay?"

The frazzled man gestured to his surrounding panels. "Yes, keeping people in isn't a problem."

"Good, we're leaving. We locked the closest passage on our way here. You better seal off this bay, fast," Scruffy said, powering up the ship's cannons, "because those doors will open for me."

The controller's eyes grew round as his face paled. "You crazy old fart, shut down before I have you arrested." As Scruffy's ship hovered and turned within the tight docking bay, the guy blurted, "Oh, shit!" He lurched out of his chair and thumped the emergency lock controls to their bay.

Elowren smirked, watching sensors screens. "He just put all inner shields up on this whole level. Nobody's getting to any of their bays for a while."

The controller's face went from pale to flushed. "Power down—this is your last chance!"

Scruffy shut off the comm. He opened fire on the huge docking bay door controls. His first blast demolished locking mechanisms on the doors, sending chunks of warped composites tumbling into open space. Red lights flared across the docking bay ceiling, alarms blared warnings, and fire foam erupted into the bay. Another blast forced the mutilated door linkage to collapse, allowing the immense docking doors to swing open.

As the *Vernacular* escaped into open space, Scruffy sang out, "That's what repair dopps are for."

* * *

When Slade came to his senses, he found himself stuck in the back of his own Zephyr, lying next to his unconscious friends. A migraine clouded his wits, and his shoulders ached from jagged gashes dug by Venamir's claws. He patted Shanto and Gus, found they had a pulse, but couldn't wake them. He tried the hatch handles, power controls, anything. The cockpit was a wreck, controls and handles blasted into rubble.

Venamir suddenly rapped on his hatch window. Slade tried to lash out mentally at his nemesis, who smiled, which from Venamir, was a bad omen.

"I see you have your wits back, all two of them." Venamir savored the seething glower of revulsion that Slade cast at him. "You have one chance to join me."

Slade yelled, "I'll join my fists with your guts! You were better off buried in the sewers!"

Venamir lashed out, an abrupt, mental channeling of energy. Slade sagged against the wall, holding his head. Blood on his hands smeared through his forest brown hair. He nearly blacked out from the instant migraine, his recovering vision dimming to a sick churning swarm of murk. Venamir's voice dripped with sarcasm. "You and the councils had your chance to protect our world." He studied Slade's expressions of confusion and rage with satisfaction. "Terrible shame you forgot how to fight like a psychic. Oh, wait, my little pet caused your memory loss."

"Come in here and I'll beat your ass into a molten puddle of toxic puke!"

Venamir laughed, scorn slithering through his words. "So *human*." He crouched for balance when two blasts jolted the ship.

Maska called out, "Captain, Earth is launching fighters."

"Splendid, release the mines." Venamir paused. "Oh, and Slade? You should buckle in." Venamir strolled out of the flight bay and sealed it off. "Eject them."

The outer door opened and ejector systems powered up. The Zephyr floated out through the *Jacobyte's* bay and drifted away into space. Venamir laughed as *his* larger ship's outer doors closed and sealed.

Snarling curses, Slade groped about in near blackness, he tested navigational controls and emergency distress signals, only to find the panels wrecked. Through the pilot's window, he saw a lower bay open and release a cluster of round probes with spikes poking out. The cluster burst apart and scattered in all directions, one barely missing his pod. The foreboding orbs maneuvered into orbits just far enough away to surround his useless Zephyr. Slade tried his personal comm, only to find it broken as well. When he tried to psy to his friends, his nerves flooded with pain and distorted visions of his friends' faces turning monstrous and raising weapons against him.

"Great, surrounded by my own damned space mines," Slade fumed.

* * *

Venamir settled in his pilot's chair and greeted his rivals on the holo-screen. "Hello, my old nemesis. Enjoy the party?" He reveled in their astonished expressions and the shocked silence.

Scruffy etched his words with menace, "Who busted you out of prison?"

Venamir rested his hands over weapons controls. "No matter. How would you like your friends back? In one piece, or space dust? Your choice."

Elowren scowled. "Never mind your demented head games. What've you done to Slade?"

"Oh, I let him live, for now. Slade and his two crewmen are in his personal Zephyr."

"Two?" Elowren muttered.

"Then let them go," Scruffy demanded. "Land the ship and release them, or else you'll be one against a fleet."

Venamir spread his arms. "What fleet? The space station fighters are locked in their docking bays. Earth has very few orbiting ships, and if they attack, I'll activate the mine field, killing your dear friends. And then, I'll attack the heart of the space station. By the time Earth launches more ships, I shall be gone."

Scruffy's eyes narrowed. "What do you want?"

"I have what I want. *My ship.* Now, I take my leave."

Elowren barked at him, "You brain-rotted psycho. I'm going to churn you into fish bait."

Scruffy studied Venamir with a disappointed leer. "Why? The councils gave you another chance."

Venamir sneered, "You call brainwashing me in deep sleep a chance? Tell your mighty Morpher Council to disband your human alliance, or they will suffer. Good luck saving your friends," His image vanished.

Elowren. activated a combat heads up display across their view panel, highlighting the mines in red and the two escape pods in green. "Those stupid mines are jamming our targeting sensors so we can't port our people out. We have to lure the mines away from Slade's Zephyr."

"Even this ship can't endure a whole field of those things without taking major damage," Scruffy warned.

Elowren reported. "There's two shuttles launching from Earth's moon, Rezoans, and mobile energy signatures, humanoid, probably clones. They're using teleporters. I bet they're porting dopps. They must be working with the hijackers. Rhoan, Tel, launch. Be ready to fight off those bogeys near Earth's moon."

Seconds later, two small Zephyrs shot out from the *Vernacular's* aft docking bay. Doors-closed lights flashed seconds later.

"They're clear," Scruffy said.

Elowren zoomed in on three life signs on her bio-screen. "Look, bio readings show Slade, Shanto, and Gus. They're alive but there are no shields. Wait a minute, Doc's not with them."

Scruffy shook his head as he sighed, "We'll find him. First, we have to lure these mines away toward us. We'll have to teleport Slade and the others onboard. We'll take damage but my old bird can handle it."

Elowren raised shields. "Shields up. I'll handle the portal chamber and be ready to teleport our friends. We have to get close. The mines are dampening our sensors. I'll transmit shutdown codes but the mines can still explode if they impact anything."

"I know, I know," Scruffy groaned as she ran out of the cockpit.

Scruffy flew toward the minefield. As he neared the outer mines, the jagged explosives drew to his ship as hungry predators to bait. The first few mines struck, their explosions gnawing at the hull. Scruffy watched his target, one disabled Scout Zephyr with three life forms inside. "Slade's bird is powered down, with only life support on. The mines should leave him alone."

* * *

Slade watched space mines floating all around his Zephyr. "Even if I could start engines, we'd be screwed," he muttered, drumming his fingers. He wrestled with every panel control he could find. "Come on, something has to work in this heap." He twisted around and tried the aft controls, having to wrestle Shanto aside. "Dammit, Shanto, lose some weight," he fumed. He smacked Shanto and Gus. "Wake up!"

Shanto groaned, eyes unfocused as he tried to fend Slade off. "Get off me...."

"Shanto, it's me. Quit punching. Quit," Slade replied until his friend recognized him. "Listen, Venamir kicked our asses. I need you to help shut down these mines."

Shanto sat up, rubbing his head. "Ow! What mines?" His eyes widened when he looked out the nearest side window. "Oh, man."

"Yeah." Slade tried to rouse Gus again, with no luck. "Can you reach the medkit?"

"Yeah," Shanto muttered as he pulled a medkit from a side panel. "We can run life support, just no engines, no weapons. Shields are risky." Using his wrist comm for light, he opened a pouch of green goo that looked black in the darkness and pressed it against a lump on Gus's head. "Can you get us some light?"

"They busted the controls," Slade said as he wrestled a hand down behind the panels and withdrew a power pack. He removed a broken power pack and worked the new one in.

A hologram of a tiny pilot appeared before Slade. "Orders, Captain?" the avatar asked.

"Maintain our atmosphere. Wait for my command to raise shields. Leave thrusters off."

Shanto started messing with the Zephyr's comm. He quickly felt the cracks in the housing. "Figures, the comm's broke. But we're already coded as a friendly ship. That's probably why we're still alive."

Slade peered out the windows, seeing movement past the mine field. "It's Scruffy's ship. He just launched his Zephyrs."

* * *

Rhoan and Tel circled the minefield, their screens calculating possible routes through the mines. As soon as the lines connected showing a good route, mines would drift into the safe paths like hungry sharks waiting for the scent of blood. One mine barely contacted a neighboring mine and the viewers braced themselves, fearing a chain reaction of explosions. Instead, the two mines opened their shells and burst into three smaller mines each.

"Figures, they breed," Rhoan fumed.

"Yeah," Tel agreed, "Scruffy said they're attracted to heat and movement, typical of mines."

"I have an idea," Rhoan said. "What if we blasted the outer mines?"

Scruffy replied, "Those mines will track your weapon fire and lock onto you. Stay clear for now. I'll try some decoys."

A swarm of tiny fighters the size of toys launched from the Vernacular's weapons. The miniature fighters flew farther below the ship and cruised toward the closest mines. Within seconds, a clump of mines pursued the drones and detonated. The instant a few mines found Scruffy's large ship, more mines followed suit. The mines slammed against the *Vernacular* and crumbled into twisted metal carnage, their spikes stabbing at the ship's hull. Puffs of smoke belched from the *Vernacular's* hull before her shields shimmered with power again.

"We can handle it," came Scruff's even-toned voice. Clouds of debris formed around the *Vernacular* as mines started exploding, starting a chain reaction.

"We can lure some mines away," Rhoan said.

"Stay clear of those mines," Scruffy ordered, his voice crackly from static.

Tel butted in, "That stuff only works in movies."

"Where do you think they got the idea? Someone knew about removing mines from space."

Rhoan and Tel grimaced as they watched a cluster of mines drift toward the *Vernacular.* The mines converged and began exploding around the *Vernacular,* shrouding the old ship from view.

"They're getting clobbered," Rhoan fumed. "We have to try luring the mines away."

"Okay," Tel agreed. "We pull some mines and go to stealth."

"Like war-gaming," Rhoan replied, grinning.

They fired at the nearest mines, punched thrusters, and dropped power to stealth mode.

A few mines targeted their small fighters, then more, until within slow dragging seconds, clusters of mines tagged along after each of their ships. Some mines split into smaller versions, swarming after Tel and Rhoan.

"We pissed off the mines," Tel commented.

"I said I got this. Back off," Scruffy ordered, muffled explosions carrying over their comms.

"Whoa, my wing took a hit," Rhoan blurted,

Tel made a quick scan. "Those shots came from Earth's Moon. I'm reading cyborg and lizard life forms. I'm hailing them. No answer. They're powering weapons again."

"Let's git'em."

Rhoan and Tel punched full thrusters and barreled through the remaining mines, blasting some into oblivion. Most of the remaining mines activated thrusters and followed them.

"Targeting shuttles," Tel said.

Rhoan and Tel took a few shots at the approaching shuttles, and then shut their guns down, diverting full power to shields. At first, their Zephyrs bucked from clumps of shrapnel and shock waves. They held course and shot between the enemy shuttles coming at them from Earth's moon. The rogue shuttles fired back, their shots striking some of the mines. Rhoan and Tel dropped engines to idle and coasted while the shuttles blasted thrusters to attempt escape. The mines detected larger power signatures from the shuttlecrafts, changed course and attached their spiked shells to the new targets. Timers on the mines expired microseconds apart, setting off explosions in clusters as the shuttles tried to escape to deep space.

Daring to look back, Tel saw one shuttle explode. The second shuttle retreated with failing shields, pursued by mines with the hunger of frenzied sharks. Rhoan and Tel whooped in triumph and jetted away, looping toward the few remaining mines.

Tel looked back, to see the last mines exploding around the disabled Zephyr. "How's our guys? Crap, the mines are all over Scruffy's ship!"

Slade's disabled Zephyr spiraled away, with remnants of mines stuck to her hull. Scruffy's ship was surrounded in debris from mines.

"Scruffy, are you guys okay?" Rhoan queried. Nothing.

Telari pulled alongside Rhoan and flicked up her visor. They exchanged worried looks.

Scruffy yelled in glee over the comms, "We got them! Great job, you crazy kids! Now get back in the docking bays."

"That's what we get, crazy kids?" Tel mocked. She looked over at Rhoan's beat-up Zephyr and laughed.

"We rocked," Rhoan gloated.

Once the two docked their limping Zephyrs into Scruffy's underwing bays, shields went back up around the old *Vernacular.*

Next door to their medbay, a clam-shaped chamber opened its doors to reveal their friends, Slade, Gus, and Shanto. Slade sat down on the edge of the portal chamber. Scowling and wincing, he squinted against the light shining around Elowren's shapely form as she jogged in holding two handfuls of green, glistening, goo. She dropped the goo onto his shoulders, which appeared to be the worst areas. The goo spread, forming a shimmering green layer, soaking into every injury as creeping moss would fill in gaps and wrap around trees. Then the glow faded, energy transferred to the target body.

"Rhoan, get the other two," Elowren called out.

Gus groaned, rubbed his head and pointed at the ceiling. "Mines," he said in a small voice.

"The slimy bastard's out of prison," Slade stated, anger swelling again. "He stole my ship. *Stole it.* What happened on that space station?"

Scruffy moved over with a medbag, looking miserable. "The whole damned place went crazy. Venamir must've hypnotized half the guards because they crashed the grand opening party. Someone took out the command post, so no alarms. What happened on your ship?"

"Venamir showed up, and his old goons came to help, Maska and Noxus. I didn't recognize the female, and I don't know how I lost. He had one Deeps singer with him, little critter, but it could fly."

"It could fly? Those bottom-feeding deep aquatics must be making new hybrids," Scruffy grumbled, helping pull off Slade's jacket. "I shouldn't have let so few of you remain on board."

"Really Scruff," Rhoan argued, "they took out the whole space station, took a chunk outta you, we all had to battle our way here, and you're blaming yourself? We all got screwed."

"Shut it," Scruffy retorted.

"No," Rhoan started, "you're not being logical."

"Junior's right," Slade cut in, "no blame on any one of us. Wren, sweetie, one thing."

"Yes?" She leaned closer so that her long, wet hair tickled his chest.

Slade admired her cleavage in that tight, foam splattered party dress, ogling over how it clung to her body like a model's waterfall centerfold. "You have the most *beautiful* breasts." He blew her a sailor's kiss.

Elowren drew back a bit, blushing. "Are you drunk?"

"Oh, that's my strongest goo," Scruffy admitted, "gets you stoned fast."

Telari moved into the *Vernacular's* cockpit, and pulled off her flight helmet, freeing her long, disheveled, black and purple streaked hair. She plopped into the captain's chair, where she ran systems checks, hull scans, engine temperatures, and a manual flight control check. She tapped the ship's comm. "We're solid enough to endure reentry and land planet-side. This ship took a lot of damage. Our temp shields won't last but a couple flights."

Scruffy answered her, "We'll have to repair at our depot on Earth. Go to stealth."

Ignoring orders to land on Earth, Telari turned off the comms. The *Vernacular* banked away, her bulky, birdlike image melting into the darkness of space.

Chapter 6
Stealth

The *Vernacular* laid low in remote spots on Earth. Acting as Ambassador for his friends, Zared informed top Earth dignitaries of only minimal news: Venamir escaped, and had claimed, rather, gloated about the success of disabling the Orion Space Station and reclaiming the *Jacobyte*. How Venamir escaped prison was under investigation. Their medical team had their injured recovering, and Slade and Elowren would resurface to their diplomatic roles within the week.

As Zared served as the Atlean emissary and held off the shaken public, Telari, Wulvur, and Gus made inspections and repairs to Scruffy's old ship, and the Zephyrs, mostly outer damage from the mines. Slade's personal Zephyr, after sabotage by Maska, was receiving more extensive repairs. Zared's crew, the feline, Jasko, and Shanto, a half-Atlean, called on their offworld allies, and local military to acquire parts. Rhoan remained in medbay with Elowren. Their chief surgeon, Doc Nelzyr, was now reported missing.

Slade walked into the ready room, where Scruffy pawed through a long list of damage. He knew the *Vernacular* needed heavy repairs before weathering the turbulent winds of war yet again.

Scruffy glanced up, shaking his head. "This old bird's survived worse, but I wouldn't fly and fight like this. We need parts from the Atlean depot on Earth."

Scruffy and Slade entered the *Vernacular's* cockpit, both heading for the captain's chair. Slade paused, shrugged, and settled for the copilot's chair.

"With your ship gone, this is your flagship, now," Scruffy said. "You want the pilot's seat?"

"No, the *Vernacular's* yours," Slade said. "It just feels weird. I need to call your sister. Cleodna's our most most trustworthy Earth ambassador."

"My sis is waiting for you to call," Scruffy grinned. "She's been nagging me while you were out cold. Rumor has it our Morpher

Council has been more secretive than usual, Cleo has our best spies poking around."

"Still no sign of our real Magistrate?"

"No, but as bad as Venamir's become, I'd be surprised if he killed Magistrate Parleigh."

"I suppose you're right," Slade mulled, rubbing his forehead. "Venamir is power hungry, and for that, he needs allies."

Scruffy made the secure call down in the cockpit, logged the attack on the Space Station and called an Atlean lady on his most secured channel. He smiled in relief when her gracefully aged hologram appeared before him. Behind her were large screens showing a vast display of news from Earth and other worlds. Past the screens were large windows overseeing the ocean. Her pale, green hair was elegantly put up, and she was dressed formally in soft green and blue colors of her clan.

"Hello, Cleodna," Scruffy greeted. "Any news?"

"Good to see you," Cleodna said. "Zared and I have heard from Atlean and from Earth. Everyone wants answers, and nobody knows where our Magistrate went. All we know is he sent a message that he's alive and is going undercover."

"Venamir already impersonated a number of people," Slade reminded them. "How are you sure it was really Magistrate Parleigh?"

Cleodna smiled, her voice patient. "He was close enough to use telepathy. For now, he wants to investigate things himself. We go way back. It was him."

Scruffy nodded with a sigh of relief. "Our Magistrate's a Merfin, so he'll likely go for the ocean."

"Our councils and the diplomats of Earth want to meet with you, now, Slade."

"We're staying low for a few days," Slade replied. "I hope you're doing the same."

"I am, to a point," she replied.

"Cleodna," Scruffy objected, "you know how bad they infiltrated the space station."

"Aw, you're worried, how sweet. I have Berku's morphers guarding me."

Scruffy grinned, running scans for incoming ships while they talked. "Good ol' Berku, he likes a good fight."

"True," she agreed with a brief smile. "So, Orion Space Station, what happened there? I was on my way to the grand opening when the station locked down. I heard Venamir and his goons hacked the space station, ported troops onboard, and he stole the *Jacobyte*, our newest prototype."

Slade frowned, fighting back a scowl. "Yeah, that's the short story."

She turned a perplexed gaze onto Slade. "How did Venamir win? You're a better fighter than he."

Slade made a bitter frown. "He cheated. He had a mutirian caller, but the creature was a hybrid. Her wings resembled drakir wings, like a tiny aquatic with dragon wings. The strange thing is, most of us could not use telepathy anywhere near the creature, but Venamir still could. He must have conditioned himself to the creature's song."

Cleodna's expression went a bit pale. She tapped her computer, "Display mutirian caller experiment Merdrake. I've heard of the hybrid, but I didn't know that any existed."

A hologram appeared beside her of a mermaid-like creature, with delicate scales, leathery wings like a tiny dragon, and the pearlescent eyes of an aquatic person.

"Beautiful, tricky, and better at cancelling out our telepathy than any technology we possess. They're a hybrid discovered a few years ago on Atlearon, on the shores of our old battlefields."

Slade pointed angrily at the creature's image. "That's the creature. I bet the breed wasn't an accident. The Deeps aquatics are proud of their genetic experiments."

Scruffy rose and started pacing. "Cleodna, *how* did Venamir escape prison? He was in the deep sleep chambers. He had to have help."

"Yes, but who?" Cleodna shook her head. "Somebody must have busted him out weeks ago, for him to travel to Earth."

"The Morpher's Council should have known if someone broke out of prison," Scruffy argued. "We may have insiders helping him."

"Someone either busted Venamir out of prison, or snuck him out," Slade said. "We need to go back to Atlearon."

"We have good Rangers there, Slade, from your clans as well," Cleodna started.

Slade rubbed his temples. "It's a hunch. When Venamir and I were in psy combat, we relived some of the old wartime flights. It was back when he and I served together, flying for Atlearon's defense. I saw the deep sleep prison, and wrecked starships. Venamir's obsessed with getting back to our old ship and regrouping his followers. I'm sure that he wants to take over the council, again." He thumped a fist on the table. "Something has made him stronger. I can barely use telepathy and I can't morph."

Cleodna blurted, "What? He nullified your *powers*?"

Slade rose, showing his hands. He tried to morph, wincing with the effort. He could barely grow fur and canine-like claws for a couple seconds. The rest of his body remained in his coppery-skinned, pointed-eared, humanoid, form. "When I try to shape-change or use my telepathy, I see flashbacks of crashing in our old lead ship, the *Spectre*. Every time, Venamir and I are in the cockpit, and we're under attack. The ship's on fire. Something's different, though. I'm not sure what."

Scruffy winced, as if sharing a headache. "I see our old ship too, about to crash, every time Slade has the flashback. We have to get your mind shields back up, pal."

"Sorry," Slade said, "I'm trying to control it. Venamir or his pet canceled my memories of how they escaped, but they woke my flashbacks full force. We crashed in the *Spectre* almost twenty years ago. I thought the worse of those memories were behind me, but now, it's like we crashed yesterday."

Cleodna scowled, drumming her fingers. "Did you gain anything from the mind link?"

"Yeah," Slade nodded. "I did read his mind, some. Venamir's main mission isn't on Earth. It's on our world. I'm sure of it. We have to hunt him down."

Cleodna reached over and shut off the creature's image. "If Venamir truly is starting another uprising, then he will need his closest cohorts. Doctor Cruentin is one of his few, trusted, friends."

She went on as her friends scowled at the name. "Cruentin is imprisoned on the avian world, Crawshen. So are a handful of others who worked for Venamir. I'll send a few spies to scout around. Last I heard, there's still a human outpost on the bird world, and feline colonies."

"Venamir has allies on the bird world," Scruffy said. "Someone there has to know something."

"We should check out the prison on the bird world, Crawshen," Slade said. "The infamous Doctor Cru, those two go way back." His voice drifted off in thought. "Venamir would want to rescue him."

Scruffy looked at Slade, who was scrolling through galaxy maps. "You don't think he'd use your ship to attack the prison? That'd be crazy. He's sneakier than that."

"He's gotten crazier," Slade argued. "He attacked us within the council chambers and made arms deals and poisons with lizards before we could make a truce with them. And then, after he escaped prison, he attacked Earth."

"Yeah, yeah," Scruffy sighed.

Slade conjured a map of a virtual fortress that covered the table. Tall, rock walls and force fields protected the outer perimeter. Two guards manned heavy artillery at the top of each guard tower.

"There's three main entrances big enough to drive vehicles through the gates," Scruffy observed, pointing to highlighted gates on the map, then to the tallest buildings. "They still have two rooftop landing sites. Each landing platform can hold a couple shuttles, but not a ship like ours."

"This is the most high-tech prison on Crawshen," Slade said in thought. "The Hrokah are bird people. Most of them can fly, but for combat, they prefer single seat fighters. Most of the prison is underground. I'm sure the *Jacobyte's* stealth mode can hide the ship from Hrokah detection. Local scanners won't see her until it's too late. Even without her main guns, my ship's defense guns can deal heavy damage." Slade replied in a disgusted tone. "Venamir knows we're coming after him. We don't have time for lengthy diplomacy. We need to pursue him."

"Agreed," Scruffy said. "Cleodna, I need you to stall the diplomats here on Earth. Do us a favor, Sis. Watch your back,"

"Don't worry. Your clan's top morphers are guarding me. Berkiru chose them for the job." Her image vanished.

"I think we should have chosen Cleodna's bodyguards," Slade remarked.

Chapter 7
Bermuda Tourist Trap

A sky taxi cleared for landing carried a few dozen passengers, mostly human tourists. The tourists chatted as they viewed architecture built by offworlders. Several dome-topped buildings linked together, typical of Altearon towns, with large skylights and trees jutting upward from around the buildings. The eager passengers gathered their carry-on luggage once the taxi landed.

"Welcome to Bermuda's latest, greatest theme park. Keep an eye out for pirates, mythical beasts, and the like," said their pilot in a bored voice.

Before his incarceration and escape from prison, Venamir was sure his days of infiltration were over. Yet, here he was, posing as a man with dreary, blonde dreadlocks, wearing tourist attire. The shirt was itchy, the khaki pants too loose, but at least his morpher shoes were his own. *Reduced to taking an Earth form yet again.* He touched the comm band around his left wrist, activating little holograms of ocean terrain that flowed up his forearm. His coordinates were near beyond some ancient shipwrecks, around an hour out to sea by local boats.

A burly customs agent boarded the air taxi and lectured his captive audience, wasting more precious time. As the agent moved closer, Venamir cancelled the map and presented a fake ID that read Terome Zeon, some actor, according to Moradin.

"Nice tech toy," the customs agent said, sneering at the ID. "Did a raving fan send it to you?"

Venamir stared back, trying to figure out how this badge-toting man could fight his way through anything besides an eating competition. "What an impressive badge, did you win it somewhere?"

The agent's face reddened. "Look, big shot, don't get your head swelled on my watch."

"The mighty badge has spoken. Someone fetch this man a doughnut," Venamir jabbed, eliciting chuckles from passengers as he donned the slender backpack. "No autographs, my schedule is rigid."

The customs agent barked, "Get out!"

The pilot watched silently, eyes narrowing behind his sunglasses.

Venamir sneered at the customs agent, snubbed the pilot, and elbowed his way through the shuffling tourists departing the air taxi.

The pilot watched him leave, and then returned to the cockpit where he waited for the last passenger to depart. Once alone, he grabbed his comm. "Zared? Hey, I may have your man, raggedy looking actor with a pristine ID and a weird attitude."

Zared's tiny image floated above the comm. "Define weird."

"I haul lots of celebs around, and I've seen this guy before. There's something strange about him. His accent's weird, and he's usually cool. Today, he was a prick. He wore a high-tech comm band and a diving backpack, that fit him like a second skin. It has to be offworld gear." The pilot scrolled through his security cam's images until he found some of Venamir and viewed them with his comm. "I recorded him. Watch."

Zared's eyebrows slowly rose. "Zoom in on his eyes."

The pilot adjusted an image of the suspect's hazel eyes, to see a strange, gold gleam in the pupils. "Whoa," he murmured, "they're like golden pearls."

"Those are Merfin eyes," Zared said. "Where'd he go?"

"Toward the docks."

* * *

Flushing the annoying sky-taxi experience to the back of his mind, Venamir explored a new spaceport built to host offworld species. Paths wove to a series of extensive theme rooms that resembled scenic bits of other planets. Only two of the rooms were cooler than outside. Humidity leeched his energy like a sauna and sunroofs welcomed the bright sunlight so humans could wear less and tan faster. Music from clashing bands hit his ears from two directions, and vendors of all kinds competed for sales, as if anybody wanted a wooden monkey, or other childish trinkets.

Venamir began wading through the mostly human tourists. There were scattered offworlders, one feline family, a few reptile races, and a few Atleans. The aliens reminded him that, without doubt, there were telepaths nearby, probably Atlean tourists. He didn't understand seeing people with sunburn. *Why do they burn their bodies? Oh, of course, because they're cavemen.* He concentrated on not holding his side or limping. Even though he had already healed the worst of the damage from his fight with Slade, moderate heat and his aching body wore him down.

He could barely wait to morph and relieve himself of his ghastly human appearance. His skin itched, his feet hurt, and he was dreadfully thirsty. One scent on the air actually tasted good, so he answered the rumblings of his stomach and headed toward an outdoor sushi bar. "Raw fish," he mused, "how bad can it be?"

* * *

Wulvur felt strange, not hiding his true form, especially on a hunt, but he knew Slade's style. He could play the bait, hoping to draw the attention of Venamir's followers. Dealing with humans was another matter. Breaking news on overhead monitors showed a resurgence of local protesters warning Earth of fish people, showing pictures of Venamir. Wulvur saw some people starting a tour and jogged to catch up. The tour guide was embellishing fearsome legends of the Bermuda Triangle. When asked about a resort in hurricane alley, she elaborated on their new high technology that protected them from such storms.

"Atlean technology," Wulvur muttered.

One of the older men in the group elbowed his buddy. "Great, now we're safe from storms, but not aliens."

"Damn fishes," the other man agreed.

The tour gave him the easiest path through a cluster of buildings facing the ocean. He soaked in the surroundings, noting how themes mimicked other planets. Holograms of wild beasts from his world, not so different from Earth's woodland creatures, except many of them had paws with five digits instead of four. Many species excelled in blending into their environment, and herbivores had sharper teeth than those on Earth. The next building smelled of salt water and cooked fish. A few Merfins were lounging in a colorful, spacious aquarium, snacking on unusual fish. The beach theme building was quite hot, with people basking beneath artificial sunny skies cast from the ceilings. And there were women, lots of them, many in swimsuits. Wulvur found a convenient batch of decorative trees to duck behind, and emerged as a hefty, brown retriever wearing a thick, padded harness and collar with a dog-bone tag.

Scruff's voice whispered from his collar's tiny comm, "Wulvur, report."

Wulvur whispered back, "Scruffy, there are some telepaths here, but not Venamir."

"Quit watching the ladies."

"Aw, man."

Wulvur trotted along the beach, his Druwen senses put to the test. The tourists made it hard to focus, with strong smells of food, loud music, and the sight of bikinis. His tail started wagging at a lady whistling to him, but he pried his eyes away and pressed on. Something felt familiar, strong psy shields swirling like the ocean tides—he sensed anger. Wulvur ran toward the ocean, where the presence felt stronger. A wave of pain and contempt washed over him, sending his hackles on end and his ears back. Wulvur halted, sniffing, listening, not noticing a few men give him a wide berth until one of them urged his lady friend to leave the mean dog alone. Wulvur snapped back to his senses, and whined in embarrassment.

Zared's hushed voice came from his collar, "Anything?"

"Venamir's nearby," Wulvur muttered. "He's using psy *blockers.* I got a crazy migraine and couldn't focus."

"Same thing he used on Slade," Zared replied. "Grab our Huvzters. He'll go for the ocean." He tapped his comm. "Berku, respond." He waited a few seconds, tapping his fingers on the firgun beneath his shirt. "Berku!"

Berku's image appeared over Zared's comm, hastily grabbing a holster. "What?"

"I have a lead on Venamir," Zared quickly replied. "I need all your spies and Rangers in the Bermuda spaceport to track me. Alert your contacts in Merfin cities report to the undersea Deeps resort. Those who can breathe water, lock onto my signal and be ready to apprehend Venamir."

"Hot damn," Berku nodded, hurrying over to his desk comms. "I have some spies there, will activate them right now."

Zared saw numerous blips on his comm of his allies accepting his order.

The image of a silvery blue Merfin woman appeared on his comm. "I'm already at the Deeps city. Track my location. Venamir called me a little while ago. I'm going to meet with him."

"Vanysa, don't trust him," Zared warned.

"I don't, but he trusts me," she said, fading away.

* * *

Venamir could feel them, Atlean kindred, their thoughts tickling his mind like the unwanted intervention of a wild dream. He reached out with his psy and concentrated on the minds around him, ignoring the chaotic jabber of human minds as he searched for any more telepaths. He recognized one mind, a psy presence thinking in Atlean, his old colleague, Zared. There was another Atlean nearby, one with primal shields, like the instinctive thoughts of a beast. Venamir hissed in realization. *One Atlean is morphed. He is familiar. The other telepath is Zared. Did Slade not survive the mine field?*

Heavily distracted by voices and the obnoxious thumps of party music, Venamir sighed and withdrew from his trance, slowly remembering where he was, sitting at an open bar overlooking the ocean with a plate of sashimi on the bar beside him. He sipped the tall, bubbling drink, only to set it down with a clunk. "Disgusting." He dropped a piece of fish into the drink and swirled it around. Noticing the bartender staring, Venamir stabbed another chunk of fish with his straw and dropped it into the drink. "Now, it is palatable."

The bartender grimaced a bit; nevertheless, he gestured toward the rows of liquor. "Sure you don't want something else?"

"Certain."

As the bartender moved off, Venamir began to watch the annoying happiness oozing from tourists. He had to get off this beach. The hot sun was torturous. Vender booths and endless milling of tourists cluttered his escape. The comm band around his wrist pulsated and he saw a message from Vanysa, along with an ocean chart. *Finally!* He sprang up from his barstool and jogged to the nearest path.

One tent, a yurt of sorts, stood out from the other money-suckers and their flimsy stands. Soothing music and voices of whales sang to him, and he tasted the gentle aroma of incense. Venamir swiftly entered the yurt of the fortune-teller, Madam Sees All.

"I've been expecting you," said a sultry woman's voice.

Venamir paused, remembering his disguise. "I came here for privacy."

One of the long curtains moved, swept aside by neatly manicured fingernails. A woman dressed in flowing attire of many colors and at least three layers of skirts. "We have privacy here." She swished over and took his hands into hers. "I see so much in you, tension, ambition, and yet, you are seeking something. Perhaps, a happier life?" She turned his hands over, her eyebrows lifting. "You have the longest lifeline I've ever seen. You must let me give you a reading."

Silly girl with delusions of greatness. Venamir took a seat at a table with an odd, smoke-filled ball in the center. "On one condition. I give you a reading as well, and then, we shall see who foretells all."

The Madame swooned as she caressed Venamir's hands. "Oh, you are so passionate." In a heartbeat, her voice filled with pity, "You are lost, trapped between your dreams, living in a cage."

Venamir's tone darkened with suspicion as he leaned closer. "What?"

"A soul trap, one that burdens you with all the grief in your life."

Oh, she wishes to know of grief. I can help her. Venamir rested his chin in one hand, his patience thinning as she rambled on about his grief-stricken, poor, childhood, a torn family, and all emotional trials that kept him miserable every day of his life. He glanced down at the pouch on his belt and eased his hands around a warm control device. The mind-numbing effect even slowed his psychic power, but the gadget prevented other telepaths from focusing on him. He pulled his hand free of the babbling woman's grip. "Get to the point."

A muscular man emerged from the back section, packing a Taser and a big attitude. "You need help? I'll throw this guy out for you."

"No, I'm making progress." She folded her hands. "For a fee, I can pray for you and meditate to all the goddesses. I can relieve you of your anguish, all the things that hold you back from happiness. Think how wonderful your life would become."

Venamir rose, laughing harder than he'd laughed in a long time. He raised a hand toward the advancing bodyguard. "Goodnight, toy-boy," he said, a quick psy attack dropping the man to the floor, snoring. He turned on Madame Sees All, who froze, aghast. "You, a lower life form can cure me? Outrageous!"

She gasped as Venamir grabbed the crystal ball. It filled with images of her own life, hidden memories now vibrant in her mind. Venamir's form morphed as if green water poured a new skin over his body. Sturdy fins sprouted from his back, forearms and legs, and webbing spread between his fingers.

His voice imperious, he retorted, "Woman, for tens of your lifetimes I have lived, and only now, drift near the years of elders. You seek to control every poor imbecile around you to make up for your failures in life. You were too young a mother, failed in five marriages, and alienated your family so they will no longer help you." As she gaped at him, he let the images fade from her imagination. The crystal ball showed nothing. "Now, you will hire a boat for me, the first available. Tell nobody of our meeting. I see into your hungry little brain. I know where every lost soul you care about lives. Now go." He slammed a fist on the table, laughing as she scampered out swifter than a deer in flight.

The Madame tore out of her yurt, heart hammering. She froze when Venamir's voice filled her head with more orders. She stood, nodding, until he released her mind. One last glance at the famous sign made her stomach lurch. She wrestled some lipstick from a vest pocket and scrawled, OUT OF BUSINESS.

Venamir followed her out, laughing. The sweet, salty taste of the ocean drifted through all the harsh odors and beckoned his parched body toward the nearest cliff, where waves crashed in a melodic, ominous rhythm. He zipped open his shirt at the sides, then kicked off his sandals and flung his shades aside. *How can they wear these things?* Venamir adjusted his body-hugging backpack and gazed around, leering at people in their bright swimsuits, playing ball on the beach. *Adult children, bah!* With his pack clinging to his body, Venamir broke into a jog, then a run as he neared the cliff, his feet growing wider with fins at the ankles and webs between his long toes, allowing him to tread across slippery rocks. How he longed for the towering cliffs of his home island, so rich with wildlife and overgrowth, where he could feel the icy spray of waterfalls. Here, one must settle for rickety framework thrust together for bungee jumping over the surf. Due to gusty winds, workers were shutting the attraction down for the afternoon, and shooing away lingering customers. Venamir took the lift to the top. Ignoring a lifeguard yelling at him, Venamir jogged to a ledge overlooking foaming pools below. He leapt off the edge, noting a few squeals and shrieks from a family sunning themselves on the beach.

Venamir's diving form sliced the air and plunged into the rough sea with the grace of an Olympic swimmer. Not wanting the gullible humans to send a rescue party, he surfaced and waved. "That one was free," he yelled, and swam away, ignoring their applause.

Once out of sight, Venamir dove toward the soothing darkness below. He resumed his true Merfin form and sped downward with powerful kicks of his webbed feet. The rough surf swallowed Venamir's now graceful form. He swam with glee through the sweet ocean water, not as sensual as Atlearon, but soothing enough. He summoned the frazzled Madame to the boat docks. Her mind was easy to find now, a familiar, frenzied ball of chaos between Madame Sees All's overly pierced ears.

* * *

Zared watched from afar, using his comm to zoom in. He sensed Venamir's presence and knew the old fish felt his psy powers as well. Zared felt a surge of anger swell up against his old rival. He watched Venamir surface from the lazy surf in human form. The exhausted Madame Sees-All met him on the beach, where they made a brief exchange. They parted ways, the Madame hurrying away while Venamir sauntered toward a tour boat.

Zared considered altering form but was tired of hiding his identity. At first glance, he appeared as a weathered, middle-aged man, just another tourist, until people spied telltale Atlean ears poking up through his pewter tinged hair. As the boat drew away from the dock, Zared spoke softly into his comm, "Track me. We're following Venamir." He strolled down the hill toward the family.

The parents paid scant attention until their two children noticed the offworlder's odd, humanoid features and alien ears. The kids abandoned their sandcastle and ran over to him, pointing and blurting out quizzical remarks.

Zared smiled at their energetic slew of questions. "Oh, that crazy diver? He does that all the time. No, I don't make toys," he added before they asked.

The little girl tugged at his arm with much persistence. "Nobody's supposed to high-dive here and he shape-changed into a green guy. Are you after him?"

Zared replied quietly, "You're right, he broke the rules. If he comes back, and he shouldn't, it's best to leave him alone."

The girl's bright, green eyes registered caution as she nodded.

Zared shrugged when the parents rose and called their children, the mother giving an apologetic look as the kids pried themselves away from their new alien friend. "It's fine. They're charming."

Bidding them well, Zared jogged farther down the beach, where he found Wulvur sitting beside two jetrigs in water configuration, their lower treads and thrusters resting on the wet sand. He loosened his Hawaiian shirt, revealing a similar wetsuit with layers indicating morpher gear. He rolled up the clothes and stuffed them in the sidebags.

Telari flew over to them, riding a dark purple jetrig with jagged claw marks painted across the body panels. "Hey, fellas."

"Be careful. We're going after big game," Zared said, his voice terse. "Venamir's on a party boat. The passengers scanned as normal humans. Let's go."

Within minutes, they caught up to a boat cruising along with colorful sails and loud music. Zared, Wulvur, and Tel slowed and ran scans to see only human life aboard the boats.

"Damn," Zared said. "I'm going to scout ahead. You two check out this boat." Morphing into a midnight blue Merfin, he dove with casual ease.

"I don't like this," Wulvur grumbled. He pulled up alongside the party boat while Tel approached from the other side. Captain Wally from his name tag, had three couples and one assistant onboard. One man paused from mixing drinks.

"Hi, folks," Telari sang out, "waiting for your hitch-hiker?"

The self-appointed bartender pointed at Telari as he smirked at Wulvur. "The girl can stay. Not sure about you, dude."

Telari smiled at the scantily clad party animals. "Fess up. We know you're missing a passenger. He has dirty blonde hair in dreadlocks, and he turns into a fish when angry."

The partiers glanced at each other, their smiles fading.

"We didn't do nothing wrong. You're cops, aren't choo?" the captain demanded.

"Not from this world," Wulvur replied, "and you just helped a baa-ad criminal." His voice remained strangely calm, even soothing as his hypnotic gaze traveled over each of the party group. "You're lucky he left you all alive."

The captain tried to keep a straight face, but his cheek twitched with worry. "Dunno' what you're talking about."

Wulvur glared at the captain's very tan friend, whose extra padding was reminiscent of thick walrus skin. "Come on, 'Wally the Walrus,' we could arrest you right now, and yeah, we can read minds. There's no lying to us, right, Tel?"

"Yeah." Telari and Wulvur pulled off their helmets to show their Atlean features and pointy ears. "You're lucky all that guy did was hitch a ride, very lucky. What's your real name, Captain?"

"Wallace," the captain replied. "He was a passenger. So what?"

"I'm not here to arrest you, Wally. That guy is Earth's most wanted. He sabotaged your planet's new space station, and you all helped him escape capture."

The captain received shocked, accusing looks and banter from his passengers. Wally tried to calm his group, but they started arguing about their mystery passenger.

The youngest male started making up wild tales of monsters in space prisons. "Damn fish-people, told you not to trust them! They probably have tentacles and fangs. They'll pull you under and suck your blood!"

"Shaddap," Wally grunted.

"That's accurate," Wulvur goaded them, "no telling what you'll find in off-world jails."

The captain held up his hands. "It's not our fault. I thought he was an actor, until he turned all green and freaky. He called us imbeciles and jumped overboard."

"We need to inspect your lower deck," Wulvur said.

The bartender lumbered up to Wulvur and pushed him toward the rail. "You need to join that fish guy. Get out of here."

Wulvur grabbed the guy's wrists, and with a few body manipulations, flipped the stronger, heavier guy into a crumpled pile of pain on the deck. "We may be space aliens, but we can enforce the law. You helped a criminal escape the beach. I know he used you, so let's pretend all this never happened. It's best that you return to shore."

Wally helped his disgruntled friend up and turned to Wulvur. "You believe us? Just like that?"

"Mind-readers, and we know Venamir." Wulvur shrugged. He jogged down the few steps to the cramped lower deck. After a few moments he emerged, looking satisfied. "No fish guys here."

"Let's get this over with. I hate swimming," Tel stated. She flashed a smirk at the boat crew. "Leave the waterbikes alone. You won't like their security systems."

Telari and Wulvur donned their masks and plunged into the water.

Chapter 8
Old Colleagues

Finally, he took a good swim. Venamir abandoned the searing rays of midday sun for glimmering lights in the churning depths of ocean caves and tunnels, illuminated by glow orbs and gems, scattered along rock walls like bits of lost treasure. He winced as the first gasp of salt water burned through his gills, but soon the pain faded to an energizing sensation from being in his element once more. Venamir reached a state of rare contentment in the rhythmic, soothing ocean currents, where the blissful depths drowned out the harsh noises of land machines. He paused to admire a school of fish, waited for them to draw close enough, then lurched into their midst and grabbed one with his teeth. He savored the midday snack as he swam. The water's energy helped him focus, to channel his attention to his next task. When he swam through a shipwreck encrusted with sediment and barnacles, he envisioned how the human sailors must have doomed themselves.

He swam along a sheer rock wall until he spied heavy plant growth. He wiggled past thick seaweed vines to find a cave that branched into three tunnels which he knew was a labyrinth of passages. Venamir swam with the tenacity of a predator in flight, eyes adjusted to the darkness, body maneuvering around jagged rocks with supple grace. He spied faintly glowing orbs and mineral veins along the way, muted signs and markings left by his people. Venamir slowed his pace, cautious, for now he was the hunted. The thought of being predator and prey teased and enlivened his fighting spirit. When the novelty of the cave labyrinth wore off and the caves grew tiresome, he sensed intelligence ahead, others of his race, their minds open just enough for cautious mental contact. The sea tunnel opened to a canyon booming with life, brightly lit where the glow fish and pulsing energy orbs were thickest. The city, built centuries ago from salvaged wrecks and smuggled Atlean technology, remained much as he recalled. Pillars and arches reached up from the ruins, supporting gently waving forests of kelp.

Venamir neared the ornate gateway in the largest pillar. There, he waited. A group of five Merfin people approached, their emotions ranging from jubilance to trepidation. He recognized two, and directed his attention to the sole feminine form, with golden, thick locks swaying in their loose braids. How relieving it was to speak naturally with his kind, using telepathy and ancient Merfin language.

Venamir greeted her mind and even graced her with a rare, genuine smile. *"Vanysa, my dearest niece."* He favored calling her *niece* over my great, great, great, grandniece.

She responded in kind, with that warm smile he trusted. *"Uncle, we knew you'd return."*

Venamir's gaze traveled to each of her consorts, his psyche probing their minds. He tasted their distrust, but mistook it for envy of his superior powers.

"My followers are gathering," Venamir said. "Will you join me?"

A Merfin stayed protectively in front of Vanysa. "The councils order your surrender. Come with us. You're under arrest."

Vanysa smiled, patting the dauntless young man. "This is Faron, my bodyguard."

Venamir's expression turned humorous. He swept close to the young consort, mere inches from ramming into his chest, but the youth refused to stand down. "Do you think you can stop me?"

"I'll haul you in myself," Faron countered.

Venamir's voice dripped with ironic sweetness. "My dear, I believe this schoolboy desires you."

Vanysa blushed. "Uncle! He is my bodyguard. Stick to business."

Faron's webbed hands clenched around his spear gun. "Why did you attack the space station?"

Venamir laughed outright and swam a circle around the youngsters. "Did you think Slade would simply give me back my ship? The space station was a warning shot. So many could have died, yet I spared them, and the Council still seeks to prosecute me?"

"Five humans died," said one consort.

"Pfft, small change," Venamir scoffed.

"And one Atlean, our Magistrate," Vanysa added with a morbid, analytical stare that made most men reconsider their next statement.

Venamir appeared unruffled. "No, he went into hiding, the diplomatic coward. This is your chance to serve our people, not humans."

"I'm here to help both," Vanysa replied.

Venamir sighed. "We've helped them enough." He turned, gazing at the caves. "We have an eavesdropper. Well, well, my old friend Zared still thinks he can hunt me."

Zared ducked behind an ancient pillar just beyond the Merfin city's edge, his deep blue skin and black wetsuit melding him in the near blackness of the deep. He felt the emotions of Vanysa and her consorts, mixed emotions, clashing agendas. All too soon, his wariness proved true. Zared recoiled when Venamir's sharp, searing thoughts carved their way into his mind, and cast aside his mental defenses like nobody else could. He grabbed his belt, jabbed attached controls and called out to all telepaths within range of his strongest psy voice, "*NOW Rangers, capture Venamir!*"

From the tranquil city, alarms went off as swirling orange searchlights penetrated the ocean darkness with glaring beams. Merfin swarmed around the city, some fleeing for shelter while others turned against townspeople. Merfins and the undercover Druwens challenged each other, many starting fights. The glittery, placid, charming town degenerated into chaos.

Two of the five consorts also turned on Venamir, whipping energy weps from their holsters. The senior patroller said in a level voice, "Surrender. Better with us than landwalkers."

Venamir glanced at Vanysa, needing only a light thought scan to read her inner turmoil as clear as her taut features revealed, and he knew that her mind felt loyal enough for now. "You should flee."

Faron grabbed Vanysa and activated a power cell in his shoulder pack. Swirling energy engulfed the two, created a vibrant safety field and with a flash of light, they were gone. Faron appeared surprised to glimpse of Venamir giving him a half salute.

Venamir chortled, "See if your domestic forces can beat my loyal spies." He motioned toward the city as the populace burst into chaos and social upheaval. Merfins were challenging each other, many shocked and confused, others trying to tackle Zared's spies. He swam for the tunnel where Zared blocked his path at the cave mouth.

Zared flexed his hands and talons sprang free from his gloved fingers. Venamir morphed into his reptilian iguana monster form and charged his rival, the force driving them into the cave. Venamir's mind focused on protecting his gills from further injury. Zared slashed for his throat and found burly shoulders with thick, scaly hide instead. Venamir sank his teeth into Zared's left forearm, trapping the hand, while he ripped at the lethal glove.

The fight took them farther through the caves, toward the surface. Venamir had not bothered to communicate with Zared until they exhausted themselves. The surface drew near as they wrestled for kill strikes at the upper cave mouth. Only then did Venamir sense more intruders. He could hear whispers of thoughts from two morphers, one female, and debated for a moment. Something about them made him curious.

Venamir taunted, "Zared, we don't have to be enemies. Send your helpers away. Work for me, and I'll spare their lives"

"I'll haul you in, piece by piece," Zared retorted.

Venamir clenched his fists, triggering spikes to raise up from his wristguards and the tops of his gloves. He slashed at Zared's forearms, drawing blood, but his old peer still wrestled him into a headlock. Zared then grabbed a pouch from his belt and spewed the contents into his opponent's face, effectively blinding him. Venamir broke free and headed for the cave. Something clawed at his leg, more talons, he surmised by the deep pain of parallel gashes. He glanced back and saw a long-haired woman with blood lust in her eyes, a look that clashed against her youthful, almost innocent features. Wulvur swam at her side, firing small, self-propelled blades from his armbands.

Out-racing them underwater, Venamir spun away and activated an energy shield from his backpack straps. Blasts reflected off the pack, while another seared past his left ear, and something sharp pierced his skin. He quick released the backpack straps and flung the pack at them. The pack ripped apart, activating a stun mine, knocking everyone away from each other, and churning up a monstrous, blinding cloud of debris. Venamir retreated into the darkness.

Telari gasped as she surfaced first and ripped her mask off, then commenced her favorite form of venting. "Scaggy, bottom-feeding bastards." On she went, enough to make Wulvur wish that swear words alone could slay Venamir. They looked around and saw only the jetrig in the distance. No sailboat, no surfboards. "Foggy, come here," Tel called. The jetrig, some hundreds of feet away, started its engine and cruised over to them. Tel climbed up on her rig and patted the back seat.

Zared climbed up behind her. He blew water out of his gills before resuming his natural, air-breathing form. One of his taloned gloves was gone and he bore multiple gashes. "Venamir started a riot. He had a number of followers down there, looked like at least a couple dozen. I can pilot this."

"No way, you're a mess. I'm driving. Let's go. We're big time shark bait." She initiated hover mode and her watercraft lurched upward, several feet over the water's surface. Sighing, embarrassed, Zared grabbed her around the waist.

Some fifty feet away, the party boat people watched with keen interest.

Wulvur yelled, "You all better run before fish-man comes back. He's really pissed!"

They didn't argue this time. The boat captain revved their engine and sailed toward the shore.

Wulvur whistled, summoning his jetrig to him. He climbed on and took off alongside Telari.

Wulvur and Tel were digging into their medkits when Elowren's shuttle flew down and landed on the water, tail mounted engines roaring. A cargo door whooshed open, large enough for them to dock, and slammed shut behind them. Tel wasted no time in using cargo straps to secure their rigs.

Elowren threw them a worried look, seeing Zared in a bandaged mess, and all of them drenched. "What happened?"

"Damned fish frenzy," Tel replied. "Venamir was there, but he got away. He took a chunk out of Zared here. The boat people were just pawns." She activated her tracking comm and waved it over the nav panel. "Blue boat's the sailboat."

Wulvur chimed in, "The red is Venamir. I shot him with a tracker."

Elowren debated for a split second and buckled into the nearest seat. "We're too outgunned." She rounded on Zared, "And you, of all people? Trying to fight Venamir in his natural element?"

Everyone onboard was glad not to be Zared. He tried to wave Elowren off, but her glare made him sink farther down in his seat. Zared rubbed his arm and started, "Yeah, yeah, I didn't expect Venamir to have so many followers willing to fight. The Merfins went crazy down there. The town barely had enough guardians to fight back"

Elowren sighed. "Couldn't you have waited for reinforcements?"

"No," he replied. "I'm rather insulted. Have you lost faith in me?"

"No, but look what happened on the *Jacobyte*. Venamir dismantled every defense on that space station, and on Slade's ship. We can't treat Venamir like a normal target. He may even be more powerful than before the Council convicted him to the deep sleep chambers. You're all drenched. Was the boat that wet?"

Wulvur replied, "We dove in for a piece. Zared needed help."

Elowren fell silent, not sure if she owed them an apology or not. "You survived against Venamir. That's admirable."

"No, I'll tell you what admirable is." Zared defended his friends, "I *was* in trouble and these two fished me out. Tel, I want you to train with us full time."

"Woo!" Tel bounded over and gave Zared a hug, despite his wincing. "Look," She said, pointing to the window. "There's a ship coming out of stealth. It's the *Jacobyte*—there." She started jabbing comm keys. "I'm sending out distress signals."

"Elowren, get Venamir to trade me for the Doc," Wulvur said, leaning forward in his chair. "I'll throw out one of his crewmen and infiltrate that ship."

"No." Elowren snapped. "You're not taking on his entire crew." Grumbling, Wulvur sank back in his chair.

The stolen warship hovered over the ocean waves and turned, her steady pivot moving slow enough that they could read *Jacobyte* across the bow.

Elowren held up a warning hand. "All power to shields, no weapons. Don't power weapons. If we shoot first, we're dead." She sent out her psy, and found Venamir's mind within seconds.

Venamir replied, *"Ah, the regal Coven Ranger herself."* He hailed them and opened the comm channel. His image appeared on the screen, in natural Merfin form. "After all the years, the eons we spent evolving, our people decide to regress and help humans. When did we become the parents of infant species?"

"So you steal a ship and turn renegade," Elowren replied.

"The renegades are you," Venamir countered. "It's time for a new High Council, one willing to ally with powerful species, not infantile humans."

Zared rose and limped over beside Elowren, his tone seething, "You still want to take over. We'll hunt you down, Venamir. You should have stayed in deep sleep."

Venamir eased his hand down over the weapons control. He flicked off the safety and targeted them. Nothing happened. He jiggled the firing handle. Eyes narrowing, he glanced at the weapons screens, to see the ship's Herja, and one word flashing across the screen: "UNAUTHORIZED. Access Denied." Weapons remained powered down.

"What in the depths?" he muttered. He glanced at his copilot, Moradin, who sat in the copilot's chair. "What is that stupid computer doing?"

"The Herja program is doing her job," Moradin said.

Zared's hologram appeared on the comm screen located over the weapon's panel. "Give up, Venamir. Surrender now, and our councils may be lenient."

Perplexed, Venamir replied, "We gave you back your Captain and his crewmen. You should have retired from spying and hunting, Zared."

"By dumping them into a minefield," Elowren fired back. She glanced at her screens. A circle of red appeared around her shuttle, but it faded. They were safe, for now. She tapped a red key marked for distress signals. If she could just stall him. "The council doesn't want to execute you, not yet. What are you trying to do, start a civil war?"

Venamir leaned forward and with much satisfaction, replied, "Oh, come now, my vision has already begun." His image faded. The *Jacobyte* shot skyward.

Tel reported, "Two fighters pursuing Venamir."

"They won't catch him," Elowren replied, also watching her sensors. "That means they'll live." The retreating ship on her screen vanished. "The *Jacobyte's* gone to stealth."

"Why didn't Venamir try anything? He could've blown us up, or ported us out," Telari said.

"I'm sure he wanted to," Elowren replied as they flew off. "I don't think he could."

* * *

As the *Jacobyte* left the shuttle far behind, Venamir released the weapons controls and rounded on his copilot. "Moradin, why could we not attack them?"

Moradin pressed her fingers against scanner ports and skimmed over the screen's data. "I've been trying. It's a Herja program, didn't surface until we tried using the weapons."

Venamir drew a long sigh. "This ship has a Herja program. The councils promised to ban those."

"We need four of us from the original crew to override the main computer," she replied. "It may let us fight in defense, but the only way to find out is to be attacked."

"You must be joking."

Moradin withdrew her fingers from the ports. "You know I don't joke."

Venamir snarled, voice oozing with fury, "SLADE!"

Chapter 9
Enter the *Vernacular*

At first glance, a spacer might look at Scruffy's patchwork ship and blow her off as an old relic, just like her captain. A grizzled bear of a ship, she looked like a morpher from her war scars and modifications. While most of the Atlean fleet's victories faded into whispers of memories, the *Vernacular's* reputation was well known in stories of war and rescue. She responded to Scruffy's light touch like the old friend she was, her engines whining their usual moaning song as she touched down on a vast, icy landscape. Stealth mode adjusted to the surrounding landscape and within seconds, shielding activated and adapted to the new surroundings. The *Vernacular's* patchwork hull turned white as snow to match the terrain.

Within easy visibility, what appeared as a snowbank dropped its own stealth, revealing Zared's elite scout ship, *Lady Mythos*. Elowren and Zared disembarked, pausing as a brisk wind greeted them. Elowren fastened her coat, shivering despite her warm, casual attire of a sweater, jeans, and tall boots.

Zared still appeared somewhat formal, even in winter clothing. "Good thing you're not in that wet party dress," he joked.

Surprised, she turned, eyebrows raised, "What? I'll never hear the end of that."

Zared chuckled as they strode through ankle-deep snow, "No, you won't."

Telari and Wulvur followed, seizing the chance for a quick snowball fight.

Scruffy opened the ramp to the *Vernacular* and let them in. The old ship's ramp took its time, creaking even more than usual. "Like the scenery?"

"We left the beach to freeze here," Zared quipped. He glanced at Wulvur and Tel, just in time to duck. A snowball beaned Scruffy in the chest.

"Really? You two can stay out there," Scruffy threatened, reaching for the controls. He rolled his eyes as the rebellious duo jogged inside. "Pups. Yeah, we're here because there are too many fish spies in the tropics right now. Come on, I've got snacks in the ready room. Wulvur, you know where the stealth gear is. Load up my Huvzter." Scruffy shut the creaky ramp.

"You got it," Wulvur replied.

Rhoan joined Telari at the pantry. "Hey, you know Slade wants that damage report."

"Yup." She was topping off a mocha with whipped cream. "I'm making this for him, might cheer him up." She winked, picked up the mug and data pad, and sashayed out. She found Slade pacing in the medbay, wincing as he wrestled with a shirt.

"This goo feels like a straitjacket," he grumbled.

Tel set the mug and her datapad down on the small table and tugged the shirt down for him. "Try a respirator and harness over cold weather gear, fun times."

Slade paused, noting her unusual camaraderie; then again, she was a maintenance woman. She showed no embarrassment at catching him with his shirt off and fastening his pants belt. Slade sat down and tugged the steaming mug over. "Thank you, Telari." He took a few sips. Some of the tension began to melt away. "How'd it go?"

"Call me Tel," she said, passing him the data pad. She began with summarizing hull damage to the *Vernacular* and Zephyrs, her tale sprinkled with fish-men insults, from the web headed bandit, to a puking slug-humper. Then she concluded that nobody could find the *Jacobyte.*

"Of course, my bird escaped. The *Jacobyte's* a prototype. She outclasses most Atlean fleets, and our ships are light years ahead of the Earth's tech." He reached over and patted the nearest wall. "Scruffy rebuilt the *Vernacular* with tech that even our councils don't know about. We'll find the *Jacobyte*, or she'll find us." He sipped the mocha.

"Venamir must have left the *Jacobyte* in stealth mode near Bermuda's spaceport. Why didn't he open fire on us?"

Slade grinned, "Venamir probably couldn't fire. The Herja program limits weapons use in case of hostile takeover. If someone shoots first, the ship can defend herself. Your shuttle wasn't a threat. The main guns won't work unless Venamir hacks the guardian program."

"What exactly is a Herja?"

"It's more than a program. Herja means guard. Usually, only flagships or high dignitaries have one onboard. Most ships have just the defense program. The *Jacobyte* has prototype weapons. Her main guns shoot plasma weapons."

"I thought Atleans banned plasma."

"My *Jacobyte's* needed more security. You know of the lizard wars?"

"Yeah."

"The lizards, Rezoans, were loose allies for centuries, until they fell into civil wars. Around a hundred years ago, the Rezoans' war carried to our world. We ended up warring for a couple decades. The Herjas are one of our best secret weapons. We have the same thing in our drakir hatcheries—humans call them dragons."

"What," Tel piped, "you mean dragons are real?"

"Yeah, I'll show you later. Anyway, the Herja chamber is protected from sound, scanners, and has psy-blockers. It's hidden between medbay and engineering. I've been scrapping with the councils to remove all the chambers. Now we have to save Doc and Kestral." He glanced around. They heard Scruffy snoring. Rhoan sat a distance away, studying holograms of Merfin anatomy. Slade lowered his voice. "Tel, you speak with vivid honesty. Can I ask you something personal?"

"Sure."

"I need to call a conference with other dignitaries. Do I look as bad as I feel?"

Telari chuckled, "For real?"

"Never mind, your reaction says it all."

"No, it's just, I just came out of a fish fight in the ocean and you're concerned about looks? Well, you are moving like a zombie."

"Great, thanks," he grumped.

"You still look good. I mean, women check you out. You haven't noticed?"

"They wouldn't today."

Tel slapped her palms on the table. "Look, women want to jump your bones, in a good way. You charm them, you're hot cha cha, sexy, still got it going on. Capiche?" She paused, wondering if he was actually turning red? "I bet even drunk, you have the nads to outwit a buncha' overstuffed, bullshit artists."

Slade took a couple of long hits of his drink, finally grinning. "Thank you, Tel. That's an ego boost. Besides, you don't need to primp. You would fill a mermaid with envy."

Tel blushed. "That's uh, gentlemanly of you. Cap, when we get home to Atlearon, you've gotta show me some dragons."

"I will, promise," Slade chuckled.

Only then did they notice careful footsteps approach. Rhoan stood in the doorway, arms folded. "Boy, Slade, you are smooth. Tel, you don't make those for just anyone. How sweet."

Tel shoved her way out of the chair. "You're freaking nosy."

"I work here, you incorrigible flirt."

She marched over and poked him in the chest. "How was that flirting? It was a pep talk, you doofus. If you want to *work*, go use your big muscles at the parts washer." She stomped off.

Rhoan turned to Slade, chuckling. "You made *her* blush? Wow, you're the man."

"Rhoan, I know that you're a fine pilot and medic, because here we are." As the young man grinned, Slade raised his voice. "Too bad you lack finesse with ladies."

They heard Tel's footsteps halt. She sang back, "Hah!"

"If you're lucky, I'll coach you," Slade said as he strolled out.

Tel burst out laughing while Rhoan complained, "Man, straight for the jugular."

Slade's brooding returned once he left his jovial friends in medbay. He grabbed snacks from the galley on his way to the ready room. Hours crept by while he researched the news and called his contacts.

Scruffy found Slade in the pantry, wearing formal attire and sipping an espresso. Slade glanced over at him. "Lucky me, I'm meeting with the President."

Scruffy blocked his path. "Where? On *that* space station where you got hijacked? No."

Slade brushed past. "It's a conference in the ready room, you old nanny. You can stand guard."

Scruffy followed, grumbling, "Funny man."

Slade led the way into the ready room. It seldom hosted dignitaries, so instead of primp and polish, the walls held memorabilia from scattered worlds, for memory or humor, not bravado. A pantry was nestled in one corner, stocked with drinks and snacks. Large screens displayed the news, with Venamir showing up on numerous channels. Top stories also flung out theories with grating titles: Atleans Conspiring Already? Merfin Hijacks Diplomat's Ship! Gills and Chills. Amazing Fish Prophecy.

Telari joined them and dropped into a chair. "Chat rooms are crying alien invasions."

Slade shut off the news and activated the hologram table. Rhoan walked in and linked a wall screen to medbay. The screen showed Shanto and Gus's body images, both sleeping, bio signs stable. Elowren strolled in and sat down beside Slade. Her long, wind-teased burgundy hair looked all the better to Slade. Zared entered, sipping a cup of tea, and eased into a chair.

Slade's mood lightened when he saw Elowren. "Hi, Sweetie."

Elowren winked back. "Hi, troublemaker."

"So tell me more about this morning's hunt," Slade prompted.

Zared blew steam off his hot tea. "We almost had Venamir."

"Like when he flew away," Elowren jested.

"I meant in the ocean," Zared countered. "I had some agents in the Deeps town, but Venamir had followers there too. When my agents tried to stop Venamir's followers, it caused a riot." His embarrassed gaze drifted. "I couldn't stop him. He's more powerful than I recall."

"Yes, he is," Slade said. "Did you get anything besides a good clobbering?"

Zared wrapped his hands around his steaming mug, still trying to warm up. "That makes two of us who got clobbered." He exchanged sour looks with Slade. "Good news is, we saw your ship, and made brief psy contact with Doc. The *Jacobyte's* guardian contacted us, too. When Venamir took over the ship, he caused overloads in the defense systems. Your ship's Herja Kestral didn't wake up because the sleep tube electrocuted her. Medbots helped her recover, but it took a few days. She's still in the guardian chamber onboard the *Jacobyte,* and Doc's onboard somewhere. I told her to stay put and spy on them."

Slade rose and grumpily retrieved a power bar from the pantry. "The Morpher Council isn't helping. We told them to ditch the deep sleep tubes. Kestral had no chance to fight when we needed her," he said between chomps. "Freaking councils insisted on putting her in deep sleep. I should have woken her up anyway."

Zared went on, "Kestral sent a cryptic message early this morning. The *Jacobyte's* hiding on Earth until they make repairs. We followed Venamir from the Bermuda Spaceport to an aquatic colony. Vanysa and her guards met Venamir. I had some spies down there already, but so did Venamir. A big fight erupted and Venamir fled the scene. He must've had the *Jacobyte* stealthed nearby. I don't know where our aquatic diplomat Vanysa went. Your brother called in more Druwen Clan rangers to help find Venamir."

Slade dropped into his chair. "My brother, Berku, good. He never trusted diplomats, not after some of our own people defected to join fish 'n' lizards."

"All the councils are tight-lipped," Scruffy grumped as he munched on a peppermint stick. "Our Morpher Council, and aquatic clan leaders. First, our Prime Magistrate traveled all the way to Earth. Then Vanysa got promoted to Ambassador after she used to side with Venamir, and now, the Magistrate's off the grid. I hope he's in hiding and not dead. Oh, and my sister Cleodna's filling in for the Magistrate, and your brother, Berku, took charge of our Druwen spies."

"I hope Cleo stays out of the limelight," Slade replied.

"Of course she will," Scruffy said.

Zared refilled his cup. "I suspect we have new traitors within the Morpher Councils. Venamir took over the space station and your ship too easily. All the diplomats are drooling for info. Good thing the American president's your buddy."

"We're not exactly buds," Slade defended.

"You get along well with Earth people," Zared countered. "Besides, you happened to save the President's life, and the Ambassador Caitlin's."

"He wasn't even the president yet," Slade grinned. "The lizards just thought he was."

Slade turned on the ready room comms and started making calls. Within minutes, little images of the president's group took form over the hologram table, the U.S. President Dean McGreffor, European Ambassador Caitlin, General Barrow, and several bodyguards.

McGreffor smirked tightly. "Good to see you, Slade."

Slade spread his arms and grinned. "Did you lose any bets on the news stories?" He saw one bodyguard elbow another, who shrugged. "Hah! I knew it."

Ambassador Caitlin smiled warmly. "We surmised the media was way off."

The general's face reddened as he butted in, "How do we know you're the real Slade? Even your people don't always detect who's who until it's too late. We need to meet face to face."

"We're better off spread out," Scruffy replied with forced patience.

"He's right. You could be imposters for all we know," Dean argued.

"So could you," Elowren replied.

Insulted, the bodyguards and the general spouted off, bragging about their modern security. Ambassador Caitlin rounded on her colleagues, arguing that they should have listened to the Atleans.

While the humans argued, Elowren scanned the White House grounds and looked over at Slade. "They still have no shielding against alien technology," she said.

Slade leaned back with a long sigh. "Elowren, Scruffy, come with me. The rest of you, stay in the meeting. Let's go visit the President." He rose and strode out, making his friends hurry to catch up.

Scruffy hounded Slade all the short way to the teleportal chamber. "This is a bad idea. The trigger-happy humans will freak out. You're not up to another fight yet."

"But you said the president's my buddy," Slade chided as they entered the portal room.

The portal room had two exits, one on either side. The teleportal chamber consisted of a round platform protected by transparent walls in the vague shape of clamshells. The control panel stood near the doors near a tall cabinet with screens and alarm controls.

Slade pressed his palm to a security panel and opened the cabinet to reveal a weapon rack holding Atlean technology. The rack held five firguns, alongside defense gear for hand-to-hand combat, guantlets and bracers with power cells. The next racks displayed combat gear designed for morphers, belts with body shield modules, kilzers, stealth gear, and pouches of mystery artillery.

"Body shield tech only," Slade said, donning a belt.

Scruffy heaved a sigh as he and Elowren also donned shield belts.

Elowren smirked. "We won't need tech gear. Scruffy and I can hypnotize them."

Chapter 10
Surprise Guests

President McGreffor watched the images of Slade, Scruffy, and Elowren vanish from their hologram projectors, leaving only the images of Rhoan, Zared, and Telari.

"Where'd they go?" McGreffor asked.

"Meeting you in person," Telari replied.

"Slade and two others will port in any second now," Rhoan informed. "Stay calm and don't shoot them. You wouldn't win, anyway."

Everyone in the President's office jumped at the sight of energy rings appearing at the far end of the room. Bodyguards clambered into the line of fire, weapons ready.

"I remember those rings," President McGreffor said. "Stand down, everyone." As he spoke, the blinding light dimmed, making the newcomers recognizable. His bodyguards jumped in front of him anyway. McGreffor ordered, "I said, stand down."

Slade, Elowren, and Scruffy stepped out of a virtual doorway that faded into nothingness, leaving them in the room with the US President, a smiling European Ambassador, a defensive general, bodyguards trying to block their view, and a few nervous staff members. Elowren and Scruffy psy-linked with the group, casting a hypnotic sensation, dulling the bodyguards' reactions for a few moments. The bodyguards swayed like sleepwalkers while Elowren and Scruffy kept them hypnotized.

Slade shook his head. "Oh, people, we should *not* be able to port in like this. I told you that when my surgeons fixed your eyes, Dean."

A few people glanced at the President, who shook his head. "Yes, you did," Dean admitted. He strode closer and shook hands with his new guests. "Everyone, calm down. Have a seat, please."

Presidential bodyguards whipped out their guns as they shook off the hypnotic state. "You can't just pop in here and get into our heads," one bodyguard complained, stomping up to Slade's party. "How're we supposed to trust you?"

Slade held his ground. "You wanted to meet face to face. This is how spacers do things."

Dean intervened. "I said, stand down. Now!"

Slade started off. "We're safe enough for now. My crew is monitoring us. We're here to discuss Venamir." He gazed around the room. "Wait. Are you sure nobody knows we're here?"

"How could we call out? You hypnotized us," a bodyguard retorted.

"Wow!" Slade read embarrassment on the humans' faces. "You have to upgrade your security, and I mean, today."

"You're right," the President admitted. "That means you can make that happen today?"

"I can have technicians get it started. The process might take a week."

Nerves settled down. Coffee was offered around the table, and the meeting commenced. The president's office had holograms showing small images of Zared, Telari, and Rhoan on wall monitors. With the swiftness of a pack of wolves, the conference deteriorated into a heated debate. First came the casualty count and shattered defense measures. Then, the stiff-necked general ordered Slade to drop shields and allow them to board *Vernacular*, to prove they weren't hiding anything.

Slade chortled outright and stuck his finger toward the man's face. "You stop right there. Are you serious? That ship's in stealth for a reason. We're trying to lie low until repairs are done."

"Then let's go to the space station," General Barrow stated.

"That'd be a blast. Meet on the foam-soaked space station with boxing gloves," Slade replied.

"You're on," Barrow mock accepted.

Elowren rolled her eyes while Slade sat back, chuckling.

"We're not going back to that space station," Scruffy stated, his ear tips twitching with fervor, "not yet. Our rangers caught infiltrators on the space station. They're still investigating the area."

"The general's eyes narrowed. "You could also help with repairs, starting with the space station's blast doors. You could at least do that. After all, *your* people blew them up!"

Surprise washed over Slade's face. "Oh, really now?" he asked, looking around with raised eyebrows. Elowren returned an innocent look, while Scruffy drooped his shoulders like a guilty kid.

"Ambassador, you can only push diplomatic immunity so far. Control your people."

Slade's expression soured at each condescending word. "That's Consul, not Ambassador. Don't reprimand us."

"Wait, you're not even an Ambassador?"

Everyone in the room could feel Slade's flashbacks begin to sift through his mental shields. Slade reined the storm in his mind just enough to hide his thoughts from his friends. Still, his heated temper lit a fiery gleam in his eyes that made the general's smirk fade. "Don't slam on my crew. One of the council's strongest telepaths hit us, and he had our psy-dulling tech. Venamir infiltrated the space station, took over command center, and stole a ship. Where were our joint defenses? They were either fighting off lizards or trapped in docking bays."

"We launched help," Barrow argued. "By then, the whole space station was being held hostage."

"Yes," Elowren said. "Venamir's strike was so efficient that he had to have help from both our people. Earth launched fighters to help, but Venamir's allies had shuttles waiting in stealth to fend them off. Our security was breached on all levels, yours and ours."

"Your report said Venamir's people, his infiltrators, attacked you from our moon," Dean said, "using our shuttles. Earth's shuttles weren't built for combat."

"It doesn't take much to upgrade them. The shuttle pilots opened fire on my crew." Slade said. He gestured to the holograms of Telari and Rhoan. "Tell them."

"Yeah, they shot at us," Tel replied. "The shuttles had lizards, fish, and cyborgs in them. The pilots were threatening us and targeting the mine field next. We had to disable them."

Slade went on, "Those shuttles hauled in Rezoans, I mean, lizards, and teleported them onto Orion Space Station once infiltrators knocked out security. They'd been upgraded with alien tech and stealth mode. Most of the available ships were stuck in docking bays. Your biggest problem you're dealing with real aliens, not humans. Orion Space Station's defense system is programmed to track life forms. If Venamir killed anyone, sensors would detect loss of life and sound the alarms."

"Makes sense," Dean said.

Barrow wasn't convinced. "For all the good it did. The station's a shambles."

"Our alarm system kept people alive," Slade countered.

"How did Venamir escape?" Dean asked.

"He had help," Slade replied. "It's still under investigation."

"Venamir has moles in high places," Zared's hologram said.

"Well, Slade, how do you plan to catch Venamir? He took your ship. That makes you the one who lost him."

Slade's eyes narrowed. "Barrow, don't be primeval. We're both dealing with forces well above what you're used to." The dull throb in his shoulders spread to his spine. He hid most of it. He glanced at two entrances to the room. "Nobody has realized we're here?"

"Apparently not," one bodyguard said.

Slade shook his head. "Wow. My point exactly! I urged you to install Atlean security. What's the holdup? You all could be dead by now."

"Yes, I get that," the President confessed, "If Venamir hacked the station."

"Venamir had help," Scruffy replied. "I bet he had spies working against us while the station was being built. We can install the same defense tech here, life detectors, portal jammers, and shield generators so nobody ports in without permission. Barrow, you've been putting up the most resistance since we first met."

"With good reasons," the general retorted.

"More like old grudges," Caitlin surmised. "Slade's right."

Annoyed, Barrow countered, "You're far too trusting."

"That's enough," McGreffor cut in. "Elowren, how are your patients? Are they comatose like some of the guards on the space station?"

"Venamir put them into a psychic induced sleep," Elowren replied. "Our medics helped wake the patients. No deaths. Everyone

Venamir's forces attacked are recovering. Our ship's medic, Dr. Nelzyr, and our Magistrate Parleigh are missing. I believe they still live, because they're too valuable."

Barrow shifted in his chair. "So what if we don't install your gadgets? How bad can it get?"

"Famous last words." Telari's holographic image spouted. "All that stuff you see in sci-fi movies, much of it's possible. You have great mentors right here, so don't blow it."

Barrow stared at Tel's transparent image. "You people really watch our sci-fi?"

"Heck yeah," Tel replied. "I figured you could relate to that."

"We learn much from watching a world's entertainment, or lack of," Slade said.

Barrow leaned forward. "Well, our sci-fi has full scale invasions, terraforming, and world destruction. Will that happen?"

Slade waved him off. "No, he won't ruin a living planet. That's movie stuff."

Caitlin gestured to her colleagues. "Can't you help us gain powers like shape-change? It's not all inherited, is it?"

"Much of it is," Slade replied. "We found ways to enhance our psy and morphing abilities."

"They want us to stay behind," the general supposed aloud.

"That's ridiculous," Elowren defended. "We've tried to make good first contact for centuries. Visitors leave because humans are notorious for witch-hunting."

Slade intervened. "I see the problem. Why should humans take us at face value?"

"Because we helped build their shiny, new space station and spaceports," Scruffy threw back. "And we've started colonies with each other."

"The problem is, we still don't understand you as a people," Dean stated.

Tensions flared and ebbed as dignitaries exchanged frustrated looks. Bodyguards stayed tense, glancing around as if more pointy-eared people would jump through the walls.

"Okay, I'll tell you a story," Slade sighed. "Our morphing ability already existed, at a lesser level. Of course, we enhanced our genetics. So do humans." He eyed the general, who didn't argue. "This would be easier onboard our historian's ship. Zared, I need your wall of history. That is, if everyone here is willing to use a portal."

The President and his staff exchanged looks of surprise and apprehension. After some quick deliberation, they agreed, looking more eager than not.

Slade saw an annoyed look on the general's face each time he called the President by his first name. "Dean, you may want to tell someone you're leaving so your staff doesn't freak out."

* * *

Within minutes, Zared ported the group to his main hall, three by three. He also ported Telari and Rhoan over to his ship so they could join the group. The Hall of History spanned double the width of a normal corridor. The visitors didn't appear to mind, their faces eager like kids on a new fantasy ride. Even the somber general smiled as he gazed around.

Vibrant colors emerged from the corridor's walls and ceiling, cloaking the holograms of Slade's friends. Images burst into both comm links, expanding into life-sized visuals throughout both Scruffy's ready room and Zared's history hall.

The humans gasped, some in alarm, most in admiration of lifelike, mythical creatures among vibrant forests full of wildlife, brilliantly colored birds. Flowers turned toward passing life forms, shining from beams of sunlight through a wavering canopy far above.

Zared joined the group and began lecturing them. "This is Atlearon before the lizard wars from centuries ago. We still have areas that haven't recovered." The scene shifted to daylight fading, not from natural means, from invading forces and ship battles that blackened much of the sky. "Guardians helped evacuate as many people and animals as we could. We cared for creatures of sea and land, some facing extinction. They lived alongside creatures from our world, mythical beings in human legends."

"We've all had wars," General Barrow said, folding his arms.

"You wanted to know about us," Slade butted in, "so let him finish."

One of the President's bodyguards muttered, "Oh no, a filibuster."

"Yes, the 'F' word," Slade confirmed.

Holograms depicted aerial battles of mostly small to medium ships emerging from land and sea to fend off huge, bulky ships whose shadows blanketed villages with moving darkness. Docking bays on the raiding ships opened to release swarms of small fighters that began dogfights with Atlean forces.

Zared went on, "We were at war against invaders. Reptilians weren't all bad, but the aggressive subspecies gained allies. We were losing, Merfins retreated to the water, and our clans to the forests."

Images shifted to demolished landscape scenes, followed by laboratories that floated beneath the tides. Other labs had round walls with views of dense forests, as if they among giant trees.

Zared continued his lecture. "We're not so different. Humans try to make super soldiers. We tried to make super guardians. One devastating battle took place in one of our sanctuaries. These were near extinct species we'd collected from other worlds, many of them, like us, gone. The Rezoans and their allies targeted our protected species, our animal kindred. Our wildlife Rangers were inconsolable. They would do anything to protect their animals and our world. Luckily, we still had DNA for some creatures who went extinct on our world."

Barrow said, "So, Atleans experimented on the creatures?"

"No, Barrow, that's a human habit," Elowren replied.

"It isn't now," Caitlin defended.

"Not so much," Elowren half-agreed.

Slade cut in, "No, not the animals, their DNA from their fur. Our Rangers made serums, trying to become more like the strongest creatures who survived."

General Barrow asked, tone skeptical, "You don't mean werewolves and other lycanthrope?"

"Yeah, I do," Slade nodded. "Where do you think legends come from?"

"How can you change shape? We don't believe in magic," Caitlin said.

"Technology and tweaked DNA," Slade replied. "The Deeps Merfins are even more advanced in medicine than we are. Go on, Zared."

"Thanks," Zared said. "When the war reached our bestiaries, we started losing our rare, strongest creatures. The main caretaker, the Coveness, she combined samples of all the serums and drank the brew. It put her in a coma."

The holographic scene in the room conveyed the story more vividly than he could. The President's surroundings appeared as a sanctuary full of frantic beasts and people. Their ceiling turned into a dome shape and appeared to cave in, making everyone but Slade and his friends duck. The group watched air battles peppering the sky with black explosions from unearthly types of ships. Inside the sanctuary, Atleans herded creatures through portals. A handful of heavily armed Atleans lingered behind, salvaging cases of supplies from a laboratory.

One lady was securing racks of small, capped tubes. She was taking samples from each tube and combing them into one larger vial. One guard turned to her, his expression questioning. The lady scientist gulped down half of the contents and capped the vial before she went into a severe tremor. Fur sprouted all over her body. Her hands turned into long-toed paws with formidable nails that shredded the carpet. She struggled up to all fours, body shaking as she morphed into a shaggy predator with tiger-like stripes appearing through her fur. She morphed from a canine beast to a bearlike creature with eyes that gleamed with intelligence. The lady changed again, growing feathers, fur, and wings, akin to a dragon and a chimera. Then she collapsed, her body reverting to her normal, coppery-skinned, humanoid form with pointy ears. Trembling, she pulled the samples from her pocket and was about to finish the tube when a man ran over, took it from her, and drank it instead.

"They were in it together," Slade elaborated. "They were scientists and best friends for life."

The vibrant scene faded as Zared spoke up. "It worked. Before the serum, our clans could only change our skin hue or mimic species close to our own. Her mate couldn't stand being without her. He did the same thing, took massive injections in desperate hope that they'd either survive together, or be reunited in the afterlife."

The next scene showed the two head scientists changing into different Atlean beasts. Their faces were bright with joy, their forms equals to the animals they lived beside.

Zared went on, "The head caretakers survived, waking in the shape of their most kindred beasts. They became our first morphers to morph into animals. In time, they gained more shapes, like creatures from your wildest mythologies. The Coveness made a huge breakthrough that day. The caretakers became the first guardians, or Herjas, and Atleans formed the Morpher Councils."

Baffled, the general asked, "Your people chose to become *more* like animals? Why?"

"Animals are more virtuous," Tel replied without hesitation. "They also have better instincts."

Barrow glanced at Telari. "Who are you?"

"Mechanic, animal trainer, armor forger," Tel replied, "to name a few."

"Your people started infiltrating other worlds," Dean presumed.

Scruffy sighed, "Of course we infiltrated our enemies."

"Morphing eventually became hereditary," Elowren said, "which forced our medical arts to evolve. It's hard on the body. Most who can morph prefer their natural forms."

"What about Venamir? He morphed to infiltrate us," Dean said.

"Humans are easy to impersonate," Tel commented.

"Merfins, fish people, can morph, but it's usually just their gills or fins," Slade replied. "That changed during the wars. Venamir's kin joined up with other tribes. They became better shape-changers, like my folk did. Difference is, they're amphibious. That's part of why Venamir feels his race is superior. They can live on land or at sea."

One of the bodyguards spoke up. "Is that why Venamir turned against you?"

Slade shifted in his chair. "Deep subject. Allying with humans complicated our treaties. We had a tentative peace with the lizards, but there was one problem. The lizards wanted dibs on Earth."

"For what?" Barrow said.

"Trade routes," Slade replied, "that's their story."

"Yeah, I heard about secret meetings between Rezoans and humans," Dean mused.

Slade filled him in. "You remember a few years ago. Atleans were trying to make good first contact, but it was dicey. When the lizards kidnapped you and Caitlin, we came out of stealth and drove them to the ground. That was our first good chance to become allies."

"Why can't you turn our people into shape-changes, morphers?" the general said.

"We're morphers, not magicians," Scruffy snarked.

"Because your skeletons can't take it," Elowren clarified.

"Hybrids morph," Barrow said.

"Some can," Scruffy replied. "Humans are afraid that we're always in secret shapes or reading your minds, right?" Most of the humans nodded. "Well, maybe we don't want to morph or read minds all the time. It'd drive us batty."

Seeing looks of skepticism, Telari added, "Humans can't morph. They change from within. You look the same, but we never know who's going to flip sides. At least when we morph, it's obvious, or detectable." She met the general's annoyed look with a smirk.

"How do you defend yourselves from telepathy?" Dean said.

"We learn to mask our minds," Slade replied. "Humans can learn. It's like ignoring a spouse, only harder." That elicited a few chuckles.

"Anything in the universe you don't want to tell them?" Scruffy psyd sarcastically to Slade.

Slade grinned slightly. "First, we need to upgrade security so people can't teleport in here."

"How'd Venamir beat the space station's security?" Dean said.

"Venamir infiltrated the place so his henchmen could take out your command post. Once they dropped the space station's shields, they ported in a hit team," Elowren replied.

"We already had Atlean tech protecting the space station, and we got our butts kicked," the general complained.

"Venamir's exceptional," Slade admitted. "He's not your normal threat."

"Why are you helping us? What's in it for your people?" Caitlin asked.

Slade shrugged. "Haven't you ever wanted to keep a good neighbor? Install our security systems here before real troublemakers decide to teleport inside your primary headquarters."

"We will," the general promised.

"Give our spies time to work," Elowren added.

"Very well," Dean agreed. "We need to meet again in a few days. I'll invite other ambassadors."

"Good," Slade agreed. "Do it soon, because I'm leaving."

Among shocked utterings, Caitlin's voice stayed the calmest. "You promised to help us!"

Slade's voice lowered, "I'm going to hunt down that sunnuvabitch Venamir."

"You're a diplomat," Caitlin argued.

Slade shook his head. "No, not so much. I'm a Druwen. That means I'm a Ranger for the Morpher Council. We train rangers in combat and survival. We also hunt criminals that others can't take down. It's what I do best." Gesturing to his crew, he added, "What we do best."

The general's defensive look faded. "What support do you need?"

Slade paused, surprised by the offer. "Work with Atlean techs to upgrade your security and flush out spies. Our space station's vulnerable, and so is this planet. Merfins have lived here for centuries. You can learn much from them."

Barrow chortled, "Centuries, right."

Elowren answered with a patient smile, "Many species have visited Earth since your renaissance era. A few colonies stayed, a few thousand people. They enjoyed this planet, except for all the witch-hunting and pollution, and your Navy's intrusions."

"Three colonies of Merfins stayed in your oceans," Slade added, much to Barrow's concern. "Most of them are peaceful and reclusive. Now we have Venamir to deal with. The new tourist trap on the Bermuda islands is a popular place for Merfins, right on the ocean. Venamir probably has contacts in the area. We need to send humans and Atleans there. Have them hunt for spies who need a cold jail and a hot interrogation."

The humans slowly lost their frowns, and even the general's forehead veins simmered down.

"For someone who isn't a diplomat, you make sense," Dean commented. "How soon can we install your defense system?"

Slade shrugged. "Right away. I'll make some calls."

Dean moved over and shook hands with Slade, Elowren, and Scruffy. "Thank you, for the help and the history lesson."

"My pleasure," Zared smiled.

Dean glanced at his comm, which was blinking like crazy. "Yes, yes, I'll be right there. No, don't call anybody. There's no emergency!" He sighed, "You'd better port us out." He was on his comm trying to calm his security when Slade ported him and the other guests back to the White House.

* * *

Scruffy laughed as they returned to the *Vernacular* via portal chamber. "You told off the freaking president's staff."

Slade tried to sound angry as they returned to the ready room. "Scruffy, you blew the doors off a *space station*?"

"Eh, we blew them open," Scruffy admitted.

"How can you not totally blow them off?" Slade pressed.

Scruffy sighed. "Well, one was hanging there, and the other collapsed inside. They still have dual containment."

"I may have tapped the aft guns on our way out," Elowren said. "Whoopsie."

Slade took a long draught of Scruffy's shamanistic brew. "*Scruffy*," he attempted to mind whisper his friend, but war visions flooded his senses until he broke contact. "Why can't I use my psy?

When I try, I get a mad headache and flashbacks I haven't had for years."

Scruffy scowled. "I think Venamir tried to mind-wipe you."

"I don't know why you can't morph," Elowren admitted.

Shanto and Gus came and joined them, Shanto limping, running his hand along the wall. Gus headed straight for the pantry, where he rummaged through snacks.

"We've had enough of medbay," Shanto said. "I think I know what happened, how the station was hacked. Venamir was posing as our magistrate. He hypnotized people at the party," his gaze lowered, "and took us out at your ship. I'm sorry, Cap. We didn't last long against him."

Slade gestured to a chair. "Shanto, sit down. I obviously didn't stop him, either."

Shanto sighed and sank into a chair, nodding in thanks when Scruffy poured him a drink.

"Venamir hacked the whole damned station," Slade went on. "He had spies waiting, onboard Orion Space Station, and Earth's moon base."

"We can be damned sure some Merfins on Earth helped him," Scruffy stated.

Gus looked up from fixing a mocha. "Wait, Venamir who?"

Slade paused as if Gus asked if the world was round. He looked at Telari and Rhoan. "You don't know who he is either? Zared lectured about him. Venamir tried to overthrow our councils. We jailed him for war crimes some ten years ago."

"Oh," Gus grumbled, "that stinky fish. Didn't he get locked up in the sleeping caves?"

"Yes, the deep-sleep caves near the Starship Boneyard. His closest followers were locked up in other prisons, so they couldn't conspire together," Shanto replied. He looked around. "Where's Doc? I thought he'd be in medbay."

Elowren replied, "Doc's been press-ganged." She went on over Shanto's doomed groan. "Doc's valuable. He's a great surgeon, and Venamir knows it."

Shanto shook his head. "I tried to psy and warn you, Slade."

"I couldn't hear it," Slade confessed.

"Why couldn't we stop him?" Shanto asked.

"'Caz he's a badass," Gus ranted, "a slimy ringleader of alien thugs."

Slade stalked over to the pantry and pulled out some fruit and jerky. "Gus is right. Venamir's a strong telepath to begin with. He'd captured a mutirian caller. That's why my telepathy didn't work on my ship."

"Wait, Gus said, "a what?"

"Little Merfin pets, like teeny mermaids on your world. They're a secret weapon," Slade sighed. "Computer, show us a mutirian caller. Magnify."

A small creature appeared over the hologram table, tiny, at first, like a fairy from Earth's fantasy stories. The creature grew in size until it resembled a mermaid child with wings that appeared more like elongated fins. Its eyes were like glowing pearls. The skin tones were fiery colors of coral at first, colors that darkened to deep red and blue. It flittered around, laughing.

"Those wispy wings work in the air or underwater," Scruffy informed. "They can change size, shrink into the palm of your hand, or grow as big as a human child."

"She looks so innocent," Gus said, gazing at the creature. "You don't mean beings like this really hypnotized sailors of the past?"

"Yeah, they live with Merfins," Slade nodded. "On Earth, and many worlds."

"Wow," Gus muttered. He added a shot of schnapps to his cocoa.

"They're powerful," Slade added. "Their song can be nearly silent, but will block our telepathy. They can even do some hypnosis, and so can Venamir. That's why the slimy bastard flew off with *my* ship—and I don't remember how he won!"

"What do we do?" Shanto asked quietly.

Slade canceled the creature's image. "Well, for now, we're all on shore leave, so enjoy it. We'll get the *Jacobyte* back. We will."

"Why? Let's go after him now," Shanto argued.

"When we're ready," Slade replied. "We need repairs and supplies. So go on, visit anywhere on Earth, except for the Bermuda spaceport. Too many fishes down there."

Chapter 11
Rocking the Station

The *Vernacular* was quiet. Most of the crew picked at their dinner and reviewed tourist locations. Elowren barged into the messroom and turned on the news. Images appeared over their table, depicting a scene of new chaos onboard Orion Space Station. Reporters were rattling on about a bomb scare from a battle dopp bearing the yellow-green skin of a Merfin, while beneath the skin was a half-destroyed cybernetic body.

"Breaking news," Elowren replied, "active bomb scare. Looks like Venamir left some presents behind."

Gus perked up. "I'm a bomb guy. Send me in. Lemme help the big puss, Jasko."

"You have a concussion," Scruffy cut in.

"I've had worse hangovers," Gus defended. "If you don't send me, who's gonna respond? Jasko could end up with some lackey, or one of Venamir's spies."

"I say yes," Scruffy said, "good thing your head is so hard.

After a brief debate, Gus geared up.

* * *

Earth and Atlean fighters flew patrol around Earth's *Orion Space Station*, weaving an ever-changing blockade, though some believed it was like protecting a leveled warzone after the pillagers had gone. The station's structure was intact, and the smoke had cleared. Only three days after the attack on grand opening night, most levels had artificial gravity, lights, and fire foam. The starship bay's floors were either clean or still slick with fire foam. Some vendors had already opened their shops. Flights in and out remained limited, and public admission remained only a growing wish list.

Bomb crews sectioned off a large conference room where a dopp lay strapped to an examination table near the emergency pressure door. Two fully geared bomb techs, in their sturdy, flexible armor, hunched over the still form. A barricade surrounded them with one low place to jump clear, and a force field engulfed the barricade. The taller technician was a Draolith cat with coal black fur and sparse speckled midnight blue spots. His long tail twitched as he used his dexterous claws and dissecting tools to carve a few millimeters deeper beneath the dopp's jawline. He plucked free what could be a chunk of bone, except for the numerous etches and dual connector holes. Ignoring the smears on the chip, an odd mix of oil and blood, Jasko opened the tiny object's case with a claw. "There you are," he whispered.

"Nasty," Gus muttered, "weird place to stick his memory."

"There are worse places to stick it." Jasko's tufted ears lay back as he distanced his attention from the many distractions yet again, and with narrowed eyes studied their captive dopp. The dopp's skin felt warmer. Tail lashing now, he elbowed his partner and pointed to one of his five diagnostic probes attached to the prone dopp. Jasko secured the pouch to his belt. "I think the body's heating up."

Gus was starting to sweat. "Man, we already blew its shoulder half off and there isn't much living body tissue to come back to life. Creepy."

The body twitched, the attached scanning displays flashed with escalating readings from the dopp's muscle structure and power cells.

Jasko hissed, "The body's powering up." He scooped his tools into his toolbag. "Game on."

Gus tapped his link to the loudspeakers and ordered, "Evacuate section three!"

Two reporters stood among medics, cops, and firefighters, all watching when the dopp's eyes snapped open. Jasko slapped a red button set into the side of the table. The sound of the blaring alert caused everyone in the room to jump back or snap into defensive positions. The dopp snapped its bonds and sat up. "Hello, humans."

Some of the spectators grabbed weapons or recorders as the dopp opened one hand and a hologram of Venamir appeared in front of it. The image spoke in a droll tone. "I am Venamir, Deeps Merfin the true Atleans, and Grand Inquisitor of the High Council. You see the destruction that resulted from our brief encounter. This attack was 'a shot across your bow'." His image rotated as he seemed to look about the large room. "Your entry into cosmic relations was premature, and you neglected to choose your allies well. This dopp is not a bomb, although the power generator within could breach your hull, if I wished it."

Jasko's eyes narrowed into slits as he backed out of the room into a hallway. "Elowren, come on, pick up." Even his sharp ears had trouble hearing her faint voice over the clamor of people.

Elowren's image hovered over his comm. "Jasko? What's happening?"

"That damned dopp just woke up. It's talking like Venamir."

Elowren considered for a second before asking. "And?"

"It's using a holovid of Venamir to spout contraband, the gut's loaded, and I already pulled its memory chip."

"Shut it down."

Jasko slapped the comm shut and bared his fangs with an eager grin and headed toward the door into the room. Evacuating people rushed past him, and one reporter backed into him while still taking motion shots. "Morons," Jasko growled as he shoved the reporter toward the smarter, fleeing people. His neck and tail fur hackling, Jasko dropped to all fours and leapt over a human in his way, bounding through the doorway.

The dopp turned toward the approaching feline. "If you turn aggressive, I will retaliate."

Jasko took a steadying breath and mustered a smile that bared those sharp teeth again, matching the attitude of his puffed fur. "Relax. I just want my tools." He walked past the dopp and put his favorite tools back in his bag, "and my *toybots*."

The dopp watched the big feline carry his tool bag to the entrance and hand it to his partner, who nodded with some reluctance. Jasko unleashed the safety from his holster and sauntered back toward the dopp.

The dopp warned. "Halt."

"Shut down your power cells," Jasko ordered.

When the distance between them closed to two feet, the dopp activated its last spare power cell. The energy surge hit Jasko like a stun weapon, knocking him on his tail. The big cat curled into a roll and scrambled to his feet.

Gus slapped a remote in his hands, and like magic, the dopp's force field sparked and fizzed to nothing. He hit another control gizmo on his belt and two toy fighters perched along the wall fired up engines.

Jasko heard the faintest of whining sounds, one that grew in decibels. He snarled and claws whipped out like wicked black surgical lasers. He leapt like a rabid beast, tackled the dopp and slashed the power conduits in its throat. Taking a metal-boned fist upside his head reminded Jasko that the dopp's remaining functioning parts, one arm and a good leg, proved stronger than even the feline's muscular bulk. The dopp's head bobbled like a broken action figure, but it continued to fight as Jasko drug it toward the pressure hatch.

"You'll all die," the dopp said, turning unfeeling eyes toward him. The big cat felt like he was fighting a robotic zombie as a cub, and remembered how it creeped him out.

"I got nine lives," said Jasko as he buried his favorite tool in their former surgical playground of the dopp's midsection. While his target clawed at the lodged tool, Jasko charged toward the safety of barricades and the awaiting doorway. He tumbled through the outer pressure door with the dopp, then leapt back through it. "Now!" he yowled, after it slammed shut behind him.

Gus hit the emergency door controls.

The spectators watched through the windows in the wall as the dopp shuddered and groped at itself when the pressure door opened and sucked it out into space. A parting gift to the hapless heap of artificial intelligence, the pair of miniature fighters rocketed toward their prey, their tail cones opening to release cables with wicked claws which bit into the dopp's limbs. With their small engines screaming at full power, the toybots towed the struggling evictee away from the space station, farther and farther, until the Venamir's threat became real and the dopp's last operating power core exploded. The space station barely shuddered at all, much akin to feeling a miniscule earthquake tremor.

Curled up on the floor with his big paws over his eyes, Jasko peeked through his fingers at the sound of cheers. He sprang to his feet with a wide fanged grin, just in time for camera flashes to splatter his vision with pulsating lights. He blinked and rubbed his head. "Stop trying to blind me," he growled, then laughed at the tenacious reporter and swatted him on the back.

"Sucks we had to sacrifice our toybots," Gus said.

"Mine was faster," Jasko taunted.

"Was not, you big puss."

Chapter 12
Venamir's Hideout

Venamir coaxed the *Jacobyte* into a low orbit over a small clump of islands. To his relief, Moradin reported that almost every life form was Merfin, with a few alien species, many on fishing boats. While the Volcano Islands still bore the ruggedness of volcanic origin, little farms dotted the rugged hillsides. The largest, middle island was almost all landing sites. He landed in a huge docking bay, camouflaged as wild terrain from above. Once the *Jacobyte's* engines shut down in the darkness, he strode down the ramp with Moradin at his side.

A young, green Merfin landed a zoomboard before them. "Welcome," he greeted. "I am your guide. Thirty years ago, these islands had barely taken shape. We developed this entire settlement."

"Humans would take another century to match this progress," Venamir stated.

"True," said their guide. "The only reason humans are starting to question this area is because our people are helping improve their technology. For now, we're still safe enough. Repairs, supplies, we should have anything you need."

Suspicion unhidden, Venamir asked, "You are half of your shell. Why should I trust you?"

"We are honored to help your cause for greater Merfin power. This is our last sanctuary above Earth's waters. Soon, humans will challenge us for it."

Moradin gazed at a spectacular waterfall that glistened against lush mountain growth. "How do you keep the humans off these islands?"

"We eat them," the guide said.

They all laughed.

"No, honestly," Venamir pressed.

"Oh, ghost stories, volcanic dangers, and so on," the young fellow chuckled.

"I like you," Venamir smirked. "Lead on. I need more crewmen."

"I shall fetch a ride for us," the youth said, hopped on his board, and zoomed off.

"Like a medic, Captain?" Moradin's concern was obvious. "Your meeting with Vanysa was supposed to help, not make your condition worse."

Venamir scowled. He was sore physically and mentally from the unexpected fight with Zared, and facing higher resistance than he hoped for. Even Zared's sidekicks had put up a better fight than he expected. Thanks to them, Zared still lived. Worse, when he had Slade's friends locked on target, somehow, his own ship wouldn't let him open fire.

When Noxus and Maska walked out to investigate the surroundings, Venamir grabbed the chance to interrogate them.

"You two, here, now," Venamir ordered. "We need an expert hacker. I could have incinerated that haughty High Council fool, Elowren and their pathetic sky taxi. Killing her would have dealt a fantastic blow to Slade. Instead, she lives to warn the council leaders."

Maska's gaze darted about. "We've troubleshot systems all the way here, Captain. There's nothing wrong with the guns."

"We could have rammed that sky-taxi and buried them at sea," Noxus said, scowling.

Venamir's eyes glinted. "Ramming them would not solve our problem. The Herja program won't let us shoot first. Moradin, the Herja on my old ship was programmed after you. Any ideas?"

"The Herja will let us defend ourselves," Moradin reasoned. "You merely need to act and fly like you're a threat. Once a target shoots at us, we can open fire. To override the program, we need four original crew members that the Herja deems as the original crew."

"We can't use our main guns because of a stupid program, great ship," Maska groused.

Venamir shook his head. "We will improvise. Noxus, you oversee repairs. Moradin, add fish to my swimming pool, and a make a pool cover. Maska, I need a hacker. Maybe we can disable part of the Herja's program. Well? Why are you standing there?"

* * *

Tranquil waves surrounded a small island that was lush with varying shades of blue and aqua leaves, and trees loaded with many strains of vibrantly colored fruit. Orchards and vegetable vines wound through all populated areas, from homes, shops, and commerce. Two docks stood out above the ground level, their exteriors and roofs covered with shield generators that protected the island from human discovery. The *Jacobyte* rested within the southern large dock.

Venamir stood in the cockpit of the *Jacobyte* as he finished a piece of fruit. "Captain's log," he pondered aloud, "we are safe for now. Ship repairs are almost complete. My followers continue to report in. Too bad my great niece Vanysa still remains neutral, for now. My people have made this tiny island much like home. With Atleans working with humans now, this island's days of hiding are numbered. 'Tis a shame that humans cannot leave us alone. I must make my people see true colors within everyone. Ever since I inflicted Slade with renewed flashbacks, I see them, too. I may as well still be in the old *Spectre* flying alongside the land morphers." His voice dropped to a grumble, "I see flames burning through walls, hear the battles, feel like the ship's flying apart. Close Captain's log."

He withdrew a flask from an overhead cabinet and took a swig. He gazed out the cockpit's windows to see distant ocean waves crashing along the beach. Try as he might, he couldn't shake the memories of his combat service with Slade. Sometimes he would look at a wall and see flames appear. He often smelled the stench of fire burning through the walls, heard laser blasts from other ships, and felt the turbulence of impact. He took another swig from the flask.

"Slade still thinks the *Spectre's* crash is his fault." Chuckling, Venamir settled into the pilot's chair for a nap.

Sounds of distant waves lulled Venamir to sleep, but the noise of repairmen outside the ship heightened his memories of gunships and weapons' fire. Within minutes, he sank deeper into his subconscious fears.

He managed to submerge his flashbacks of combat, but not prison. His heartbeat rushed with trepidation of entrapment, just as when the High Council had sentenced him. The surrounding cavern felt like a tomb, slowly enclosing around his temporal stasis pod. He lay trapped in dreams, with subliminal messages filtering into his head, trying to make him a 'better' person again. Barely sentient, with his brain functioning below a comatose state, his raw emotions and incredible resistance overcame any outside attempts to soothe or reconfigure his intentions. This was different from prison stasis. Tentacles pulled him downward, where pressure crushed all air from his lungs. Then Slade loomed over him, morphing into a fierce woodland beast, lunging for the kill.

Venamir jumped with a gasp, grabbing at anything until he latched onto the arms of a pilot's chair. He glanced around while his heart settled to a normal beat. "Murky leeches and blithering nightmares," he snarled. "Will they never end?" He didn't understand how water could frighten him. He was Merfin, unable to drown unless his gills sealed shut, but he never truly acclimated to deep space. Venamir rubbed at his drying skin and knew he'd better spend some more time in the pool to hydrate.

Slowly, Venamir morphed through his land-walking form, Merfin true form, and back again. Each time he changed shape, the process of returning to his true form helped his damaged gills heal further. Swelling lessened, bruising faded, ragged tissue fused together. The healing process left him exhausted, but it helped. His lungs could breathe almost normally. Slowly, he sat up and looked at his hands. The webbing between his long fingers felt tender and appeared cracked. He sighed and sat back, hoping for a more peaceful nap this time. "I need sleep in my ocean, not these polluted waters," he said in a shaken grumble, leaned forward and started a new entry.

"Captain's log. Sensor sweeps register high pollutants in this inlet where we are docked. Maska has filled a tank, but water transfer is sluggish through our filters. I need to expedite my return to home waters. Soon, the Council will celebrate their first air show with those miserable humans on my world." Venamir tried to activate the ship's computer avatar. "Wake up, *Jacobyte*." Seeing screens light up to his voice, he continued. "Weapons keep malfunctioning. Run a full systems scan."

To his surprise, something scanned him, leaving a tingling sensation through his body. The computer's feminine voice took a colder tone than the submissive personality he expected. A holographic woman appeared, seated upon the central control panel. She wore morpher armor with weaponized bracers. Her youthful, hard features leered at him. "Identify yourself," she ordered. "You are not Captain Slade and do not have permission to access my classified files. Enter the pass code."

"What?"

"Enter the pass code. You have one minute to comply or security measures will commence."

"What security measures?" He heard the unmistakable sound of the ramp retracting and slamming shut. Venamir struggled to rise, but artificial gravity intensified, sucking him into the chair as if he were pulling high-G maneuvers. From somewhere in the ceiling, he heard the hum of weapons charging. Venamir lurched out of the chair, just as yellow-hued light flashed and two stun blasts dropped him to the floor. Blotches of lights flashed before his eyes.

"Identify yourself," the Herja ordered.

Venamir morphed into a replica of Slade. He had to sound perfect. "Defense system, power down!"

"You are not Captain Slade. He's a beast morpher. You are aquatic."

"I am Captain Slade, you obnoxious can of fake intelligence!" Venamir caught himself and fumbled for calmer words. He leaned heavily on the chair, not letting the machine scan his retina. "You are a tactician, not a medical dopp. Disable your defense protocols"

"Enter your pass codes and do not try to manipulate me."

He chuckled at the irony of arguing with a machine. "To the depths with you. My true identity is Venamir, original Captain of this ship. I order you to run *that* diagnostic and accept my body readings as your Commander. In accordance with our Atlean High Council Order of Were-Worlds survival tactics, I am in command of this ship. Atleans are at risk from hostile forces. As your former commander, I am authorized to commandeer this ship under times of crisis and war. You should know that I outrank Consul Slade."

The Herja took her time processing the command. At length she said, "That is among our oldest orders of the High Council, originating when our related psychics joined forces eons ago." Her relentless gaze dissected him.

Venamir loathed how he couldn't control her. Was she basking in vanity like a real woman hiding a secret, or searching the databanks for a way to override his command? Would she even cooperate? Seconds crawled by.

"I will comply," she replied, eyes glinting, "for now."

Venamir heaved a sigh of relief. He limped to the lower level, where Maska had modified a cargo bay to hold a large pool, much like an oversized hot tub, complete with a large tank. Lines from portable tanks gradually filled the new aquarium. He gathered alchemy materials for testing the water. Fifteen degrees too cold, not salty enough, no friendly growths or exotic fish yet, but it would do. Venamir stripped down to diving shorts. Tenderly, he rubbed his right gills closest to his lower heart. His gill flaps resembled gnarled tissue and the fight with Zared left rows of gashes from those metallic talon gloves. Swelling diminished and he felt better, but the healing talent had its cost. Hunger gnawed at him. He felt dry of wit and drained, mentally and physically.

Perhaps snarling his most nasty swears would help, with Slade's name fused by heartfelt venom. "Blithering Slade, I wish I could have killed him already, the rabid, walking mongrel."

Noxus approached at a bored walk. "Everything works except main weps."

"Leave it to that rotten Slade to leave his ship under the protection of a cyber wench." *A very familiar cyber wench,* he thought. "Find someone who can hack into this ship's Herja program."

Noxus nodded and stalked away.

Snarling, he imitated the Herja, "Tell me the pass codes." He dove to the bottom of the pool, onto a matt of soft rehydrated seaweed.

120

The soothing tank helped Venamir regain his physical strength, but nightmares still troubled his sleep. Now, he dreamed of combat in his element, deep beneath the sea, in ships designed for air and water transport. He recalled back when he and Slade were friends, and Scruffy equaled his rank in the High Council, but all their voices rose in heated debate. Then *they* turned on him, his *loyal* council brethren. There were a few neutral members, very few. His distant great, great, grandniece Vanysa. He knew she wouldn't turn, being his distant niece. Still, he never forgot how she stared at him, doubting, analyzing. The council voted. Venamir couldn't even try to escape. He was sentenced and stuffed into a suspension tube, oblivious to everything except whispers in his dreams from psychiatrists trying to rehabilitate his subconscious.

Venamir woke with a start. He looked down at his gills, watched how they fluttered open and closed. The nap had helped reduce swelling and fatigue. With a small amount of self-gratitude, he laid back and nibbled at his seaweed bed, pondering over the Herja program. *Why should I waste time on this trivial matter? She is only artificial intelligence, thus perhaps even my crew may be able to outthink her. No, those are high expectations.*

He wondered why he woke so early, until muffled voices of Noxus and a stranger again carried from down the corridor. Venamir rose and headed for the surface. Graceful and powerful underwater, a few seconds of effort sent him surging out of the makeshift tank. He wrestled on his loose pants and strode toward the noise.

Noxus intercepted Venamir in the hall. "We looked for hackers on this island. Moradin and I are the best you have."

Venamir shook water from his hands and took the pad. "We must disable the Herja program. What is all that noise in medbay?"

"We press-ganged someone from the space station."

Venamir's eyes narrowed. "You know my distaste for surprises."

Undaunted, Noxus led the way to medbay. They found Maska leaning over a closed suspension tube. Venamir stomped in, a snarl on his cracked lips. "I ordered you to keep no prisoners."

Maska straightened at that low tone. "Captain, we had a good reason. We didn't have a doctor, so I kept this one on ice. Couldn't you use him for now?"

Venamir halted and cocked his head. "We had Slade's doctor all along? Why Maska, sometimes you impress me. Wake him."

Basking in a rare compliment, Maska activated awakening sequence and stepped back. Power cells along the tube glowed vivid yellow, while a wall screen above showed a silhouette of the slumbering man and elevating body readings.

A disheveled, bruised Atlean man in the suspension tube gasped and woke with a start. Reflexes dulled, he sat up with stiff movements, glancing around. His eyes narrowed at the sight of Venamir, his voice unsteady with alarm and grogginess. "Where's my crew? Where's Slade?"

Maska spun and grabbed the man by the collar. "Doesn't matter who we are, you're a healer, so shut your bait-hole and do your job."

"I'm not helping any of you."

Venamir smiled, a dangerous expression for him. He pushed Maska aside and leaned on the suspension tube. "Doctor, I left your crew alive when I commandeered this ship. You owe me."

Nelzyr glared back at him. "I don't believe you're the real Venamir, and I'm not helping you."

"Maska, keep trying to find a computer hacker, and well done."

Maska beamed at yet another rare compliment, bowed, and hustled out of the medbay.

Venamir turned his full attention to the doctor. "Tell me, have you ever walked out of an escape hatch, in space?" He saw instant fear light the doctor's eyes, though the poor fool tried to hide it. "That would mean no." He closed the gap, pressed his hands to the doctor's chest, and forced his psy into their disoriented prisoner's mind.

The surroundings of the medical bay faded to blurred shadows, the scenery twisting and morphing to the crushing darkness of ocean depths.

Doctor Nelzyr shuddered at the sudden invasion, his collapsing mental shields leaving his mind more vulnerable than a drunken stupor. He thrust his arms out as if falling off balance, but all he could feel was water swirling around him, even though he knew they were standing on the ship. The harder Doc tried to cast Venamir out of his mind, the worse his body shivered against the imaginary cold as serpents swam up from the waters. Blackness wrapped around his body. *Serpents... what is it with cultists and serpents?*

Doc saw the waters pale from the real light in the room as his frantic mind kept denying the reality of drowning. *It's just an illusion... just an illusion,* until he jumped at the sharp pain of fangs piercing his flesh. *Illusion!* Doc grabbed the sea snake and squeezed just behind the head until its eyes turned blood red and it released him. Once Doc convinced himself it wasn't real, the snake vanished, along with the holes in his arm.

"Doctor," Venamir chided, each word laced with sadism, "I remember how your captain values his friends. We are above primitive torture methods. However, I know you still have surviving family, *for now.* How much do you want them to live?"

Nelzyr clenched his shaking hands into fists. "What do you want?"

Venamir smiled, gesturing to the treatment bed. "Serve on my crew."

It wasn't long before Venamir left the medical bay, renewed energy in his stride, and the Doctor back in the suspension tube. Venamir walked through the *Jacobyte's* halls at a slow pace, pondering. He could inhale a full breath without pain now. Even in Merfin form, his gills fluttered at a comfortable rhythm. *That doctor is good,* he thought, *now to solve my other problem.* As he neared the flight deck, lights and power flickered an instant before zaps and loud cracking sounds from the cockpit drew his attention. He heard the Herja woman's voice demanding proper pass codes. Venamir knew what to expect before he walked in. His technical experts struggled to rise from the floor, with the Herja standing over them.

"Incompetents," Venamir grumbled, and then glared at the Herja hologram.

"State your intent," she said.

Venamir marched up to the Herja until he stood nose to helmet with her glimmering body projection. "I want access to all systems, including weapons."

"Denied. You were granted limited access to the arsenal for defense only."

"Doctor Nelzyr entered the code. Scan the medical bay and do note that your chief surgeon is alive, for now. If you refuse to grant me bridge control, he will die and you will have failed to protect your crew."

The Herja didn't respond at first, debating in silence. Two codes received from a hostile being. Subject Venamir had broken proper procedures. Venamir claims council rights, yet threatens to murder a crewman. Engage covert defensive strategy.

Venamir let a few seconds tick by. "Have you scanned the ship yet?"

"I know he is there."

"You knew all along, but held that a secret?"

"You realize the implications of your actions?"

"Tell me your name," Venamir demanded.

"I am the *Jacobyte's* Herja," she replied. "You may call me Jac's Byte."

Venamir clenched his fists. "I am sick of your games! I need this ship now! The primary role of a Herja is to protect the crew, and secondary is the ship. Granted, we hacked your systems. You failed to protect your crew. I give you five seconds to save your doctor." Venamir glanced at the power grids the Herja used to shoot stun blasts. He suspected she could only stun and not kill with those energy bursts, or else she probably would have earlier. "If you deny me control, I will destroy this ship! If you incapacitate me, others will kill your medic. Decide now!"

The sections of triple artificial gravity deactivated under Noxus and Moradin, allowing them to climb to their feet.

Only Noxus had the nerve to laugh. "Captain," he said, "you just yelled at a machine."

Venamir pointed at the avatar. "This machine is empowered with Merfin-Atlean artificial intelligence, the blithering cyber wench."

124

The Herja asked, "Venamir, you are aware of the consequences?"

"Noxus, kill the doctor. Make it gruesome."

Noxus nodded with a lustful sneer, "With pleasure." He turned to go.

"HALT!" the Herja demanded. When Noxus refused to obey her, she activated the flight deck doors and slammed them shut.

"Give me back weapons control, or I promise you, he will die." Venamir watched the computers flicker on and off, their screens a mass of data stream. "Go ahead. Crash the computer. I prefer to replace it."

Moradin raised her open hands up and down as if she were weighing gold. "You've created a clash in her program. Kill the crew or save the ship."

Noxus folded his arms. "She can't think that hard."

The Herja scowled at Venamir with a hungering vengeance far too real for an avatar. Her image fluttered as she growled, "Primary weapon control is yours." With that, she vanished, and the doors unlocked.

Venamir savored a long, "Aah, I knew Slade was weak enough to put the crew first."

"Can I still kill the doctor?"

"No."

Noxus dropped into the gunner's chair, fuming.

Watching the controls respond and hearing a whining click hum of the forward turrets activating gave Venamir some relief. "And?"

"They're smooth," replied Noxus, "like a vulture swooping over a field of prey, Noxus panned over the cavern of mechanically inclined thugs and zeroed the sights on one exceptionally strong worker thug. His trigger finger twitched with bloodlust until Venamir reached over and shoved the controls. The cannons bucked and spit a burst of laser blasts within three feet of a worker nearest the cave entrance. The lasers sizzled into the churning ocean surf, sending rocks, sand and plumes of water spraying near fifty feet upward. "It's still not the main guns. We have everything but Slade's best weapon."

"This will do, for now," Venamir replied. He strode outside to watch the workers. One repair tech stood out from the rest, a gray, shaggy feline who used delicate scanners to inspect the engines. Hearing the light footsteps even over a clamor of voices and power tools, the feline's ears twitched back toward him. "Tell me, cat, why are you here?"

The feline faced him, ears cocked sideways. "I need work."

"Do tell," Venamir commented. "If you want an interview, open your mind."

Before Motley could argue or even curse, his muscles stiffened and, with a wave of nausea, he saw their rocky surroundings swirl and blur into writhing shadows. Venamir's voice and image barged into his mind and read his thoughts with the casual boredom of a librarian scrolling through a database. Venamir backed out of his mind, leaving Motley shaking his head to clear it, his brawny paws holding a crate for balance.

"Ah, you are a malcontent," Venamir summarized, "and have a knack for programming. Noxus should have brought you to me. We have a computer issue."

The feline straightened composure under strict control. "That tattooed thug of yours didn't bother to ask. Said cats are stupid."

"Interesting. How is your son?"

Motley's fur hackled. "Leave my cub out of this."

"Relax. My time is too important to waste terrorizing my workers. I find your talents worthy of a high sum. How are your hacking skills?"

The feline said with a cocky smile, "I could impress even you."

Venamir gestured toward the *Jacobyte*. "Excellent. Leave this drudgery behind." He clasped his webbed fingers together as they left the work area. "We have the most annoying Herja bitch in the ship's network. I need her deactivated."

"For how much?"

"Name your price."

Noxus and Moradin glanced over as Venamir entered with the feline man. Noxus scowled and continued running manual flight control systems check. "We must have rats," he chortled.

* * *

Deep within the hearth of the *Jacobyte,* a backup computer hummed to life, its lights and activity subdued to draw only minimal power from its own emergency source. This computer lay in a hidden chamber with a clamshell dome surrounded by catwalks and power grids, and an octagon of walls lined with military surplus cabinets, a secondary computer hummed to life.

Up spoke the Herja's icy voice. "Spy mode activated. Terrorist threat. Ship's doctor held hostage in temporal stasis tube. Transfer of database to primary Herja complete upon next restart. Hologram program, suspend to dormant mode. Emergency defense on standby."

Chapter 13
Trial by Festival

Slade and his crew spent the day wandering around one of Earth's largest multi-theme events of early spring: a huge park that incorporated a science fiction convention, a renaissance faire, and multiple other areas dedicated to fantasy realms.

Elowren arrived at the Fiction Fantasy Convention where the sights set her imagination on overload. People dressed in all kinds of costumes flooded a cluster of buildings surrounding a park bustling with cosplay and vendors. It reminded her of her first visit to a multi-species city as a child. She didn't stand out so much here, even in her Atlean form, with light coppery skin, pointed ears, and cat-like eyes.

She walked past a costume tent, smirking at the cloaks, toy weapons, wands, staves, and other fake magical items. Some garments looked quite realistic to her. She touched a medium weight cloak that was comparable to dragon scales and moved into a dressing room.

"At last, a quiet moment." She tapped her fancy wristband, activating a blank holographic dome form above her arm. "Shanto, come in. You're supposed to be on the space station. What's going on?" No reply. "Odd," she muttered.

Elowren let her psy drift free, allowing her to scan the minds around her. Her range bested most Atleans, but she focused only on the festival. It was easier to hunt a telepath here, compared to her homeworld, Atlearon, where most people were telepathic, or at least empathic. After several minutes, she felt a familiar kindred mind among the sea of human brains.

"There you are," she whispered. She pried at his mind and tried to see through her target's eyes. She hoped for a glimpse of his surroundings, only to see sharp memory images onboard the space station. Shanto struggled to close his mind to her, but for a few moments, she felt his emotions conflicted between guilt, anger, and a hunger for vengeance. Elowren glimpsed psy images of Venamir morphing into a gentlemanly old diplomat with blue skin.

128

The diplomat vanished into a crowd of hazy partiers on the *Orion Space Station.* "He posed as our magistrate."

Elowren brought her psy back to her mind. She sat down in the dressing room, frowning. She reached up and tapped one of the glittering gems in her headband, releasing a piece of the band that swung forward alongside her left temple. "Map fairgrounds at my location."

A map splayed on the wall before her, giving an overhead view of the grounds, dotted with tiny shapes depicting life forms.

"Filter out humans. Track Atleans," she said.

The many dots vanished, leaving only a handful, most of them in a building. "There's Slade and the crew. Shanto's closing in on them—but he won't answer me? Zared, come in."

"Go ahead," Zared's voice whispered from her headband.

"Did you assign Shanto to follow us?"

"No, I put him on shore leave, like the rest of the crew."

"Well, I saw him and made psy contact because he's not answering his comm. I saw a memory of him speaking with Venamir before that attack on the space station. I think it was the real Venamir because he morphed. It looked like our magistrate."

Uneasy silence fell between them.

Zared lowered his voice. "Shanto's been acting strange ever since that hijacking event. I'll alert the crew. We need to round him up."

Elowren swung the belt and cloak over her clothes, pulled the tags off, and found the vendor. "I'd like to buy these."

* * *

Fireplace logs muttered in teasing crackles and pops from their brick hearth. Slade lounged in an old, creaky leather chair and sipped from a foam-topped stein. It was the heaviest thing his medics would let him lift just yet, making him enjoy the sixteen-ounce curls even more. *A real fireplace,* he mused. *I haven't seen one of these since my crewmen were scrapping brats.* Slade wished he could morph into a human and go incognito, but he couldn't even change his body that much, not after that psy fight with Venamir.

His gaze panned across patrons, humans, their features darkened by the shadowy ambiance of dark wood walls and modest lighting. Most humans still regarded Atleans with swaying emotions, from high curiosity to suspicion. And that was on a good day, even after a few decades of helping them build their first spaceports and space station. At least the Fiction Fantasy Faire helped him feel at home. All weekend, he was glad to see even weirder species grab people's attention—the springtime all-genre convention, from renaissance to science fiction. In the past few hours, Slade had already autographed a stein, a hat with fake ears, and random souvenirs.

His thoughts drifted back over the afternoon as he scrolled through the day's pics. His favorite was their visit to Italy, where Telari hugged naked statues for tourists snapping pictures of 'real' aliens. He resumed watching his crew. Tel attracted the men, not only by her subtly copperish skin, streaks of purple in her ebony hair, and tiger stripes on her pointed ears, but her jokes. Her sailor's jokes had even the men blushing, Gus was haggling with a leather vendor, and Scruffy was teaching the locals ancient drinking songs. One of the three entertainment screens played a documentary that explained the major species on Atlearon: Werefolks, Draoliths, Merfins, and a newer species, amphibians who were related to Rezoans, or cynically known as dogs, cats, fish, and lizards.

Even with all the warm karma, Slade's mind drifted. He loosened his aviator-style jacket, brushed chip crumbs off his jeans. Beer and snacks didn't help stop his brooding. Nobody had figured out exactly how Venamir hacked the Orion Space Station a mere week ago. Then there was the mystery of his missing medic and lifelong friend. He turned and glared at the fireplace.

Slade's brother, Berku, sat in the next chair, nursing a dark stout. Berku's burly frame, braids in his beard, and tooling in his leather jacket and boots, gave him the image of a modern Viking. Voice low, he leaned toward Slade. "Brothah, are you still thinking about that old fish? Your psy defenses are getting loose. I can see your brain's images. Get your flashbacks under control."

"Damn," Slade grumbled. He focused on reigning in the memories of ships crashing and wartime storms of aerial battles. "I can't remember what happened on my own ship. I get close, and it slips away. I need you to get into my head and look at the flashback memories with me. Come on, you were there. You were on our crew."

"Like I can forget," Berku grumbled. "Fine." He downed the beer and set his mug aside. "You owe me a refill."

Slade fell silent as old memories again immersed his conscious thought back into his combat days from decades ago. He allowed Berku's psy into his mind and tuned out their surroundings. The bar noise, voices and music all faded to whispers, replaced by scents of burning composites and synthetic oils, a barrage of warship alarms, and tense voices snapping systems failures. The memories used to haunt Slade until he pushed them into the dark recesses of his mind decades ago. Now, the memories were fresh in his mind again.

As the flashback gained clarity, Slade saw his younger self in the co-pilot's seat as if he were gazing into a crystal ball. He eased his conscious mind out of the memories. After what felt like being yanked from a swirling tunnel, Slade and Berku looked around. The safety of a warm, cozy bar surrounded them, and Scruffy stood in front of them, arms folded.

"Will you stop doing that?" Scruffy complained. "You're giving us headaches, and a few of the locals think they're seeing things. I can't blame *everything* on the beer."

Tel lightly elbowed past Scruffy, carrying a round tray with shot glasses, and sat down on the spare logs. "Why you guys all serious?"

"I need a think tank," Slade said, voice drifting off to admire the Bavarian shot glass and its intricate art of a busty bar wench. As if lured by her scent, he picked up the shot glass and swirled the warm, fruity amber liquid. "Something's wrong with my memories."

Scruffy pulled up a footstool and planted his rear. "What do you mean?"

Slade continued, "In that memory of *that* flight, where we crashed, I was ordering myself around or someone else was, like in a dream. I can't order myself around if I'm me."

"You know," Tel said as she handed Berku a shot, then took her ale mug and sipped at it. "I saw enough of that flashback to see Slade in the cockpit with a warzone all around them. Venamir was the captain back then, right? Isn't a flashback more of a historical reality stuck in your head?"

"You think that clearly after three hard ciders?" Scruffy said.

Tel waved her mug under his nose. "It's normal cider." She smirked at their surprised looks.

Slade lowered his voice, contempt spicing his words. "It's like I'm not seeing that flashback from my perspective anymore. I'm looking at me from the left seat. *Venamir* was in the left seat on that ship. *He* made me remember this shit. I quit having these flashbacks years ago. Now, every time I even think about using my psy, I see and hear the damned warzone when our ship crashed. Yet, I think there's a difference. I bet that since Venamir revived my memories of the *Spectre's* crash, he's been reliving them, too."

"But he was using his psy at the beach, and in the ocean. Didn't seem to bother him," Telari commented.

"I think I know why," Slade replied. "The crash, losing half his crew, didn't antagonize Venamir like it did me. He never bonded much with us. He must have known reliving the flashbacks would affect me more than him."

"We've been guessing he brought up those memories to make you forget other memories," Berku reasoned. "I bet Venamir doesn't want you to remember how he, well, how he stole your ship."

"Right," Slade nodded. "So Venamir relived the old flashbacks of our crash landing after a big air battle. He made a big mistake in reminding me of the whole scene." His voice darkened. "Now, maybe I can solve the mysteries of the crash!"

Scruffy groaned, "Will you stop dissecting whose fault it was? The ship took so much damage, we were all lucky we didn't blow up."

Elowren entered the building in true form, swept back, tapering ears, catlike eyes and burgundy hair suggesting what she wore was no costume from Earth. She drew some looks from the men as they ogled her trim figure. Her warm cloak cascaded over morpher gear that appeared as a long faux leather tunic and snug pants. Zared walked in behind her, his warm coat more formal, yet strangely retro. While Elowren returned flirting grins with a cool smile, Zared noticed some patrons glancing at him and chuckling.

Slade couldn't help but grin when Elowren and Zared joined them near the fireplace. "Did you and Telari go shopping together? Who are you, queen of dragons?"

"I like that," Elowren replied. She eyed Telari's long, hooded cloak with Celtic trim and pagan clasps. "Magic user?"

"Druid, sort of," Tel replied.

Zared reached over and tapped Slade's brandy cup. "You're easy enough to find."

"Nice coat, Dick," Slade tossed back.

Zared paused, cocking his head. "What?"

"You look like Dick Tracy. He was a detective," Slade laughed. "Some historian you are."

"I don't count comics as history," Zared countered.

"You can learn a lot from cultural entertainment, or lack thereof," Slade elaborated. "Join us for a drink."

Zared smiled a bit. "Tempting, but I'm here with news. Shanto may be a problem."

"He's your best spy aside from Wulvur," Slade commented.

"Venamir must have worked on Shanto's mind. For the past few days, Shanto's been distracted, almost paranoid. He's been following you, but he won't report in. I know he's on shore leave, but usually he'd answer his comm. He won't respond to psy, either."

"Shanto's been edgy ever since we found him knocked out on the space station," Berku mused. "He remembered psy contact with Venamir, and losing track of our Magistrate, but that was all he conveyed. You'd think he'd stick with us, not avoid us."

The group exchanged concerned, puzzled looks. Slade rose first. "Well, let's go get him, make sure the slimy fish didn't screw up his head." He moved to the bar, outwardly jovial as he paid the tab. Slade and his friends got their jackets and headed outside into the brisk cold and bright sunlight.

"Let's spread out," Slade said. "Tel, Wulv, you're up. Find Shanto and distract him."

Telari pulled a wand and wizard hat from her backpack. Her tunic-style shirt and tall boots fit in well with fantasy cosplayers. She pulled on her long, dark green coat and flipped up the hood. Wulvur morphed into his Retriever dog form again and trotted off with her. Wulvur rubbed fondly against her leg, tail wagging, all senses alert. They walked through the swarms of people, taking in endless sights and scents, until a familiar sight caught his attention.

Wulvur reared up on his hind legs and licked Tel's ear. "There he goes," he whispered, "into that vast concert hall."

Tel and Wulvur jogged until they closed in on their target. They watched Shanto glance around, disappear behind a hot dog booth, and stroll away with human features.

"He morphed," Tel reported, "but we have a visual. We're moving in." She glimpsed Shanto moving through the crowd, trying to look casual as he lengthened his strides.

A few vendors down, Tel spotted Rhoan approach wearing a cheap replica of robo-guard armor. Smirking at them, Tel pulled her shades out of a shirt pocket and slipped them on. She sang out, "Dog show at the main stage. See my dog do magic tricks and jump through fiery hoops."

Wulvur stopped and got an accidental knee in his butt. "Ow!" he mumbled.

Tel raised her voice even more. "Meet my dog in the kissing booth. Fund raiser to help the deranged." Hearing Wulvur's low whine only spurred her on. "He's a great smoocher."

Wulvur groaned, but grabbed the wand, flung it up and caught it in his teeth again, his sharp teeth leaving fresh chomp marks on the wood. Some onlookers laughed.

"See magic tricks with his special wand." Tel announced, drawing chuckles from onlookers. Wulvur spat out the wand and glared at her.

"Looks like you already took him camping," a burly man laughed.

Tel offered her wand to Wulvur, who clamped his mouth shut. "Take it," she said. The dog shook his head no. "Take it, now. Now. Oh, man, okay, you can't have it." She chuckled and gave it to him.

Spying Shanto, Tel released the leash, letting Wulvur trot ahead. "You there, Atlean cute butt guy." She frowned when he ignored her, "in the combat boots with morpher hunting logo."

Shanto went pale. His stride faltered, but he tried to play it off and quickened his pace.

Wulvur caught up and whacked Shanto's knees with the wand. Keeping hold of the wand, he bared his teeth and fangs.

"Ow!" Shanto yipped, trying to look calm as he stared at Wulvur's dog form. Even for a retriever, the dog's bulk and teeth were formidable. He shot Telari a worried look. "Lady? Call him off."

Tel strolled up to him, smiling. "Oh, don't worry about him. He likes you. I need a volunteer for the show. You look good."

Shanto stared at Tel's human shape features and her dark sunglasses, suspicion clear in his eyes. "No. How d'you know about my boots?"

"Those are Atlean wolves on your boots. It's obvious."

Wulvur bouncing like a pup, shaking the wand with a taunting play growl. Each time Tel tried to grab the wand, the dog maneuvered his wagging butt in her way and kept his head just out of her reach. Relaxing a bit, Shanto rolled his eyes and tried to leave the narrow walkway between vendor stands, but the dog smacked him with the wand again, this time to his left knee. After being tripped a third time, he wrestled the wand from Wulvur's mouth. "Give it, you obnoxious mutt!" He thrust it into Tel's hands.

She studied through her dark shades. "Thanks. Now look away while I stick it up his rear."

"That's no way to train a dog," Shanto began, "I mean, never mind." He tried to stroll away again, trying to look casual as he glanced around.

Tel and her other telepath friends heard Scruffy's voice. *"I've got eyes on Shanto. He's acting really nervous."*

She grinned, ran to catch up and grabbed the Shanto's arm. Wulvur broke free of his leash and took off.

Shanto jumped. "Huh? You again?"

"What a lousy greeting. Help me catch my dog. I'll get you concert passes."

"No. Why me?"

"He likes you," Tel insisted. "It's only a few minutes of your long life. And quit staring at my boobs."

Shanto tried to hide his clear frustration. "I wasn't. I'm not stupid. You're acting."

"Well, most of us are. This is a role-playing event, duh." She took a firmer grip on his arm. "Tell you what, you feel really stressed. I can get you a free massage from my friends." She leaned close and whispered in his ear, "A really good massage, and beer, because you're really cute."

Not wanting to make a scene, and eyeing her shapely figure, he blushed. "Really?"

"You could be on stage with my awesome dog."

"No."

"Oh, come on, he hasn't even humped your leg, yet." Tel looked around as they walked, appearing as lost as she could. Tel spied Vanysa a few vendors away, holding a large, strange-looking cat on a stout leather leash. Vany turned away when Shanto looked toward her. The cat was Atlean, a mysterious sight for humans, and at least fifty pounds under all that fur. Seeing Telari, the cat emitted a rumbling purr.

"This is too weird," Shanto started. He tried to break free of Tel's hold, but that only sparked a wrestling match. He quickly found she was quite strong and knew some moves. She twisted his wrist and tripped him, sending him sprawling to the ground.

"You're the lucky winner of the stocks," Rhoan informed him. He called out, "We have a prisoner for the stocks! Does anyone have rotten fruit or beer-soaked rolls?"

A guy sang out, "Soggy hot dog bun right here!"

"That'll work," Rhoan said as he pulled Shanto upright, starting a wrestling match.

Tel beamed and smacked Shanto on his behind. "I thought you wanted a quickie. Come on, the queen wants you for questioning."

Shanto retorted, "What queen? You're all overgrown children."

Rhoan began shouting off fake charges of heathenism, creating a ruckus, over drinking, and humping the milk goat in public, whereas molesting the goat in private would be okay.

Shanto snarled a curse as he wrestled his way free and bolted, not caring about anything, not Tel's sharp whistle nor whether the cops were real or fake. The cat sprinted in powerful bounds across tables, over squealing children, and zigzagging through people like a cheetah. Wulvur, still in dog form and bounding like an overgrown pup, helped herd Shanto towards their friends. While Shanto was trying not to trip over the cat or get leg humped by Wulvur, Rhoan grabbed him by the shirt.

"Come on," Rhoan said with a big grin. He and Tel wrestled Shanto into the stocks.

Sweat beaded on the prisoner's forehead. "This isn't funny—let me go."

Rhoan leaned close to their stockade prisoner and whispered, "Don't even think about morphing into something scary, because we'll smash you."

Elowren stomped into view, still in costume. "What's going on here?"

Rhoan groped for a comeback. "This man confessed to running a goat brothel."

"Alright, haha, you got me," their captive started in a shaky voice. He yelped when Tel smacked him hard on the rear. "Yeow! You raunchy wench, what kind of place is this?"

"Raunchy? You wanted the massage," Tel warned, her tone revealing how she reveled in the moment. "I should let my dog hump your leg."

Shanto fidgeted and tried to cock a glance at her. "I don't do animals."

"He lies about inches, too," Tel announced.

Rhoan was having fun with the gathering crowd. "What is the punishment for kissing a goat?"

"Depends on the sex," a guy replied.

Others grabbed the chance to throw in their arguments, no longer caring about the conversation between Elowren and Shanto. The boisterous crowd uttered all kinds of ideas, from marrying the goat, to kissing other animals in uncouth places, and other deviant acts.

Lady Elowren crouched right in front of Shanto. "Why didn't you report? Why avoid us?"

"Abandoning his post. It's a good thing we don't have a ship for keel hauling," Tel goaded.

The crowd laughed and jeered until Elowren waved them back. Most of them were enjoying the scene and played along. A few were bored and walked away or to shop from vendors, while most patrons were distracted.

Shanto's face took on the image of a busted juvenile when he noticed Slade standing with folded arms, and Scruffy wearing a mask of disinterest, either posture forewarning a severe reprimand. After a moment, something shadowed his submissive attitude, and ice chiseled his words. "Oh, you think you're all so funny, sublime in your silly little games. That includes you, Queeny."

Elowren prompted, "Go on."

Shanto's face contorted in desperation to remember not his own memories, but images forced into his recent memories. His words were hesitant. "Slade, I have a message for you. To solve your problems anew, solve your greatest mystery at the source."

"What?" Slade started, his arms unfolding.

"Only then can you move forward. That's what the fish said." Shanto's voice drifted off as he blinked and shook his head, then glanced around with sleepy eyes. "How in all frantic realms?" Even though he jerked at the stocks, the venom left his voice. "Ow! Get me out of this thing. I'm not that kinky."

Tel jumped on that one. "How kinky are you?"

Shanto growled, "I'm not."

"Wuss," Tel sighed.

Elowren nodded to Rhoan, who opened the stocks and helped their captive up. Fuming, Shanto straightened his clothes. His anger subsided as the crowd applauded him for the show.

As the festival carried on and people wandered away to find other amusement, Slade strode closer, his expression impassive. "Shanto, what else do you remember, and why'd you run?"

Shanto rubbed his neck, then shrugged. He replied in a bewildered voice, "Cap, I left the station because I picked up a lead on the next hit. Rumors, really. Jasko's bomb cop buddies told him there's hardened spacers afraid to go to the spaceport on Earth. Seems logical to me that if Venamir hit the Space Station, why stop there? Earth's planetary spaceport could be next."

"Makes sense," Slade nodded.

"There was one crew," Shanto went on, "real heavy in cyborgs, real shady. They were among the first to get clearance off the space station after Venamir's goons hacked the place."

Slade gazed around but saw only humans nearby, all enjoying the festival. "To the spaceport. Let's do some infiltrating."

Wulvur grin was downright wicked. "I know some guys, musician spies." Noting weird looks from his friends, he shrugged. "That's how I get cash. I worked as a musician and a stunt double."

Scruffy groaned, rubbing his eyes, "Yeah, I've seen your stunts."

Slade watched Elowren sashay off with Shanto on her arm and Zared escorting them, all appearing like fun-loving cosplayers.

Gus nudged Scruffy. "Who'd throw someone out the airlock, anyway? That's crazy."

"Venamir would," Scruffy said in a low tone.

Slade walked backstage, where Telari sat on the floor to cuddle the cat and baby talk about how much she'd miss working with the furball. While his crew mingled and joked with the band members, Slade folded his arms and studied the feline. *That cat's an Atlean hybrid, maybe even a morpher?* He strolled over for a closer look. "Telari? How long have you known this cat?"

"Months. Vany and I've been training her. Problem is, Vany isn't too good with felines."

"Training her for what?"

"Search and rescue. You know how cats are in hunter mode. They're very focused."

"Now, that is interesting," mused Slade, "that a water-breather would have a cat. This breed can detect morphers." He smirked at Telari's peaked interest. "Let's go find Vany."

At the sight of Slade's friends regrouping, Maska made his escape, losing himself in the crowd. His grumbling belly and the festival's sights soon diverted his attention from his spy duties. Posing as a human, Maska bought a hot dog and a beer and tromped through the All Genre Sci-Fi Festival patrons, smiling at every set of cleavage.

"I wish all of Earth was like this, like one big spaceport," he said between bites.

He purposely brushed past ladies dressed up as aliens, and female aliens dressed as humans, ending up slapped twice and chased once by an angry boyfriend. Maska escaped by switching forms in a hallway and adjusting the colors on his coat. Despite his efforts, humans managed to single him out. Seeing the boyfriend and two angry women stalking him, he ducked into a bathroom and morphed into something close to a woman's form. One of the women passed right by him, stuck her nose away in clear distaste, and skulked into the bathroom he'd just polluted.

Maska's comm cancelled all enjoyment for him when a low voice growled in his earpiece, "Have you found Shanto yet?"

"No," Maska grumbled, wiping ketchup on his pants. "I'll find him. Get lost, Noxus."

"Don't say our names out loud!" the voice snapped. "Report in before they recognize you."

"That was a long time ago," Maska sighed, turning off his comm. "I'm not leaving." He headed toward the beer stands, not seeing a large retriever trotting after him.

Maska found a beer garden, where he bought a large, frothy beer, and sat on a bench to watch women. He paid no mind to the shaggy retriever until the dog sat down beside him.

"What do *you* want, mutt? I got nothing but a bad name," Maska complained.

"Yes, you do," the dog agreed.

Maska snorted beer up his nose and started coughing, driving the nearest people hurrying off in clear distaste.

"Relax," said the dog, "I don't fit in, either."

"I fit in. Wait, who are you?" Maska growled under his breath. "Why are you tailing me?"

The dog replied, "I'm a talent scout," and stared into Maska's squinting, untrusting eyes. "I can tell you're new around here, still working on a good human image."

"My form's good enough."

"No offense," Wulvur continued. "No, it's not. Let's talk. I'll buy. I know some great places where the women are hotter. Worst case, you get a drink and slobber over women."

Maska glared at him with beady, suspicious eyes. "You gotta be Atlean. I can't get past your psy shields. How about you let me read your mind?"

"Caz we're not intimate."

Maska snickered. "You got me. Well, there's one problem. Only one drink?"

"Many as you want."

Chapter 14
Disgruntled Crew

Doc Nelzyr sat in an exam chair, fuming, "The *Jacobyte*. What've they done to my medbay?" Hesitating, he reached up to find a snug band around his head and rubbed the contraption. It felt like scrap metal fastened over a hat liner. When he tried to wrestle the thing off his head, tiny clamps bit into his skin. Worse, power cells greeted his touch with a minor zap to his fingers and his head. Doc jerked his hand away with a gasp.

Moradin glanced from the lab station and stormed over to him. "I said, don't touch it. Get up. Let's go, no tricks."

"Mori, we didn't give up on you," Doc started. Images flooded back to his mind, similar to Slade's flashbacks, air battles, evacuating their old crew when their ship went down, and losing over half their crew from combat and a crash landing. They hid or morphed to avoid capture, spending weeks posing as forest creatures or enemy militia.

"Don't call me that name," she retorted.

Doc pushed himself out of the chair. "Damn it all, listen!" He grabbed her arm despite a sharp feeling of doom that slapped at his better judgment. "We searched for months. I won some scars trying to find you." He jabbed at a faded scar beneath his chin.

Moradin freed her robotic arm. "You got a teeny scar. Poor you, boo-hoo."

"When we regrouped, Venamir told us you were dead. He hid evidence."

"Likely story."

"He said your body was never found. Doesn't that bother you?"

"I swear, just shut your hole," she growled, and pointed to the door. "Move."

Doc sighed and complied, glancing over to see her flanking him, her face in a tight mask, but he could see the clash of fire and sorrow smoldering in her eyes. *Fine, I'll let her chew on it,* he thought, his features cold and sullen as they passed through the research lab. He slowed, eyeing a layout of vials and containers that appeared as innocent as game pouches worn by children. His eyes narrowed at the cryptic markings on the larger vial, and he strayed closer toward the workbench, until Moradin took him by the arm and redirected him.

"I'm warning you, wanna-be heroes meet an ugly fate around here," she said in a flat voice. "You're going to help hack the guardian program out of existence."

"I'm not a hacker. You should know there aren't enough of us onboard to do that," Doc muttered.

"Find a way," she ordered.

They walked down the halls that once felt like home, but now Doc understood what subjugation felt like. His mind raced as he pondered ways to escape.

Motley glanced up with a start. He glared at Moradin, not noticing Nelzyr.

Moradin waved one arm toward the feline man, "Meet our mascot, Motlion ze furball bomb. Rats dragged him in."

"I said, call me Motley," hissed the feline. "You furless pimps can't pronounce my name."

"Quiet before I muzzle you." Moradin turned to Doc. "You may as well cooperate, Doctor Pee-on, or Noxus will be watching you instead of me."

Doc couldn't hear any footsteps until Noxus turned the corner. He and Noxus gave each other scornful stares of recognition.

"The turncoat doctor," Noxus sneered. "See what you get for throwing Venamir in prison?"

"You're his experiment, that's all," Doc countered. "Why don't you go plug yourself and recharge your batteries somewhere, like in a lava pit?"

"Sooner or later, the captain will let me at you," Noxus replied. He turned to Moradin, "You must enjoy this reunion."

She sneered back, "Didn't the captain give you chores, like scrubbing the waste chute?"

Noxus chortled, a sinister noise that reminded Doc of a choking crocodile. He smacked Doc's headband, making the elder jerk away and spit curses, then strode out.

The sulking doctor bit back his retort, feeling vulnerable enough sitting beside Motley. Moradin's posture was relaxed, her demeanor aloof while she scrolled through ship schematics. Motley returned his attention to business as the Herja faded from the cockpit screen. "Come on, baby, hack," the cat muttered, his whiskers twitching in time with his bushy tail. His voice faded off and he rose with a start, bonking his ears on the overhead panels. He ignored the sharp, brief pain, far too aghast with the sight of one shuttlecraft's open ramp, and jumped at Venamir's voice on the open comm.

"Oh, cat, you have a visitor," Venamir proclaimed.

Motley gasped a "No, he didn't." He charged through the ship and out the nearest hatch. He saw what he dreaded, a clone of Moradin ushering a cat boy.

The wavy fur along Motley's nape hackled. He flung his headset aside and tore out of the ship. "You. Get your thug gloves off him."

Mora-clone shrugged and released the boy's collar, allowing him to spring in agile leaps to the adult feline man. "Captain's orders."

Motley hugged his son before turning to the ship and roaring, "VENAMIR!"

"Wow," the cub muttered, watching even some heavily muscular thugs shrink back at the sight of his dad's bared fangs and claws.

Motley used utmost control to keep from snapping at his boy as he said, "Watch your language. These are not our kind, so spare them any lessons." He winced at Venamir's voice in his head, a summoning that left him with a lingering feeling of amusement. Ears pinned back and fuzzed tail lashing, Motley swept an arm around the boy and ushered him into the ship. He whispered to his cub in their tongue, a language full of rolled r's and hisses, "This changes my whole spy mission. I have to act like a double agent."

The cub glanced around, fur hackled, but his eyes were wide and his ears twitched from the many strange voices and sounds. "Where?" he said, hushing his cracking voice. "What's going on?"

"You're unharmed, yes? I'll rip that bionic bitch apart."

"I'm okay. Don't flip your lid," the boy assured, trotting along to keep up with his father's long strides. "She gave me desserts to shut me up."

"Then just play along."

"What? Do I get to see what you do now?"

"No. Yes, unfortunately." Motley had lost all productive thought, thanks to his new dilemma. He had to help Venamir now, but realized he could bend the rules. Motley proceeded to hack into the ship's computer, using several tries before using his own password. "Venamir can't read my mind, not well," he whispered to Doc, "or else he'd know more about me. Oh, Doctor Nelzyr, meet my cub, Leifur."

"Hi, Cubbie," Doc said.

"Hi," the cub sighed.

Motley reached over and clamped a paw on Doc's shoulder. "Nelzyr, your pass codes."

Doc shrugged the paw away, but heaved a sigh, giving one last lingering look around. *A ship full of thugs, led by a madman, one manipulated Ranger and one former ally.* Doc reminded himself that there was always a way out. Or was there? He could picture it all, resisting and ending up with the blood of a child on his hands. Then Venamir or the bunch of thugs would murder him anyway, with Motley leading them with a roar of vengeance. He knew secrets of this ship not even Venamir could find, or so he hoped. Doc met the gaze of a desperate father, and a formidable enemy, and a possible ally against a common enemy. Doc nodded to Motley and pressed his hand against the screen. "Herja, request critical access, Chief Surgeon Doctor Nelzyr."

Motley heaved a sigh of relief, whether premature or not. The screen flashed with the blackness of doom, but only for a few lingering seconds. Next, multiple windows popped alive with ship's condition, crew life form readings, engine performance, and a dizzying sensor display. Ignoring cheers from the thugs watching, Motley located the choices for EMERGENCY PASSCODE approved, and set the time frame to lowest setting. Leifur watched every command his father made, reached down to the gamebot in his pouch and activated the recorder.

The computer beeped, flashed on and off in a steady rhythm, scrolled gibberish until the screen finally displayed, Complete Reset?

"Yes."

Are you sure?

Motley sat back, one ear flicking forward, his head cocking a bit. "Yes."

Are you certain? This can NOT be undone!

By now, Motley was thumping the touch panel harder each time it kept asking questions, until his last whack cracked the formerly resilient surface.

"Yes, for all infested hair guts, just do it!" Motley snapped. His voice drifted off as the ship's systems began resetting, some solo, some in groups, including the engines.

An intense presence swept into the room, strong enough to make even the non-telepaths straighten up or glance around for invisible fiends. Motley and Doc knew who it was, and sensed a sinister pleasure.

Motley whirled and growled at Venamir, who had crept up behind them, so quietly that only the felines and Moradin with her enhanced senses could hear him approach. "There, now release my cub."

"Impressive," said Venamir. His twinge of a genuine smile suggested hope. "Not just yet. Why are you so worried? Guilty conscience? There is no honor in assailing children, especially those graced with potential." He strode out.

* * *

On the outskirts of the Fantasy Faire, Wulvur sat at a bar and watched Maska try to flirt and brag about his many vague talents, only to fail miserably at scoring a date. Wulvur slipped some powder into Maska's drink and shoved it over to him.

"Hey, Romeo, take a break."

Maska stared after yet another woman who stomped away from him. He sighed and plopped onto a chair beside Wulvur. "You bought a stupid logo shirt and looked like you stepped out of a boring office and they like you. I don't get it."

"Earth women," Wulvur shrugged. "They have to think it's their idea. Try this. It's called 'Getting Laid with Style.' You'll like it."

Maska swayed in his chair as he eyed the layered drink, clear on the bottom, bright swirls of blue and red in the middle, and foamy on top. His gaze drifted to Wulvur's nearly empty beer mug. "You don't want one of these funny drinks?"

"I like ale. That funny drink's for you. It looks complex. Women like that. I'm trying to help since you're hooking me up with an interview."

Maska grinned, a scary sight with his yellowish teeth, the two front ones needing new caps. "Maybe the captain'll like you after all." He sniffed the drink and took a long draught. "This booze is all right."

"Anything else you can tell me?" Wulvur asked.

Maska slurped the drink, swaying more by the minute. "I can't promish you much luck. Jus' be at dis planet's spaceport when I told you. It's a recon mission. Captain wants data and some human transports." He chomped down the last chips in the closest bowl.

"Hey those were mine," a disgruntled man said, turning.

Maska shoved the bowl at him. "Gimme a refill."

Wulvur vacated his chair and stepped between them. "Sorry," he told the human, "he just broke up. I ordered more stuff. You can share."

"I can see why, and, eh, okay, I guess," the man said, turning back to watch the game.

Wulvur turned to scold Maska. "Dude, you start any fights, and our deal is off. Besides, there's an all woman band here tonight. Come on." He led the way upstairs.

"Oh, baby," Maska drooled, following with uneven steps.

True to his word, the bartender delivered another tray of bar snacks. The insulted guy watching the game glanced around, shrugged, and claimed the food.

Maska chugged the rest of his drink. "I want more o' dis."

Wulvur hid most of a snicker. "That's your fourth tonic. That's what we call special drinks, for a special kinda guy. So, the name. Who do I go see?"

"Oh, uh, Axehat. He'll be with a couple twin doppelgangers who look like Moradin. Captain is weird that way. Where's the strippers?" He swayed, holding his gut. "Where's the crapper?"

"That way," Wulvur pointed across the busy dance floor.

As Maska staggered away, Wulvur strolled outside, laughing. A safe distance away from the bouncers, he activated his comm. "Slade, I'm with Maska, and he's spilling his guts."

Slade's image appeared on his wristband. "Maska? That worthless leech! Go on."

Wulvur watched the locals, his voice hushed. "He knows about Venamir's next hit. Some guy named Axehat is going to hit the inland spaceport tonight. It's almost dark here. We'll only have a few hours. Want me to bring him in?" He heard Slade talking to his crew.

After a few minutes, Slade said, "No. Where is he now?"

"Probably getting slapped," Wulvur smirked.

"Ditch him and report back."

"Will do." Wulvur put his comm on record and swaggered toward the nearest bouncers. "Hey fellas, did you see that moron in a neon bright jacket? He's been harassing the ladies."

"Yeah, real creep," the gnarly bouncer nodded.

"I think he's a dealer, in just about anything," Wulvur said. "I was trying for a sting tonight, but he doesn't know much. All he's doing is scamming on every chick in the joint, and a few dudes."

The other bouncer spun up, "Hold it, you're a cop?"

"No, but he is," Wulvur pointed to the gnarly bouncer.

Wulvur snuck away as an argument between bouncers ensued. He strode down the busy sidewalk, reverting to his true form. He touched a few decorative claw-shaped marks on his collar. The style and colors of his clothes changed from a casual hoodie and jeans to dark blue and black tactical gear. Whistling, he kept strolling as a security car sped past. Scruffy pulled up just ahead and Wulvur hopped in, snickering.

Scruffy shook his head, grinning. "I hope those bouncers smash him."

"He's slippery. Next hit is tonight. Yeah. Let's jet." Wulvur said.

"Good work," Scruffy said. "We need to send our Druwens to the spaceport."

Wulvur grinned, "Mine are already there."

Chapter 15
Spaceport

As Slade landed the *Vernacular* at the spaceport, twilight crept across the horizon. Renovated hangers and new dome-shaped buildings separated the city from runways and landing pads. His crew gathered inside and started gearing up. Gus, Jasko, and Shanto made final checks on concealed weapons.

"Gimme what you know," Slade said, activating the ready room screens.

Elowren tapped the long table. "*Vernacular,* show us the Bermuda spaceport, highlighting non-human people and cyborgs." A miniature spaceport formed, complete with images of ships and life forms. She pointed to a cargo ship buzzing with troops, non-humans and cyborgs, with a few humans, floating energy signatures that glowed like fireflies. "An Atlean cargo ship docked a few hours ago. The crew left, probably on shore leave. They have a class three stealth shield, but I'm sure Venamir's people could bypass it."

Zared leaned on the table's edge, noticing smaller clusters of people moving irrationally about. "There're already some skirmishes popping up. I bet they're trying to scatter the cops. A handful of cyborgs are heading toward the veteran party hall."

"Maska said the hit-guy is a cyborg named Axehat, who works for Venamir. One thing you should know is they're packing plasma weapons, and it gets worse." Wulvur held up a pendant, which splayed scenery across the dashboard, zeroed in on two humans slipping weapons into their coats.

Zared's eyes narrowed at the weapons. "Wait, are those... *diser* firguns? Earth cops aren't geared to defend against those."

"Our force fields won't hold up past a few shots," Shanto added.

"I brought backup," Wulvur said, "my brother's rock band. We bumped the other band."

Shanto snickered, "You call a band backup? They gonna sing the criminals to sleep?"

"They're morpher spies," Wulvur countered, "and yeah, they can."

"How d'you punt the other band?" Zared started. Seeing a wicked grin, he decided, "I don't want to know. Why would Axehat choose this place?"

Rhoan walked in, medbag over one shoulder. "This whole spaceport is a major info hub. How d'you weasel into their fold, Wulv?"

Wulvur shrugged. "I told Maska I'm a black market dealer. If he hooked me up with Axehat, I'd get him disers, a crew, and the latest, greatest, sex-robots."

His friends stared as if they weren't sure whether to doubt him or congratulate him.

"I don't like splitting up, but we need to," Slade said. "Keep in contact. Stay covert long as you can. Scruffy, stay here. Elowren, with me. Use all necessary force. Venamir likes to use cyborgs. Capture Axehat dead or alive. I'll have teams ready to disable explosives."

"Give me a few minutes to bait him." Wulvur morphed into his favorite alias form he'd used with Maska, a personality his friends called the angry rock star. He ran to the cargo bay where three hover-cycles were parked, strapped through heavy rings along the wall. "Huvster bikes, fun times." He unstrapped the nearest one and mounted up.

"We better split up," Zared said. "Alert the local force, cops, medics, whoever will listen."

Wulvur left the ship first, hoping to draw some cops as he sped to the party hall. No luck. He parked in the VIP section and posing as one of the band members, schmoozed his way past the bouncers. He strode toward the stage and waved at the lead singer, who nodded. Wulvur turned up his tiny headband comm a notch. "I'm in."

"Talk to us," Slade replied.

"Most people are acting normal. I see two Moradins, no, three, near each exit. Their faces are a little different, weird. Each one's near a couple of humans wearing higher tech guns, not Earth-made. Target located." Wulvur made direct eye contact with Axehat. The man sat with a couple Mora-dopps in a corner booth, frowning as they conversed in hushed tones. Wulvur smirked as he approached, meeting Axehat's icy glare with a cynical grin.

"Sit," Axehat ordered.

"This changes the deal," Wulvur said, eyeing the Mora-dopps. "You already have sex-bots."

One of the dopps started to rise, scowling, until Axehat pushed her back down.

"It's okay, honeybunch," Wulvur jived, "I don't need a test-drive."

Zared's psy voice nagged him, *"Don't start a fight, not yet."*

"Take his goons at the doors, Z-man," Wulvur psyd back as he glared at Axehat. "I hear you're a cyborg experiment gone sour. That probably means you can't psy."

"Who are you? I'm here to either make a deal or kill you," Axehat stated. "Choose fast."

Wulvur spread his arms. "Let the girls jump me first."

"Who are you with?" Axehat demanded.

"Dude," Wulvur leaned on the table, "I think you already know. I'm giving you one chance to surrender. You call off your infiltrators or else my Druwen pack will use your parts for scrap metal and grind the fleshy head into fish food. You won't even get the chance for deep sleep prison. The name's Wulvur. I've chewed up plenty of your kind."

Axehat rose slowly. "The Captain will reward me big time for you." His dopps followed suit, coming at Wulvur from both sides.

Wulvur psyd, *"Lyriad, you're up."*

The lead player shifted to another song. "Arrite, party animals! It's time for our nightly murder ballad." More spotlights on at his cue and traveled over the crowd in lazy passes as his band sang, "Night's done, lights out, time for hot toddies." Lyriad, recited, "Go home, peeps, to safer dreams. Nightmares awake, your lives at stake. Cyborgs come to town to bring you all down." As the murder ballad rambled on, the audience swayed to the beat, many lazily heading for the exits.

The dopps by the exits shoved some of Axehat's human thugs, who were falling under Lyriad's hypnosis. "Useless," one

Mora-dopp scoffed, shoving the thug outside. As soon as the emergency door opened, alarms sounded.

Axehat and the Mora-dopps remained unaffected, focusing on Wulvur.

A fight erupted in the corner booth. Wulvur morphed as he sprang onto the table, leaping over the nearest Mora-dopp, kicking it head-first into Axehat. He landed on Mora-dopp number two in alien wolf form, stabbing it through the throat and twisting, showering Axehat with sparks. The dopp fought back, knocking Wulvur off. He rolled to his feet and grabbed a boot knife. "Catch," he taunted, flinging it. The blade started glowing, melting the dopp's fake skin, digging itself farther inside until seconds later, the dopp's midsection exploded, showering Axehat with fluid.

Wulvur laughed as Axehat and the nearest others backpedaled, groaning and complaining in sheer disgust. "You're next, fish-bot," he goaded Axehat. "Come on, I'll sell your parts at auction."

When the band's tune faded, the spell-struck audience regained their wits, looking around with quizzical squinty eyes or twisted lips. Muffled sirens grew louder. A few big guys squared off with the Axehat and his cyborg flunkies.

Wulvur called them off. "Leave them alone, folks. They're not fleshy."

Axehat's thin lips twisted into a sick leer. He cast unconcerned glances at the partiers and a handful of bouncers. "You're quite the bloodhound, Wulvur of the Haunted Grove. These humans should flee in terror from you."

Wulvur stiffened, only a secretive lifestyle and merciless training keeping his features from showing anger. *Where's he getting this info?* "Don't insult us with fairy tales. Get on the ground. Now!" He added, "Ladies and gents, step away from the terrorists."

Axehat sneered as people backed away. "We are elites, unlike your tribe of scavengers."

Wulvur grinned. "Don't you think it's strange that a band of morphers just happens to be here during your little raid? We're here because your spies can't keep a secret."

Sirens wailed louder now, just outside the exits, and then silenced, replaced by commanding voices and pounding of feet to no avail, when the doors jerked and shuddered, but refused to open.

Outside, a stern voice barked, "Damned force fields! Bring them down." They heard shots and zaps commence.

Wulvur touched his headpiece. "Slade, there's an energy shield outside the doors.

Axehat's Mora-dopps surrounded Wulvur. "Come with us, Druwen. You humans surrender if you want to live. Your puny race stands no chance against offworld forces."

"Hear that?" one rough voiced biker said through his shaggy beard moistened with beer foam. "They wanna play Cowboys and Aliens."

As multiple people laughed, Axehat turned his wary gaze to the older patrons. The old farts bore the deadpan, haunted eyes of war. They wore war pins in their caps and patches on their jackets or vests, hustled over to weapons hanging on the walls, or drew firguns from their personal holsters.

"We don't take kindly to party crashers," said the bearded biker.

Wulvur wanted to step down and disarm Axehat, but the thought of being riddled by friendly fire made him wait. "You're one stupid criminal," Wulvur stated. "You're in the Veterans of Allied Worlds Hall. Duh!"

"Don't surrender," another old cuss said, "We'd rather shoot you."

Axehat waved them closer. "Try and kill us, cavemen. Shields!"

Energy shields popped up around the Mora-dopps.

Wulvur gestured at sleepy-eyed thugs scattered throughout the party hall. "We already disabled your hired hands. They're hypnotized because they're stupid. Come outside, Axehat, just you and me."

Axehat looked around and saw his thugs not responding, halfheartedly swaying to no music while wearing stupid grins. The audience looked around as well, some poking the dazed goons, while a few undercover cops cuffed the strongest looking ones. His band of thugs shook off their hypnotic states and turned to fight, but too late. Good Samaritans popped out of the crowd and pounced on them, firing up a full barroom brawl between thugs, vice-cops, bikers, and long-haired stoners.

Jasko climbed in from a balcony window and descended with feline grace. Hackles up and fangs bared, he leapt into the fray.

Axehat noticed some crazy humans among a display of antique weapons. They were turning a historical cannon toward him and lighting the fuse. Axehat sneered, "That junk heap is centuries old."

The craziest looking man with his cap loaded with war pins smiled and tapped the controls on the back of the cannon. The rusted outer shell faded to reveal a shining turret with sites that popped up. A hungry red beam kept locked onto Axehat's chest and followed his movements.

A white-haired man glowered at his target with eyes somber from war. The crazy old guy grinned, hollering, "Fire in the hole!"

People reacted with everything from curses and shrieks to cheers. The smart ones dove for cover.

A merciless "WHABOOM!" echoed for blocks, triggering an orchestra of alarms and an old-fashioned free-for-all bar fight.

Axehat dove for cover behind the bar. The cannon ball demolished the bar, its shock wave disintegrating his energy shield. He crashed hard enough to collapse another set of cabinets loaded with booze and snack food. Behind him, racks of booze collapsed, shattering bottles and glassware. Smoke curled from a jagged, blackened hole in the wall behind the bar.

Someone yelled, "That's alcohol abuse!"

The smoke cleared, and people regained their bearings, searching for Axehat.

Zared burst into the bar's entry hall, flanked by a handful of cops. Jasko barged in from the café and leapt onto the nearest Mora-dopp, bowling it over. Gus and Shanto worked their way through the crowd while ordering the nearest bystanders to get outside.

The Mora-dopps and thugs took on the cops. Axehat plowed past a foolhardy drunk who was helping himself from the beer tap. On stage, Wulvur called out over the surviving surround-sound speakers, "He's making a break for it. There he is, glowing whiz yellow."

Axehat slunk along the wall until a spotlight surrounded him. His head snapped around to lock a murderous glare at Wulvur. "You'll pay for that," he growled, hopping onto the bar. His right hand blurred as he drew a boot dagger and flung it. Eyes focused, Wulvur caught the dagger by the handle and sneered as he and Axehat locked knowing scowls. The weapon heated up within seconds, burning his palm. He yelped, dropping it. The hilt cracked, spewing a cloud of noxious smoke.

"Get off stage!" Wulvur yelled, kicking it toward the farthest wall. His band scattered, except one man blocked behind his drum set. The dagger's handle exploded, toppling the tallest amplifier. Wulvur tackled his buddy, and they ducked behind the next speaker.

Somewhere in the smoke, the drummer groaned as his cymbals crashed over, "Aw, that's just not funny." He morphed into a hyena-faced humanoid, fur hackling through the gaps in his clothes. "Get 'em!" He led the other musician Druwens against Axehat's thugs.

Lyriad, the bandleader, was shoving his favorite guitar under the stage. Wulvur grabbed him by the shoulder. "Find those weapon pieces. Don't touch 'em. You got our stuff?"

"Yeah," Lyriad panted. He climbed up onstage, looking for the dagger pieces.

Wulvur pulled instrument cases out from beneath the stage, yanked them open, and smiled. The cases were loaded with Atlean weapons, old school, yet high tech. He collected his firgun, bow and quiver full of arrows, and one odd, wider stick. Wulvur donned his weapons and glanced around. He saw most of the remaining partiers shooting at the sparse invading force, yelling, "Die robots!"

Jasko sprinted after Axehat, but saw something more insidious. One of the Moradins opened fire on the ceiling, shooting through the walls into hidden power boxes. Lights went out through most of the bar while sections of the wall oozed to the floor.

A cop yelled, "They have disers! Take 'em down before those guns melt you!"

Zared spoke into his comm, alerting everyone across his defense networks. He resumed his true Atlean form and tackled one of two Mora-dopps, while Jasko took the other. An arrow hissed halfway through the Mora-dopp's weapon wrist, breaking its grip. One shot squeezed off and melted a nearby table and booth into molten goo.

The crowd gasped at the sight of the diser's power, but only for a moment. Few fled, while most remained and helped pummel the Mora-dopps or chase down escaping thugs. One Mora-dopp knocked everyone away with a stun blast, the last burst of power from her energy shield generator. Most people nearby absorbed a low dose, which did not stop them. The cyborgs now faced an even angrier mob, if that were possible. Mora-dopps tried to flee, only to be shot at and pulverized. Too late, they realized the ferocity of enraged humans.

Wulvur yelled, "I'm on the leader. Dopps have energy shields. Keep shooting them 'til the shields collapse." He followed Axehat's path of leaked fluid through a doorway at the far end of the bar. He found a stairwell with a crushed "employees only" sign on the floor. Wulvur charged up the stairs just in time to see Axehat assembling a short rifle with a fat scope.

"Come, little mutt, I'll rip your skull open," Axehat said through a bloodthirsty grin.

"You can't rip a skull. It's bone." Wulvur morphed into beastman form as he lunged at Axehat. They battled with the fury of lifelong enemies, going for that perfect jugular rip or organ stab. Instead of breaking bones and crunching cartilage, Wulvur's best hits left only dents and scrapes on cyborg parts, where leaking blood gleamed with metallic fluids. Axehat twisted around with inhuman strength, even past Wulvur's ability to overpower. They rolled apart and sprang back into combat, some of Wulvur's strikes causing lesser damage than hoped, for Axehat's ripped skin hardly bled, and their agility nearly matched.

"Freakin' zombie-bot," Wulvur growled while reconsidering his approach. This cyborg was limber and skilled, like fighting a martial artist on steroids. When Wulvur lunged again, Axehat leapt off the roof, one hand sticking to the wall to slow his fall, where he landed on his feet, the walkway cracking around him. Axehat leapt over a few parked vehicles and sprinted down the closest alley.

Wulvur ran downstairs, reporting over his headset, "Axehat's on the run toward the hangars. He jumped off the roof like it was nothing." His only reply was static. "Crap." He threw down his broken headset. Ignoring protests, he fished a spare earpiece from a pocket just in time to hear Zared's order of, *"Regroup."* He tore down the stairs and stared. At the bottom of the steps, they saw an odd sight in the dance hall, steaming piles of cyborgs, surrounded by gloating humans.

Jasko looked at his favorite weapon to find the muzzle bent and the handle crushed. "She broke my gun," he complained.

The shaggy biker pulled Jasko back to reality with a slap on his shoulder. "You're okay, puss, even if you're not a dog."

An old Brit handed Jasko a jetpack. "Here, mate. Metal-head dropped this."

Jasko gave his new human buddies a heartfelt, "Thanks." He ran outside, buckling the pack on. A light touch activated the thing. He tested the controls, hovering this way and that, grinning.

Wulvur ran over to him. "Big J, where you been, licking yourself?"

"I wish," he replied. "I'll be eyes in the sky."

"Don't take on Axehat alone," Wulvur yelled as Jasko flew off.

* * *

Scruffy flew the *Vernacular* low over Axehat's ship, shining her landing lights on it. A few strategic shots to the cockpit ensured that the ship wasn't taking off any time soon. He orbited around the spaceport, arguing with flight controllers while tracking Axehat's retreating life form.

"I'm trying to help you," Scruffy insisted to a frazzled controller. "Our main target's headed for your northern docks. We just disabled his ship. He'll look for another way out. Call the cops. Call your fighters, but I'm on your side."

Scruffy brought the *Vernacular* to a landing at the north end toward Axehat's location. The old ship's engines warned those on the ground as her thrusters sang like a tenor among shrieks of banshees. The *Vernacular* landed in the largest clear area on the ramp, blowing over docking markers and sending people fleeing away from landing thrusters. Tel followed suit and landed a Zephyr alongside the flying tank.

The *Vernacular's* ramp creaked open, and Slade disembarked.

Tel ran up to them. "We got dopps, led by some half fleshy. They're packing disers, got the spaceport going crazy."

Slade looked like he wanted to shoot every villain alive. "Wulvur's comm went dead. Scruffy, lie low for now," Slade said. "Come on, grab jetpacks. Medics might need the Zephyr."

Jasko's voice came over their comms. "I see the cyborg, Axehat. That name sound familiar? Oh shit!" Shots fired squelched the connection.

"Jasko?" Slade tried again. "All hands, track Jasko."

* * *

Jasko's arm bore a laser burn, but his jetpack took a direct hit. He piloted the sputtering thing toward the nearest roof. He didn't quite make it before the engine died. He slammed against the wall a few feet below the gutters. Claws digging into the wall, he slowed his momentum before falling to the street. He landed on all fours, cursing, groaning, and wrestling the smoking jetpack away from his body. Seeing Axehat approaching fast, Jasko flung the jetpack, bowling his target over.

"He's here," Jasko panted, pain in his voice. "Track me." He heard familiar voices from the far end of the alley.

Shanto and Gus entered an alley and found their quarry waiting for them, holding only a pool stick. Shanto eyed him uneasily, his rifle pointed at the man's heart. "Weapons down. Get on the ground."

"Out of my way or die," Axehat retorted.

"You're crazy *and* stupid." Gus said, in a matter-of-fact voice. "Get down or fry."

Axehat crouched to lunge, and they both opened fire. With incredible dexterity, he tucked into a roll between them. One shot struck him in the leg, but the other shots deflected off the force field, ricocheting back at them. Shanto yelled out as a laser caught him in the ribs, burning into his armor. His gun clattered onto the pavement. Trusting his muscles and skills, Gus lunged.

Axehat bent away with the fluidity of water. All Gus saw after that was a volley of strikes from each wooden end, first to his head, chin, left knee, and then the right. He buckled to the street, growling and groaning. Behind the force field, Jasko scaled a power pole, stealthy, silent. Axehat glanced up to see green, slitted eyes glaring through the darkness. Jasko launched from his perch on a window ledge, casting a monstrous shadow. He caught Axehat in a tackle, slashed his prey, and sprang away to land, claws bloody, tail lashing.

Gus cheered him on. "Get him, Jasko! Slice him up!"

Even against the Draolith's feline dexterity, Axehat manipulated the cat's grip, and rolled free. They squared off again, crouching in the dark alley.

Axehat felt blood run down his left arm, but still smirked. "You're not bad, but still disgusting, fleabag. I bet the buffoon over there castrated you before you could sleep in the house at night."

Jasko snarled, hackling. In a flurry of fur and claws, he pelted his prey with rapid strikes until he sat atop a prone man. Axehat attempted to wrestle free, but Jasko slammed him onto his back and raised a paw, claws shining in the dim light.

Axehat kept both arms wrapped around his midsection. "I give up. Why do you work with Slade, worse, with humans?"

"They're my friends, you rancid, depraved, cave-ape."

Axehat raised his hands. As the cuffs drew near, he grabbed the feline's arm. Jasko toppled onto the pavement. He summoned every shred of determination to jerk that probe out of his arm. He collapsed, wheezing, his muscles clenching in knots. His ringing ears drowned out rapid, fading footsteps. As the world spun, Gus's voice sounded like a distant echo.

Gus burst into the alley, firing at the fleeing form. His lethal shots made Axehat stumble, but nothing more. Gus skidded to a halt and reported to his team. "Man down! I mean, it's Jasko. Cat down! Need a port for him. Target's running southeast of me. His armor's damn good, couldn't drop him."

Scruffy's image appeared over his comm. "I got them," the old geezer said in a war-weary calmness. A few seconds later, a swirling portal appeared around Jaskuro and the big feline vanished. Portals engulfed Gus and Shanto, removing them from the war zone. Scruffy's voice came over all their comms. "Crew, I need Rhoan and Elowren in medbay."

Chapter 16
Spaceport Roundup

Slade landed his jetpack beside a new, busy hangar. Troops, medics, civilians, all trying to help or escape. Sirens had multiplied, and the giant voice was announcing a no-fly zone over the spaceport. Slade moved into the nearest alley, calling his friends, "Crew, regroup with me. Head count."

"Scruffy here, Jasko's staying in medbay. I'm sending Berku and Gus."

Within minutes, two huvzters landed beside Slade, one making a hard landing. Zared opened his visor. "You started a riot without me?"

"Saved some for you, didn't I?" Slade replied with a shrug and turned to the other pilot, "*General?* From our council meetings?"

"Not every day I get to shoot aliens," the general said. "Vanysa tipped us off, said you're working covert to hunt our terrorists, so I brought some help. So let's shoot something." He patted a new, Atlean-made firgun.

Slade grinned, nodding. "Let my crew and I go in. You stay with Zared, since he's a telepath. In case comms go down, we'll still move as one."

"Axehat went for the main hardened shelter. There's a cargo ship in there," Zared informed. "Scruffy tried to port us in, can't get through the hangar's shields."

"So we'll go in the fun way," Slade said. "General, go with Zared. Meet up with the cops. Zared, be our psy link to the cops."

"Call me Glen," the general said.

Zared nodded with a grin. "Scruffy, port Glen and me near that hangar where all the cops are." He grasped Glen's arm just before a glowing sphere formed around them. As Glen glanced around with wide eyes, they vanished. "Scruffy, round us up. Port Wulvur and Telari to me."

Within a few minutes, energy rings formed like swirling hoops of lightning that opened into shifting doorways. Wulvur stepped through one, and Telari through the second.

"The hit-man," Slade said, "what do you know?"

162

Wulvur's comm band was gone, chest armor blackened, jacket torn, Scruffy's green goo showing through the rips. "Axehat's the name, hits like a martial arts dopp. He's more machine than flesh."

"He must be carrying spare power cells to keep it active this long," Gus mused. "Can't you get an arrow through that shield? Or bullets? They're usually made to deflect energy weps."

"Even if we kill him, his cyber parts could take over, or he might blow up, or kill himself." Slade informed. "We have to subdue his living body and his cyborg power at the same time."

Telari caught up to them, panting. "The cops are surrounding a cargo ship. I can disable it." She pointed back the way they'd come. "I'll need to borrow some tools. There's an overhaul dock."

"Let me get Axehat," Wulvur said. "I know his soft spots, not that there are many."

Slade nodded. "Tel, break that ship. Wulvur, find Axehat and bring him down."

They set out, spying two aircraft hangars that lacked the luster of corporate offices, their windows bearing "All Air and Spacecraft Refurb," and "We Fix-Um." Moving inside, they found a shop full of work in progress. A few lifts gave access to the upper level and the basement.

"Most of this stuff's new," Tel commented, "and it's offworlder tech."

"Fan out," Slade ordered. "We need to sabotage that ship."

As the others explored, Tel strode through the cluttered shop, full of test stands, racks of tools. She found what she wanted, a small welder. She grabbed it, along with a mask and gloves. To Wulvur's questioning look, she replied, "A hunch."

Tel and Wulvur moved halfway down the three flights of stairs, pausing at double doors where they heard stoic voices of more dopps. They looked at each other, sighed, and burst through the doors with guns blazing. After a few minutes, Tel emerged carrying another Mora-dopp head, with Wulvur close behind. He glanced back and hefted a confiscated diser.

"Guards are yours," Wulvur murmured.

"Yep." She stuffed her gloved fingers into the Mora-dopp's hollowed eye sockets and hurled it down the stairs as she sang out, "Bowling for Bootie!"

At the bottom of the stairs and another hall away, two guards stood watch in front of double doors marked Hangar 18, Overhaul Dock, NO ADMITTANCE.

"Huh?" the ugliest one grunted.

"What'd you say to me?" the other thug taunted.

"Wasn't me, stupid."

"Who you callin' stoopid?"

They shut up and jerked their guns to ready, toward odd thumping sounds.

The Mora-dopp head rolled down from the steps at the end of the access hall, gaining momentum. They recognized the shape of a skull, its mouth gaping open, teeth clamped on something dark and protruding.

"What the?"

"Shoot it!"

Tel waited through the sounds of dull thumps and thuds, yelps, shots fired, followed by an explosion, and weapons clattering to the floor. "Oh, you don't like stun grenades? Wait'll you get cavity searched," she sang out.

Behind her and further up the hall, she heard further commotion, Wulvur's snarls, thuds, "Oofs!" and obscenities. She started his way to assist, but then the battle fell quiet, except for Wulvur saying, "Chew on that." Her amusement faded when she heard more scrambling feet running toward her, heavy menacing thumps of boots on dopps.

By the time another Mora-dopp tore up the stairs, diser rifle in hand, all it found was an abandoned stairwell ending at hallways and an open door.

Tel remained pressed against the wall, her holographic cammo gear protecting her from immediate detection. She held her position, her breathing controlled, and eased her firgun upward, the deadly red dot creeping up to the base of the closest dopp's skull.

Something made the hair on Tel's neck tingle, a cold, lurking feeling that made her almost fire prematurely. She realized that what the dopps lacked in cunning, they made up for in sensors. Tel fired. The Mora-dopp's head jerked to one shot in the throat, but still lunged as it fell. Its mechanical fist caught Tel in the thigh, knocking her off balance.

The pain triggered something deep within, that mentors had been trying to help Telari summon. Her natural were form. The closest dopp collapsed while the other dopp leapt up the steps to grab at her throat. Tel partially morphed, more humanoid than cat, but her fingers were like long-toed paws with long claws. She blocked the attack, swiping the dopp, to little effect. The dopp didn't flinch as grey fluid leaked from gashes in rubbery skin.

Tel opened full automatic at point blank range on the dopps legs. It made the monstrosity drop to its knees, but the Mora-dopp grabbed Tel's gun arm and squeezed. Telari fired a shot, grazing the head, and leaving a jagged gash of stinking lab-grown flesh and a charred slash in the skull, but no kill. The dopp still clamped onto her arm with its least damaged hand.

Then, instinct took over.

Telari uttered a feral snarl as her nails morphed to claws and thin, shiny black fur thickened from her body hairs. She could tell she was more like a cat than the last time she morphed. Tel felt her ears flick back, and the curious sensation of her tailbone straining against her belt. All she saw through blood-tinged vision was her claws ripping into the dopp's arm until its hand dangled, useless and twitching. Once free of the cruel grip, she ripped out the throat of the Mora-dopp until she'd crushed the power cells hidden beneath fake skin. After a few seconds of onslaught, the mechanical carcass crashed to the floor, its gleaming eyes dulled to inert lumps.

Wulvur sprang through the doorway in a similar demi-human form, claws and teeth bared. In a feral rage, they dismantled the dopps. "You okay, wild girl?"

"Sure." She patted him on the head with a smile. "You look rode hard." She dropped to her knees and unscrewed the smoking head and looted the body's ammo packs. "Woo, a shield generator, cool."

They continued down the stairs, to where the guards lay sprawled on the floor next to ominous diser rifles. Tel picked one up, surprised by the sawed-off style and lightweight, holstered her pistol and walked in with a torch over her back, and rifle in one hand.

The hangar housed a class three cargo ship, large enough to need three bulky engines to haul its swollen gut of a cargo hold. Workstands, lockers, and tall toolboxes formed a brief entrance barrier just inside the double doors she'd entered through, allowing only a few people in at a time. The barriers also blocked Tel's view of the entire ship, unless she moved out into the open. She knew an entrance was located directly across the huge bay, and felt sure some form of trap awaited those foolish enough to tamper with the tall hangar doors. She heard someone trying to sneak closer in bulky boots, and a man's voice whisper, "Dead, right?"

Tel's hands tightened around the diser. Then she saw it, the top of a power panel on the wall. She'd have to greet her stalker to fry it. *Oh, screw it.* She raised the disers and let molten havoc sear through the makeshift barricade. Having never fired such an outlawed weapon, it filled her with gleeful excitement.

Her shots seared through the top of a flame and explosive resistant chemical waste shed and melted through the power panel. Hangar lights overloaded, casting darkness throughout most of the hangar. At each exit, flickering emergency lights activated, their beams hazy in the smoke.

"I'm in," Tel said.

Wulvur emerged from along the wall units, took the looted diser, blew her a kiss, and then vanished again. Tel shifted her tool bag to her front for easy access and headed for the nearest engine.

Chapter 17
Cyborg Wrangling

Axehat familiarized himself with the cockpit controls. "Venamir, I'm on the Atlean ship, as planned. Activating jammers. It has teleporter chambers. It's old. I don't see a stealth control. It can carry great loads."

Venamir's hologram appeared on his arm. "Stealth is a mere luxury. Bring me that ship."

A Mora-dopp walked up beside him and activated a scanner that showed body images all around the hanger. "Troops are converging. The cop with the loudspeaker wants to talk."

"Idiots," Axehat scoffed. He tapped the ship's mighty voice button. "You wish to know why I'm here? This is the second time in a row Venamir is proving that you humans need to evolve more. You're not ready for us. I mean all offworlders. Stay home, Earth people. I've left you presents all over the spaceport. Clear out, or I'll start blowing things up."

The Mora-dopp sat down in the copilot's seat. "They've taken back the control tower. Atleans are helping, and local cops. The locals have turned combat command over to Slade."

Axehat activated the ship's giant voice. "Now you listen to me. I am going to fly out of this archaic excuse of a spaceport. This is your last chance. Just before I leave orbit, I will send directions on how to disable the bombs safely. Lucky for you, I'm following orders from Ambassador Venamir."

Outside the hangar, defense forces didn't budge.

The police chief yelled back, "We don't take orders from terrorists."

Standing with the cops, Zared scanned the hangar. "I don't see evidence of explosives. Keep stalling them.im," Zared said.

Axehat waved to his dopp to end the transmission, and ordered over the ship's speakers, "All hands, target Slade's telepathic henchmen. Fire at will."

Tel chose the left, lowest engine, and gave the exhaust turret another long burst with the torch. Seeing movement in the dock, Tel shut off the torch and flipped up her face shield. Hatches were opening all over the ship.

"I got this, Tel," Wulvur said as he walked past her. Watching three forms sneaking closer behind power distribution units across the large bay, Wulvur morphed into his best doppelganger of Axehat. "Change of plans. We have a cracked thruster, could catch the whole damned wing on fire. That tech is fixing it."

The goons holstered their guns, gruff faces wrinkling as they squinted at him.

"The repair won't take long." Wulvur imitated Axehat's stride, his limp, the accent, and the demeaning tone, leaving the henchmen scraping for apologies until he waved them off. "This may be an Atlean ship, but if she doesn't repair it, we're stuck on this rock. That fool in the cockpit is my clone. The feds will shoot him instead of me. Go on, guard the door."

They nodded and walked past, right into the line of fire from Berku and Slade, who dropped them within seconds.

Wulvur jogged over to the aft emergency escape hatch that hissed open. He stayed in his morphed appearance of Axehat and strode deeper into the ship.

"Gus, do your thing," Slade said in a hushed tone. "Once Telari disables that engine, help her flush that cyborg out of the cockpit."

"Copy," Gus whispered. He put on headsets and gamer glasses and released a small robotic lizard from his vest pocket. The lizard ran ahead, relaying visuals and sound. Gus snuck past stunned thugs.

Slade and Berku morphed into man-beast forms. They leapt onto the lower engine and climbed onto the wing. They knew Tel had done her job when an alarm sounded off. "Fire… engine fire… evacuate! Fire… engine fire." The warnings silenced.

From what sounded like the aft end of the ship, Axehat's baleful voice commanded attention. "Come aboard. My dopps will tear you apart. Then I'll use your carcasses to make more dopps."

"Was that Axehat or Wulvur?" Berku asked in a hushed voice.

"Must be Wulvur," Slade whispered, "he likes to dramatize. Gus, why the bomb threat?"

Gus replied. "My recon lizard overheard him saying he wants to lift off and return home, so why blow up this ship? And he's running jammers so nobody can use portals."

"That's a Merfin strategy," Slade said. "Silence the comms so only telepaths can talk. Disable any teleportal chambers."

"We don't have portal chambers yet," Gus informed.

"This ship is like the space station. Atleans helped build it. There are portal chambers," Berku explained. "This hit is similar, too. Venamir's playing terrorist while collecting massive data."

Slade and Berku were just encountering another dopp and blasted it into a smoldering pile.

Gus blurted, "Don't shoot the head! I need the Mora-dopp's head."

Berku shook his head. "You need help."

Gus caught up to them. He whispered, "I reprogrammed the chips so I can do things to her you can't." He knelt beside the fallen dopp, twisted her ears, which caused a chip to slide out of each one. Glancing up and grinning at Berku's disgusted frown, Gus dug an odd globe from his backpack. He looked around for danger, and let out a relieved breath, seeing Slade and Berku moving to defensive positions around him, guns ready, and they tossed him questioning looks. The globe resembled a cross between a brain and a multicolored planet, yet squishy to the touch. Gus inserted his command chips into the brain's gooey opening. Gus whispered to the globe. "Connect to clones. Activate emergency shutdown. You have been compromised. Shut down."

Berku chuckled, "What the heck is that, a toy brain?"

"This is a brain from one of the dopps on the space station," Gus defended. "I spent a lot of time hacking it."

Glancing all around, the trio pressed on into the next open area, the command room, with two other shut doors, red glowing controls showing locks engaged.

From behind the right door, a dopp's icy voice stated, "Intruders have infiltrated our program. Revert to individual mode. Kill them."

From behind them, footsteps also drew near. "Kill them all."

"You sure pissed them off," Berku murmured.

"Telari, where you at?" Slade whispered.

"Forward nose, hell hole," Telari's hushed voice replied. "We got a plan." She started yanking open panels to reveal a colorful array, mostly manual overrides with warnings in bright red. "I'll get Wulvy in there. Gimme five seconds, then hit that cockpit. From my sensors, it's just him and one dopp in the cockpit."

Fire foam belched from all along the ceiling vents until, to their immense gratitude, Tel shut down the extinguishers.

As the others clambered onboard, the real Axehat tried to start the engines. FAIL symbols splayed across the screen. Indicators showed all hatches opening. The upper windows in the roof opened and swung apart with mournful groans of imminent destruction. Axehat waved his firgun toward the windows. Seeing no attackers, he looked over at the Mora-dopp in the copilot's seat. Instead of rising for combat, the dopp sat and twitched, hands trying to dig at the chips in its ears.

Gus's voice spoke through the dopp's mouth. "Hi, asshole, bet you wished you killed me at the bar. Lesson number one: you are stupid. Two, that dopp's gonna' kill you. Three, refer to one and two." The dopp rose with stiff movements. Eyes dull, it turned on Axehat, zombie fashion.

Axehat shot his Mora-dopp in the head. One shot only made the head jerk, so he peppered the dopp, stray shots burning into the insulation and frying delicate instruments on the copilot's overhead panel until the dopp toppled to the floor.

He never saw Wulvur step into view above him on the roof of the ship, but he felt a deadly presence. The slightest sound from behind alerted him, too late. Axehat whirled to see Wulvur's shadowy form in the dim light.

Wulvur plunged the arrows into Axehat's body, one upward into his heart, and the other through his throat. "Hey, Asshat, thanks for the poison, and enjoy the virus."

"You can't make me sick," Axehat scoffed, voice fading with each breath.

"Not that kind of virus. It shuts down cybernetic neural pathways."

Behind Wulvur, the door had whipped open from the evacuation programming. Slade and Berku burst in, and seeing the situation, lowered their weapons.

"Nooo!" Axehat moaned, collapsing onto his back. "You can't defeat Venamir, not without help. What've I… done?" Axehat's body jerked, sparks dancing off the arrow shafts until he sagged into a pile of recyclables.

"He had the nerve to feel guilty." Wulvur studied the cyborg's corpse. "He may have been mind-controlled. Can we fix him?"

"I could try to wipe his program if our medics can revive him," Gus mused. "But we can't unprogram a killing machine in one night."

A hologram of Venamir appeared over Axehat's chest. "Congratulations, Slade. I watched your encounters and gained valuable data. Decent of you to help."

"Come and face us yourself, you slimy bastard," Slade growled at the hologram.

"Soon, rabid dog, soon," the image replied.

Slade manned the cockpit controls. "I'm dropping shield generators and activating the portal generator. I'm teleporting our fallen hitman, and the holographic fish to the bomb squad, where he'll be dissected after we're sure he won't blow up." He turned to the hologram standing on Axeman's chest. "You've chosen a primal path, Venamir. Good riddance, for now."

Slade tapped the controls again, porting Axehat off the ship. "All hands, stand down. The ship is ours. Tell the cops to stand down."

Outside the hangar, people cheered.

Chapter 18
Ships and Mascot

Slade's crew scattered, most to tour Earth, and to party. Telari went to a couple of animal rescue places she worked at, somber as she cuddled her furry friends for hopefully not the last time. After a few days of that, Wulver lured her away to tourist traps of castles to cheer her up. Not knowing when they'd return to Earth, the crew split work and play with scant time for sleep, making the most of what might be their last week or two.

Wulvur met Telari in a wildlife reserve, the next day at a dog park, and the next at her favorite place, a cat cafe. She was curled up in a beanbag chair, reading a comic book, surrounded by felines. Wulvur grinned, petting a few as he walked through the habitat.

"You don't have any personal pets here, do you? I think Slade would take them."

"Really? Um, lemme adopt like ten right now."

"So no. Sorry."

Tel sighed, closing her comic book. "I wish, but, you know, work, school, I'm usually gone too much, short trips but often. That's why I volunteer. Here, they're all mine, for a while."

"Never been to Atlean?"

"I was really young."

Wulvur found a long feather and lured out the most curious kitten. He picked up the little guy and sat down on the nearest pillow. "Tel, there are some Earth animals on our homeworld, even cats and dogs. They'll love you too. It's your second world, it'll be like magical."

She smiled as she petted the nearest cat. "You're really sweet, sometimes."

"Don't tell anyone. Wanna do castles after this?"

"Yeah."

* * *

While his crew made the most out of shore leave, Slade found half the enjoyment. He spent his mornings with repair techs and diplomats. He missed the hunt. Venamir was out there, recovering, gaining followers. At least Venamir's damage was fading

172

as repairs went on. Earth's space station and spaceports gained extra security since Axehat had ravaged most of the defense systems. With shops open again and flights resuming normal turn-times, the locals interacted with Slade's alien guards with growing trust.

He managed to steal away a couple of evenings with Elowren. Their last night on Earth, they toured a bed-and-breakfast atop a lighthouse, where they could watch the ocean. Earth's seas were less green, and more blue than on Atlearon. Lights from boats dotted the darkness like fireflies beneath a blanket of stars, painted with wispy clouds. This world sometimes felt as serene as their homeworld.

"Remember when we talked about retiring?" Slade reminisced, "Start up our own dragon sanctuary?"

"Yes, but dragons hardly need sanctuaries," she chuckled.

"Yeah, and so much for retiring."

"You'd get too stir-crazy. Being a Consul is hard enough on you."

"I'll say," Slade agreed. "How did I get roped into that? I'm as diplomatic as a wild dog."

"I believe the metaphor is fox in a hen house."

Slade chuckled. "Thanks a lot. Well, my ship disappearing had one good effect. We're back on the same crew. We need to keep it that way."

"Agreed," Elowren smiled, leaning closer. "I don't believe either of us is ready to settle down." She kissed him on the ear, on the cheek.

Just when Slade began fantasizing about intimacy, inevitability crept up on them. The comm demanded attention.

Slade heaved a sigh. "Really? Scruffy, again?" He answered it, not caring about his rumpled shirt or disheveled hair. "What?"

"You wanted to know when the ships are ready." The old geezer wrinkled up with a wide grin. "Oh, am I interrupting anything?"

"No, I always look like this. I mean, it's windy. We'll launch in the morning," Slade grumped. "Good night."

* * *

He approached the *Vernacular* with the Atlean wildcat from the festival padding alongside him. "Oh Telari, I have something for you."

The cat raised on her hind legs with a rowwrl. Slade released the leash and patted her on the rump, sending her bounding ahead.

"Okay, hang on," Tel said, straightening, and piped, "Holy crap." The cat landed inches away with a rigorous purr. "I thought Vanysa was keeping her until we got home."

Slade strolled over and handed her an envelope. "She's officially yours." He grinned, watching her eyes go round and her jaw drop. "I finalized the deal you made with Vany. The cat's driving her crazy, keeps growling at her bodyguard and mangles her bed." They shared a laugh. "Griffa is now registered as your working search and rescue animal."

"Woooo!" Tel grabbed him in a body hug and kissed his cheek.

Slade chuckled and stammered despite himself, "Oh… well now, you ah, have an hour or three to stop that."

Tel glanced around as if waiting for angry women to pick a fight with her, then shrugged and took the envelope. "I mean, thanks. You're the greatest!"

Gus looked up from behind some crates, cargo straps in hand. "What's the big deal with that furball?"

"She's half Atlean Fiersa," Slade replied. "She can detect morphers. We use these cats and some canines that can sniff out a shape-changed person like Earth dogs sniff for drugs. Sure would've been nice to have one around that night at the space station."

"I don't want her in combat," Tel said. "I want her alive."

"We'll all look after her." Slade patted Tel on the shoulder as he strolled past. "Scruffy," he called out, "the crew's ready. Let's go."

* * *

The *Vernacular* hovered clear of the populated spaceport before igniting full thrusters and streaking toward the sun. Behind her followed the *Mythos*, and three fully loaded cargo ships. Once the flight crews completed the official chatter with flight controllers and cleared orbit, they left Earth behind for their long flight home.

In the boredom of deep space, Tel half nagged, half sweet-talked the crew into hanging onto some extra storage boxes. She created an environment with makeshift stairs, perches, and tunnels. Scruffy ran with the idea and rounded up most of the crew to drag some spare crates into the workout room. They repurposed storage boxes, netting, and shipping blankets into a jungle gym for one large feline who liked to claw and chew on everything. They barely still had room for workout equipment, a treadmill, and weights. An escape ladder hung across the ceiling, with planks running across it, and somewhat easy access to perches along the wall. Cammy netting and branches simulated jungle trees, and halfway hid the oversized cat box in one corner.

Tel ushered her extra-large feline into the room. The cat twitched with excitement as exploration promptly commenced. Griffa took right to a fat scratching post that spanned floor to ceiling.

"My favorite's the stripper pole," Wulvur chuckled.

"I love you guys!" Tel exclaimed.

"Here's the kicker," Scruffy elaborated. "You're a morpher trying to find your first new form. This is for mostly her, but all of us. I want you to do what the cat does, climbing, stalking, all that. Telari, you're morphing into a feline, so do what your cat does."

Tel hugged Scruffy and Rhoan, and swatted Wulvur on the rear. "I'm not using the catbox."

* * *

Slade's crew made use of the *Vernacular's* ready room for virtual simulation. They splayed a prison layout over the large hologram table and practiced ways to find Doctor Cruentin. Zared and Elowren uploaded their latest maps, acquired from spies and friends in low places.

"There's over twenty prisons on the bird world, but only a few that can handle most species and telepaths," Zared said. "The one we want is nicknamed Bunker Maze. Part of their security is keeping the inmates lost. Over half the compound is underground. My sources reported that Cruentin is still a prisoner, maximum security. That'd be in the basement levels. Venamir's sure to try to bust him out. If Venamir rescues Cruen, well, I doubt our Doc will survive."

"I thought you said Venamir didn't like to kill Atleans," Rhoan said.

"The fish has a big vendetta against me, and my crew," Slade replied. "I want a medic on each team. We don't know what shape our doc is in."

"I'm going to help break out Doc," Elowren said. "If you pair me with Wulvur, I'll be their medic and we both can access the *Jacobyte's* systems."

"That'll work," Slade replied. "Scruffy, stay onboard your ship. Nobody flies the *Vernacular* like you. The prison is on the avian people's world, Crawshen. We need to stop at Ferally Station." Seeing questioning looks, he clarified, "It's an outpost run by felines."

Telari perked up. "A real cat house? I have to see this."

"Cats and birds share an outpost, and have colonies on the bird folk's world," Berku supplied, "never boring in on that planet."

"I need to talk to the cats at that outpost," Slade said. "One of our spies has been out of contact. Name's Motley, a feline, good troop. Maybe the cats have some news."

"Good place to do repairs, too," Elowren commented. "Those cats and birds will be all over our ships like kids on a jungle gym."

Slade went on, "We'll meet our contacts at the Die Hard Tavern."

Scruffy groaned, "Be careful what you eat. Those Hrokahs cook anything, *if* you can call that cooking. You're lucky if they even kill it first."

"I hear one bird cooked his own gizzard," Wulvur said.

Berku grinned as he leaned back in his chair. "When we get to Crawshen, I say we look up the Wild Paints gang. A few of their members do repairs for the prison."

"I was thinking about them," Slade admitted. "You think Shocks' father is still alive?"

"I know he is," Berku said. "I sent out a recall order a few hours ago, summoning all Werefolks and supporting troops. Grumpy old Max replied right before our meeting here. He sent us charts on the prison and local area. So he's still a decent mole, but it doesn't mean he'll fly and fight."

Slade conjured maps from his brother's new files. Virtual maps appeared over the table, showing layers of cellblocks at a prison, as well as a map of the region that highlighted a spaceport near a peninsula, caves up the coast, and farther inland, a prison compound. "Max was becoming a good diplomat for humans until Venamir turned a major council meeting into a warzone. Last I heard, Max still has his old crew."

Elowren displayed images of two brawny humans, the older one leaner with grayer hair, both wearing vivid tattoos of cartoon-style art. "Max and his son, John Shocks, were so mad at Venamir's revolt against humans that they left our fleets of allied fighters. Can't blame them, after almost getting killed protecting our diplomats. According to reports, Venamir's followers have been meeting in sea caves near the prison. More aquatics have been trading weapons and sea treasures. Max and his gang think the Merfins are recruiting followers, because activity of cultists has shot up sharply since a few months before Venamir busted out of prison."

"They may be right," Slade said. "I'm sure Shocks and son are bitter, but we need their help. Wulvur, take Gus and Shanto. You helped save lives when Venamir turned against us. The Shocks crew should remember that. For now, we'll get our repairs, supplies, and intel, and leave the cargo ships at the outpost. We'll take only Scruffy and Zared's ships near the prison, and stay in stealth as much as we can. The mission is to rescue our people first. Most of us will go into the prison after Venamir. Wulvur and Elowren will look for Doc Nelzyr. Zared will fly wingman to Scruffy. We'll fine tune the plan on the way there."

Berku rubbed his braided beard in thought as he zoomed in on the spaceport's nearest cities. "I can send word to Max to expect a visit, and that his friends at the prison should take time off."

"Do it," Slade said. "With or without their help, we rescue our people. This is our best shot to rescue Doc and our Herja, Kestral, and take my ship back.

Chapter 19
Walk the Airlock

Doctor Nelzyr worked his eyes open through another pounding headache and greeted one more hell-bent day with growing scorn. Movements stiff, he sat up in the hibernation pod that looked and felt very much like a high-tech coffin. To think that he put patients into these things now filled him with revulsion. This time, when he looked around medbay, expecting Maska to bully him, he saw Noxus and Moradin standing guard. Doc steadied himself as their presence sent ominous vibes through him. In walked Venamir.

"What do you thugs want?" Nelzyr demanded.

"Let us talk," said Venamir.

Doc grimaced inside. *Another session.* Each session had grown worse, because each time Venamir questioned him, Doc refused to unveil the secrets of the *Jacobyte*. He felt Venamir begin probing his mind, initiating their daily battle of wills.

Venamir started out with his usual question. "Doctor, tell me the ship's codes. Why delay the inevitable?"

Doc folded his arms. "Are those stun burns on your hands? Still can't command the ship's Herja, can you? That's really bad for you water breathers with those delicate webs between your fingers. You should go soak in your pool and add more salt to the water."

Venamir ignored the taunt for the moment. "I know how to deactivate the Herja program. We need more people from the original crew. Or you can help hack it."

Doc faked a look of puzzlement. "I don't know how to hack. The lizards couldn't hack the Herja of Mori on our old ship, either. You remember the *Spectre*, the ship you allowed to crash."

Venamir's tone darkened, "Slade crashed her."

"Oh, no you don't," Doc retorted. "It wasn't Slade's fault. You flew left seat. You were in command." Seething with reckless anger, Doc went on, "The very people trying to kill us became *your* allies. How did that happen? Oh, I know, conspiracy, that's how."

"Rezoans were not my allies. They were merely tools."

"You can justify anything to yourself," Doc retorted.

"You're an imbecile. We are above the ways of humans." The two met with glares while Noxus and Moradin soaked in the show. "Earth will bring nothing but pain and degeneration to our people." To Doc's surprise, Venamir's voice turned friendly, even soothing. "You know I was the Morpher Council's best inquisitor, and you, their best surgeon. We should be allies."

Doc refused to take the bait. "You enjoyed wearing down the will of your captives. You're sick." He tried to imagine snaring Venamir with a giant fishhook and watching the fish dangle with his fins flapping and eye bulging out, but his defenses caved in. As his captor kept talking, trying to reason with him, Doc's mind drifted into a relaxed state, far too relaxed.

"Doctor," Venamir whispered his lies, "we are in deep space, headed home to Atlearon." He gestured to his thugs. "Bring him, light grips, mind you. Do not wake him."

Noxus and Moradin took Doc by the arms and guided him along as if handling a lost sleepwalker. One crewman noticed, and another. Doc gained an audience of half the crew following, all eager for twisted amusement.

Doc Nelzyr's weary mind raced to rebuild his mental defenses against relentless psy interrogation. He felt like he was in a dream where he was the only fool left alive. Even back when they were colleagues, Doc never liked Venamir. Anger distracted him from concentrating on protecting the secrets in the back of his mind. Hands clenched his arms. He knew he was walking somewhere, but his vision was as blurry as a drunken man staggering through the fog. Something hissed and clicked behind him. Then, with Venamir's voice silenced, Doc's vision cleared, and he looked around.

Doors ahead opened to reveal a small pressure chamber used for emergency spacewalking. Doc took one look at the window and saw fuzzy stars against the blackness of space. He found a reserve of energy and fought against his captors, but his strength paled against their overpowering grips.

Venamir's hands rested over the pressure door controls. "I ejected your friends into their own mine field. Granted, they were in a flyer. Would you like to be next, without a space suit?" He reveled as Doc's face contorted between panic and fury. "Tell me the access codes to this ship's weapons."

Dr. Nelzyr yelled, "Are you insane? Wait 'til these brainwashed scags mutiny, this pressure chamber will have another customer!"

"Tsk, tsk," Venamir nodded to the pressure chamber. His thugs threw Doc inside. The pressure door slammed shut.

Doc scrambled to his feet and pounded sweaty fists on the inner window, bellowing every curse he could think of, and then made up a slew of new ones. "You know it takes more than two of us to override a Herja. You need original members of the old crew."

"After we raid the prison, we will have our four—myself, you, Moradin, and Cruen."

"Then why am I in here? I've done what you demanded," Doc fired back.

"Have you?" Venamir waved a tiny, spear shaped blade where Doc to see. "You allowed this to remain in my leg, so your friends could track me."

Doc tried to steady his voice, even though his heart tried to rattle itself out of his rib cage. "Well, of course, I did. Who wouldn't try to escape? Soon, you'll need a medic to patch up all of you, and after this treatment, I won't want to help."

Venamir had raised his hand close to the ejection controls, but he lowered the hand, and his eyes narrowed into raging slits. "What do you mean, soon?" He saw Doc smile. Ignoring grumblings from the henchmen, Venamir demanded, "What did you do?"

"You'll see," Doc promised, eyes narrow.

As they stood off in checkmate, Venamir could sense the doctor's fear and delighted in the sensation. Still, he knew Doc. *The senile old doctor may have found a way to sabotage the ship and still be afraid.* Behind him, some crew members muttered and glanced at one another.

Doc knew he couldn't keep Venamir out of his head for much longer, but one thing gave him a twinge of comfort. *The old fish needs me.* "You try to blast me into space, I'll take you with me."

Only Noxus and Moradin appeared unmoved, but their faint smirks surfaced as they watched the rest of the crew worry and fidget.

With his usual smile before committing a vindictive act, Venamir broke the restless silence. "Yes, I will see, after your blood sizzles with the molten sun. Farewell, Doctor." Venamir thumped a large, red button. Clunks and hissing from the outer pressure door left no chance for redemption.

Doc whirled and tried to plaster himself against the door as if it would save him. "NO!" he cried out, face ashen. He squeezed his eyes shut. An unbelievable coldness gripped him, blackness and utter futility. "Herja, shield me," Doc pleaded, "and let me back in!"

Instantly, he heard a woman's soft voice. "Activating life force shields."

As a foggy substance shot from tiny ports in the floor and ceiling, Doc felt a tingling all over his body and noticed a faint sparkly glow around him. He imagined effects of decompression and the extreme damages that would kill him in seconds. His heart pounded harder when the outer hatch opened full. His mind's eye saw the vast graveyard of space. He was sure it was too late. Then he realized that he wasn't dying. The stars didn't look quite right either. The door hissed and slid open, and Doc collapsed onto the floor near Venamir's feet, panting.

Only Venamir, Noxus, and Moradin remained where they stood. The scavenged crew of thugs shrieked like startled carrion birds, ran in panic, the larger ones bowling over the smaller cohorts in their crazed efforts to outrun decompression.

Venamir called after them, "You idiots, I told you it was an illusion."

Farther inside the ship, the pounding feet came to a halt, and angered groans and complaints arose from the crew.

Doc Nelzyr couldn't fathom what just happened. He was still breathing, not floating, but shaking. He struggled to his feet and stared through the two open hatches, where Venamir's final stand was supposed to be. Instead of stars and cosmos, he saw darkness of a dim, damp cave.

"You were hypnotized," Venamir laughed. "We have been docked here for days."

Doc ranted, "You motherless hell-spawn. You know how many ways I can kill you?"

Moradin's eyes narrowed. "You were going to blow us all out of the hatch? We could have all died at your hands. I shouldn't be surprised, doctor of death."

"You shouldn't make a man desperate," Doc shot back.

"Oh, but it worked," Venamir gloated. "You proved you can override the Herja's lock on this ship's systems. She answered to you. Now I know that you can help crack the security program. Take the good doctor and fit him with a subjugator." He sauntered away.

Doc ranted even as Moradin grabbed him by the back of the shirt and herded him up the corridor. "Venamir. You worthless, psychotic scag, you're a disgrace to your race. Slade's Druwen clan will tear you apart."

"Let them try," Venamir countered. "My plans are far greater than simple revenge upon Slade. I will show our people the destruction of human influence. When I am done, the clans will reveal their true colors against each other. The councils will be too busy with their own people to deal with humans imposing more colonies on Atlearon. Even the High Councils will be forced to reject their alliance with Earth."

"Who are you replacing the humans with?"

"Amphibious Rezoans."

"Hybrid fish-lizards," Doc clarified in slang, "under your command."

"If you must, yes." Venamir nodded. "You can either join me or remain an enemy?"

"You're crazy—ow, let go." Doc winced as Moradin pulled him down the corridor.

"Shut your trap hole." Moradin whispered as she pulled Doc through the ship and into medbay. "I've seen Venamir blow people out the hatch. Since when did you become suicidal? Do what the captain says and maybe you'll live."

"Do I know you?"

Moradin's glare hardened farther, as if that were possible. She pushed Nelzyr toward a reclined therapy chair.

Doc tried to backpedal. "Oh, no you don't."

She easily man-handled the haggard, bruised elder into the chair. "Restrain," she said, and flex cables shot up from their sheaths and looped around arms and legs.

"Shit!"

"Don't do that," Moradin said.

Doc Nelzyr found the more he studied her, the more familiar she appeared. "You sure modified this chair fast," he grumbled.

"Yes, it was fun. Comfy?"

Doc watched her turn away and stomp over to a supply cabinet to scrounge for some delicate instruments and what else, he didn't want to know. "Why do you work for him when you act like you want to help?"

She shot him a glare. "Don't get personal. You're just another nosy, egotistical prick."

Doc strained against his bonds for a better look at her. Even with shallow feminine features on a near manly face, his surgeon's eyes identified subtle evidence of reconstructive surgery, likely multiple procedures, he suspected. There was something about her, the toss of her head, the tint of her eyes, and that unusual swearing proficiency in multiple human languages. "Moradin," his voice quavered, "Mori'alya, is that you?"

The cyborg stiffened.

"Is it? What's happened to you?"

Moradin's voice iced over, her words stone slow like a creeping iceberg. "So, you do remember your ex-patients."

Doc's voice fell faint, as if dug up from the grave. "But—we—you were dead!"

"Dead?" She whirled, holding a wicked headset in her shaking hands. "No, I wasn't dead, but that's what you left me for." Moradin stomped over and held the headset above him, a terrible headband-looking thing of curved energy rods and a few probes made to grip the skin. "I want to know one thing. Why'd you leave me for dead? WHY?"

Doc sank farther into the chair. "I swear you were dead! We were in combat, couldn't land, and even if we could, there were no life readings. The Merfins must have revived you. Their medicine exceeds even ours. We were in combat when you first vanished. There was nothing we could do until we regrouped."

"*Nothing we could do*," she echoed, teeth bared. "Poor excuse of a doctor, that's what you are," and roughly fitted the headset in place around the back of Doc's head.

"Wait-wait-don't be like Venamir." Doc rattled. The poison in her snarl told him that was a bad, vile comparison. "I can help you, Mori."

Her voice took on a flat morbid tone as Doc watched the heat of emotion drain from her face, replaced by a mask of casual disdain. "No help, no more procedures. I used to be beautiful and now look at me, a robotic lab rat. You meat carvers have done enough, so shut up."

Moradin gave the headset main control a thump, causing the probes to grip his scalp with the wickedness of an intelligent branding iron searing into flesh.

Doc swore in his native tongue until the tiny clamps gripped his skin. There was a short zap when the unit activated, blinded him with flashing lights of pain. "Freaking witch." he yelped with all the air in his lungs until blacking out a second later.

Moradin looked down at him and grunted, "Wimpy fleshling." She tapped a control on the back of the chair's headrest and the flex cables withdrew back into their sheaths. She stalked in circles, tossing glares at the doctor. After several laps around the medbay and scorching profanity at the overall universe and especially doctors, she touched her earpiece and reported, "The subjugator's on."

"Bring him to work with our new hacker," said Venamir's voice.

Moradin poked Doc until he began to stir. "Wake up."

* * *

An Atlean woman lay, clad in what appeared to be sleeping clothes, in a hibernation tube. Her burgundy hair cascaded around her pillow, her coppery skin a bit darker than most Atleans. She'd taken burns around her cybernetic implants, notable around her joints and forearms. Tiny dopps bearing injectors in their metallic arms worked until their power cells drained and they emptied all their small reservoirs of drugs and medical supplies. The med-bots had applied concoctions to accelerate tissue healing, but once their energy ran out, they collapsed into dull, gray heaps.

The computer at the head of her hibernation bed showed the woman's bio readings, now with a strong, steady heartbeat and healthy readings. A holographic avatar in the form of the same woman, except wearing armor, emerged from the computer and hovered over the sleep tube. The avatar spoke in a tranquil voice, "Med-bots have exhausted their life cycle. Herja Kestral, healing process satisfactory. Activating waking sequence."

Within seconds, the Herja took in a long, shaky breath, followed by another, until she reached a steady breathing pattern. The suspension tube creaked open and slid out of her way. Her eyes slowly opened.

She looked toward the sleep tube alongside hers. The tube was dark inside, as were the controls, but she could see a man inside, morbidly still. Her voice came out raspy, her throat sore. "Report on other Herja."

"The prime Herja was electrocuted. He is in stasis. Chance of reviving, calculate ten percent. All functioning medbots diverted to save you."

"No... they will pay for that." Shaking off heavy grogginess, Kestral forced herself to sit up. Her armor began expanding from her bracers, belt, and chest piece, forming a lightweight combat suit as she clambered out of the sleep tube.

The hologram flew over to a cabinet that opened at her gesture, revealing rifles, firguns, and weapons cases. "Ship has fallen to hostile takeover," the avatar informed. "You have messages from Consul Slade, Ambassador Zared, and the Morpher Council."

The real Kestral paused from pulling on armor that hung on the wall. "Is my crew onboard?"

"Yes. The only member of the crew onboard is Doctor Nelzyr. Venamir commands this ship."

"I'll use stealth armor. Display all messages," Kestral ordered, pulling open another cabinet full of food and drink rations.

* * *

Doc Nelzyr and Motley sat in the main engineering room, munching on rations that Doc could swear had expired a decade ago. Motley's cub sat nearby, slouched in a chair too large for him, tapping away on his game pad.

"Any luck?" Doc asked, hoping for another "No." The last thing he needed was to help Venamir gain full weapons control.

"I'm not sure," the cat said.

A hologram appeared before them, an Atlean woman, wearing ornate body armor. Doc and Motley scooted farther into their chairs, captivated not so much by her athletic shape, but by her eyes, how her midnight blue eyes glowered with intensity, glinted with anger.

Leifur glanced over, his curious eyes widening before the rest of his body reacted. "Whoa!" he yipped, springing out of the chair. "What'd you do?"

"You will never control this ship," the Herja informed. "With all the crew gone, that ship's control falls to me."

Doc squinted as he examined her stiff movements, wondering, was she flinching? As she faded away, Doc heard her whisper, "Doc Nelzyr, it's me, Kestral. I'm the ship's Herja, in the sanctuary chamber."

Moradin walked over to them. "What're you up to?"

The thugs left their posts and started closer, one cracking his knuckles, the other drawing his firgun with a carnage-hungry grin.

"We're doing what you ordered," Motley said, "looking for a way into the Herja program, not your kind of back door."

"Huh?" the uglier thug grunted.

"Yeah, he meant you," the fat one said.

Moradin rolled her eyes. "Speaking of back doors, we're going to raid the main prison on Crawshen. I need full layouts of Broken Crag Prison." She sent the guards out of the room. "Start working on those prison schematics, cat. We need them good enough to bust into the lower levels." Leaning closer, she whispered, "I don't work for Venamir. I work for myself."

"Sure," Motley replied cynically.

She kept her voice hushed as she loomed over his shoulder. "Venamir can't read my mind very well because of my cybernetics, and he can't read yours because you think in cat language, but he can read your intent, Nelzyr. Bear in mind, I know about Herjas, so don't try to trick me."

"What are you getting at? You're telling us a lot," Motley whispered.

Moradin raised her voice. "I said, get to work. Hack into that Herja so she can't take control of the ship. I'll get you lunch. We should have some rats onboard. Remember, we're watching you." She stalked out of the room.

Doc, Motley, and the cub exchanged bewildered looks.

A miniature image of Kestral appeared on the control panel, looked at them, then vanished. Her voice spoke in Doc's head. *"Nelzyr, I'm Kestral, the ship's Herja. I was incapacitated during the ship takeover, but I can help you now,"* the faint voice murmured in Doc's head.

Doc risked replying, *"We'll find you."* The psy-duller built into his visor sent a sharp tingle around his head, giving him an immediate headache for using his telepathy. It was worth it.

Chapter 20
Space Kill Café Mission

Scruffy eased the *Vernacular* through the outer barriers, rings of atmospheric generators and defense weapons. In the center of the layered defenses, was a space station that dwarfed Earth's newest space station. Following instructions from a thickly accented spacecraft controller, Scruffy landed at a spaceport that spanned the mass of several cities. Ships from Slade's caravan followed suit, landing on nearby docking platforms.

Slade, Telari, and their feline crewman, Jasko, disembarked from Scruffy's ship. Telari could barely keep from running ahead.

Telari was smiling with delight. "Look at all these cats! Hey, I speak some Drao, took five years when Zared taught on Earth."

"You can't keep them," Slade teased.

"This is only a space station, an outpost made to resemble our homeland," Jasko explained. "The horizon and sky are holograms that change with the seasons."

"I want to vacation on the real world where there are lots of cats like you guys," Tel said.

Jasko ruffled her hair, chuckling, "So cute. Our main world is Atlearon."

Cats were everywhere on this outpost, upright, slightly humanoid, Draolith cats. The artificial sky appeared quite real, aqua with grey and lavender clouds to soften bright lights high on the walls. Trees dominated the artistic horizon, and cities of tall buildings interlinked together with swaying ramps, shrouded behind misty clouds. Draoliths by far outnumbered other races here, even on the main space station that served as their outpost to other worlds. Most structures invited climbing or flying species. Avian creatures easily navigated the multiple levels of warehouse and living sections. Humans and humanoids used scattered lifts or hover technology.

A clever-eyed orange Draolith approached, his ears twitching, fangs bared as he grinned. "You must be Slade and crew, yes? My name is Brewber."

Telari hesitated, enthralled. "I want to see your world too, not just this outpost," she replied in Drao, meeting his gaze with a slow blink.

Brewber smirked, his whiskers straight out, alert. "Not bad."

Tel went on in common tongue, "Coome on, Brewie, let's shake some legs. You get me and Jasko. We have a parts list, and Gus wants takeout from the Space Kill Cafe."

The cat fought back a hacking noise. "From the bird cooks? Their food is disgusting."

"My friend really wants to try it," Tel said.

Brewber shrugged. "We'll pick up something to calm his stomach. He'll need it. Shall we?"

Telari lingered as they walked. She was gazing upward at the various building levels, watching cat people and bird people. Many floors had balcony structures large enough to hold a two-person transport. "It's like a city of giant cat trees," Telari piped. "I love this place. We have to come back here—and the cat world." She pestered the felines with all kinds of questions as they walked. "Can we hit a local cafe, too? I wanna try what you guys eat."

"Cat food," Brewie said.

* * *

Slade and his friends regrouped that evening in the ready room—Zared, Elowren, Gus, Scruffy, Rhoan, and Telari. Wulvur and Shanto walked in, still heckling each other on who had the best new firgun. The group was sharing and making fun of the odd smelling carnage in a box with an obnoxious, neon yellow logo, Space Kill Café. The food truly resembled road kill. One open box had feathers and claws sticking out of dissected pieces of meat linked together with stretched stomach lining. Gus splattered more hot sauce onto the carnage and poked it with a hunting knife, found something juicy, and the thing squirted on his shirt. Gus shrugged and stabbed it again, this time hitting Scruffy with juice.

Scruffy smarted off, "Boy, you know where I'm going to cram that dying bird?"

Gus held a chunk of meat out on a fork. "Want some?"

Scruffy made a sour face. "No way. Even our mascot won't eat this stuff. Don't eat too much of that. We don't need you sick on the raid."

"Oh, alright," Gus sighed. "Maybe I'll make meatball leftovers."

"I didn't know you ate fish balls, Gus," Tel commented, spurring groans from the others.

The other plates didn't look much more enticing. One food box contained long, twisted pieces too deep fried to recognize what was beneath. Scruffy's fish platter was the favorite at the table. Even the Atlean hybrid cat, Griffa lay gnawing on chunks of steamed fish instead of the takeout food.

"You're all braver than I thought to eat space hash made by buzzards," Slade said, and helped himself to Scruffy's cooking.

Jasko trudged in, one paw over his gut. "I'm here, stomach's still queasy."

"I thought cats ate anything," Rhoan said.

"No, that's dogs," Jasko replied. He wrinkled his nose. "What is that smell?"

"Dinner." Gus grinned and held up a dripping chunk of mystery bird organ.

Jasko started forward for a closer look, but instead made body-wracking, heaving sounds. His neck stretched, his fur hackled along his back. "I'm fine, really." He grabbed Gus's hat as something slimed its way up from his throat. He shuddered and retched.

Gus yelped, "Dude, you yakked in my cap!"

"Sorry." Jasko licked drool off his arm, eliciting a groan from Gus. Ears drooped and tail twitching, Jasko moved to the pantry and made himself a large, meaty wrap.

Telari moved over and then poked the slimy thing with a chopstick. "It's not barf. It's a hairball. See?" She tilted the cap and jiggled the hairy mess for Gus, who covered his eyes.

"I lick when I'm nervous," Jasko admitted.

"Where?" Gus asked. When his friend poked fun at him, he snatched his cap and dropped it beneath the table. "Never mind."

Slade chuckled, filling a tall mug. "Let's go over the plan."

Scruffy activated the hologram table where Slade had spent the past nights pondering. The crews piled up their leftovers, mostly the Space Kill Café food, and set it aside. Telari's overgrown hybrid cat sniffed the boxes, turned up her nose, and returned to a large bowl of fresh meat and bits of greens.

Gus pointed to Griffa as the cat lay chowing down, content. "Hey Tel, you said this cat's trained? She could help in the raid."

Tel waved him off. "No. She's trained for rescue, not combat. I want her to live."

Slade began, "Our mission is delicate. I know we all want to charge in and rip Venamir apart, but we have to focus. Our Herja, Kestral, is onboard the *Jacobyte*. She sent another message last night. She and Doc are still alive, and Venamir's flying to Crawshen. Doctor Cruentin is locked up there. That prison has tech to restrain telepaths. If Venamir tries to break out Cruen, he'll take down the prison's psy blockers. The prison is an hour's walk between the nearest town and a fishing village.

"You mean Shocks and son? Yeah, they ran a bar and engine shop on Crawshen," Zared said. "Venamir's first uprising caused turmoil between our councils and the human colonists. Shocks and his bikers swore they retired from the Council fleet. They may not be happy to see us."

Slade shrugged, grinning. "Oh, Shocks likes a good brawl. Vanysa has been spying on the Crawshen trading posts for us. There are Merfin colonies in their oceans. Rumor has it, Venamir will try to rescue his doctor, Cruentin."

"How much do you trust Vanysa?" Scruffy chewed on a candy stick. "She's a great spy and diplomat, except where Venamir's involved. Problem is, she's related to Venamir and doesn't want to see his true colors."

"Yeah, well, she'll find out," Slade agreed. "I've sent her on ahead to warn the Hrokahs. The prison has good defenses, but the *Jacobyte's* stealth mode far outclasses their scanners. Lucky for us, Vanysa said she found our old allies on that world."

Elowren sipped a cup of hot tea. "What old allies?"

"The Wild Paint gang, human bikers, war vets," Slade replied. "My brother dug deeper and found out Shocks senior and son are still there."

"Shocks, is that a nickname?" Telari said.

"Surname," Slade replied. "Max and his son, John Shocks were bodyguards when Venamir turned against the councils and tried to kill or subjugate us. Shocks and son, and their gang of bikers, had good techs and fighter pilots in their gang. They all told the councils to screw themselves and went off on their own."

"They like to fight," Scruffy mused, "and they hate Venamir."

"Right." Slade nodded. He activated a map of the Craggly Claws spaceport and the nearest cities. "Wulvur, I'm sending you. See if the spaceport auction house is really selling Atlean ship parts, and find Shocks and his gang. Bribe them, challenge their honor, just get them on our side."

"Fun times." Wulvur grinned.

Slade went on, "Keep our mission simple. Get Shocks to help if you can. We find the *Jacobyte,* and rescue our people. Stage two, if we can, take my ship back. Elowren, I want you and Wulvur to go after Doc and Kestral." He gave Elowren a knowing look. "Use stealth."

She smiled, "We will, somewhat."

Shanto, who had been quieter than usual, waved his mug. "Why does Venamir need to bother rescuing Cruen? He already has Doc Nelzyr. Attacking a prison, that's a big risk."

"Venamir and Cruen go way back. They crewed together in the Atlean-Rezoan wars before I even served with them. Even without using the main guns, he can stealth in and knock down most of the prison's defenses before they can even call for backup. We used to do that in the lizard wars. The Rezoan ocean lizards were fighting over Merfin territory. We'd stealth in, blast the hell out of their shield generators, rescue our people held captive, and be off while they were still chasing their tails."

Scruffy tapped the table controls, summoning images of Noxus and Moradin. "We'll need to watch out for Noxus and Moradin. They're both cyborgs."

Slade put a hologram of his ship on display. A small, yet formidable image of the *Jacobyte* hovered over the table. Even at toy size, the ship loomed like a hungry hawk, her lower belly cannons searching for targets. "The *Jacobyte* has better stealth than we do, so we have to make the ship more visible. I hate to say it, but don't hold back. Wulvur and Elowren will go for the *Jacobyte*. Scruffy, you and Zared will fly defense. We'll rehearse our hit during the flight to Crawshen."

"Let's hope they don't get access to the main guns," Scruffy said.

"What's the big deal with the main guns?" Gus said.

"They're Atlearon's newest weapon on a starship. Her torpedoes don't blow things up. Rather, they heat up like lava, and melt what they hit. I plan to have those main guns dismantled," Slade fumed. "If Venamir brings those main guns online, destroy that ship or get the hell away."

Jasko, who had been chewing on his big wrap, finally joined in. "I know some folks in the local defense militias. Want me to contact them?"

"Yeah," Slade nodded. "Tell them their prison is in danger of a direct attack from Venamir." He rose and finally started fixing himself a large fish sandwich. "Listen, I don't want the *Jacobyte* grounded on that world. If she crashes, we'll have to destroy her. If those plasma cannons fire up, they'll melt through most any ship's plating, including Scruffy's flying tank."

Chapter 21
Wild Paint Gang

The world of Crawshen was home to many space-faring species, but primarily avian. Bird people flocked to the forests for the clan-style settlements built in tall, swaying trees. The birds modified most caves for living quarters as well, places not easily accessible to non-flying folk. Not all bird species could fly great distances, and even those who could still harnessed hover-cars and ground vehicles. The Avian races were everywhere, big birds, small birds, most of them with nimble claw-like hands near the ends of their wings. Even the clouds appeared like massive avians swooping over the masses below. Dark, looming clouds stretched out in layers over the sprawled out town that surrounded an old spaceport. The horizon darkened with nightfall, allowing fog to shroud the city.

Shanto flew Slade's dented, scarred Zephyr onto a cracked, faded landing platform. The mockup paint job made the rescue fighter appear old, faded, and plagued with body corrosion. Shanto, Wulvur, and Gus climbed out. They worked as a ground crew to service the craft themselves, then locked her up, activated the protection protocols, and set off to explore.

The town spread out around them, hustling with many alien species, large and small, from scaly lizard species to humanoids, and creatures with more fur than attire. Hrokahs stood out the most. They were tall, birdlike beings, some grey, some vividly colored. Most of the spacers wore weapons of some sort. Other small ships and buildings didn't look much better than their Zephyr. The moon was high and shrouded by clouds, making the place look even more dank and dismal.

"This poor Zephyr may look like crap, but she's fixed where it counts," Shanto admitted. "It took a beating from the minefield."

Gus pulled on his jacket and rubbed his hands together in the cold air. "I thought we'd get pelted with bird crap, flying in here."

Wulvur chuckled, "They have bathrooms, might look like nests, though." A gust of wind howled, the cold trying to bite through their jackets. Wulvur pulled on a cap from his pocket and flipped up his hood. "I'm the only one here who's met Shocks and the gang. If

194

you guys drop me off at the gang's bar, you can go check out the auction house."

As they walked, Gus pointed out bright signs around a bunch of hovercars parked atop a garage full of all shapes of vehicles. "That looks like a Huv Rental place. If we rent a junker, we'll fit in. It should be easy to find a paint shop and bar run by humans."

Shanto nodded. "They didn't quit on good terms."

Shanto rented a heap with free leftover mystery snacks that smelled a week old on the dash.

"Don't look in the trunk," Wulvur said as Gus flung the snack bag at the nearest overflowing garbage can, or, at least he thought it was a garbage can.

Gus shot him an eerie look. "Why? Think there's a dead guy in there?"

"Maybe, couldn't smell him," Shanto replied.

"Gross," Gus mumbled. "This place sucks. Was it always like this?"

"Nah, the town's gone downhill fast." Shanto sighed. "It's still a good hub for spaceship parts."

Wulvur drove them away from the rental building. "Shouldn't be hard to find a biker bar among this flying circus."

The trio drove past a mix of small shops, overhearing aggressive haggling from vendors and raunchy flirting from a massage parlor. They bartered a ride on a local shuttle to a vehicle rental place that looked more like a junkyard.

"Boy, it's been a long time. The auction house is this way." Shanto said. "This is a fun world. We should come back here for shore leave. Next town is near the cliffs, big tourist trap. The main hotel is a casino with cage fighting."

Gus sank deeper in his seat. "You know a lot about this place. Get that from spying?"

"More or less," Shanto said. "The cage fights are infamous."

Gus sounded nauseated. "To the death?"

"No, almost never. It's often virtual, or drones, and they have Deeps medics."

Wulvur pulled over and hopped out. "Check out the auction, and get back here, quick."

His friends gave him skeptical looks, but drove away.

Wulvur took on a drunken swagger as he approached a ramshackle bar. The rumors were true. Most of the patrons were human. This place had fallen into even more disrepair than the other buildings along the block, and a demented form of house music blared from within. The smell of mystery bar food was strong and the smell of smoke, pungent.

A bunch of bikers sat on benches outside the door, trading foul jokes. Their tattoos depicted militaristic or cartoonish scenes of battles between dancing weapons, or a collage of erotica or other self-entertaining centerfold scenes. However ratty and worn, their rigs bore similar murals and weaponry built into their power systems. One particular cycle was fully dressed, complete with low profile saddlebags, guns built into the handlebars, and vivid aviator art.

Wulvur halted in front of the bar, absorbed the whole scenario with amused eyes, and stomped up to the gang. "Yo, Captain John Shocks, you're easy to find. I can see your cartoon tats from space."

The lead guy took a long draught of his beer. "There's no Captain John here. Leave while you can still walk."

The bikers kept talking, only one throwing him a low growl, the sound of an underfed beast, even though this one had a gut.

"Kiss it, then," Wulvur said, shoving past them, making his target spill the rest of his beer "You probably don't have the nuts to help, anyway."

The brightly tattooed biker slammed his beer stein down on the table and rose with a heaving grunt. He growled to his pals. "Any of you want a piece of this runt? Cuz I'm not leaving much."

One guy shrugged while the others sat back with their drinks to watch, either too lazy to bloody their knuckles or too eager to watch the show.

The leader grunted to his friends, "You bunch of slugs." He elbowed past the bouncers, his angry, bloodshot eyes locked on target. He went to grab Wulvur, who gripped his arm and twisted it against the joints. The onlookers fell silent as they watched the wiry stranger rush in close, body against body, and slam Shocks, their local wrestling champion, to the battered sidewalk just outside the bar door.

Wulvur stepped back and beckoned him, making sure to use his middle fingers.

The bouncers' faces turned red, but one of them stomped in between the two foes. "You know the rule, John. Take it to the cage if you wanna' brawl."

Shocks waved the bouncers off. Still eyeing Wulvur in disbelief, he thumbed toward the center of town. "Screw the cage. We're going to the graveyard."

"Pssh," Wulvur scoffed, "you like humping the stiffs?"

Shocks clenched his large fists. "You won't even be stiff when I throw you in a fresh hole."

"You don't remember me? I saved your painted ass."

The old bartender stormed over and demanded, "I said, take it away from here."

Wulvur greeted the old man with casual respect. "Hello, Max. I needed to make sure you guys aren't imposters. Lotta trouble with morphers lately."

"Oh, great, an Atlean complaining about morphers," one biker snarked.

Wulvur turned to the old bartender. "Shocks senior and junior, we need to talk. I'll pay for drinks and grub. What do you say?"

Max scowled. The poor sucker looked like the years rode him hard and long. Only the bar logo on his long, stained apron differentiated him from the customers. His hair splayed out in a crazed manner like he'd pulled it to thinness, and his body appeared tired of living.

"Oh, now he wants favors," chortled a scrawny biker. He and his buddies guffawed.

Wulvur's voice turned bored as he added, "Of course, if ya don't know nothin' or nobody, maybe I should assume yer mama did the tattoos and stole the bikes for ya."

Weapons slid from holsters with clicks and scraping sounds, and multiple barrels leveled at Wulvur. More bar patrons had joined the onlookers, all looking desperate or angry either from their beaten clothes, scars, or war-weathered faces.

Wulvur smirked. "You all used to have a better sense of humor. I'm working with Slade. We're hunting Venamir."

"Venamir's in prison, you moron," one ruddy biker scoffed.

A skinny biker eyed Wulvur over the rim of his beer mug. "You don't watch the news. Turd birds said the fish escaped."

The ruddy biker rounded on his buddy, "How does a guy escape deep sleep? Did the place flood, and he swam away?"

"We're not sure how he escaped," Wulvur admitted. "Fellas, Venamir's recruiting again. I know crime's picked up around here. Venamir's followers are active again. They're trying to bust up alliances between Atlearon and Earth."

"Earth's ties with Atlearon sucked to begin with," Shocks retorted.

"And this town can't get much worse," Max added.

"Oh, yes it can." Wulvur turned to Shocks with forced patience. "Yeah, the first human settlers had it rough, but so did my people. Venamir's uprising made it worse for everyone."

"We remember," Max said. "Venamir and his goons killed good people. The avian folk are still leery of Merfins."

Wulvur gestured around the rough neighborhood that surrounded them. "You sure picked a shady area to set up shop, and it's going to get worse if we don't team up. I'm asking for you to temporarily team up with Slade's crew, so we can stop Venamir and turn this crap around. Well? Any of you still got the balls to fly and fight?"

All eyes snapped back to Wulvur, as did their weapons. For several long seconds, they just stared, floored by the audacity of this stranger. All they could hear now was heavy breathing from patrons, creaks of leather, and the cold wind through leafless trees.

Max shoved past his burly son. "It's been over fifteen years. Why are you showing up now? Maybe I'd rather watch a good brawl at the graveyard."

Wulvur read their faces and body language, some stiff with defense, others squirming with unease, some undecided, but few daring to show the slightest hint of hope. "Venamir is going to start another uprising. He's recruiting followers of many species. The fish and bird people have been scavenging parts for old council ships.

During the battles against the lizards, a lot of ships crashed on this world."

"This is bullshit," Shocks argued. "Somebody posed as Venamir. You could do that."

"Yes, I can morph into him," Wulvur nodded, "but I don't have all his abilities or connections."

"Venamir raided Earth's space station," the woman biker said. "Local Merfins are all talking about it. Some even want to join him."

"Wait a minute," Max reasoned, "Venamir's coming here? He was in prison on your world. You're saying that Venamir went all the way to Earth to steal a ship? Why?"

"Because he wanted Slade's ship, a prototype that has more powerful guns and better stealth than anything in the fleet. He is trying to undo our alliance with humans. Where better to start than on Earth? He attacked Earth's space station, stole the ship, recalled his spies on Earth. Now, he's coming here with a kickass starship with better stealth than the rest of the fleet."

Shocks folded his arms. "Why does he care about a world full of chickens?"

"There's Merfins in the oceans of this world, a great hub to get supplies, and his old medic, Cruentin, is in prison here. Come on, Shocks, Doctor Cruentin is Venamir's most trusted friend, and he doesn't have many friends."

The bikers fell silent as everyone gathered closer to eavesdrop. Someone turned off the music inside the bar.

Max asked, "So, we're supposed to defend the prison from a warship?"

"At least warn local defenses," Wulvur said. "Make them call reinforcements."

"Screw them," Shocks huffed. "They're corrupt, anyway, buying up weapons and fuel before normal folks can get a fair bid, stealing animals from zoos and training them to guard the freak show prisoners."

Wulvur jumped onto the nearest table and glared at the group. "Dammit, listen. We are risking a massive breakout of criminals from many species. You're the ones who live here." He pointed at Max. "Come on, you already slipped info to Slade's brother."

A few burly men shoot questioning looks at Max, who shrugged.

"Yeah, so?" Max defended. "I've done my part."

"Look, I'll buy you beer, long as I get info. Then if you still want, I'll do that brawl. It's a win-win." He added to young Shocks, "Junior."

"Suck it," Shocks junior retorted.

Wulver continued, "Max, you and John were in the council meeting when Venamir pulled his revolt. It was the first meeting of all clans, where we invited humans. Now, it's happening again. Venamir is trying to turn the Atlean clans against their own councils. You can't lie low anymore. Besides, these guys want beer. Right?"

"Beer. More beer," said the scrawny biker at the table, starting a group chant for beer.

Wulvur hopped down from the table and handed a pouch full of credit chips to Max. "Either way, drink up. It's on me."

"We almost got killed for helping protect the furries," Shocks countered, glancing at his dad.

Max patted Shocks on the back. "Son, the furries kept us alive." He looked around at everyone and sighed. "Well, come on in, or I'll close shop and spend it myself."

Guns slid back into their holsters as people shoved against each other to get inside. Old Max turned the music back on while young Shocks followed, scowling.

* * *

Shanto and Gus entered a large building that appeared to be half auction house, half warehouse. The place was busy with loud, squawking auctioneers in the bright, warm rooms, while quieter silent auctions took place in the other half of the building. Most of the bidders were avian people who resembled overgrown birds. All kinds of birds bumped against Shanto and Gus, some with bright plumage and others with dark feathers. Many wore loose garments with many pockets. Gus spied a few humans, even one female. Her coat, decorated with paintings of angry skulls from many species, and her double holsters with slim, sawed off rifles, made her look even scarier than the overgrown parrot-like avian man in front of him.

Shanto tried to answer Gus's many questions. "Ever since Venamir's goons killed the bird ambassadors, it's been harder to do business here. The birds have a harder time trusting morphers and if you're a Merfin, expect to pay double."

"I thought you said felines also live here. I don't see many cats," Gus commented.

Shanto plugged a bidder's chip into one of many receptacles along the wall. "Felines like the dark rooms better."

Gus looked at one of the auctioneers and stifled a laugh. The tall, brightly colored birdman looked at home in the dazzling podium light, and his feathers made a peacock look dull.

Shanto pulled his chip free and pocketed it. "Okay, got their inventory list. Let's go."

"That's it?"

"Unless you'd like to bid on an avian hooker, if you like birds."

"Nope," Gus declined.

As soon as they left the building, they flipped up the hoods of their long coats, activated the stealth reflectors built into their clothes, and faded into the crowd. They found their rental, luckily not stolen, and drove away from the auction house. Even after making faces and quiet remarks about the bird aliens, Gus still had the eager eyes of a tourist, recording scenery with his comm.

"You are part human, a little. I took Zared's course on Merfin philosophies. Venamir's a Deeps Merfin? He grew up with the solitary tribes, right?"

"Yes."

"Venamir makes some realistic points. Humans fight over stupid crap. We've witch-hunted your people. Our people can't deny it. I want to have kids. I want them to have neighbors who are chickens, or dogs, cats, wolves, fish, even lizards, and call them friends."

"Wow, and you're a bomb tech who thinks like a diplomat."

"Maybe I can do both. Wulvur's hanging out with crazy biker dudes. Not all bikers ride and cuss all day. The bartender, old man

Max, is a veteran and was next in line to be Earth's diplomat. And what's with Slade? He doesn't act like a diplomat."

"Slade and his brother are from the Druwen clan. They're not very diplomatic. They're morphers who protect the forest. The stronger ones can take a full animal form, usually similar to your wolves on Earth. Some can change into other forms of woodland creatures. We have a bearlike beast on Atlearon. Berku can turn into that form. Most of their related tribes grew up on settlements in the woods, protecting wild creatures. And they sometimes hunt criminals."

"So all the stories about werewolves aren't real."

"Our ancestors may have influenced your culture."

The biker bar came into view. Shanto parked near the wildly painted Huvzter bikes. They left their vehicle and strolled into the bar, another highlight of the evening for Gus, who studied the historical aviator and racecar memorabilia on display. His friendly candor earned him and Shanto a couple of beers and conversation with a few of the bikers. Even the mean-looking woman with the skull coat and custom hip-rifles entered the bar and joined the banter.

"Yeah, I followed you two. We keep a close eye on new people," the woman said. She eyed Gus. "There aren't many humans here."

"True. Like a beer?" Gus offered.

"Nah." She strolled off to join her buddies at a pool table.

"Oh, there're my cohorts, Gus and Shanto." Wulvur said, gesturing toward his friends.

"Morphers, I bet," young Shocks grunted.

"Gus is full human, raised on Earth," Wulvur said. "Shanto's part human."

Max ran a hand through his thinning hair as if it couldn't get any messier. In measured words, he said. "Okay, we'll help. I'll scrounge up who I can. A bunch of fish and lizards hole up in a cave with a jagged mouth, along the beach of graves. The birds here believe in ghosts. Lizards use that fear to keep the birds out, good place to have secret meetings."

Wulvur leaned on the bar. "What else?"

Old Max pulled his own bottle from beneath the bar and took a gulp. "Merfins have been sending more buyers over the past year. They only want old Atlean ships. It's bogging down our auction house, makes it harder for us to trade for normal supplies. Worse than that, there's some Maska guy who thinks he's everyone's captain."

Wulvur butted in, "Wait—you said Maska? Slime-ball morpher looks like he's always stuck between shapes, morphs into a gargoyle-bat, laughs like a hyena?"

"That's him," Max nodded.

Wulvur slapped the counter. "He's here?"

"He's been coming to this world."

"Shocks, Maska was there the night all of us were in the conference room. Yeah, that we were supposed to seal the first treaty with Earth and Venamir busted in with his goons. Maska was there, helping Venamir. He escaped during the big fight. He may have freelanced for a dozen years, but he's working for Venamir now."

Shocks and Max looked at each other, anger clear on their faces.

"I was hoping you could identify something for me. It's used by a specific bloodline of Merfins, the ones who worked with Venamir in the past." Wulvur opened a jacket pocket and carefully exposed a dagger hilt. "Like this?"

Max's brow furrowed as he stared at the design. Pearlescent green and blue fin shapes with bright gold scales, fins wrapped around the burned hilt. He paled and dropped the bottle, which Wulvur grabbed with easy grace. Wulvur wrapped the hilt again and tucked it away. He set the ornate bottle onto the bar. "It's used by fish people, namely aquatics of deep waters, the reclusive ones."

"Green fin color for Deeps Merfins," Max said, "and gold scales for Rezoans. This dagger was made to show unity between the two. Yeah, they come through town. There's been more of them over the past month at the auction house, buying Atlean ship parts."

Even Shocks lost his sarcastic look. "Fish and lizards, they really are banding together again. This sucks. Just when I thought this town couldn't get any worse."

"Slade's hunting down Venamir," Wulvur said, "but we need your help."

Shocks looked over at his dad, Max. "I thought we were staying out of their battles."

"John, Wulvur's right. We can't be idle anymore," Max said, his voice growing terse. "Take Wulvur and round up Maska. I'll call our militia contacts, see if they'll return any favors. This time, the fight's coming to us. It's been harder to get parts for our fighters and bikes, and now we find out that Venamir's followers could be the cause? Even a couple of our own bikers have vanished. What if your kid ended up with Venamir's crew?"

Shocks shook his head. "Tatts wouldn't join them."

Max pounded his fist onto the bar, making some other bikers glance over. "I am not gonna lose this business or let a scaly bunch of fish wreck our lives again."

Shocks heaved a sigh. "Okay, Pops, don't bust another artery." He grabbed a faded surplus coat with service emblems and leather wrapped claws from the Hrokah bird-people. He led the way out, with Wulvur, Shanto, and Gus close behind. Shocks declined a ride in the rental. He swung onto his armored Huvzter cycle and fired it up. "Don't fall behind, tourists," he called, and took off.

Shocks drove like a stunt driver, up over traffic, and diving to the road again, weaving between buildings, and finally landed in the back patio area in the heart of the red-light district.

The town's business section was active with locals and offworlders. Tenants found ways to create a flowering landscape among winding paths that linked a maze of businesses together. Most of the businesses were homes converted into all kinds of shops for many species.

"There he is," Shocks said. "Recognize him?"

Wulvur's gaze landed on an overdressed man who would pass as a psychedelic pimp on Earth. The scent of this guy would sour his taste buds for a long time. "Yeah, that's him"

Maska was oblivious to their approach, too busy trying out his sexiest pose, leaning on the frame of a thin furred hooker's barely open door. "Maska's the name, sweetheart," he tried to con in a slurred, hoarse voice. "How ya doin' baby?"

"Good. You?" Her voice oozed fake sweetness as she sized up her potential customer, his strong body and styling clothes, ripe with liquor and cheap cologne.

Maska kept trying. "You want a good time, right? There's a party in my pants."

"We not here to talk. You want in or not?"

"You're supposed to beg me." He blew her kisses with foul breath, making her lean back, fanning the living stink away.

She asked with forced patience, "Are you a customer?"

"You should quit this place and come with me."

She backed away from him. "Get lost. I don't like you, okay?"

Maska leaned back in surprise. "What? I bet you never had a morpher. We could go out in the woods and do it wild style."

"You're disgusting. Get out." She shut the door in his face.

"Oh, the shame." Maska spouted in his best fake bawl. He staggered back onto the main path. "I don't like you, either. It's your loss, saggy wench." He spun when Shocks started laughing. "What?"

"You got turned down by a hooker," Shocks cracked up.

"I'm a physical therapist," she hissed, and yanked down her window shade.

Maska's eyes widened when he studied Wulvur. "You!"

Wulvur chuckled, "How d'you get away from the bouncers?"

"That was you in the bar? You tricked me. No wonder I got ganked by the bouncers!"

"You deserved it. I told you I was looking for Venamir, truth." Wulvur replied. "You should've left the women alone. What're you doing here?"

"None of your business," Maska retorted, his beady eyes focusing on Shocks. "You?"

The big biker's gun hand rested on his firgun. "Yeah, me," Shocks growled. "You assholes shot me and my dad. It's payback time." He grinned when Maska flinched back a bit. "I'm gonna throw you into the pit and kidnap the medics so they can't save you."

While Shocks distracted Maska, Wulvur worked his psy into Maska's mind.

Maska cringed as he stared at ghostly reminders of Venamir's first revolt. He saw visions of the past, when he was back in the Morpher's Council of all species, where for the first time, the humans Max and his son, Shocks, had attended. Maska was there, with Venamir, Noxus, and Moradin, weapons drawn against their brethren. He saw himself morph into Venamir's form, as did Noxus, Moradin, and several spies hiding within the ranks.

Maska collapsed to his knees, hands clamped against his overly waxed hair. "Get out of my head!"

Shocks moved over and took Maska's firgun. He grabbed Maska by the collar and hauled the whimpering thug to his feet.

"There is no fighting here," came an authoritative, feminine voice.

"Hullo Madame Mayor," Shocks said. "I'm doing vermin control."

The woman moved closer, her heels clicking on the worn stone path, her many adornments around the waist and wrists jangled with her slow, graceful steps. "What brings you here?"

"Maska's working for Venamir," Shocks informed.

"Am not," Maska lied, panting when Wulvur broke mind contact. "Stay out of my head. That's psychic abuse."

"Coming from a psycho," Wulvur scoffed. He looked at the mayor, flanked by two bodyguards. "You're really human?"

"Yes," she replied. "I run the human settlement, here."

Shocks kept his eyes on Maska. "Why do you think Maska's sucking up to the bird people? Venamir's out of prison. This slimy rat works for him, and I bet he's trading for black market parts. He's also been recruiting a new crew."

Maska wrung his sweaty hands. "Not true. I'm an innocent merchant."

"There's nothing innocent about you," the mayor said, scowling. "Shocks, you want vengeance? Not here. Go sign up for the cage fights, or hand him over to me."

"Take me to Venamir," Wulvur demanded.

"I won't!" Maska's eyes widened when Gus and Shanto approached. "Oh, no, not Slade's crew." He struggled against Shocks's grip.

Shocks grabbed a fistful of Maska's jacket. Wulvur went for the other arm. Maska's gloves zapped them enough to break their grip and dull their reflexes. Maska wiggled free of his coat in a mad, squirming gyration. The coat erupted in electrocuting zaps and flame, causing Wulvur and Shocks to jump clear. As Maska fled, he jerked an amulet free from one of his necklaces and flung it toward the group.

The Madame's bodyguards standing beside her jumped in front to protect her. They spread their cloaks, activating energy shields that absorbed the power from Maska's stun grenade an instant before it went off.

The Mayor yelled after Maska, "You can't escape us!" She resumed her normal, indignant poise. She pressed a red gem on her glittery necklace. "All hands, Maska's back to his antics. Shocks and his friends are after him. Be helpful."

"Understood, Ma'am," said a gal's voice from Madame Mayor's headband.

Wulvur and Shocks worked the feeling back into their hands, cursing.

Shocks, however, was grinning. "That skanky slug likes to shock people? Ooh, it's on."

"Spread out," Wulvur said. "Keep your trackers on."

Gus winced, holding a hand over the bite in his arm. "He bit me!"

"Dammit, he bit Slade too," Wulvur said. "Get a wrap on that."

"I have a medic," the lady mayor said, moving over. "Let my ladies patch him up."

Despite blood dripping through his fingers, Gus managed a grin. "Okay."

"Listen," the mayor said, "Maska stays at the Flocker Casino. He'll most likely go there first."

"I know where it is," Shocks nodded, touching his comm. "Hey, Pops, I need our gang at the Flocker Casino." He smiled at the mayor. "Thanks, Clarisse."

She winked and flashed him a smile.

"Shanto, you and Gus catch up," Wulvur said as he and Shocks ran to their vehicles.

Wulvur and Shocks pursued Maska. The area appeared serene enough, music and voices casual among small cottage-style houses in the middle of meandering paths, until the casino came into view.

The casino resembled a multi-story haunted house with colored lights flashing through the windows from games, theme rooms, and a brightly lit stage on the side deck. Hrokahs perched on most of the balcony rails. Two black and silver-feathered Avians, one fat and one skinny, perched on the roof, watching and eating. The majority of guests were birds and humans, with some Atleans, a few Merfins, Rezoans, and other odd species. There were very few felines here.

Wulvur was scoping out the place in dog form, trotting around, appearing lost, tail wagging. Shocks looked at Wulvur's dog form, shook his head, and flew off toward the large party house.

Gus and Shanto caught up in the rental. Gus stared outright at the space aliens of many shapes and species. Gus stared at muscular women who patrolled the place alongside men of various species.

"Why'd he go dog form here?" Gus muttered.

Shanto raised the volume on his scans as he targeted groups of people. Voices came through his comm, a jumble of dialects. "People are watching for Wulvur in his normal form. See all the pet birds and lizards? Those are pets. People shouldn't care about Wulvur's dog form. Look, there he goes."

Wulvur trotted toward the most masculine woman, his tail wagging.

Shanto and Gus left their vehicle, trying to look casual. They watched in disbelief as a couple intimidating women smiled and petted their dog friend.

"I thought Maska's already seen him as a dog," Gus commented.

"The locals are pet friendly. They won't body frisk a dog," Shanto replied. "Wow. Did you see where he sniffed that bouncer woman? She would kick our asses for that."

"Man, she patted him and let him in. I want a dog costume," Gus muttered in envy. He whispered into his comm, "Slade, we're closing in on Maska."

"Great," Slade replied. "There's heavy jammer activity ahead of you. We might not be able to teleport you in. Be careful."

"Must be from the cage fighting area," Shanto said.

The dance bar and casino beat any sorority house Wulvur could imagine. The place was surrounded by decks with rental Huvzters and hooker-bots. There were even real women, but they looked and acted like bouncers. The back of the building overlooked the ocean, with double doors opening to balconies. The smell of incense and junk food saturated the air, while the commotion of gambling tables and loud music hammered his sensitive ears. As he wandered through the crowd, a hand stroked his back, tickling his spine. He looked up to see two females, a shapely human, and a four-breasted woman with horns curling around her ears.

"Hey puppy," the horned woman greeted with a knowing grin. "I'm Serica." She nodded toward a tough blonde human beside her. "This is Delphi."

Wulvur whined and barely remembered to do the tail wag as they knelt on either side, ruffling his fur and ears. Serica scratched him and pressed her lips against his twitching ear. "Our Madame told us to help you catch Maska. You're lucky we like animals, morpher."

"Has Venamir been here too?" Wulvur mumbled, his words clumsy around dog teeth.

"No. Should he?"

"Venamir's recruiting again, and acquiring parts for Atlean ships, black market stuff. With your spaceport and the trade hub on this world, it's a strategic place for him. You think it'll stop there?"

Delphi's humor vanished. "We knew that damn Maska was up to no good. Our Madame was trying to uncover his scheme. Last time Venamir was in power, his cultists tried to take over this area. Well, they're like cultists, loyal without question. Avians control much of the defenses but they fear Venamir's ships and his lizard allies."

"Shocks and his gang used to fly warships with us."

"I know," Delphi replied. "They're war vets, but they're all burned out, outnumbered, and outgunned."

"Not for long. I have an idea."

A couple humanoids walked over, leering at the women. "Hey, is that for the dog and pimp show?" one asked.

Wulvur looked up at them and snarled, fur hackling. He lunged at the bigger guy, bowling him over. The guy's buddy grabbed him until Wulvur morphed into his humanoid beast form and threw the second guy over his shoulder.

Delphi uttered a splendid scream. "Out! Everyone out! He's got the fever—he'll go crazy!"

Serica yelled, "The dog's contagious! Get out!"

Gus and Shanto made it inside just as customers started running out in a frenzy.

Maska sat near the costume masks, his glaring eyes fixated on the dog. "Morphers," he growled, then realized his mistake. He'd used a man's voice in a woman's form and dress.

Wulvur leapt onto the bar, morphing into his most deranged werewolf shape. He raked his long claws across the bar, threw back his head and howled at the moon.

Delphi cried out, "It's a werewolf! They're real!"

"He's a morpher, you dumb bimbo," one drunk replied.

Delphi stormed over to him, joined by other bouncers. "Who are you calling a bimbo?" They wrestled the guy outside, giving the resisting man bruises and scratches in his manly parts.

Wulvur pointed at Maska. "He works for Venamir. We're here to arrest him."

"Venamir's in prison," a guy retorted.

"No, Venamir busted out. Maska's been running bootleg parts," Wulvur countered. "He attacked the Madame—they want to take over this whole place."

Maska jumped up and ripped the dress away. "Lies! I only stunned the raunchy wench."

Bouncers shoved their way through the scattering crowd, brandishing fists and homemade-looking firguns. The muscled women from the front entrance ran in and swung their gun barrels toward the bar's large bouncer.

"Throw them in the cage," one gruff woman ordered.

Wulvur held up his hands. "Why are you after me? Maska is wanted dead or alive. If he helps Venamir back in power, it could ruin your whole freaking colony."

Among the angry group, one bouncer yelled, "They're both morphers. Open the cage."

"Yeah," another guy joined in, "throw them in."

Maska backed toward the bathrooms, muttering, "No, no cage fight."

The sound of engines surrounded the building. Everyone quieted down and listened, not to grand ship engines, but resonating sputters and thrums of Huvzters outside the casino.

Wulvur asked, in full dire wolfish form now, teeth bared at Maska who backed toward a wall, glancing about. "Give it up, hairball."

Gus yelled "We got backup." as he and Shanto barreled down the steps. Shanto squeezed off a shot that grazed Maska's leg.

Maska lunged through the balcony door. He morphed, his arms contorting into leathery wings. Wulvur tackled him, slamming him against an old railing that cracked under their weight. Maska scrambled over the rail and dropped onto another balcony below, that linked to an outer walkway over a huge, dried out swimming pool. Just beyond the pool was neglected landscaping and a rocky beach. Crashing waves pounded the rocks. The wind howled in gusts, forcing Wulvur to crouch for balance. The weathered, narrow balcony creaked beneath his weight.

Slade's voice came over his earpiece. "What's going on?"

"Started a riot," Wulvur replied.

"Again?" Slade quipped.

Maska flapped his wings, hovering out of reach. "I heard that. Slade's nearby." He turned to fly away when an old, skinny guy riding a Huvzter zipped around the building and blasted a chunk out of the long balcony overhead, pelting Maska with chunks of debris, and knocking him down to the next balcony.

Young shocks came roaring in on his bright Huvzter bike, yelling, "Damn flying rats!" He pulled alongside Maska and clenched a fist. The studs from his glove flew off and stuck to Maska's chest and midsection, and the electrocution began.

Maska's stuttering dance lasted only seconds before he collapsed to the deck, wheezing.

Using his morphed shape and claws, Wulvur climbed down to the next balcony with ease that surprised the humans. He dropped to his feet beside Maska. "Stay down."

Maska snarled. He lunged past Wulvur, crashing through the railing and fell, vanishing into the foggy mist below.

Shocks hovered under Wulvur. "Hop on."

Wulvur climbed onto the back seat. "Thanks."

A leathery, man-sized creature flapped past them. "You'll pay for that." Maska screeched as he flapped upward. His arms had morphed to outstretched skin and muscle, enough to enable him awkward flight and make his unpredictable maneuvers a difficult target. He turned and flew away, yelling, "You'll all pay."

Gus shot Maska in the rear, snickering as Maska swerved in flight, whining.

"We'll finish him off," the old biker said.

"No." Gus shouted. "I shot him with a tracker. He'll lead us to Venamir."

Shocks whapped his comm. "Boys, let the freaky bat go."

Two others bikers gave Shanto and Gus a lift.

Shocks elbowed Wulvur. "All those morphing shapes and you can't sprout wings?"

"Not my breed," Wulvur replied.

* * *

Rhoan and Scruffy used the medbay laboratory to compare recent bite marks they'd treated since Venamir attacked the Orion Space Station. Scruffy conjured images from their database of the marks from Slade's shoulder. He put it next to images of the teeth holes taken by Gus's upper arm, and Shanto's forearm.

"Look, the bite marks are the same," Rhoan was saying.

"You may be right," Scruffy nodded. "They do look consistent. Let's compare width, depth, all dimensions of injury from teeth and fangs."

The computer replied, "Bite imprints are a match."

The pattern showed holes from carnivorous teeth between the shape of a large dog and a man's mouth.

"They look familiar," Rhoan said. "This left incisor is smaller, perhaps chipped, and there're claw marks from six fingers. Like Slade's bite."

"Gus's, too," Scruffy agreed.

"Holy crap, it's the same guy?"

Scruffy madly searched his medical record. "The bitemarks are a match."

Rhoan chimed in, "Cap, look at these bites. The same guy bit you."

Slade joined them, his voice hopeful when called in. "Don't capture him. Maska's finally good for something. He should lead us to Venamir."

* * *

Maska dove into the ocean to try to relieve the burning pain in his rear. The cold, unforgiving ocean stung him with salty water. Grunting and whimpering at his own moronic efforts, he leapt and flapped until his wings pulled him free of the water. Maska cursed the ocean spray, the wind, his parents, and most of all, that rotten bloodhound Wulvur and those traitorous bikers.

Maska called as far as his telepathy allowed, "*Captain?* *Captain*! *They're after mee-e-e.*"

213

Chapter 22
Space Walk

Distant in thought, Venamir waded through shallow pools of cold water that dripped from the cave roof. Shanto's arrival to this renegade world meant his time in hiding was limited. The *Jacobyte* still needed work, but she could fly and fight. Now, after discovering Slade's crewmen, Maska called for help and used their hidden cliff entrance to enter the cave tunnels. Surely Slade would arrive soon and try to claim his ship.

"*Maska, fly faster. We are lifting ship.*"

"*Coming,*" came a feeble reply.

"Sniveling hybrid," Venamir fumed, easily barging into the intimacy of Maska's frazzled mind. He sensed Maska's psy defenses drop, mere images of shifting walls and shields, which dissipated at his intrusion and allowed him to see thought images without resistance. Venamir saw glimpses of pursuit, ghostly shapes of Wulvur, Gus and Shanto.

Maska emerged from a passageway connected to the cave, panting, disheveled, and with a clear limp. "Slade's crew, they found me. Wulvur, Shanto, and their pet human. The biker gang leader was with them, surprising."

Venamir led the way out of the cavern darkness, into the docked *Jacobyte*. He paused, turning. "So, the painted humans are helping Slade. Strange they would help anyone after going into retirement. The biker gang may have been a formidable flying squadron, but now they are drunks with outdated fighters. They pose little threat."

Sullen, Maska rubbed his rear, where the tiny dart stabbed him with each step. It had lodged in the upper rear thigh, neither protruding enough to reach nor grab. "Ow. Ow!"

"Report to medbay," Venamir ordered.

"No, no," A little flesh patch is all I need." Maska detoured to his room, where he wrestled out of his dripping wet clothes and pulled on a jump suit loaded with pockets. Still sniffling from sea water, he hurried to rejoin his crewmates.

Venamir detoured by engineering, where Motley, Shanto, and Doc worked at the main control station. Venamir met their uneasy gazes with a calm stare. "Doctor, mend my crewman."

Doc Nelzyr obeyed with grudging feet. "What now? Mangy cur had a rough day? Good."

"Better than your day," Maska said, still rubbing his rear, "stupid prisoner."

Doc grabbed a few instruments and easily plucked the dart from Maska's rear. Whining and wiggling, Maska swatted at him, sending the dart flying, where it rolled out of sight. Maska grabbed a bunch of gauze as he retreated out of the doctor's reach. Heaving a sigh of relief, Maska stuffed the gauze into his pants.

"Don't stain the seats," Venamir snarked.

Maska asked with clear anxiety, "Boss, do we have to raid the prison? We already have the best stealth ship, but our crew is a bunch of prison thugs. They're no comparison to a crew of Merfins."

"They will do. We'll have the most fearsome guns in the fleet, once we hack that miserable Herja program," Venamir turned to the doctor. "Continue working with the cat."

Nelzyr admitted, "We're trying to override the program, but don't get your hopes up."

Venamir smiled, not in good will, "Too much sass, and I will leave you at the prison in place of Cruentin. Trust me, there will be casualties. Shall I put you back in stasis?"

Trying to keep his voice steady, Doc turned to face Venamir. "Look, I can't keep surviving so many hibernations. I can't...." He tried to read his captor's face, but saw only the typical cool, relaxed cheek muscles, and dim, gleaming eyes.

"You'll be awake this time. We may need you during the raid." Venamir pulled out the subjugator controller, an innocent looking gadget resembling a small flashlight, but Doc knew what it was. "If you try to psy, you'll get a tingling through your unruly brain. Depending on your actions, the current could be highly amusing to me." Venamir looked him in the eyes and asked, "Can you possibly imagine how slowly I could kill you?"

Doc threatened back, "I'm a doctor. What if I decide to do harm?"

"Perhaps, later, I'll accept that challenge." Venamir smiled. To Doc's surprise, he merely handed Maska the controller. "Maska, when we near the bird planet, lock Nelzyr in the tube, awake."

* * *

Venamir looked out a starboard window to see the ocean's darkness, the ship's lights casting soothing glimpses of colorful fish. He tapped his comm. "Captain's Log: Despite being freed from prison, or recruited for greater service, my new crew-members still need to prove their worth. Some are frightened, some angry. I must know the depth of their contempt." His psy drifted free, just long enough to scan the minds around him to feel their anger, apprehension, and fear, all melted into a pool of adrenalin. Venamir listened to shuffling, thuds of boots and closed his eyes, hands lightly together in quick meditation. He knew too well the emotions of leading a mutiny, but never considered it his fault. He stalked past the ready room toward the cockpit where his hoodlums stood waiting and muttering to each other. They fell silent upon his approach, bodies stiffening. Venamir ran his smoldering gaze over the foursome.

"You, Clamp. Tell me, here you are not at your posts, ready to bear arms. You think I need to read your minds to see your lust for power?"

There were five of them, two humans, Clamp and another vaguely human man. Two Rezoans stood with Clamp, but their lizard-like faces were stoic, their tails hung low, and weapons drawn.

Clamp whipped out his firgun and shook the muzzle in front of Venamir's face. "We're taking this ship, so don't be pulling any of your mind-blasting junk."

"I knew it," the other human whimpered. "He's gonna blast our brains into goo."

Venamir chortled his amusement, short-lived as it was, before his glare locked onto Clamp. "I do not brain blast." His tone was soothing.

"I don't care what you call it," Clamp retorted.

Venamir snuck his psy vision into the minds of Clamps and the henchmen so easily it felt like looking into a library full of tablets with crayon writing. There were their thought images, primitively random and unprotected. Clamp and one other in the group were human, but the rest of them were part reptilian. They all thought in different languages, but their minds' images revealed intent like hazy faded movies of people acting out crime scenes. The crew wanted the *Jacobyte*, his ship, after he worked so hard to steal her back. Venamir watched the mind images of them pounding on him, their captain, as if they stood a chance of winning.

"Get outta our heads!" Clamp groaned as he bent over, hands wrapped around his skull. "You can't stop all of us."

"I think he can," said the timid reptilian. "Uh, s-sorry, Captain." He set down his weapon and pointed to Clamp. "It was his idea."

Venamir briefly scanned the nervous man's brain. "You may stay, for now. Back to work."

"Y-yessir." The reptilian man sped from the room.

"Your uprising didn't work last time. It will fail again," the angry lizard said. "You once sided with my people. Now I see it was for convenience. And Clamp is wrong. You should surrender the *Jacobyte* to the Rezoan fleet, as you tried to do with your old ship, the *Spectre*."

Venamir's eyes narrowed. "You need to go. And by the way, I was trying to swap technology, not surrender her. Your lizard friends almost destroyed my ship."

The lizard glanced past Venamir, noticing movement. He hissed at the sight of a dainty creature with fins and tiny wings, flying into view. The creature appeared as a dainty Merfin with long fins sprouting from her back, allowing her to fly. Her soft, sing-song voice dulled the senses of everyone in the room, everyone except Venamir.

A few other crewmen peered into the room, and then a few more, muttering amongst themselves.

"A mutirian caller," the lizard whispered. He tensed, eyes glinting. Before he could lunge, the tiny caller screeched and flew at him, slashing at his throat with her tiny claws, forcing him to backpedal.

As the creature veered away, Venamir morphed, his aquatic features altering into a menacing form with a longer face and pointy teeth, his body taking on thicker scales like a monster from the deep. His growl was deep and bloodthirsty.

Furious, the lizard lunged, as did the humans at his side. Venamir blocked swings with ease, and threw the lizard over one shoulder, sending his prey crashing into the two humans. Venamir dropped to all fours like an enraged beast and leapt onto the three, driving them to the floor. When one managed to rise, Venamir spun and kicked him over again. His psy voice goaded the three to fight, laughing. Each time one swung, the tiny creature would latch onto an arm, biting, or Venamir would pummel the poor fool with fists and claws. In less than a minute, he had them hypnotized and climbing to their feet, wincing in pain.

Venamir resumed his far less threatening form of a Merfin man with green skin and hands with thin webbing between the fingers. He gazed around him at the onlookers. "Anyone else?"

The crew replied with hasty denials, backing away.

"Cannon fodder," Venamir said, shaking his head. As easily as thumbing through a travel journal, he found pleasurable images in their primitive minds and led their focus to happier memories, instead of their imagined victory of claiming his ship. His ship, the nerve. *"Oh, the bliss of lucent daydreams. See how easy it is to whisk your troubles aside? You should never let your fears succumb to the mythology of monsters and magical powers."* Venamir's voice turned to ice as he snarled, "Drop your weapons."

Clamp and the three remaining henchmen dropped their weapons and stood with dumb, relaxed expressions. Their eyes shining with fear, they realized too late that Venamir's lips had stopped moving, but his thoughts were louder than their own. They felt compelled to do anything for him—run, fight, dance, anything.

Venamir smiled, picked up Clamp's firgun, and adjusted the setting. "Is life not better without tension and barbaric slaughter?"

"Yes, Captain, our mission is to serve you," the foursome replied, voices quavering.

Venamir lightly gripped the burly man by the back of his shirt.

This man was larger, stronger, and despite physical advantages, let his fists fall open as all emotions washed away from his tense features. "Help," Clamp murmured.

"Come along," Venamir ordered.

The other three rebels obeyed, their eyes glazed over.

Venamir saw images of a handful of the crew attacking, only figments of this lousy oaf's imagination. "In Atlean court rooms, intent seen within memories can stand as evidence."

The burly crewman under his grip shivered as his mind demanded his body to regain control. He fell helpless to Venamir's will. His eyes shifted to his companions, who waged the same losing battle.

Venamir's voice rang with glee as he announced, "We shall settle this with a race." He called out, "Moradin, come join the party."

Moradin came jogging around the corner, expression dark with disgust. She looked at Clamp and the other would-be mutineers, who stood with dumb, dazed expressions. All tension washed from their faces, except for the lizard. The Rezoans eyes blazed with anger. His tail twitched, which was all in vain, for he couldn't shake Venamir's control over him.

"Mora, take the helm and surface. Fly low over the water. Our mutineers are going for a swim."

As Moradin nodded and ran out of sight, Venamir pushed Clamp. "Move along."

Clamp and his henchmen obeyed and shuffled down the hall. Only the panic in their eyes betrayed the relaxed movements of their bodies. They moved as if sleepwalking under the rule of a fearsome dictator, sweat beading on their faces.

Moradin jogged to the cockpit and plopped into the copilot's seat. "Captain's orders. I take the helm," she told Maska. "Go stand by a hatch. He's kicking out some goons."

Maska's lips peeled upward into a grimy grin. "Ooh, why didn't you say so?" He jumped up and took off to watch the show.

The *Jacobyte* lifted off and cruised out of the cave between forbidding rock teeth. Her engines growled, longing for action as they soared over the surf. Maska opened a hatch. Venamir shoved Clamp off the ship, and then sent the three other rebellious crewmen screaming into the waves below. A single shot sizzled through water, and one of the men cried out in agony as the laser blast struck him.

"Oh, look, blood in the water." Venamir sang out. "How fast can you swim? Perhaps if you race each other, only the bleeder will be eaten."

"You crazy bastard." Clamp hollered, floundering to stay afloat.

The hatch closed, and the *Jacobyte* soared away.

* * *

Slade and friends sat in the war room listening to the voices of Maska, Venamir, and Doctor Nelzyr coming in loud and clear until Maska removed the projectile from his buttock. Some clinking noises followed, and the sounds became muffled.

"Sounds like Maska got the dart out, but they didn't destroy it," Scruffy reasoned.

"They may not realize it's a tracker, especially Maska," Elowren said.

"That's good, for now," Slade nodded. "Doc's alive, for now, but if Venamir rescues Cruentin, he'll kill Doc for sure. Break up in two groups. Scruffy, let's take the *Vernacular* and hit that prison. Zared, keep stealthed. You and Elowren have the longest psy range. Try to find our Doc. With any luck, we can just disable the *Jacobyte*, and not destroy her." He added to the long range comm, "Wulvur, you'll get to that cave first, since you're closest."

"We're almost there," Wulvur's voice replied. "We just saw the *Jacobyte* take off."

"Dammit," Slade fumed, "scout the cave and report back."

* * *

Gus, Shanto and Wulvur docked their Zephyr in the Cavern of Rituals. Their boots splashed in shallow pools, littered with droplets of oil and freshly crushed rocks in the footprints of the *Jacobyte's* landing gear. They found nothing but discarded building supplies and empty crates.

"The shapes are right, but she's gone," Gus said, eyes on his scanner. "This sucks."

"Quiet," Wulvur said, "someone's coming. Hide."

"Man," Gus said, "you're faster than my scanner."

They hid and waited. Minutes passed, long enough to make the others doubt Wulvur until they heard a faint, rhythmic splashing, and winded curses. A shivering man stumbled up the short beach, where he dropped to his knees. He shook water from his sopping, stringy hair, and coughed and sputtered so hard the shiny clamp fell off his nose. "They're dead, all dead," he wheezed, raking his fingers through the sand for his adornment. Only then did he notice three sets of boots in a half circle around him. Slowly, his eyes traveled upward, to see Gus, Shanto, and Wulvur, their weapons drawn.

The guy uttered something between a whimper and a screech, belched, and tried to run. His legs, rubbery from exhaustion, folded, and he splattered onto the sand.

Gus snickered. "You really wanna go back out there?"

"No. Don't arrest me, don't kill me, and don't make me do any crazy races."

The trio glanced at each other with mutual looks of "Huh?"

Wulvur hauled the guy to his feet. "Where'd Venamir go?"

"How d'you know?" He put up little resistance as Wulvur and Shanto muscled him into the cave. His eyes landed on the abandoned cooking site where some rations still lay unopened. "Can… can I at least have… a last meal?"

"Why should we feed you?" Shanto badgered him.

"How about a truth serum cocktail?" Wulvur said, then poked the man in his well-fed side. "On second thought, we could turn you over to the Hrokahs. The birds hate Venamir for killing their ambassadors. The old fish scared the birds out of our councils."

Gus joined in, "By the way, Venamir thinks humans are nothing more than cavemen. You and I are human. Why were you working for him? Was the pay that good to be a traitor?"

Clamp glanced about, desperate. "Yeah, I figured that out. We tried to mutiny, but he morphed into a half-lizard thing and stomped us."

"Wait," Wulvur said, stepping closer. "A lizard?"

"Yeah, man, it was freaky. His face got longer, mouth full of sharp teeth, and he bulked out and grew a tail." His voice drifted off as he looked up at his captors. "Is that normal?

"Nothing about Venamir is normal," Gus stated, disgusted.

"What's your name? What'd you do for him?" Shanto demanded.

"Clamp," their prisoner replied, shivering, dripping wet, his legs shaky. "I'm a computer guy. He wanted me to hack into the ship's Herja, but I haven't even seen a guardian program like that one."

Shanto brandished his firgun. "What a stupid name. Nobody is named Clamp."

Clamp held up his shaking hands. "It's what I go by, see? Why you want Venamir? You have a death wish? That fish is crazy and powerful. If I tell you too much, he'll find me."

Wulvur morphed into one of his canine forms, not the Retriever that girls adored, but the shaggiest, ragged-eared, dire wolf he could think of, and pounced onto Clamp's chest, bowling the guy over. "Enough flack. Start talking."

Chapter 23
Prison Raid

Desolation comprised much of the landscape of Merchant Colony Techgars. Bleak flatland surrounded an old fortress of a prison. The streets leading to it offered a handful of run-down repair shops and migrant vendors who sold bare essentials. Lights cast a dull haze from an over-farmed forest to the north. To the south, a small town dotted the edges of a huge lake.

A bored Rezoan manned the tallest control tower. Surveillance screens surrounded him, showing the entire prison grounds. He set aside a piece of jerky that had feathers protruding from the crusty skin and hailed an approaching ship. No response. He called again. The controller sighed and tapped the warning level alert button.

An equally sleepy guard appeared on his screen. "What?"

"Incoming ship, not answering hails."

"What is it?"

"Atlean ship. Wait, I'm getting something." He answered the hail to see a hologram of a green-skinned Merfin with mean, yellowish eyes, and a smug smile. "What's a fish doing way out here? What's your name?"

"I am Venamir. We're here to visit Doctor Cruentin," Venamir replied.

"Land in the next town, and we'll think about it. Now veer off."

Another lizard behind the controller swiveled in his chair and stared at Venamir's hologram. "You look like him," he hissed. "When were you released from the sleeping caves? State your purpose."

"Oh, I hate red tape," Venamir drawled. "Here is a token of our good will."

The *Jacobyte* veered away, her artillery bay leaving behind a cluster of mines. They spread out over the prison, each moving ever closer to the structures emitting the most power, such as control towers and generators. The mines blew in rapid sequence, causing a chain reaction of explosions across the large prison yard.

The lizard's mouth hung open, his sharp teeth and twitching tongue shining in the light. The blinking ship on his screen tripled its velocity, now headed straight for them. His eyes widening, he hit the large alarm button that triggered defense guns to fire at the incoming ship. The *Jacobyte* returned fire, blowing the control tower's lower frame into shrapnel. The structure toppled into a splintering avalanche of smashing a patrol vehicle parked below.

The other guard spat out a mouthful of candied bugs. "Pfft! All defenses! Help!" The screen went blank as the tower crashed to the ground just outside his entrance post.

The controller lizard bellowed over all prison comms, "We're under attack! Shields! Aaah!"

The *Jacobyte* thundered toward the prison, so low that ground forces dove for cover. Ground defense opened fire. The *Jacobyte's* wing cannons blasted vehicles into flaming piles of wreckage before the ship screamed upward, into the clouds.

"Our defense cannons are good. Still no main guns?" Venamir complained.

"No, they won't come online," Maska reported. "I could distract the guards and port you in."

"No, it's a prison," Venamir reminded him. "We can't port in. Bring us closer to the top security main around. Blast a hole in the weakest part of the shielding and drop us in."

Venamir ran out of the cockpit, through the ready room, and down the central lift. He rushed to the lowest hatch where Moradin and Noxus joined him, each carrying a Merfin hydration kit made of pressurized canteens with spray nozzles. They made last-minute adjustments to each other's jetpacks.

The *Jacobyte* made a second pass, returning heavier firepower than the prison threw at her. Turrets from beneath each wing spit molten death upon the prison's southern walls nearest the main entrance chambers. Smoke billowed as people swarmed in all directions. Searchlights dotted the dark, cloudy sky, trying to target an armored ship that kept going into stealth. Venamir grabbed an extra jetpack.

Maska flew lower, barely fifty feet above the streets outside the prison, and returned fire, sending guards scrambling for cover. While smoke bombs shrouded Venamir, Noxus, and Moradin's descending forms, the *Jacobyte* pulled up and vanished into stealth mode.

A mad exodus erupted. Prisoners, guards, and the pit beasts coexisted long enough to flee the *Jacobyte's* crazed attacks. Some prisoners stole the nearest vehicles, renewing a free-for-all with the remaining security forces. A handful of scavengers lingered to loot weapons, namely a pair of Hrokah who resembled overgrown crows.

"Ooh, guards in big trouble," the skinnier crew-avian chittered. "What do we do? We are not fighters."

The fat crew grabbed his friend by the wing. "This way, to the chow hall."

"You must be joking," the skinny bird groaned.

"Chow hall is on most protected level, and close to weapons vault," the fat one retorted.

From the brooding clouds over the city, the *Jacobyte* swooped again. Her defense guns blazed havoc upon the prison, toppling a guard tower into the yard below, crushing helpless stragglers. The guns targeted shielded structures protruding from the central building until the energy shields crackled into dissipating sparks, and the armor plating exploded into jagged scraps of metal. Maska had a great time making multiple strafing runs, blowing up generators to knock down power. Much of the prison was dark now, except for scattered fires.

Two of Scruffy's Zephyr medbirds landed behind a half-demolished wall. Slade's crew piled out. They drew scant attention since most people either fought fires or fled for their lives. They left the Zephyrs in stealth mode and took cover behind some wreckage.

Slade snarled as he watched his beautiful warship melt into the murky sky. "He's using my ship to raid a prison? We'll never live this down."

"It could be worse," Berku said.

"Tell me how," Slade replied.

"It's only backup gunner fire, not the main weapons. That means he still can't use the main guns against us," his brother replied.

Slade paused before admitting, "True. Scanners, anything?"

Gus was making slow, wide sweeps with his scanner, as distracted as the others. "So much movement," he murmured. "I'm reading three Merfins. Two of them are cyborgs. Looks like they're headed underground. I'm losing the signal. This place has strong jammers."

"Let me search for telepaths," Elowren said.

"I've got your back," Wulvur assured. He stayed beside her in his beast-man form. His ears twitched as he sniffed the air, his lips curled in disgust.

Elowren was silent in meditation as her psy explored the frantic minds nearby. She struggled to ignore a multitude of fiery emotions and just look for their friend, Doc Nelzyr. She opened her eyes with a start. "Venamir's nearby. Doc is farther away, probably onboard the *Jacobyte*. I can't sense Cruentin. It must be the psy dullers on the lower levels. They know Cruentin is a strong psychic."

Slade tapped his comm. "Zared, Scruffy, what's going on up there?"

Scruffy reported, "The *Jacobyte* comes out of stealth, attacks the prison, and vanishes."

Slade scowled, his tone tight. "My ship's infamous. Wulvur, Elowren, you rescue Doc. The rest of us will go after Venamir. Find the *Jacobyte* and drive her to the ground."

"Don't worry, you crazy g-dog. We know where to hit her," came Scruffy's voice. It almost sounded comforting.

* * *

Maska brought the *Jacobyte* around for another strafing run when Scruffy and Zared brought their ships out of stealth and opened fire. The blasts rocked the *Jacobyte*. Battle shields activated around the multi-layer cockpit view panes, leaving only slits of direct visibility, forcing Maska to rely on his head-up displays. He swerved the *Jacobyte* away from the *Vernacular*, only to find another starship, the *Mythos*, looming above him.

Maska gasped. "How'd they target this ship? We have better stealth than they do." He slapped on the ship-wide comm and shouted, "Motley, get our stealth back online." Maska received no response, except for shots and yells coming from inside the ship. He silenced the comm. "If I let Nelzyr escape, the captain will kill me, or who knows what. I need to get out of this job."

Leifur, the only child onboard, found it easy to be ignored by the harried crew. He grabbed his game bag as he headed to engineering.

Motley caught up to him. "Leifur, can you find the Herja?"

"Like fresh meat," Leifur whispered back, his tail lashing with excitement.

Motley gently nudged his son away. "Find the Doc and the Herja. I'll catch up."

The cub ran through the ship, ducking behind everything he could, as if trying to find the best place to hide. He heard a ruckus near medbay and caught her scent. She didn't smell of thick perfumes, more like armor stored for a long time, with a light layer of oil, like the stuff in his father's shop. A few seconds clicked past, with no reply. Alarms blared, sending the crew running amok. The cub wove through the hustling crew to medbay, where he peeked inside to see some tough thugs trying—and failing—to flatten an enraged woman.

The only opponent offering a challenge was a Mora-dopp. Leifur sprang onto the dopp's back and stuck a spare power pack down its shirt. He leapt off, ducked behind a bed, and activated the charger. The Mora-dopp staggered, still trying to swing at Kestral, who twisted the dopp's head out of alignment with a sickening crunch.

Kestral looked around, smiling. "Thanks, cubby." She ran over to the sleep tube. She thumped controls until the doors of Doc's prison opened and he stiffly sat up. "This ship's a disaster."

"You're telling me." Doc couldn't help but lose his focus at the sight of her athletic figure. Doc tried to stick to business, pointing to the hated headband clamped onto his scalp. "Can you get this hell-hat off?"

She helped him out of the tube. "One way or another."

"That's not comforting." He glanced around. "You okay, kid?"

"Yeah." Leifur handed Doc a firgun. "Here."

Kestral strode over to one dopp that was still twitching, and slammed her boot on top of its head, creating a sickening crunch.

She glanced back at her new companions. A couple more thugs barged in, firguns raised. Kestral flung a glowing boomerang from her belt, sending them into the dance of death. The boomerang zinged back to her hand, and she slapped it back onto her belt like a gunslinger.

Doc ran to a cabinet and grabbed a med kit. "Let's go, kid." He made one last detour to the computer, tapped in rapid commands, pulled out a chip, and dumped it into his pocket.

Over the ship's comm, they heard Maska's frantic voice. "We're landing? Why are we landing? Damn this Herja program!"

The Herja's voice came over all comms, "This ship is receiving orders from allied Atlean ships. Main guns are not authorized for use against allies."

Maska yowled, "Aaargh!"

The cub came out of a cabinet and ran over to Doc, laughing. "Dad hacked the computer to help us, and Atlean ships are forcing us to land. Yay."

Doc jumped when Motley burst into the room, roaring. Doc, Kestral, and the cub all swung around and pointed weapons at him, deflating his bravado. The grey feline skidded to a halt and looked at the crewmen laying on the floor.

Kestral hugged him and patted Motley's furry head, making his ears sway in embarrassment. "I knew you'd come through."

"Ew, get a room," Leifur said, sticking out his tongue.

"Junior!" Motley scolded.

"Wait," Kestral said. "We have to get his headband off."

Doc turned nervously to her and touched the evil control band around his head. "How?"

She strolled over, saying, "Sorry."

Seeing her half-gloves glowing, Doc backed away. "Wait, what're you doing? WAIT."

Doc tried to block her, but Kestral's touch set it to overload. As the old doctor shook from the equivalent of a taser to the head, she yanked the headband free and tossed it aside.

* * *

Elowren flew a Zephyr past the demolished prison that was still lit up with strobe-lights and wailing with alarms. Wulvur sat alongside her in the copilot's chair, manning weapons.

The *Jacobyte* was taking a serious beating from Scruffy's armored tank of a ship, and Zared's hybrid, which looked more like a racing ship than a fighter. The *Jacobyte* shifted in and out of stealth, unable to escape, nor to stay hidden from her pursuers. All three ships had smoke trailing from them.

"Hrokan forces are headed this way," Elowren warned him. "We'll be surrounded by bird-folk within minutes."

Wulvur smirked. "I guess we'll have to 'wing it' like the birds do." He chuckled when she rolled her eyes.

Motley's image appeared on their comm panel. His grey fur was even more disheveled than usual and speckled with fire foam. "Slade, anyone on the *Vernacular's* crew, respond! Elowren? Motley here. I hacked the *Jacobyte* to make it land, but we won't stay grounded for long. We're landing near a cluster of warehouses. Tall buildings should give us some cover. Doc's okay, and so's the guardian, Kestral. You have to get us out of here. My son is onboard. Venamir cubnapped him. This whole crew is crazy."

Elowren nodded. "How many onboard?"

"Uh, only a dozen, but Venamir's bringing as many convicts as he can set free, cannon fodder," he said, glancing around.

"Can't we retake the ship? A dozen isn't so much," Wulvur said.

Motley shook his head. "Maybe, but Maska closed off the cockpit. Even I can't hack it, and it's not just the crew. He'll come back with his doc, his top hit-man, and a bunch of Mora-dopps. Slade's not the only one who wants this ship. He's gotta fight off birds, local mercenaries, and defense troops." He glanced away when someone yelled at him. The comm went blank.

Elowren and Wulvur glanced at each other as they neared a clump of warehouses. Numerous life forms appeared on their scanner, all surrounding one parking area in the center of the complex, large enough for one ship. The *Jacobyte* was headed right for the landing area.

Elowren landed on the loading zone behind an old warehouse. "We'll need a diversion. I'll park on the roof."

Wulvur popped the hatch and climbed out, grinning. "Fun times."

While Elowren flew away, Wulvur ran toward some transient people coming out of the back doors. "Guys," he yelled, "enemy ship landing—they're gonna blow up the prison. I know you don't care, but there's a trick here. They have food and munitions." When more people came out of the warehouse brandishing weapons, Wulvur swung an arm toward the prison. "The guards are coming, prisoners, everyone. But we're here first. A big ship's gonna land here. It's full of stolen goods. If we do nothing, the prison guards will take it all. There's a skeleton crew. We can take the ship."

"He's a loon," one guy said.

The other man beside him turned, his voice earnest. "What if it's true? The prison's an inferno. Maybe we can get off this rock."

Wulvur counted four so far, with two more coming out of hiding "If you stay here, you'll be hunted and interrogated by every bird cop in the flock," Wulvur said. "They're crazy mad. You want to deal with a jail cell and worms for dinner every day?" He saw a few lips curled in disgust.

"He's right," a Rezoan said, one of two lizards in the group. "Haven't you heard Venamir is recruiting again? If we help him get his power back, there will be no more scavenging. We will have good lives. We need to board that ship. Who is with me?" He began to spin up the desperate and greedy members of the group.

Wulvur stepped forward. "I'm in."

The lizard turned to Wulvur and eyed him with equal distrust. "Who are you, a bounty hunter?"

"Jack of all trades. Get me off this bird's nest planet."

As the group ran toward the central parking area, Elowren landed atop an old warehouse, climbed out, and watched the sky. Just as she left the stealthed Zephyr, the first prying eyes set upon her, and a man emerged from an emergency ladder.

"I'll take that ship, woman," he announced.

Elowren morphed, wings sprouting from her back, her hair curling into twisted horns as she stretched and contorted into a silvery dragon. She didn't appear much larger until she reared up, spread her wings, and shrieked.

The guy scrambled down the ladder, slipped, and fell butt-first on a transition level, where he grabbed the next ladder and kept fleeing. "Don't eat me," he cried out, running away, "I just quit drinking."

The other spectators laughed until dragon-Elowren soared over their heads and swooped around to land beside Wulvur. She wasn't a huge dragon like in fairy tales, barely taller than a man at her shoulders, but her outstretched wings, claws, and bared teeth made the locals shy back, staring, all except for Wulvur and the brave Rezoan.

"So, your kind do exist," the lizard said, "most impressive. We join forces?"

"Yes," Elowren hissed at him, reverting back to her feminine, Atlean form, "we storm the ship."

Some of the group cheered, while others remained silent, and a few muttered to each other. Weapons slid from holsters, belts, or pockets, all held at ready, most eyes showing hope amongst darker emotions of fear and foolhardiness.

The Rezoan took charge, or so he thought. "Listen. I've kept you alive. The best chance we have is to work for Venamir. He knows the ship. One cannot simply walk in and command an Atlean ship until the computer accepts him. We take over the ship and be free of this miserable bird-world."

The group of allies watched the *Jacobyte* as the ship landed in the parking area, her gear creating large footprints in the cracked ground. The *Vernacular* and *Mythos* pulled up, unable to fit. Both pursuing ships veered away to higher orbits. Others gathered as the ship's engines slowed to idle.

Wulvur ordered, "Now! Take that ship."

The *Jacobyte's* lower hatch opened, and Mora-dopp came flying out while a disheveled feline man roared in her wake. Elowren landed just outside the hatch, buffeting the dopp when it tried to rise, before leaving it to the mob. She morphed to her Atlean form and ran up the ramp into the ship, with Wulvur close behind.

As the *Jacobyte* sank into chaos, Maska tried to reset the ship's computers to emergency retreat mode. The crew attacked the Kestral's hologram clones, while dopps attempted to fend off incoming locals. Wulvur dumped a pouch full of Gus's toybots on the floor. The little, shiny critters skittered throughout the ship, dropping their smoke bombs.

Kestral pulled Doc to his feet and led him through the smoky halls.

"Damn you, woman," Doc sputtered, "if it weren't for your amazing boobs...." His face reddened. "I didn't mean to say that!"

"Uh-huh," Kestral chuckled.

"Really? More slobbering?" Leifur complained.

A series of muffled explosions went off through the ship, followed by panicked screams and Wulvur's laughter. "You better run!" More shots and stampeding noises followed. Wulvur glanced at the Kestral and Doc. "No making out. Run."

As his friends ran out of the hatch, Wulvur morphed into Venamir's form. He turned just in time to face Venamir's bravest thugs. Wulvur silenced them with a seething glare, causing a confused standoff. *Boy, these guys are mentally whipped.*

A young crewman stared at him. "Captain Venamir, you're back already?"

"The plan changed," Wulvur lied, his tone and demeanor flawless. "I need a jetpack. Go fetch one."

The thugs ran off, yelling over the sounds of alarms and fire extinguishers.

Wulvur fought back laughter, and muttered into his comm, "All hands, rescue complete. I'll be along. Want me to retake the ship?"

Slade's voice replied over sounds of combat. "How many goons onboard?"

"A lot, and the cockpit's closed off."

"Get out of there," Slade answered. "Track me and regroup."

"Damn," Wulvur grumbled. He went back into character when crewman ran up with a jetpack, panting. The man was young, face pale as he helped Wulvur adjust the straps. Leering at the youth for being a peon, he started the jetpack. "And the gun."

The youth handed over his weapon, looking more nervous by the second.

"Thanks. Hey, you all should get off this ship." Wulvur said in a humored tone.

"Why?" the youth asked.

Wulvur morphed into his true form and cracked up. "The real Venamir's gonna' be pissed if he figures out you helped me escape." He turned and shot off into the sky.

* * *

Whispers of a familiar voice lured Doctor Cruentin from his evening meditation. He felt his body caressed by gentle ripples of calm ocean water as he lay within the surf's reach on a sandy beach, where lush growth of giant foliage swayed, draped above in a canopy of sensuous greens. Cruentin lingered there, struggling to regain his blissful feeling of warmth and solitude. A chilling swirl of water churned from the pearly waves, a twinge of reality, ordering him to answer the telepathic call.

"Venamir," Cruentin grumbled, "I must be delusional." *Better to keep dreaming.* Again, he tried to escape into meditation, breaths slow and deep as he willed his body to relax. Each time took him longer, for his body and mind had degenerated and now survival became a series of games and willpower. Again, the name called him, clearer this time, making him flinch. *"Cruentin, wake up. Now!"*

His serene, wonderful beach formed shadowy splotches on the sand erupting around him. Cruen sat up on his cot. Those guns, those engines thundering overhead, pounded his dulled senses. Cruen snarled at the very thought of Slade, captain of the Werefolks, who testified against him and put him in this torturous pit. Good thing he was a doctor. That alone kept him alive.

He rubbed his hands together, wincing as several delicate, withered scales fluttered to the floor. Even the protective scales along his forearms had turned brittle over his months of captivity.

Down the odorous halls, voices of many species rose to a raging chorus of demented taunts and pleas. Fellow inmates found things to pound and clatter as guards opened fire beyond his sight, and shots sizzled through the stale air. Tentacles, claws, arms, and a few long tongues lashed out between the bars, grabbing some guards and slamming them against the cages.

Somewhere towards the entrance, chunks of wall burst free and bludgeoned the nearest prisoners. Realization spread throughout the prison. Cell doors rolled open, releasing a stampede of prisoners, leaving others yelling and pleading to be freed. The halls filled with clashing species, guards fighting and losing.

A guard tumbled and hit the bars of a locked cell, tried to roll away before a pair of six-fingered hands grabbed him, fingers joined by green webbing. He only lasted a matter of seconds before the inmates smashed his head against the bars, took his controls, and set themselves free. The web-handed man let his cell mates run first before poking his head out and looking at Cruentin, who shooed him off. The green man nodded and disappeared through the ensuing carnage.

Cruentin knew his own cell was stronger, thanks to his higher abilities, so not just anyone could open it. He listened to the noise of thundering engines and cannon fire. "Venamir's strafing the prison," he gloated. A high-pitched zap caused most lights to overload, and power to the bars fail. Mayhem exploded all around him. Prisoners pounded at their doors, their yelling sporadically interrupted by heavy artillery defense guns, firing along with explosions from above.

Cruentin only cared about one sound that suddenly fell dead.

The agonizing hum within his head that dulled his psyche rendered him unable to use his telepathic powers. When the psy dulling machine fell silent, Cruen's mind cleared. His telepathic senses burst to life as he took a deep breath and exhaled, allowing his body to savor the rush of adrenalin and the tingling in his long, leafy shaped ears. His mental prison shattered. He could sense other telepaths again.

Cruentin yelled in triumph, "My psyche is free!"

The nearest guards spared an instant of startled glances, then saw his bars still glowing and exchanged laughs.

A guard powered up his scattergun. "Cruen, you crazy old fish, shut up, before I give you another sand blasting."

Eyes narrowed, Cruen focused psy energy upon all guards within his range and yelled into their minds, *"Come to me. I'm a doctor. I can help you."*

Two injured guards headed toward him, at which point, Cruentin sent his psy deep into their confused minds. Being out of practice, he wasted precious seconds as the guards drew closer, one reaching for the controls outside his cell door. The guard's hand trembled, the hardened expression contorting to rage as he turned on the other guard.

"You traitor," the guard rumbled, "you've wanted to free the fish all this time."

The other guard stammered, "Huh? He's a telepath. He's in your head."

"No, he's in yours. Get on the ground or die."

The guards lunged at each other, tumbling to the ground in a flurry of punches.

Watching with a sick smile, Cruen savored the first taste of revenge. "Oh, yes, I'm back in business." He yelled to the prisoners, "Let me out. Help my rescuers and together, we can leave this festering hole."

A few of the guards shot at the Doctor's cell, but their shots failed to pierce the bars and energy wall that their prisoner stood behind, laughing. A frantic captain shouted for their aid, so the guards pressed on, battling in an effort to subdue escaping prisoners.

Cruen moved closer to his glowing bars, reveling in the rush of images from surrounding minds. He locked his gaze upon the nearest guard and focused, channeling his consciousness into the young humanoid's mind, infiltrating his thoughts, taking over. *"They're all against you,"* he whispered. *"the prisoners, your partner, all of them. Kill them all."*

A silhouette approached through the smoke and mayhem, flanked by two battle-gear clad companions. They strode through the rioting prisoners. Their flanking guards killed inmates stupid enough to challenge them. The center being in the lead was in his true form, his yellow, gleaming eyes visible through the smoky haze. Venamir pointed downward.

Cruen laid flat against the far wall. In seconds, the trio opened two cylinders at the base of the bars and ducked aside. The bars shrieked with energy, showered sparks and random pulse beams that left some nosy prisoners and hasty guards dazed and blinking as if they'd stared at the very sun's rays, just long enough for others to flatten them. The carefully targeted blast and meltdown left the doctor's cell bars warped and sagging. Noxus and Moradin bent the bars apart with ease.

Venamir sauntered through smoke and churning dust. "Hello, Cruen. We stole my old ship back. I expected you to have better accommodations."

"I expected you sooner," Cruen replied.

Venamir and his duo moved into the cell, and his partners activated canisters over their backs. Cruen jumped, startled when dual water sprays hit his body. He rose with a grateful laugh, his gills fluttering with only a little pain for the first time in months. Moradin and Noxus then discarded the water sprayers.

Moradin helped him don a flak jacket. "Stay between us."

Venamir led the way out of the cell. "Now I can leave Nelzyr in this slime pit."

"Nelzyr? It's his fault I'm in this prison."

"Vent later," Venamir ordered, "let us blaze a trail."

The assault of two powerful telepathic minds joined the forces of fighting prisoners. Guards staggered as the doctor's and Venamir's joined voices burned through their thoughts and will power. Prisoners swept over the fallen in a crazed rush to freedom.

Venamir yelled, "Whoever helps us escape wins a job on my crew."

Cruen's voice held traces of excitement writhing with caution. "Slade's nearby. Let's get him."

"Keep moving," Venamir ordered.

Chapter 24
Pit Beasts and Rangers

Explosions silenced more of the prison's power generators and most of the alarms, feeding the chaos on all levels. People, guards and prisoners, were fleeing more than fighting, but a few stubborn honchos remained and activated their next level of defense. Alarms blared as doors opened on walls, floors, and ceilings.

Slade and his friends stood back to back, listening and scanning with their bio-readers.

"Oh, no good," Berku said, eyes widening at multiple dots on his wristband. "They got pit beasts, heading our way."

They snapped up their weapons as footsteps and scuffling closed in. Nearby, screams and fierce growls announced the prison's sadistic guards of last resort, pit beasts. The creatures loosely resembled overgrown canines mixed with giant badgers, long claws and thick fur, with stripes down their backs. One creature had greater stealth than the others. It had a different growl, lower, more ominous, and kept farther in the shadows, as if ready to attack them in one giant leap. Each pit beast wore form-fitting armor that protected much of their heads and upper bodies.

"One shot and they all charge," Gus muttered. "Man, why'd they have to be animals?"

"We don't have to kill them," Slade whispered. "Maybe my flashbacks can scare them off. Get your psy defenses up."

Slade closed his eyes and released the flashbacks from the old crash that had rattled him for decades. He made no attempts this time to hold the visions within his own mind. Instead, projected them to every vulnerable mind around him. He couldn't see the pit beasts recoil, their hungering eyes flashing with surprise, fear, and confusion. Absorbed within his visions of the past, Slade grabbed for balance as his ship from the past bucked beneath him. His memories of the ship's hull moaning over voices of his crew sounded different this time, filled with shadowy images of the real world, where animals shrieked and whimpered as they galloped, slithered, or scampered away. The familiar cockpit faded to dark walls and a shadowy form in front of him.

"Get off me!" Slade threw the assailant over one shoulder, elbowed another shadowy form, and rolled clear of their grips. He lowered his fists when he recognized his friends, illuminated by dimly glowing wall markers and lights from their combat helmets.

Gus climbed to his feet, wiping at his bloody nose. "Thanks, Cap."

Slade glanced around. "Sorry. Where'd the pit beasts go?"

Berku flipped his visor up and returned a broad grin. "The beasties saw your nightmares and ran off, bawling."

Another flight of ships thundered overhead, flying low enough to make the passage walls tremble. Chunks of ceiling panels broke free, one bouncing off Gus's burly form. They felt the floor trembling, followed by rumbling. The group sprinted in mad flight as debris fell in their wake. Once outside, they kept close to the wall and activated their stealth gear. They almost made it away from the central buildings when two large, flapping creatures bore down on them. What looked like overgrown crows seized Rhoan by the arms and tried to lift him away from the group.

"See you, smell you," the skinny bird chittered.

"Are you shitting me?" Slade barked, firing a shot that winged one of the birds. The wrestling match was on, birds clutching at Rhoan, who reached for the birds' tail feathers, legs, and wings. Rhoan grabbed the skinny bird's leg and twisted, causing it to screech and tumble down with him. The other bird, larger and fatter, landed on top of his captive like a psychotic chicken desperate to incubate her eggs.

"Tried to make it easy," the fat bird ranted, "but people are greedy. We need medic." He flexed hands that were more like bird feet and dug into Rhoan's combat vest. "You come with us."

"What the hell?" Rhoan wheezed, trying to wrestle his hand farther under the bird's overfed mass. "What do you eat, fatso? I'm gonna make you into a two-course dinner."

"We always hear food jokes," Fat Bird retorted. He dug his talons through Rhoan's jacket. "You come with us."

Slade growled, "Let him go, or we'll roast you right here."

"No, no, we need medic. We'll be rich, rich."

"Told you to ask," the Skinny Bird whimpered.

238

"You still suck mama's craw," Fat Bird retorted. "Shut your beak." He added to Rhoan, "Stop wiggling. We not on date."

"You're the one who jumped me," Rhoan said, wrestling hard to dig into his med bag.

"What you doing? That tickles," Fat Bird complained.

Rhoan taunted back, "You shouldn't mess with a master of anatomy."

Fat Bird screeched, leaping off of Rhoan with all his might. He flapped frantically into the air, all feathers on end. Rhoan barely had time to roll away before Fat Bird crashed to the ground, curled up and rubbing his crotch. Fat Bird peeked through his wing feathers, to see guns wavering at him because the group was laughing.

Rhoan climbed to his feet, stuffing the heart zapper into his bag. "I can't believe I found any junk under all that flab."

Skinny Bird whimpered, "You keep him, strangers. We too stringy to taste good."

Slade stepped on Fat Bird's closest wing feathers. "You were in this prison. What do you know about Doctor Cruentin?"

"Cruen? Oh, bad doctor, that one," Skinny Bird said.

"We know nothing much," Fat Bird lied. "We no speak Atlean too good."

Slade made a bunch of squawking noises that made his friends stare in surprise.

"Oh, you from Druwen clan," Fat Bird said, "works for high fancy councils. Lot of good it did. Our ambassadors died trying to keep the peace."

"I know," Slade replied. "I was there. Shut your beak and listen. Venamir's raiding this prison. You're gonna tell us what you know, or else I'll have the top buzzards on your merchant business like scales on fish."

Skinny Bird whimpered, curling his head behind his wings.

"What do you know about Cruen?" Slade interrogated. "Where's he going? Did he know about the rescue?"

Fat Bird started rambling, "Cruen, bad doctor, worked as medic until they found him doing experiments, putting implants in guards, said to control them easier, no news for escape plan, said he wanted to take over whole prison."

"This rat-hole?" Berku asked in surprise.

"Not only this prison, every place Venamir uses. Said he has fishes in the Deep, more crazy than Venamir. He says ghost ship in grave come save him. Take him to Deeps friends, I swear. Don't fry our brains."

"Be too small a meal," Rhoan heckled.

"Ghost ship," Slade muttered in thought. Slade waved his firgun from one bird to the other.

"We sorry tried to steal young medic," Skinny Bird whined, "make good cash from him, then let him go, borrow, see?"

Slade let Fat Bird up. "Shut it. Remember, you owe me. Now get outta here, you stupid buzzards." He fired a few shots, singeing their feathers as they scrambled away. Feathers fluttered to the ground as they flapped into the air.

"What'd he mean by ghosts?" Rhoan asked.

"Ghosts and graves," Slade mused. "Now it makes sense. I know where Venamir's going."

* * *

Across the prison yard where generators had been reduced to piles of smoking rubble, the prison lay in a vulnerable state of thinning chaos. Search lights made a few random passes, then moved on outside the demolished prison walls. Blaring zaps of weapons fire and screams of ships' engines swelled with new intensity. Surviving guards had called for help, summoning inland security forces. Most were unmarked ships, suggesting mercenary forces, but help was help.

Noxus crept along walls, glancing about as he darted from one hiding spot to another. "Venamir, Slade's party is just beyond the far wall. Give the kill order."

Venamir replied over the noise of approaching engines. "Return to the ship."

"I can shoot them from here," Noxus argued. He paused along an overturned patrol rig.

Shots came from above, searing his shoulder and sizzling into his sniper rifle. While Noxus ducked around the other side of the rig, shots to his jetpack knocked him off balance. Too busy searching for cover, Noxus didn't see a form closing in behind him.

Another shot hit the back of his leg, driving him to the ground. He rolled aside just in time to avoid Wulvur's boots landing atop his back. Noxus scrambled to his feet and backpedaled a few steps, raising his hands in mock surrender.

Wulvur landed, blocking his path, firgun leveled. "Power down. I know you're a cyborg."

"Venamir has an offer. You work for him, or I kill you."

"Okay. Let's rumble."

Pit beasts were approaching from all sides, two giant bats, a pack of canine creatures with thick fur and armored harnesses that protected much of their body. The feline's hackles and tail fluffed at one whiff of Noxus. The swirls in his deep, blue spots were mesmerizing, his gaze hypnotizing. Noxus started to lower his weapon until he caught himself and stomped at the pit beasts. The pack of animals snarled at him, teeth shining in all their fanged glory.

"Get back, you pack of vermin. You won't be eating me." Noxus snapped. "I'll skin all of you."

Wulvur moved into his path. "You're worse than the spaceport terrorist. I figure he's being dissected about now. Weird thing, he had a change of attitude. He acted regretful at the end."

"Slade will pay for my brother's death."

"You gave Slade the credit? I brought down that crazy cyborg."

"You mean, you-u killed him?" Noxus froze, panting, fists clenched, oblivious to everything around them, even a mangy hyena-like creature edging closer to sniff his rear. The creature took one sniff and backed away, gacking. Noxus snarled, "Axehat was my brother!"

Wulvur curled his lip. "Eww, is that possible? Someone screwed your mama twice? Gross. It had to be test tubes."

Noxus yelled in rage as he lunged. Wulvur started firing large, hollow-point bullets into his armor. Noxus staggered as shots dug into his helmet, pierced one arm, and finally destroyed the shield generator on his belt buckle. Winded, he flung a pouch off his belt at Wulvur. The pouch released thick smoke as it expanded into a net that barely missed its target.

As Wulvur backed away, saving his ammo, a grenade flew toward him. Instead of exploding, the grenade-like gadget tracked his hot gun barrel and melted around it. Searing heat traveled to the handle, Wulvur flung the weapon toward the nearest wrecked vehicle before it exploded. The overturned transport burst into flames, evicting Noxus, who emerged, coughing.

"That's messed up," Wulvur complained. He drew a staff from over his back. One twist to the handle morphed the weapon into a double–ended spear.

When Noxus charged at him, Wulvur blocked, his spear slicing off a chunk of armor and biting the cyborg's weapon hand. Blood spewed as Noxus backpedaled, angered all the more. Wulvur struck Noxus in the leading knee, buckling the leg. Undaunted, the cyborg rolled aside and rose with sadistic contempt in his glare.

"I don't feel pain like you do, fleshy," Noxus jeered.

Wulvur dug deep within to fend off the enraged Noxus, each block jarring every joint, each dodge demanding all his speed. This cyborg was a better fighter than Axehat.

Noxus suddenly stopped, shaking all over and panting, then backed away. His reddened face throbbed with blood vessels as he glanced at the creatures surrounding them. "Land rats," he scoffed.

"You may be a half-flesh robot, but you can't beat a yeti."

His face a nauseating scowl, Noxus advanced. "There's no such thing as a yeti."

Wulvur rolled toward Noxus and made a wide sweep with his bow, slicing through boots and flesh. As Noxus stumbled, Wulvur stuck him with the bow's spikes, shoving him back toward a massive form.

Noxus heard rhythmic grunts that resembled laughter as a monstrous shadow loomed over him. He turned, his bloodshot eyes widening as a ten-foot tall creature eyed him, its broad humanoid face bearing a look of disgust. The creature's large, oblong ears pressed back against its twisted horns. The yeti beast roared, a thundering, ear-rattling scream. With a twisted grin, the creature lunged, shaggy arms reaching, maw spread wide open.

"Bye," Wulvur said, waving.

The pit beasts closed in. Noxus made wide swipes with his staff, clipping one of the monster bats. The bats buffeted him with their wings as they surrounded him in a frenzy. Noxus crashed hard, covering his head. He reached into pouches and hurled stun grenades. Most of the beasts fled while the enraged the monster bats shrieked and swooped around him, baring jagged teeth.

Wulvur cheered as the yeti-like creature grabbed Noxus and carried him off at a lope. "Wait, don't eat him. He's nasty!"

* * *

Venamir, Cruentin, and Moradin crouched behind some wreckage and watched the ground battle through the bodycam on Noxus. The fight between Noxus and Wulvur made Moradin smile as she saw the other Druwen Wulvur, fending off a bloodthirsty cyborg. Their view ended when the yeti's great teeth smashed the bodycam.

"Oh, what a shame," Cruentin said in mock pity. "I didn't like that cyborg, anyway."

"Nobody likes him," Venamir said. He turned to Moradin and pointed after the retreating beast. "Go rescue that failure."

Moradin opened her mouth to argue, but bit back her retort, turned, and ran down the stairwell.

"We need to capture Wulvur. He knows too much, and he's stronger than Noxus," Cruen said, following his rescuers. "Wulvur is known for hunting cyborgs. At least disable him, or he'll cut down Moradin next."

Venamir halted. "Disable him."

Maddened by months of interrogation in prison, Cruentin drilled his psy into Wulvur's mental shields. The raging doctor found Wulvur's thoughts protected by trees and rabid beasts, all writhing together, creaking and snarling. *"Feel what I've been through."*

Wulvur felt his lungs compress. He dropped to his knees, weapon clattering out of his hands. His sides ached, giving him a strange sensation of his skin twitching and air moving through it. He grabbed one side and felt gills. Gills? They felt so real, as if someone blasted hot sand into his lungs. Venamir's mind joined in, both psychics prying apart his shields, and digging into his mind as a miner would tunnel through layers of earth.

He couldn't show fear or weakness for long, or the beasts would chase him down next. Keeping his psy barriers up demanded all his concentration, while Cruen's illusions still sucked the energy from him with every breath.

Venamir whispered into Wulvur's mind, *"Why do you work for Slade? You are no more than their trained pet. The morpher councils use you. I mean to make our kind greater than ever before."*

"Sure, hire me so I can kill your asses," Wulvur retorted.

Cruen's anger raged through Wulvur's mind. *"Your people put me in this prison, Wulvur. You owe me. Serve us, or I will drown you with normal air."*

Wulvur saw his surroundings of gnarled beasts and battle-torn yards swirl into soothing ocean waves, rising over his head. All underwater sensations washed over his senses. Weightless, trapped in a whirlpool, craving dry air, he could only imagine his best defense, an air bubble around his body. He understood why Elowren had called Venamir their infamous interrogator. Wulvur's had no idea how long he could fight off those two.

Slade's voice came over his earpiece. "Wulvur, you're surrounded. Wait for us."

"No, stay away," Wulvur shot back. "Venamir's in my head. Back off."

Slade's voice nagged from his headset, "Regroup with us. Now. We'll snap you out of it."

Venamir's psy voice sneered, *"Disobey Slade, and you will see how bloodthirsty he is. He wants to murder me for taking back what was mine. I mean to remake the Morpher Council, but to do that, I need Slade's help. You must capture him for me. If he can be swayed, he can live."*

Cruentin added, *"Slade should be in this prison, not me. This is your chance to join us."*

Defending against two telepaths in his head, Wulvur swayed on his knees. When his eyes clenched shut again, he saw Venamir's fake vision—him fighting Slade, and winning. He imagined killing the council's top Werefolk. He could taste blood and victory, no more taking orders, no more long hunts through cultists

and spies, so someone else could take the reward. Hands
unsteady, Wulvur activated his stealth gear and blended into his
surroundings.

Slade's voice nagged at him, "Ignore them. Block them out."

"Listen to reason," Venamir psyd again, *"I am trying to spare
your friends if you join me."*

Wulvur saw brief glimpses of a shared past between Slade
and Venamir, visions of them being council brethren, flight crew
comrades, battle survivors. *"Let me think about it."*

"Think quickly," Venamir's psy voice warned.

As Venamir and Cruentin started arguing, Wulvur grabbed his
polearm, twisted the top spike, and pulled it free. "Arrow," he said.
The spike lengthened in his hand, splitting and reshaping into three
arrows. Wulvur ran his hand along a silvery line down the polearm's
long handle. The two other blades on the weapon retracted. He
leaned on the staff, bending it into a bow-shape. The grey, waxy line
along the handle sprang loose from the handle, forming the bow
string.

Venamir's voice invaded his mind again, *"Decide, now."*

Slade's voice nagged over Wulvur's comm. "Don't listen to
them. Report back to me. NOW."

Wulvur's head pounded as Venamir sought to control him
again. His view of reality faded from the battle-scarred prison
buildings to pillars shrouded by aqua blue hued water. Wulvur
dropped his stealth, standing out where he stood unprotected in the
prison yard. Notching an arrow, he pivoted toward a guard tower
that stood in shambles. He saw silhouettes through the smoke,
shapes of his friends taking cover.

Wulvur dropped stealth and moved into view. He yelled, "All
of you, shut up!"

He still heard Venamir and Cruen in his mind, their voices
gleeful as they urged him to fire, giddy at the thought of watching
Slade fall. Wulvur's hands shook. He realized with a twinge of dread
that he was turning toward his friends. He spied Slade across the
prison yard, and knew he had an easy shot at his friends, but not
Venamir. He glanced up and around, through smoke from scattered
fires. He couldn't see the *Jacobyte,* but he heard the engines,

roaring and steady, like they were hovering. *I can't keep them out of my head, not two of them, not for long.*

Venamir was losing patience, his psy voice feeding Wulvur's anger, *"Join me. You're a Druwen Ranger with rare talents. I know you can channel healing energy from the forest. You beat my top hitman. You have the skill to capture Slade. Bring him to me. We will make a new Morpher's Council, one that does not bow to humans. Tis a simple choice. Join me, or watch your friends die."*

"Last warning, Slade," Wulvur said. "Get out of here. I work alone."

Slade's fearless voice growled over Wulvur's earpiece, "Don't argue with me. Report back, now. Don't use a firgun, either. Prison defenses will target you."

"I don't need a firgun." Wulvur drew back his arrow, aiming toward his friends.

* * *

Sporadic weapon fire thundered all around the prison. Reinforcements from nearby towns began to converge around the grounds, helping injured guards and rounding up prisoners. Shocks and his gang were still taking shots at the Venamir's Mora-dopps.

Slade and Berku ducked behind the lower guard tower walls. Slade pointed toward the tallest buildings, and beyond them, the *Jacobyte*. "There's my ship. Venamir's about to escape!"

A dull *thwack* sounded above Slade's head. An arrow half-buried itself high in the sooty guard shack beside him, just beneath the roof.

"Whoa!" Berku pulled his brother back farther behind the wall. "That's Wulvur's arrow!"

"No." Slade pointed to the arrow. "You think Wulvur ever misses by that much? That was a warning. He could have used scatter-arrows to pepper us." He touched his comm. "All hands, Venamir's trying to control Wulvur's mind. Distract the damn fish."

* * *

Wulvur collapsed his bow and flung it aside. He morphed into beast form, hoping it would keep Venamir and Cruen out of his mind. It didn't help much. He could sense Venamir and Cruen arguing with each other over how to kill him, but something else grabbed their attention. Venamir started yelling to return fire. Finally, the fog of painful mind-control lifted from Wulvur's brain.

"Now get back here," Slade ordered.

"Whew," Wulvur sighed. "Sorry 'bout that arrow. Wait, I'm gonna have a pow-wow."

Slade's tone dropped, "You're gonna what?"

Wulvur stood encircled by the beasts, but instead of attacking, they circled him, whining as he met each of their penetrating gazes with his lupine eyes. He swirled his bow, where glowing orbs appeared, capturing the attention of the animals around him. His voice was soft and hypnotic as he shared his psy images of a peaceful forest with their excited minds. "We are kindred. No need to fight me. My people are part animals, too."

When Wulvur slowly broke the hypnosis, the animals milled around him for a few moments, sniffing him, some whining. Their body language had settled into a somewhat relaxed state.

"Go on, hide," Wulvur urged, motioning away.

Prison creatures ran away in all directions. Bat-like creatures took flight, their escape shrouded by smoke from waning fires. The creatures closest to canines, and a large feline strayed only a short distance, watching him with wary eyes.

Wulvur grinned up toward the *Jacobyte* that loomed over a nearby building. This time, he allowed psy contact with Venamir and Cruen. *"I commune with beasts. You'll be the ones wearing spiked collars when I'm done with you."*

This time, Venamir and Cruen recoiled from his mind.

* * *

Moradin ran through cell blocks, losing herself in thought as she passed fallen people, most of them prisoners. The end outweighs the tactics, Venamir would say. Her life, her enhanced abilities, were because of his medic, Doctor Cruen. The thought of having Cruentin back excited her, filled her with hopes of appearing more like her old self, more feminine. Maybe old promises would be kept after all. They would make her beautiful again.

Moradin slowed her pace, fuming, "Why can't Noxus die?" She hoped to be rid of her blood-lusting crewmate. She hung her head. "Venamir would suspect I killed him, like it's a bad thing," she mumbled. Scowling, Moradin approached a mangled rock wall. As she found an exit, she heard gunfights mixed with howling and snarling.

Heavy feet thudded toward her from the other side. Large, thick claws as long as her hands gripped the top rail. Twisted horns atop a grizzly head with a snout shaped muzzle appeared, gripping a familiar man by the torso. Gleaming eyes fixed upon her under a scarred, furrowed, man-like brow. The beast cast a monstrous shadow around her as it leapt over the wall and landed in front of her. Noxus was trapped in its drooling maw. Moradin's jaw slipped open as she stepped back and snapped up her rifle, which only enraged the beast. As it rose to at least full height, she could clearly see it was a male. The yeti spat Noxus out, growling when his prey landed hard on the ground.

Moradin smirked. "You're okay by me. Go on." She gestured away from her.

The beast was too angry to leave. It bore scars from the past on its chest and arms, and oozing burns from the current battle. Moradin felt a pang of respect and sympathy for the creature, until it lunged for her.

She backpedaled, firing on her lowest setting. "Stun, stun."

As the beast staggered forward, his massive hand-like paws grabbed at her. Moradin leapt high on the wall, using one hand to hang onto a window ledge while she swung the rifle around and thwacked the setting with her thumb. When the beast crouched to spring at her, she blasted the ground at its feet, forcing it to stagger back. She grabbed Noxus by one arm and retreated until she heard a near-human moan, followed by loud, dull thuds. Moradin peeked around a building.

"Stun setting? Weakling," Noxus mumbled.

Heaving a sigh, she wrestled him into a fireman's carry. "Shut it, you sadistic puke. Last thing I want to do is carry your worthless hide."

"Good thing I poisoned it."

Moradin gasped, "What? You didn't have to do that. You're a sick, slug-faced piece of shit that kills everything." She had vivid fantasies of blasting Noxus limb after limb until only a steaming pile of him remained. Cursed Venamir for ordering his life be saved.

"Soft little Mori, pathetic," Noxus sneered.

"You're lucky the captain wants you alive." She dropped him, watching his head bounce on the ground, knocking him out. "Bastard."

Chapter 25
Stalemate

The *Vernacular* remained in stealth, Scruffy and Elowren at the
helm, and Jasko in the gunner's chair. Telari stood just inside one
lower ramp, her scope panning for targets.

"The guards aren't looking for us," she observed. "They're too
busy fighting prisoners."

"If we come out of stealth, locals won't assume we're
friendly," Scruffy replied. He pointed at their friend or foe scanner.
"There's Venamir and his crew on the roof across the yard. They're
using the crumbled generator barricades for cover. Slade, come in.
Do we attack your ship or not?"

Slade replied over the shrieking noise of engines and
weapons fire. "We can't let anyone steal the *Jacobyte's* technology.
If the ship crashes, we'll have to blow up the main guns if we can't
dismantle them. Shocks and his gang are giving us cover," Slade
replied. "Go distract Venamir. Try to knock out the *Jacobyte's* portal
generators."

"Finally," Scruffy said as he powered up the engines. "All
hands, I'm closing the ramps. We're lifting off."

"Scruffy, I'm going sniper mode," Telari yelled, and leapt off
the ramp as it started closing. Her loyal feline followed, landing
close beside her.

Telari morphed into a feline humanoid and slung her rifle
across her back. She glanced down at the hybrid Atlean cat by her
side. "I said stay inside." She signed and petted her self-appointed
bodyguard. "Well, let's test out your gear." Tel adjusted the cat's
collar, activating armor that spread over the feline's back and
matched the surrounding colors. "Stealth mode on," Tel said as she
and the cat bounded away from the *Vernacular.* Telari's long
combat vest morphed with her, covering her with a leathery garment
that also matched the terrain. She and her cat raced through the
prison yard battleground, scampering over debris. A fallen prisoner
was climbing to his feet and reaching for a firgun when Tel and her
companion bowled him over, grabbed the weapon, and kept
running. Telari threw the weapon near a couple guards, who ducked

behind a crumbling fence. The guards spun, trying to find a target, unable to zero in on footprints and blurs.

"Guard me," Telari whispered, panting at the edge of a half-mangled control tower. She sprang up the rickety structure to a remaining stretch of catwalk near a charred hole that used to be a door. Slade, I'm up on a wall tower. Venamir's dopps are climbing to a roof. That whole roof has landing pads, but for small ships. The *Jacobyte* is hovering with her aft ramp open," Telari reported. "Venamir's got Cruentin. They're taking pop shots at ground troops. I have good line of sight."

"Disable both those fishes," Slade's voice replied in her earpiece. "I need Venamir alive, for the councils to interrogate."

"Copy that." Tel's feline eyes slitted with inhuman depth perception. She aimed her rifle.

* * *

Venamir climbed up the last steps of a creaking emergency exit staircase, panting. He opened a door to the flat rooftop and stepped into the open. Cruen and two other prisoners cleared the stairs before the stairwell collapsed, taking stragglers along with it. The unlucky fools plummeted to the lower floors. Their screams were cut short by crashes. Venamir led the way across the roof, seeing cracks forming as they ran. All the landing pads on the roof were empty, except for one small hovercraft reduced to twisted wreckage.

Venamir yelled into his comm, "Maska, port us out!"

A hologram of Maska appeared before them, the image shrouded by smoke. "I can't port you," Maska reported in a scared voice, "We're being jammed and took damage."

"Then pick us up," Venamir ordered.

The *Jacobyte* swooped down upon the prison in another strafing run, scattering the prison's defense troops. The ship came about, gracefully slowing to a hover over the building. The aft ramp opened, lowering until the trailing steps scraped the roof. Stress cracks, created by the edge of the ramp bouncing and scraping along the rooftop, spread toward Venamir and Cruen.

"Hold her steady," Venamir commanded. He turned and yelled at five prisoners who were running to catch up. "Everyone aboard. Move!"

The prisoners sprinted up the ramp and into the ship. Another prisoner and a damaged Mora-dopp tried to climb over the roof's edge near the ship. A laser blast knocked them off, sending dopp parts and debris flying.

"Wait," Cruen argued, "Slade's crew is down there. Let Wulvur get to us. We can take him over. He's an energy channeler. There aren't many of those left. He can give accelerated healing."

"I remember him," Venamir replied, scowling. "Wulvur healed the council people when we tried to take over. It cost us the win. He can't summon energy out of nowhere. He needed substantial plant life to draw energy from. Why do you think they live in forests?"

Cruentin looked toward the horizon as an old flying tank of a ship thundered into the sky and opened fire. "It's the *Vernacular*. Get down!"

Venamir, Cruen, and the prisoners hit the deck, covering their heads with their hands.

The *Vernacular's* first couple shots hit the *Jacobyte,* sending chunks of armor plating flying. The next shots hit the landing port building. The *Mythos* flew over them, also firing, blasting away chunks of protective hull plating.

Zared's voice came over a loudspeaker. "Surrender, Venamir. Dead or alive, we're taking you in."

"You die first," Venamir hissed. "All hands, no time for prisoners," Venamir snarled. "Both those ships are with Slade. Lift ship on my command."

The roof shuddered, huge chunks collapsing the upper stairwell into the levels below. Venamir and Doctor Cruen ran and jumped onto the *Jacobyte's* ramp, a Mora-dopp close behind, until another chunk of the roof caved in, taking the dopp with it. More stress cracks spread from where the ramp slammed onto the roof as weapons' fire barraged the ship.

Moradin climbed up the fire escape ladder, with Noxus over her shoulder. "Captain, wait. We're here," she yelled. She climbed up the wall and ran toward the ship's unsteady ramp. Her cybernetic legs groaned in protest as she sprinted, leaped onto the ramp, and dumped Noxus onto the cargo deck.

Scruffy's *Vernacular* and Zared's *Mythos* were coming around to attack again when warning shots streaked across their path. Two scout-sized warships appeared, only large enough for a crew of three each, but built for almost nothing but engines and weapons. They took position on both sides of the *Vernacular* and the *Jacobyte.*

A loudspeaker from the planet's defense ship bellowed, "We have a fleet on the way. Power down weapons and land, now!"

* * *

Max Shockinzo and his son, Shocks, rode their brightly colored Huvzter cycles up underneath the *Jacobyte.* The wind from the ship's thrusters overhead buffeted their small vehicles. Max did a shooting motion to Shocks, who nodded.

Telari saw her targets lingering on the *Jacobyte's* aft ramp, ushering straggling Mora-dopps onboard and shooting at her friends. She didn't have a clear shot at Venamir, but Cruentin moved into view. Cruen was holding onto a Mora-dopp for balance as he took pop shots at people below.

"Time for payback, biatch," she hissed.

Doctor Cruen knelt near the edge of the ramp, holding on to the side railing. His eyes fixated near a guard tower. "Look, some of Slade's crew. Let's finish them." He focused his attention on Slade's nearest crewmember, the young medic, Rhoan. *"I hear your psy voice, trying to stop us."* Cruen gloated into Rhoan's mind. *"Oh, you're a combat medic. how gallant. Come out in the open."*

Rhoan moved against his will, sneaking out into the open, leaving a gravely injured guard with a hastily applied compress on the ground behind him. Domination. He'd never felt it before, a force that made his thoughts feel far away, like a dream where somebody else was truly him. It really pissed him off. Rhoan's anger fed his psy strength as he focused on Cruentin. *"No, you come to me, Cruen,"* he psyd back. *"You think you're such a badass. Come and get me."*

Cruentin froze, his smile fading. He moved toward the end of the ramp like a sleepwalker, his mind whirling in disbelief of a novice controlling him.

As ordered to "stay close," a dopp proceeded alongside him.

Cruentin peered over the edge of the ramp and beheld the chaos below, jagged framework of demolished buildings, survivors shooting at them. He tried to yell, to psy, but was only able to obey.

Smiling wide with victory, Venamir backed farther up the *Jacobyte's* ramp where the structure protected him.

Across the prison, armored vehicles from the prison were converging around a bulky, oversized defender ship. Smoke curled upward from one of the old ship's engines.

"Another victory for us," Venamir crowed as the ramp started to close. "Doctor, come along. Stop toying with them." He glanced around at a splash of colors and the sound of small engines approaching from both sides of the building. It was two brightly painted hover-cycles, ridden by the familiar forms of Max and Shocks. The crazy biker gang opened fire.

The dopp standing beside Cruentin staggered and fell out of the ship, crashing through the weakened rooftop below. Venamir reached out to grab him, but he slumped to the deck. Moradin grabbed Cruen and Venamir. She pulled him farther inside, leaving a blood trail.

"Maska," she yelled, "close hatches. Retreat!"

Venamir raised his weapon, snarling, "Who did that? Where is he?"

"Like to say all three of us plugged him," Shocks yelled.

Moradin staggered as a shot hit her leg before the ramp started closing.

The aft ramp slammed shut.

Venamir and Moradin half helped, half dragged Cruentin toward medbay, staggering when the ship shuddered from heavy fire, making a few seconds feel like a long nightmare. Helplessness gripped Venamir as he turned to his fallen medic. "All my abilities, why did I not study medicine?"

Doctor Cruen chuckled through gasps of pain, "Because you… hate people."

Venamir looked around, expression helpless as his voice dropped to a hoarse plea. "Tell me what to do." Coming from a leader who hated following anyone, the desperate words stunned them both.

"You've done what you can. I need a surgeon, a real one. Now."

"He escaped."

"Then put me in stasis... lowest sleep setting." Cruentin said in weak voice as Venamir helped him to the stasis tube. Seeing the controls, his eyes widened. "What were you thinking? Turn these settings down!"

"We used the settings on Nelzyr."

Cruentin collapsed onto the soft cushions inside. "Amazing. The fool survived."

"Our Deeps family can save you," Venamir said with fake certainty. He set the controls to induce deep sleep. He leaned on the tube, reeling from his perfect plan gone wrong. "Moradin, fly to the nearest Deeps hospital."

Amidst all the fighters on their tail, only *Jacobyte's* enhanced stealth mode allowed an escape. Their flight proceeded in sullen, stunned silence. Farther and deeper the *Jacobyte* plunged into the ocean's depths until her lights only illuminated churning sand and murky waters. Venamir sat in the captain's chair with Moradin in the right seat, sharing a silence of deep discomfort.

Moradin said in quiet hope, "The Deeps can fix Cruen. They fixed me."

Chapter 26
Raid Games, Shocks Style

Prison guards regrouped as local forces showed up to fight fires and capture escapees. Although the *Jacobyte* was no longer a threat, many prisoners still were. Hoping for help, prison guards waved and made downward gestures to men and women flying overhead. Shock's gang flew low in the prison yard, helping to herd the prisoners into hastily fashioned cages.

Shocks and his father, Max, landed their brightly painted Huvzters in front of Slade's battle-weary friends. Max chewed on the nub of a cigar for a moment, as if posing with his prized machine, its body almost covered with all moods and styles of cartoon art, matching his own visible tattoos, and familiar leather riding attire.

Wulvur jogged over to meet them, limping a bit, still carrying his longbow. He twisted the top end of the bow. The weapon shrank into a staff half his height, the string vanishing from view.

Shocks slapped Wulvur's shoulder. "You're a good troop. You need some inks."

"Don't wanna blind myself from paint," Wulvur chided back.

"You old bloodhounds." Slade strode over and shook hands with Max, and then Shocks. "I knew you were alive. Of all places, you set up shop on this world?"

"Oh, well," Max replied, "everything went to shit when the high and mighty councils fell apart after Venamir's stinking fish turned against them. When we got disbanded, we took care of our own. High time we started working together again. My boys and I used to run these defense forces." He shifted his weight, "Let's just say hard times hit us." He looked up as more defense fighters soared overhead.

Slade nodded. "You got new troops?"

"Don't need new troops. My old crew dogs stayed on." He popped up the safety on the combat screen secured to his handlebars. Gun turrets and armor deployed all over his ride, while an energy shield hummed around his body. Shocks tapped his old, faded comm. "Wild Paints, we got incoming bogeys trying to pick up escaping prisoners. I know those fighters. They're mercenaries, been doing black market on this world. Bring 'em down."

"Aye, Cap," a scratchy voice replied.

Shocks revved his Earth-built Huvzter. Gun barrels poked out of his armor, making the toon murals look like they were holding cannons. Shocks lifted off, leading a bunch of mismatched fighters and several flying cycles. They flew around the prison, herding escapees and badgering them with gunfire back within prison walls.

A group of small mercenary fighters converged upon the prison. Slade's allies rose to meet them. Chaos erupted in the sky. Zared's ambassador ship, the sleek *Mythos,* flew alongside Vanysa's elegant scout ship, the *Sorsia.* Together, Zared and Vanysa teamed up with Shocks and protected the prison.

Vanysa hailed the approaching group of mismatched fighters. "This is Vanysa of the Scout Fighter *Sorsia*, Ambassador of the Atlean Morpher Councils, allied with my hunter clan friends. I'm sure you remember the Wild Paint Fight Team. We're all veterans of the Rezoan-Amphibian Wars. You won't even survive to go to prison."

Zared added, "This is Zared, Ambassador of Atlean Morpher Councils. If you attack this prison, you'll be helping Venamir start a war. I'll shoot you down with no regrets."

Shocks revved his beloved armored jetrig. "Aw, let's blast them anyway. Most of their parts are stolen. I could use the scrap metal."

The opposing flight leader appeared on their comms, a human with a birdman copilot. "Damn you, Atleans, what're you doing here?" He glared at Shocks. "John? I thought you retired."

"I did," Shocks replied, "until you all started dealing black market in our settlement. You think nobody knows you're selling Atlean goods? Land your fighter, chump."

The human's face reddened as his small, heavily armored fighter hovered over the prison's courtyard. His fighter appeared only large enough for a crew of three, but carried twice the weaponry of a normal prison defense ship. "You had a good spot being lawman and diplomat, Shocks. You quit."

"Look who's talking," Shocks countered. "Listen, Xerat, your local defenses suck. Nobody's protecting our settlements. Fish and lizards come here to recruit followers for Venamir and use our auctions for their own black market. Yeah, I know. We ousted Maska for trading Atlean ship parts and attacking our mayor gal. Now play nice and land your fighter, or we'll blast you to pieces."

Vanysa's stylish scout ship swung around and hovered near Shocks as her image appeared in the cockpit of Shocks' opponent. "Your ship is on the wanted list for smuggling weapons and exotic beasts, and piracy of merchant ships."

Xerat sniggered, glancing at Vanysa's silvery skin and pearlescent eyes. "A fish woman, and I thought Shocks didn't like fish."

"I don't like rats," Shocks replied.

Xerat's avian copilot squawked, pointing to incoming blips on their screen. The avian man still wore prison attire, and both their pilot and copilot looked as weathered as the shabby prison buildings below their shop. Still, the human captain argued, "Vanysa, since when do you pull rank on our world? I need your cooperation to help recover the pit beasts or stay out of my way." His voice faded off. He blinked, shaking his head as memories of Venamir surfaced. He recalled clear images of Maska hiring aquatic people to upgrade his once passenger ship, and relived glimpses of workers turning his ship into a mean, fighting machine. Too late, he realized, Vany was studying his memories. His eyes narrowed, "Why can't you damn psychics stay out of people's heads?"

"I remember you, Xerat." Vany retorted. "You were a decent man before too much power corrupted you. I know who runs the animal sanctuaries, and it's not you. Last warning, land your ship."

"Ladies first," Xerat retorted. "Oh, look, my backup is here." He opened fire, the first shots burning into the shielding on Vany's left wing, inflicting minor damage.

Vanysa, Shocks, and his gang swarmed around the beast-master's ship, riddling its engines before he could get off a few scattered shots.

At first, incoming attackers in their mismatched fighters swerved at the unexpected defense group. Four of the scavenger group abandoned the chase despite cursing and threats from their lead ship. The aerial battle waned. Two of the three fighters attacking the prison had to land or be shot to bits. The third attacking fighter tried to retreat, but Shocks and his gang drove it to the ground.

Shocks flew his Huvzter along Vanysa's stylish scout ship, waved, and hailed her comm. "Hey pretty lady, are we allies now?"

She replied, "We are friends."

"Ooh, I like that," Shocks said, his rough face creaking in a wide grin.

Energized by unexpected allies, surviving prison guards regrouped. They fanned out and helped some of Shocks' gang surround prisoners.

Two black and grey-feathered avians, one skinny, one fat, snuck around a transport truck. Arguing, they pointed toward the *Vernacular*. "That's our ride out of here," Fat Bird squawked. The birds sped the stolen, armored truck toward Scruffy's ship, hopes soaring higher than their brain cell counts. Skinny Bird wrestled the driver for control, turning the truck toward the nearest section of collapsed walls and screeched, "No, they mad at us." Feathery arms flapped about as the truck swerved away from the looming warship. The birds drove over chunks of debris, the sides of the broad vehicle scraping along the ragged sides of a prison wall, its engine puking smoke.

Shocks flew his bright, cartooned cycle over to Slade and gave him thumbs up. "We're good. This was fun. I need your doc to look at a couple of my guys. Nothin' fatal." He flew off, grinning.

Slade jogged back to the *Vernacular*. "Regroup, all hands, regroup on our ships. Gimme a headcount." Everyone reported in, except for his engineer. "Shanto, report," Slade ordered. No reply.

Amidst static, his engineer replied in an odd, satisfied voice. "Shanto here, I'm onboard. Get yourself safe."

* * *

Doc Nelzyr heaved a long, grateful sigh as he walked into the *Vernacular's* medbay. He sat down long enough to let Elowren put a bandage around his head. He set straight to work, looking over the crew with a bio-scanner and trained eyes. Wulvur tried to slip past the medbay, heading for the pantry as if he'd finished another workout at the gym, when Doc Nelzyr intercepted him. "Wulvur, you were fighting Noxus, right?"

Wulvur was rubbing one arm. "Yeah. Is Noxus all cyborg? He hits really hard." He glanced over at Telari, who strode past them, her large feline by her side. "Good shooting, Tel, picking off Cruen and the dopps. I didn't know you were a sniper."

Telari paused, looking a bit nauseous. "I'm not. It's not my style. I'm just a good shot."

"You helped save our people," Doc said, "first kill?"

"It was a torso shot. He's probably alive." Off she went.

Nelzyr shined a light in Wulvur's eyes. "Noxus bragged about slow poisoning everyone." He eyed Wulvur with critical eyes and a furrowed brow. "I want to run blood tests until we're sure he didn't poison you."

"But I know the symptoms," Wulvur started, "and have resistance to it."

Doc thumped him in the chest. "Pup, it's been a rough week. Don't argue with me."

Wulvur huffed like he wanted to argue, but held back. "Sorry." He followed Doc into medbay. "You were on the ship for days with Noxus onboard. Shouldn't we be testing you?"

Doc's face paled a shade. "I didn't even think about that."

* * *

Once the prison appeared under control, Vanysa flew her elegant scout ship away from the prison. She landed on a scarred beach near a cavern with a gaping mouth of stalactite teeth. The crashing waves beckoned to her, but now was no time to enjoy a splash, especially in polluted water. She hailed the *Vernacular* and the *Mythos*. Holograms of Slade and Zared appeared on her console.

"Hello fellas," Vany greeted. "How is everyone?"

"We took some scrapes, but we're good," Slade replied.

"Stop hoarding the crews," Zared joked. "Send Shanto to me."

Slade returned a befuddled look. "We don't have him."

"He's not with me," Vanysa said.

The group was exchanging looks of disbelief as morbid silence gripped them.

"Now it makes sense," the cub said. "Shanto said he was going deep cover. I thought he meant he was going back to the prison."

Motley and his cub's holograms appeared as they padded into the cockpit with Slade. "I bet Shanto is on the *Jacobyte*," Motley said.

Slade groaned, "This isn't happening. How could he bail on us?"

"I know," Zared theorized, "because ever since Venamir pried into Shanto's brain on the space station, Shanto's been on a vengeance kick."

Motley heaved a sigh. "I think Shanto's either mind-controlled or he's gone crazy."

Chapter 27
Planet Crawshen Bird Logic

"Captain's Log: We saved Doc Nelzyr and our Herja, Kestral, and lost Shanto to Venamir's crew. Did Shanto join Venamir's crew, or is he hiding out in the ship? He won't stay hidden for long, not among two rotten psychics." Slade sighed, shaking his head. "We're stuck on the bird world, Crawshen, for at least a day while our ships are repaired. Now, I have to smooth things over with the chickens because my ship raided their prison." Slade shut off his log when Scruffy and his crew entered the ready room.

Old Max Shocks shuffled in, escorting a pair of Hrokah birds. One avian was a reddish birdman with a hawkish beak. The other bird had owl features and a stocky build.

"Okay," Max said, "I brought the chickens."

The birds both turned on Max, their beaks gaping open until the wrinkly human pulled a couple of flasks from his satchel. "Now calm down, birdies. I brought your favorite drink, brewed it myself from blue shroom berries." He handed each of them a flask. "You think I buy all the booze in my bar?"

The Hrokahs quieted as they accepted the flasks, their hands resembling bird feet with shortened claws. Each bird cracked open a flask and sniffed it before taking a sip. If bird beaks could smile, these did for a few moments.

"Ooh, home brew," the hawkish bird admitted. "Most tart."

"Sneaky Shocks," the owl-like bird complimented, "good flavor." He sat down first in an awkward position, taking up the pantry counter, while his hawkish friend preferred to stand.

Vanysa joined them, and Slade called their impromptu council meeting to order. Roll call counted Slade and his crew, with images of Vanysa representing Deeps aquatics, landwalker Morpher Atleans including Atlean Ambassador Cleodna, and Max Shocks as a returning diplomat, representing humans.

"We're authorized to act in lieu of the Morpher Council, for the time being," Slade began. "Most of us here are already council members. We will bring your needs to the Morpher Council."

Avians quickly added a clamor to the already chaotic virtual conference. The bird-people spoke in a broken chittering language, even with translator tech to help them.

The hawkish bird voiced the first complaint. "We want justice. Venamir has attacked our people yet again."

The other bird pointed a feathery hand that was more like a bird's foot at Slade, "Bad enough Venamir began his uprising by murdering our top Ambassadors, and now, that fish demolished our prison, with your ship."

"He is determined to kill our people," the hawk bird hissed, his wing-like arms waving and losing a few small feathers.

"No, it was more equal opportunity this time," Max said. "You have all kinds of aliens working that prison."

"Criminals ran your prison," Cleodna butted in, startling the birds with her gruff candor. "The prison leadership was corrupt as a traveling circus run by lizards. I thought you wanted Doctor Cruentin in your prison, because as rotten as he is, he's more skilled than your doctors. Worse, you're supposed to have more real guards and battle dopps, not stolen animals taken from wildlife shelters."

Telari looked up from her damage report. "Exotic animal thieves! You deserve to be put into armor locked up with criminals!" She glared at the birds' vacant expressions.

"They did?" the owl asked.

"Wow," Tel fumed. "I thought owls were wise."

The hawkish fellow replied, "The pit beast trainer is accepting a plea bargain to help contain the creatures. I should have known that morphers care more about animals than upright beings."

Telari's grip tightened around her work tablet. No one knew she was saving the meeting on her scanning and recording device. "That so-called trainer can't be trusted, either. Let me watch him. Besides, the animals like Wulvur, now."

"I second that idea," Slade said. "Listen, ambassadors, you birds are ambassadors?"

The hawk bird straightened, his dialect better than his companion. "I am now, Ambassador Talen Raaker." He gestured to the owl-eyed bird. "This is Mayor Krizer. We tried assigning Venamir's doctor to a useful role. Doctor Cruentin earned his punishments. He would hypnotize the guards, even with our psy dulling tech. Strong telepath, that one. He nearly broke out, four times."

The owlish bird added, "You Atleans need to control your own people," he squawked, losing another couple of feathers as he flapped his wings. "Reading our minds, destroying our prison, running black market ship goods." His rising voice trailed off when the hawk shot him a startled glare.

This time, old Max leaned forward, muscles still evident beneath his faded tattoos. "Oh, so you know about black market smugglers."

"Parts are parts," Raaker said. "Why should we care where they come from?"

"You birds need to put some of your own in cages," Slade retorted, "like your auction house managers and the two who tried to fly off with our medic."

The birds looked from Slade to each other, their beaks hanging open as they chittered.

"Are you laughing?" Rhoan asked.

"Yes," the owlish bird admitted. "Medics are hard to come by."

"See? I told you the turd birds are scavengers," Max chortled.

"Quiet, painted man," the hawk bird hissed. "High time you returned to flying defense."

"Your crazy flock said you didn't need our help," Max argued. "You're lucky my crew defended your feathery hides."

"Enough bickering," Elowren cut in. "We need to regroup against Venamir. If we don't, Venamir will keep trying to overthrow our councils until he makes the rules. This world, Crawshen, is one of our best allied trading bases." As the birds puffed out their chest feathers in pride, she went on, "We know crime's been up, and good business down, more black market. We're sure that Venamir has been buying parts for Atlean ships."

"You birds need to become watchdogs," Max pointed out. "Stop helping an enemy rebuild his forces. Stick that in your craw."

"Then we need our people to take over the hunt for Venamir," the hawk-bird said.

Most of the others chortled or laughed at that.

Scruffy laughed the loudest. "Are you crazy? Your target's a Merfin, and most birds don't swim."

Slade growled, "We're not standing down. This is *my* hunt."

Berku rose, a wolvish growl in his voice, "We don't have time to pussyfoot around. Venamir's been stirring the ocean sludge all over, not just on Earth. He wants his power back and for that, he needs followers and ships. Anyone with defense forces better get their troops ready for combat."

As the council started arguing again, Slade rested his hand on the comm controls. "That's all the news I have. We're flying to Atlearon in two days. But first, we'll help catch the pit beasts. After all, they should have been there in the first place, and my ship helped set them loose. My crew has agreed that we'll get them back to their rightful sanctuaries."

The bird people eyed Slade, their nearly emotionless faces hard to read. At length, the hawkish bird nodded. "Very good, Consul Slade."

Before the others could start arguing again, Slade turned off the comm, making the Morphers council vanish.

"Thank you," Slade told the avian diplomats as he escorted the birds out. After closing the hatch, Slade returned to the ready room, to find only one person there. Scruffy grumbled as he cleaned the owl-bird's butt-feathers off his pantry. Smirking, Slade continued on. He found his brother working with Wulvur in a makeshift fabrication shop. Wulvur was customizing a rifle with a smaller stock. Berku was modifying the power cells on the weapon.

Telari lifted the stock and held it to her shoulder, nodding to Wulvur. "Better. Can you fashion some claw marks on it?"

"Just for you," Wulvur chuckled.

"What're you all doing?" Slade asked.

Wulvur looked up with a grin. "Telari's such a good shot, we're modifying this rifle for her." He glanced at Tel, who shrugged, smiling a bit. "Instead of a diser, it'll be able to launch a zapper net, shoot stun darts through water, and fire lasers. We're doing some more laser gloves, too. They can also cast a body shield so we don't have to reach for our buckles to power up the shield."

"We have a few nights before we can lift off, right, Tel? Why so long?"

"The *Jacobyte* hits hard. It wasn't even her main guns, but they cracked the plating to number one engine. There're cracks in the drag strut. If we don't fix it, we can't do top speed home. Either way, we'd lose travel time, and new cracks could make the strut fail. I need a few days if repairs go well. That gives us time to catch the beasties."

"I haven't forgotten," Slade said. "I want you and Wulvur to help the beasts' trainer round up as many as you can. You may not get much sleep."

Tel smiled. "You rock. Screw sleep."

As an excited Telari hauled Wulvur out of the room, Slade turned to Berku. "About the prison, your thoughts, brothah."

Berku leaned his rear on the worktable. "Well, I'm glad to have Shocks and his gang back on our side. Oh, there's a message from home."

Berku played a message from a canine humanoid female, who, despite her animalistic appearance, had very human-like speech. She stood in the midst of a dark, derelict cargo hold. "Pack leader, there's been weird activity at the Starships Boneyard, here on Atlearon. My spies have been very leery to call in, say there're fish and lizards claiming to be new hires. We haven't seen the drakir guardians for the past week, and most of our prison guards in the sleeper caves are missing. I'm worried about the baby dragon eggs near the cliffs. If those eggs are harmed, the adult dragons wake up furious. The new workers have been in the *Spectre's* hangar, and the surrounding ships, setting up camp. I don't see why the Morpher Council would allow the old ship to fly again. Somebody is covering up something." She glanced around. "I must go." The image vanished.

Slade queried, "Who would allow work in that hangar? The *Spectre's* a museum piece."

Berku shrugged. "A few months ago, before Venamir's breakout, the council wanted to do repairs on the hangar. Seemed fair enough. After all, the hangar and the ship are centuries old."

"Strange for even Venamir to kill many Atleans," Slade reasoned.

"Did your psy fight with Venamir give you any more clues?"

"Not that I remember. There were glimpses of caves. Maybe he put the guardians to sleep in their own cells? Or he brainwashed or killed them. The old fish has gotten crazier."

"No matter what he did, sounds to me like Venamir wants easy access to the prison, the ships, and the baby dragon eggs."

Slade's thoughtful frown darkened. "Venamir knows about the hatchery. It's near the starship Graveyard. Those baby drakirs are like Earth's dragons, only real. Aquatic people revere those creatures. There must be something more to his plan. I got into Venamir's head, some. He's obsessed with the old *Spectre,* the one we flew in the last war."

Berku scratched the braids in his beard. "The *Spectre* had a lot of restoration. With the right repairs, she could fly again. The drakir watchers have teleport chambers in the underground labyrinth. One, near the surface where the most important ships are docked. If Venamir's goons manage to power up the ship, then the *Spectre* can teleport them, too. Let's suppose Venamir has spies inside our ranks at the Boneyard. Venamir doesn't need to kill those guards. Aquatics are elixir masters. They can manipulate even our people into thinking they're doing the right thing."

Slade rose. "Venamir could take control of that place the same way they infiltrated Earth's space station. Get all the help you can find to fix our ships."

Chapter 28
The Dogs Got Out

Telari and Wulvur returned to Shocks' biker bar that evening. The bar was more lively than usual, for the biker gang was celebrating what might be their last night there in a long time. The human bikers shared pitchers of beer as they argued over who caught the most fleeing convicts, who was the biggest hero saving some hapless, overpowered guards, and who hit the *Jacobyte* the most times. Their new mascot, the young Yeti, listened with a shrewd expression on his beastly face. Already, the creature replied in human common tongue with more clarity.

One man looked way out of place, even without his prison guard uniform. He sipped a beer, keeping his cap pulled down and wearing sunglasses even in a dark booth near the back of the bar. Earfins poked out from beneath his cap. He wore loose, long-sleeved and legged attire, and sandals. His skin was aqua blue.

"The prison's beast trainer is a Merfin?" Telari muttered.

"Yeah," Wulvur nodded. "He was one of Venamir's henchmen during the first aquatic uprising."

Telari stalked over to the Merfin's booth. "You, get up."

The aquatic man peered over his beer. "Why?"

"I'm gonna kick your nuts up between your earfins," Tel growled.

He edged farther back in his seat. Wary, he set the beer aside. "That makes me want to rise?"

Wulvur strolled over beside Telari, watching. "It's only a matter of time," he chuckled.

Telari yanked the table aside, knocking over the nearest chair, and jumped knee first into the man's lap. Grabbing him by the collar, she bounced his head against the wall. "YOU! Animal abuser. How could you take them and make them prison murderers? What the hell is wrong with you? You're gonna help us find every one of those animals."

The Merfin glanced around and saw only bikers waiting for an excuse to clobber him. "OW! Why else would I be here?"

The music and patrons in the bar went silent, all eyes on the woman who'd been so jovial and nice to them the night before.

Telari snarled, "Bullshit. You're no better than dog fighters, and cock fighters."

"Cock? What do you mean?"

Tel snapped, "Shaddap!"

The aquatic man held up his webbed hands. "Crazy woman, it was do it or die. The prison commander wanted them trained to kill, but I trained them to detain prisoners. That's why they didn't attack your friends on sight. Now, get off me."

Wulvur and the bar patrons were laughing. The music came back on. Even the yeti was grinning.

"Woo," Shocks guffawed, "I knew you have biker in ya, Tel."

She flashed him a smirk. "You smell, anyway, slugbait," Tel said, shoving the fish aside and backing off a few steps. She shook a fist at him. "I don't believe you, and I don't care what your story is. Come on, we're gonna find those innocent animals and take them somewhere better."

The Merfin man straightened, rubbing his crotch. "Like where?"

"Away from you. Away from that prison." she fired back.

Wulvur laughed harder as he tugged the riled woman farther away from the brooding aquatic. "Tel, Zared's working on where the pit beasts can go. He's looking for safe places. Some came from exotic sanctuaries. We may even need to take a few to our world. Let's get to work."

Tel muttered, "Zared's awesome." She glanced down as the yeti moved closer and tugged her sleeve.

"I come too," the yeti creature said.

"It's a good idea," the Merfin said. "The animals trust him, and they trust me. And from what I hear, they trust you, Wulvur."

* * *

Wulvur, Telari, and the Merfin called Mushier, sat down with Max and his son, Shocks, outside the Wild Paint shop and biker bar. John Shocks had warmed up to Wulvur, and even more, to Telari, who told foul jokes and appreciated the mythology behind his tattoo art.

Max sat back with a look of skepticism on his weathered face. "I'm surprised Slade agreed to help catch all the pit beasts."

"Why?" Telari asked. "We can't just let the animals get murdered. It's not their fault they ended up guarding the prison."

"The turd bird Hrokas should appreciate the help," Wulvur added, "after Venamir used Slade's ship to demolish the stupid prison. The locals said the closest place that smells of food is the fishing village, and guess what, that's where the animals are gathering."

"Well, count us in," Max nodded. "The whole gang is waiting to help."

"Okay, here's the plan," Shocks said. "We gotta team up to catch the attack beasts from the prison before they all get shot."

"They're not attack beasts," Mushier cut in. "They're guard animals."

Shocks replied, "Yeah, let's hope so. I don't need my leathers or bikes getting chewed up."

Max activated a map off his comm. A lakeside town spread over the table with comical avatars of tiny dogs with big teeth. "Here're the critters. The town is called Shrieking Net. Mostly bird people live there, but there're some humans, and a couple of other species. There's already been some sightings, and the birds get scared fast, so we don't have much time. Last thing we need are hide hunters trying to shoot the animals."

Wulvur finished his beer and set the mug down with a light thump. "Slade's brother will protect the animals from scumbags. Trust me."

"Good." Max went on, "my boys and I have the tracker frequencies on our bikes. We'll fly around and set you down in the area, and Mushy can track the pit beasts on the ground." He smacked the blue-skinned aquatic beside him on the back.

"Mushier, not 'Mushy,' thanks," the aquatic man corrected.

"Whatever," Shocks said with a wry grin. "If you don't wanna become mushy, you'll help. No tricks."

"So you've told me," Mushier grumbled.

"Our trackers show avatars for general species," Shocks went on, "two giant bats, a dozen canines, and one feline."

270

"I want to catch the cat," Telari said.

"Don't you have a big cat, Tel? I thought you'd bring her," Max said.

"Griffa is under the table," Tel replied.

Max laughed until a low growl rumbled from under the table. His gaze panned down to see a furry tail swish against his leg. He leaned way back in the chair as a large, shaggy feline emerged from beneath the table, stretching as she studied them all with silvery eyes. The cat had swirly blue spots of an Atlean wild jungle cat, and stripes on the head, tail, and legs. She was nearly as tall as Telari when she reared up and put daunting paws on the table, extending her claws as she sniffed each of them. Her harness, stealth armor similar to what Telari wore, was self-adjusting, matching the surrounding colors to make the wearer invisible when activated. The feline sat down beside Telari, who stroked her chin.

"That's a big pet," a biker drawled.

"She's more than that," Tel said. "I train exotic Atlean animals. Most of them are like Griffa. She's trained for rescue, not combat. I don't want anything to happen to her."

"To her?" Shocks chuckled. "She oughta scare the pit beasts into their cages. We'll catch the dogs. It'll be fun. Bring the yeti cub, too. We'll need some muscle."

"Great," Max grumbled, "if they don't eat us. They're not dogs. They're pit beasts."

"Aw, they're mutts," Wulvur shrugged. "Most of our crews are gonna help. I think we should go after the cat first. Tel, we may need you to shoot nets on some of them."

Telari patted her newly assembled rifle, which was leaning against the table. "That'll be a good test run. I think the fastest way to gather the animals is a decoy."

Mushier looked around as the group turned, eyeing him like he was a tasty treat. "You won't need me for a decoy," he said, tone sour. "They'll come to me." Seeing skeptical looks, he gestured to a decrepit, faded rig parked across the street. "I have an old prison transport. There's food, traps, and crates inside."

Wulvur leaned forward. "What kind of traps?"

"Harmless traps," Mushier promised.

* * *

Jasko led the work crews of human, avian, and other technicians who worked to repair blackened combat damage on Scruffy and Zared's ships. Bird people who looked like they couldn't fly flapped their way atop the *Vernacular*, while more agile bird people stayed on the ground to work. A number of Shocks' crew also helped prep the ships for flight.

Berku listened to his brother, Slade, who was haggling with a pair of black-feathered avians with streaks of grey around their wing tips. They were the infamous Fat Bird and Skinny Bird from jail.

"Slade, we come to help," Fat Bird squawked. "We of big value here. You want info, we have it."

Skinny Bird chimed in, "Your friends seek the pit beasts, but so do poachers, and cops, good cops, bad cops. You won't find them all in one night, even with trackers."

"We fly around and help find them. We distract the poachers," Fat Bird offered.

"Why?" Slade pressed. "What's the catch?"

The birds paused, glancing at each other. "Humans call it brownie points," Fat Bird said.

"You chasing Venamir," Skinny Bird added. "The whole flock knows."

"They're right," Berku said, walking closer. "One night's not enough. Let me take some of my pack with bird brains here. We don't need anyone else catching them."

"Or shooting them," Slade added. "Let's go."

* * *

Shrieking Net Fishing Villa lived up to its name. When Shocks and his gang followed Mushier to the fishing village, they met Wulvur and Telari near the boat docks.

The pit beasts had taken over the small town. The dog-like creatures were running amok. They were baying, barking, some eating the day's catch, while others bounded through town. Two were playing, which looked like fighting as they chewed off each other's battle armor. Chunks of mangled leather and armor flew aside until the dogs noticed the biker gang and Mushier.

Mushier climbed out of his rig and opened the back gate. He started toward the two dogs, one of whom was chewing on a mangled chest guard. He patted the rig's side window, and called them, "Richtor, drop it. Rumble, come inside. Home."

The dogs eyed the humans, the Atleans, Wulvur and Telari, and then looked back at Mushier. The burlier dog dropped the leather and lowered his head, growling.

"Stop it," Mushier said. "Come on, now. Come."

The other dog yipped, then nipped at the bigger dog. Seeing new targets, the dogs charged toward two avians on the dock. They slowed, glancing back with mild interest when Mushier yelled at them to come back.

The bird people, trying to unload fish from their small boat when the dogs ran past, screeched, their round, shiny eyes wide as they jumped aside. One smart bird flung a large fish at the dogs. It worked for a few seconds. The lead dog grabbed the fish in mid-air, starting a game of keep-away with the other dog. The second bird dropped his slimy fish, slipped on it, and fell over into his friend. As the birds flapped to regain their balance, the dogs charged again, scaring their targets into the water. The birds surfaced seconds later, grabbing onto the side of their boat and screeching curses at the dogs.

Shocks guffawed, "Yeah, they love you, Mushy. I wish I recorded that."

"I got it," came a voice from behind them. It was Slade's brother, Berku, pointing his comm at the retreating dogs. Images replayed over his wrist comm, showing the birds flapping about and tumbling into the water.

Not being water dogs, the pair of pit beasts ran off, knocking over some crates in their wake.

Slade came out of the shadows as if he'd stepped through an invisible portal. "Mushy, are you sure you're their trainer?"

Mushier jumped, startled. "Damned stealth gear. Why are you sneaking around?"

"Because it's fun," Slade grinned.

"So are my Rangers," Berku said. "You won't see them unless they want you to. They're securing the perimeter. All we have to do is round up the animals."

Slade started toward the birds, offering a hand, but the bird people hissed at him as they climbed onto the dock. "Well, it was funny," Slade chuckled.

Shocks laughed, listening as he wrestled on his crash gear, a crotch guard, and helmet with the help of his biker pals. "Don't take out all those traps," he said. "Put some around the outskirts of town. And open up all the meat you brought. Leave some in Mushy's rig, here."

"Let's lead the cat in first," Mushier suggested. "There's a problem, though. The cat won't go into this rig. He's too familiar with it."

"Bad experience, no doubt," Shocks said. "That sucks. Now we need to find a rolling cathouse."

"Story of your life," Max jested. He pointed past the overturned boats to a delivery rig with bright logos of fish jumping into a pan. "Hey, how about that delivery rig? It's big enough."

One of the birds looked over after climbing out of the water. "No, no," he yelled. "Only fish is for sale, not our transport." He helped pull his friend onto the docks. "Get away."

Slade walked up to the bird people as they were shaking off their feathers. "Birdies, we need to commandeer your truck. I'll rent it."

The louder-colored bird with a rather parroty face picked a loud, vile argument with Slade. "Bite my beak, you molty, half-beast. You are taking nothing."

Meanwhile, Shocks and his dad, Max, moved to the passenger door and leaned in, both pointing and grinning at each other.

Slade argued back, just as loud, "You want us to catch those pit beasts or not? I hear they like the taste of chicken." As the birds hissed at him, he went on, "You'll get your truck back. Come on, we're trying to protect your flocking town."

"This here's a boating truck," Max said. "It'll ride the water. Now all we have to do is explain the fish smell to the gals." He jumped in and started the engine. "Follow me."

Shocks chuckled, turning away. "Okay, Pops." He jogged to the back of the truck and slammed the aft doors shut. "Go."

Max peeled out and drove into the water with a mighty splash. The rig bucked at first, but smoothed out and picked up speed as he zoomed across the lake. Shocks jumped on his bright huv-cycle and took off after his dad.

The birds shook their wings in a mighty flip-off toward their vanishing truck, then yelled at everyone within earshot. Ignoring Slade's offer for payment, the birds half ran, half flew, into town.

Slade returned to his friends, shook his head, and grinned.

Mushier heaved a sigh, shaking his head. "Once we catch the feline, I will help catch the others." He gazed upward toward the nearest roofs, where a number of avian people were perched on their rooftops, peering downward and pointing all around. "There they are, those two black and gray birds. They promised to be our eyes in the sky."

"Yeah, we met those two, shady lot," Slade said, tapping his comm. "Hey, Fat Bird, you copy? We're all listening."

Fat Bird's raspy voice came over Slade's comm. "Have someone follow me. I lead them to the bats. Wait." Fat Bird turned to a brightly colored bird on the rooftop. "We here to save you."

The female wore a leafy toga of sorts and rounded on Fat Bird. "Save us? Too late. The prison set the mutts free," she complained. "They mutts came to eat us."

"After prison food, maybe we're more tasty," the male bird beside her commented.

She swatted her mate with her speckled wings. "Not funny."

"Where are the pit beasts?" Fat Bird asked.

The female flapped her arms as she gestured from the boats to the nest-shaped cafes across town. "Everywhere."

The lady bird spoke truth. Dogs were pillaging food in the nearby open market, knocking over garbage containers, and splashing in the central decorative fountain. The dogs Richtor and Rumble ran through the streets, leaped and wagged their tails.

Farther down the block, he saw a merchant trying to wrestle a rug away from a bulky, blue hound that still wore prison armor. After being dragged into the street, the merchant gave up, ran back into his shop, and slammed the door.

Fat Bird flapped back to Shocks and the gang. "Not good. She say birds are scared of being eaten, pit beasts all over town, mostly dog."

"What about the feline?" Tel said. She checked the setting on her rifle. It was set to net her prey. "What's his name? Not Killer, is it?"

"Steely Claws. That's his name," Mushier replied.

"Okay, Mushy Dick. You'll be good bait. Cats eat fish."

Mushier groaned, shaking his head. "Honestly. The abuse I must endure."

Tel slung the rifle over her back and patted her leg, summoning Griffa to her side. "Guys, we're borrowing Mushy."

Wulvur walked off with her, leaning closer, sniffing. "Do I smell catnip?"

"Damn straight," she replied before jogging off with Griffa and Mushier at her heels.

Wulvur grinned, shaking his head. He spoke into his comm, "Shocks, we need that transport, pronto."

Shocks' voice replied, "Yeah, yeah, we'll find something."

Tracking device in hand, the reluctant Merfin walked with Wulvur, Telari, and Griffa through the back alleys of the town. Griffa trotted closer to Tel than usual, sniffing at her. Tel put a hand over her satchel, nudging the cat's nose away. They heard complete chaos—things crashing, humans yelling, birds squawking—all from the escaped prison dogs.

"What kind of animals do you train?" Wulvur said.

"Canine creatures," Mushy replied, glancing about, "not so different from felines."

"So, you trained the cat as if he was a dog," Tel half laughed, half groaned. "They're a totally different species. People do that on Earth all over the place. I expected more out of Atleans."

Mushier glared at her, keeping his fingers away from Griffa's curious reach. "You're Atlean. Why go to Earth?"

276

"Some of us went to school there, and some of us taught there."

The Merfin jested, "Humans have schools?"

Tel and Wulvur glanced at him and laughed.

Mushier smiled, "And you know everything about cats?"

"Dude, we know a lot," Wulvur defended her. "We've worked with other animal trainers for years, and big wild animals, too. Down, deep, they're still dogs and a cat."

"They're not dogs. They're Cziardegs," Mushier grumbled.

"Dogs," Wulvur shrugged.

Musher glanced at his tracker as they walked. "My tracker shows he's nearby, but there's too much interference to pinpoint the animals. Damned birds must have all their alarm systems on. You expect my feline to be in these alleys searching through garbage?"

"No," Tel replied. She pointed upward. "He'll be stalking us, my cat, and what I'm carrying. Does he even like you?"

Mushier looked away. "Of course he does."

The alley widened at a cluster of buildings that formed an open market, which was already a mess from the dogs, and frantic bird people trying to hide or save their wares.

Telari eased a hand into her satchel as they walked. Beside her, Griffa hissed and snarled, her fur hackling as she glanced upward and around. Tel put her free hand on Griffa's collar.

Mushier heard it too. He slowed down. "I think we're getting close to him." He looked at the tracker in his hand again. "He's right up ahead. Wait, he's moving back the way we came. No, he's right here." He pivoted, shaking the tracker.

Telari sighed, rolling her eyes. She pulled a baggie out of her satchel and pulled out a mangled, fuzzy toy covered with green dust and crumbled leaves into her one hand. Suddenly, she smacked the toy against Mushier, and bounced it off him as he backpedaled. Wulvur grabbed Mushier from behind while Tel stuffed the toy into the aquatic's shirt.

Mushier wrestled his way free of their grips. "What are you doing?" He sidestepped as Griffa pushed against him, sniffing him with long whiffs.

"It's only catnip," Tel replied. "So here's the plan. You find a vehicle, climb in, and when the cat comes after you, climb out. We'll lock him inside."

"Just like that?" he replied.

"Wait, there's more." She pulled out another item from her bag, uncorked it, and tossed a smelly oil onto him.

"Stop. What is that smell?"

Tel laughed as she backed away, pointing upward. "Fish oil."

Mushier wiped at it, only smearing the stuff. "You're trying to make me into his dinner."

"No, you're dessert," Tel replied.

Griffa snarled, louder this time, her tail lashing. Telari held onto her collar as Mushier's eyes widened. A low growl came from above. A shadowy form leapt down from a small balcony behind them, landing with muffled thuds of padded feet.

"Ssh," Mushier coaxed, "Steely, calm down, boy."

The cat's head was almost waist level, his fur striped with midnight shades of green and black. The dark alley shrouded his markings, but most of his leathery armor was still visible. His shiny white fangs and silver eyes gleamed in the light cast from a nearby window. He glared at them, even his trainer, as he stalked forward a few steps.

Mushier pointed to the ground beside him. "Steely, calm, come to me."

A giant bat started into the alley from behind Steely, drawing the cat's attention. Steely lunged up the wall, catching a balcony rail. He swatted the bat's feet before it could fly away, shrieking.

Mushier yelled, "Steely, down!"

"He's not listening," Wulvur half sang. "Do I have to hypnotize him?"

"Maybe," Tel muttered.

Steely only came down because the balcony rail collapsed from his savage claws. He landed gracefully, with scraps of crumbling balcony falling around him.

Wulvur whispered into his comm, "Shocks, where's that vehicle? Track Mushy."

Mushier whispered, "You put a tracker on me too? Horrible people." Mushier summoned his courage and stepped forward. "Steely, lay down. Down!"

The cat crouched, his tail lashing as he stared at Telari's cat. Griffa hackled up, hissing. The felines began snarling at each other, hackles fluffed up, fangs bared.

"Griffa, stealth, shh," Telari ordered.

As the cat obeyed, her armor activated, making her seem to vanish against the wall.

"I'm fricking insane," Wulvur grumbled as he stepped in between the two cats. He pounded the wall beside him, crouching to meet Steely's glare. "Here. Hey, you remember me." He tried to psy to Steely, but it was harder this time, for the beast was more riled than at the prison. The large cat was confused, lost, and quite angry.

Mushier ranted in a hushed voice, "You two need to leave. My cat is going to floor the two of you, eat your cat, and then maybe he'll listen to me. Or do you have any better ideas?"

Tel reached into her pocket and pulled out a small spray bottle, then squirted Mushier with it. "Pheremones. There, make love, not war."

Mushier gasped. "He's not fixed."

Tel rounded on him, spraying him again. "Really? You deserve to get humped."

The Merfin took a whiff, as did his pit beast cat. Mushier started backing away as the cat advanced on him, licking his chops. Then Steely halted, his mouth open as he took deep whuffs of his trainer's erotic scent. His rear end wiggling, he uttered a strange, lusty, "Merrowwrr."

Mushier backed away, his voice losing all authority. "No, no!"

Wulvur cracked up laughing as the aquatic backpedaled, tripped, fell, scrambled to his feet, and ran a short distance.

"Shoot the cat. Net him." When Steely hissed and charged forward, Mushier turned and ran.

Telari sighed, leveling her net gun. She fired.

Wulvur busted out laughing.

Mushier tumbled to the ground, struggling as the net ensnared him. "Not me, you crazy wench! Not me! Steely, stay off."

Steely had other plans. The big cat pounced onto Mushier and held his trainer with all four feet. Cat and fish rolled around, Steely licking, nipping, and clawing as his trainer demanded, "Get off. STOP!"

Telari echoed in a scolding tone, "Shoot the cat. I'm not shooting a sweet lil pussy cat."

"Sweet, my ass."

"Oh, you do speak Earth slang," Wulvur chuckled.

Steely cat lay on his side, still wrapped himself around his new toy, growling and gnawing on the net. The aquatic man's language degenerated with each playful nip and kick.

By the time Max arrived in the borrowed delivery truck and Shocks landed his infamous cartoon-painted huv cycle, Steely had settled down a bit. Wulvur was easing the armor off of Steely Claws, while Telari was feeding him strips of meat. The large, blue cat was now laying across Mushier like a police dog holding down a criminal.

Shocks laughed. "Well, I'll be darned, Mushy, you really did teach him how to detain prisoners."

"Shut up," Mushier groaned.

* * *

The rest of the night went with similar havoc, but one by one, and sometimes, two by two, pit beasts were lured into traps or vehicles. Steely Claws got the fish truck all to himself, where he passed the time shredding the storage crates. Finally, he laid down across the front seats, chewing on the biggest fish he found. Onlookers would ease toward the truck, only to run away when Steely hissed at them while mangling his late dinner.

Once Mushier regained his bearings, he remained true to his word and helped round up the rest of the beasts.

Shocks took one look at the aquatic and guffawed at Mushier's appearance. "Damn, Mushy, you were supposed to catch the cat, not make out with him."

The Merfin was a mess of scratches and torn clothing. He glared at the biker's humor at first, then grinned. "I suppose jokes are better than threats."

The bird folk calmed a little when the pit beasts found other targets to heckle. They watched through windows and from rooftops, some placing bets when they spied a hunter or more trappers trying to sneak into town. The would-be poachers didn't get far. When the first couple people raised a firgun or rifle toward the beasts, one of Berkuru's pack members would come out of stealth like a predator animal lunging from the darkness, and disarm the hapless hunter.

Shocks, Mushier, and the bikers were trying to surround the dogs, but instead, the beasts surrounded them, howling and slobbering.

"Come on, poochies," Shocks goaded as he threw some bait toward the nearest animals. He shook the net, yelling, "I got bacon." He grinned wider as a couple of the pit beasts turned and glared at him, one growling, one wagging its rear as it grabbed the food.

"You're crazy, but it's working," Mushier said, now more in his element. "Lure them in."

The yeti stayed close to Shocks. He was holding the other end of the net as the dogs closed in. As soon as a dog snapped at him, the yeti tried to roar, which came out as a childish, screaming sound. Undaunted, he charged at the pit beasts, grabbed two of them, and dragged them by the scruffs toward his biker friends.

Max and his son wrapped the two overgrown canines. They won with the help of their strong yeti mascot, earning only a few scratches. The yeti bounced over and sat on the dogs while his human friends secured the net.

Slade and his brother jogged through the streets near the biggest cluster of dogs. Slade and Berku watched from across the street, chuckling.

"Fat Bird, where's the bats?" Slade yelled.

A few seconds later, two black and grey avians, Fat Bird and Skinny Bird went flapping overhead, with two giant bats close behind them. Skinny Bird was screeching, "Here they are."

Slade chuckled, rubbing his eyes. "Somebody net or tranq' those darn bats."

Telari's voice came over his comm, "Okay, my team will save the turd birds."

Most of Slade's nearby allies showed up to help. Vanysa flew her pristine scout ship in so Elowren and Zared could wrangle creatures into the cargo bay of the *Sorsia*. Scruffy and Rhoan landed in midtown in a Zephyr, where they used their telepathy to help calm the animals.

* * *

Dawn approached fast on a weary town when Mushier took a head count on all the beasts scattered amongst a handful of demolished vehicles, animal crates, his own prison rig, and a food delivery truck. All the pit beast chasers congregated in the town square—Mushier, Slade's friends, Shocks and his biker gang, the yeti, and Griffa the Atlean hybrid cat.

The townspeople emerged from their homes, still disgruntled as they chattered and argued amongst themselves. Some of them gave the group happy waves and words of thanks, but emotions clashed as other townspeople, human, birds, and even a few feline humanoids, looked over damage to their shops and landscape.

Zared and Elowren were trying to calm the agitated townsfolk. Even Fat Bird and Skinny bird stayed to help, and tried to rummage up new customers as they bartered for trade goods.

"I can't believe it," Mushier said as he leaned on his rig's hood. "We caught all the dogs."

"Oh, you're calling them dogs, now," Wulvur chided.

For the first time since meeting him, the beast trainer laughed. "I thank you all. I am glad to see them all alive."

"Now, we need to chat," came Slade's voice.

Slade and Zared walked over, joining the group and making Mushier's smile fade.

"Mushier, tell me something," Zared requested, "I know your crimes weren't enough to be in this prison. You were in jail with Cruentin. You worked for Venamir before the uprising against our councils."

The Merfin shifted his weight. "I don't know much. Cruen kept to himself except when he needed help with something. Venamir blackmailed my family to make me keep quiet."

Slade wasn't impressed. "Tell us what you know about Doctor Cruentin and Venamir. Someone busted him out of prison. Cruen had to know how Venamir escaped. You and Cruen were in the same prison. For all I know, you helped bust Venamir out."

"No I didn't," Mushier countered. "I want him in prison."

Slade closed in on Mushier. "HOW did Venamir escape?"

When their reluctant ally hesitated, Zared also stepped in with a menacing glare. "Stop holding out. You know. Why didn't you escape the prison with Venamir?"

"I'd rather be with the pit beasts," came the uneasy response. Surrounded by looks of disbelief, he went on, "It's true. He's not exactly benevolent."

Zared kept a reasoning tone, "You want a plea bargain and protection, right? We need each other's help. You're our best insider in the prison. You worked with Cruentin and Venamir years ago. Cruentin was in the same prison as you, and he was supposed to help their medical team. There were only four Merfins on record in the prison right now. Surely, you spoke to each other."

Mushier's expression drooped from defensive to worried. "You did your homework. Cruen was lead medic for a while, until he mind-controlled some of the medics, and the guards. That's why he ended up in a cell."

"Tell us what you know," Zared replied. "What is Cruen planning? How did Venamir escape? What does Venamir want?"

Slade waved Zared off. "I say we turn you over to the bird councils. Venamir killed their top diplomats. If the birds think you're working for the rotten fish, you'll be working in the sewers."

"All right." Mushier pearlescent eyes darkened. "There's a morpher traitor within the councils, likely, more than one. Someone from within planned the breakout."

Slade set his comm to record mode. "Go on."

Mushier heaved a sigh. "Venamir's top three, Noxus, Maska, and Moradin teamed up with a Merfin. As you know, we aquatics can reach the deepest underwater gates, often without detection. My people are trusted to make repairs. Whoever helped bust out Venamir knew how to disarm security and use the teleportal chambers to escape. I presume that everyone was left alive, because the body count detectors would have alerted the Morpher Council of fatalities."

Scruffy joined the interrogation. "Yeah but we're talking about the Deep Sleep Caves. How'd they compensate for a head count? Unauthorized entry should have triggered the alarms. The guards and the councils would have been alerted."

"I don't know how they overrode the alarms," Mushier replied. He glanced at several skeptical expressions. "Honest. I believe that whoever helped them was a strong telepath, strong enough to control or sway the right number of guards into leaving at the right time. Any diplomats in the morpher council are strong enough to hypnotize people. Maybe some guards were corrupt. All I know, is they had a way in, and a clone was left in Venamir's place."

"What kind of clone?" Slade asked.

"Most likely an cyborg." Mushier replied. "Cruen bragged about making clones good enough to fool even Atleans. The only problem is if he rushes the process, they are less smart and don't look like perfect twins."

"Only Venamir clones?" Slade asked. "We saw others."

Mushier smirked, "Clones of his top henchmen, of himself, and of Venamir. He probably made some others to replace people within the sleep prison, and the neighboring areas."

"Areas like the drakir nursery, and the Starship Graveyard," Zared said with sudden concern.

Mushier nodded. "Yes."

"We fought a bunch of Moradin clones at Orion Space Station," Scruffy recalled.

"And the spaceport," Slade added. "Were the clones all living? Cyborgs? Dopps?"

Mushier paused, his expression thoughtful. "Dopps, far as I know. Cruen was going to make hundreds, but only made a few crews worth. He made clones and hired Merfins to pose as Venamir. He was short of time. The council's spies were getting wise. Cruen said the clones were hidden away and ready for Venamir's return. The newest clones aren't as good, because he had less time to let their programming evolve. They don't all look identical, but they can still fool most people."

284

"So they're not alive," Slade said. "The person in the sleep chamber has to be alive to not alert anyone. Venamir was on the loose weeks before anyone caught on."

Zared speculated, "Venamir's imposter might have been a morpher, or had a smart mask, or had something alive with it."

"That makes sense," Mushier said. "Cruen had a Mutarian Caller for a pet before landing in prison. They're powerful telepaths."

Shocks, who had been listening, chuckled. "They look like little bitty mermaids."

Slade scowled at the last scrap of information. "Teeny, flying, mermaids who can stop a telepath's abilities. They can hypnotize and bite the hell out of you. Venamir had a female Mutarian Caller on my ship. I bet she helped him get past all the Atleans on the space station." Slade and some of his psychic friends looked a tad embarrassed. "Most of them can't fly."

Mushier sighed, "Rumor has it the Deeps have enhanced the mutirian callers. Venamir's followers have, anyway."

"We need a safe place for you, Mushier," Slade mused.

"For now, the animals need their trainer," Shocks said. "Tell you what, Mushy, I know people in high places and low places. You play nice and help get the critters back into the refuges where they should be, and some of my gang's friends will help keep you alive."

The Merfin stared at the human biker, surprised, waiting for a punch line. When none came, he nodded. "You have my gratitude. I need a favor. The cat and one of the razor hounds came from Mythic Sanctuary on Atlean. They should go back to the sanctuary, together. They're bonded."

"Yay!" Telari piped, turning to Scruffy. "So we can take them?"

Scruffy rolled his eyes. "Great." He saw only stares of peer pressure around him. "Okay. Fine! But they are not getting the run of my ship."

Slade turned and looked upward, to where hawkish avians flew over the rooftops. The birds landed in the town square. They carried themselves with poise, authority, and tempered calmness.

"Here come the Council's buzzards," Shocks remarked.

"This night's gonna be expensive," Slade grumbled. "I hope your dad has more of that berry booze the birds like so much."

The council birds landed nearby and eyed them, chittering among themselves. The hawk patrol approached, walking past a small fire that the avians had built to burn a pile of mangled debris. In the fire's shifting light, they looked quite regal, with their shining plumes of bright blue, and light garb that offered body protection and full dexterity. Their heights ranged from four to seven feet tall.

Scruffy, Zared, and Elowren flanked Slade, along with Max and his son, Shocks.

"I remember the hawk guy," Slade muttered to his friends. "The lead bird's Shorewind. He used to show up at council meetings."

"Reasonable?" Zared asked.

Slade did a so-so gesture.

"Slade, the infamous wolfman," the lead bird said as they halted within wing's reach. His tone was analytical and even. "First, your stolen ship levels the best prison we have, and then, their pit beasts try to eat my people."

"I'd hate to see your worst prison," Slade replied, "with even more corruption." Folding his arms, Slade went on, "Admit it, Shorzy, you had infiltrators inside the walls. Did you even know they were using animals instead of people and battle dopps? Did they sell the dopps off?"

Scruffy smirked at Slade's typical style of defiance as he walked over to join the power circle. "He's right," Scruffy said. "The prison raid uncovered a lot of issues."

The hawkish birds, five of them, muttered amongst themselves in their own language until Slade interrupted them, in the same language.

"Damn, you speak Hrokah," Shorewind said.

"Yeah, I speak bird," Slade confirmed. "How about all the smuggling? There's Atlean ship parts being sold black-market in your auction houses while the town's square holds cage fights. A lot of shops closed up. Things are falling apart here."

One bird confessed, "The prison's use of blackmarket smuggling is a struggle. However, sales of Atlean goods have risen." Shorewind's admission and calmness settled the other birds. "I expected you to fly away and leave us to clean up after the battle, and yet, your people stayed to help. Then, you all saved the creatures, and our townspeople. We are surprised, and thankful."

Mushier had been leaning against his transport, but he straightened and strode up to Shorewind. "These creatures were taken from their homes and sanctuaries. I never trained them to murder people. They deserve to return to their prior homes or habitats, where it's safe."

Slade glanced at his friends. "We agree with Mushy. We helped the animals so they could have better lives."

Mushier nodded at Slade. "Thank you. I, uh, must admit, that I was a spy for the birds, not a prisoner. Much of my official prison record was fake."

"Now you tell us," Slade commented dryly.

"Shorewind, invite your ambassadors to Atlearon," Zared said, "if only for a visit. Our Council needs your voice, for the good of both our worlds."

The hawkish birds, like most avians, held only vague emotions on their faces. At length, the leader nodded. "You have our allegiance, for now. Since you are dedicated to stopping our old enemy, Venamir, we will see it done. Mushier, will you return to your job as beast caretaker at the refuge?"

The Merfin smiled in surprise. "The wildlife sanctuary? Yes!"

Chapter 29
Home Sweet Morpher Home

Slade and his crews were glad to leave the bird world behind and continue home. Berku flew *Vernacular* when Scruffy needed a break. The bulky, war-seasoned ship responded to his command like a race-ship, even after taking battle damage. Still, he missed the *Jacobyte*. He nudged Rhoan, who sat right-seat, browsing through Atlean tourist traps. "We're close. See if you can wake up the Controllers."

"Sure, Berku," Rhoan nodded, stretching.

After Rhoan made the call, they fell quiet as the Atlean planet swelled on their long-range screen, her colors gaining depth to show vivid blue oceans surrounding continents and multiple islands, all swept over by streams of wispy clouds.

"The border patrol's all yours," Berku said.

Rhoan tapped the comm. "Starship *Vernacular* here, requesting permission to land planet side. We need the Moonpaws Spaceport near Shamon Forest."

Within a minute, a uniformed Atlean appeared on their console. "Greetings, keep your convoy in orbit until approved inbound."

As the controller kept asking questions, Telari walked into the aft section of the cockpit and picked up the captain's Maintenance Log. The Logbook data splayed across the nearest wall. Their space travel from Earth had consumed much of their immediate resources. Over three weeks, their ship passed through three hyper-jumps and a wormhole, plus endured some asteroid field damage. She took a few notes, pocketed her digital book, and entered the cockpit. Overhearing the stubborn controller, Telari joined Slade and Scruffy by the pantry, bantering over the simple task of making coffee. "Guys, we need you," Tel said.

Slade was saying, "He wanted it black, Scruffy."

"My concoctions never fail, just like my goo, and speaking of which," Scruffy popped a coffee bean into his mouth, "I need to restock. My plants are hungry."

"We will," Slade assured. "Quit eating those. You're too hyper already."

Smirking, Telari moved in between them. "Scruffy, they need you in the cockpit."

Scruffy stomped into the cockpit and relieved Berku. He smiled at the grumpy holographic man and spread his arms. "I'm Doctor Scruffius. The *Vernacular's* my ship. Let us land."

The controller waited for his scans to complete before nodding to someone behind him. "Thank you for the visual, Doctor Scrufius. I'll transfer you to the local controllers. It's nearly nightfall."

"Thank you," Scruffy said, settling into the pilot's chair. "Wait." He whispered to Rhoan. "Do something for me. Make them dim the lights. The landing lights play havoc on my eyes." Wearing a heartrending, cockeyed frown, the old geezer watched his young protégé shift in the copilot's seat.

Rhoan's eyebrows lowered. "Are you serious?"

"Do it for the old man." Scruffy locked Rhoan with his best puppy dog stare. When it didn't work, he threw up his hands and blurted, "We'll see how you fare after centuries of space dust and firefights. Here we are landing at night and I won't get much sleep, makes my nuts hurt."

"Okay, okay." Rhoan waved him off, "just for you."

Scruffy thumped Rhoan's shoulder. "Take us in, kid. I need a nap." He leaned back in comfort and turned on the ship-wide speakers behind Rhoan's back.

Rhoan snuck Scruffy a suspicious look. "Hold on, Control. Would you order the landing platform lights turned down? Just for this ship."

"Our marker lights?" the controller echoed. "You think we have nothing else to do? Should I turn down the moon as well? It's bright tonight."

"Just turn down the landing lights," Rhoan pressed. "Be a sport, man." He gestured to Scruffy. "Respect your elders. He's really old."

"Hey," Scruffy objected.

"As you wish," came the weary reply.

Slade and Berku turned away, restraining snickers as Rhoan's conversation carried throughout the ship. Rhoan heard laughter from his friends and the controller's cohorts.

The controller chuckled, "We believe you're you, Doctor Scrufius. Nobody else asks for that. Keep your convoy in formation, weapons off, shields up for reentry. Escorts will meet you."

Scruffy laughed, "I can't believe you fell for that."

Rhoan groaned. "Wow, man, so lame."

Rhoan forgot about Scruffy's antics when he observed the world of Atlearon. It was so much like Earth, but with more aqua in the sky. Landing in twilight, he glimpsed vast towering forests, even taller structures resembling lighthouses poking through the trees, and occasional rooftops. Lights dotted the landscape, from bridges and waterways, cities, and towns.

Scruffy wore a heartfelt smile. "Ah, good ol' Atlearon, I can smell the forest already." He waved at Slade. "The controllers are paranoid. They think my cockpit was infiltrated."

Slade frowned, "Yes, they should be suspicious. Venamir stole one ship already."

* * *

The *Vernacular* led the way over Moonpaws Spaceport, followed by the *Mythos,* three cargo ships making up Slade's caravan, and a patchwork ship with a fat cargo belly and scout-fighter ship flown by Shocks and the painted biker gang.

Telari lured their extra mascots, the great silvery cat and the pit beast dog back into their oversized crates with a meal of fish and her last stash of freshly thawed meat. After securing them, she turned to admire their pet lodging. Storage room two looked like a wildlife habitat, with large, makeshift pet beds, crates of goods stacked to form stairways and perches, and half-chewed toys she'd bought from the Hrokah auction. She activated her comm. "Telari's personal pet log. We're back on Atlearon. I hope I can visit these guys. Zared has arranged for my cat Griffa to stay at the Morpher Temple with us, and the overgrown dog and Steely the gray tiger to the exotic rescue. I plan to integrate her with the search and rescue pack. Maybe the other two as well. Zared rocks!" She looked at an incoming call. "The animal peeps are here. I'd best get these furry guys to their transports."

Early nightfall settled in by the time everyone had disembarked. Maintenance techs from all crews teamed up to "put the ships to bed" for the night.

Slade gathered everyone together beside Scruffy's ship. "Welcome to Atlearon. Most of us have been here before. The hunt for Venamir is more complicated here. He has more contacts here than he did on Earth. We're on a world where many people have morphing or psychic ability. Enjoy your stay. Just keep your wits about you."

Chapter 30
Morpher Council Chambers

Morpher headquarters stood several stories above the center of town. It was one of the most ancient buildings in the city, with weather worn statues of creatures from land and sea around its base. Equally, old trees shaded much of the building. Fat vines that stopped near the balconies climbed tall pillars reinforcing the walls. Bricks along the entrances glowed as dusk cast foliage-shaped shadows across the many stone paths. Bird songs carried over the breeze, while a young couple watched their dozen wooly ewes graze on high grass and foliage.

The surrounding guards appeared casual enough, a few trading jokes, and civilians went about their business. Atleans, some from Merfin descent, some land-walker hybrids with furred morphers, and two humans milled about the High Council chambers. Their pristine attire of suits and sheer sashes elevated their demeanor as they waited in their tall, spacious chamber. It was in a Romanesque styled section of their city's grand hall, decorated by historians who used timelines their people valued. This wall of artwork depicted evolution, wars, and burial grounds, a warning to not repeat past mistakes.

Elowren and Cleodna returned to the council headquarters, reaching the council chambers first. Inside, they noticed more guards, some new. They exchanged pleasantries with other council members, who were giving a tour to a blue-skinned Merfin. Cleodna gave the blue Merfin a shrewd look as he walked away with his escorts.

"I've got your back," Elowren whispered. She moved off, removing her long cloak.

Cleodna walked out of earshot, ending up beside the entry hall filled with historical murals. "Scruffy, I'm here," she whispered. "Everything feels like it did before." She stared at a long, faded mural depicting the humanoids of Atlean at war. "Everyone's on edge, watching for infiltrators, like before the last uprising. Keep listening. Here they come." She cancelled the hologram and went to meet her visitors.

Vanysa and her bodyguard Faron strode past the sentries by the door. "Cleodna, I expected to find you here," Vany said.

Cleodna turned with equal seriousness. "Any luck with the Deeps emisaries?"

"I was trying to meet with the Deeps last night, but they never showed up," Vany replied.

"Emissaries are already here," Cleodna replied. "I saw them as we came in. Have you located Venamir?"

"We've been trying to," Vanysa replied evenly.

"Under protest," Faron grumbled.

Elowren burst in through the doors. "You can't find Venamir because he stopped following us, and you won't find Slade because he's rounding up allies." Her attire brought stares, for few of the elites had seen her wearing combat gear, body armor, a firgun on each hip, and boot daggers.

Vanysa and Faron turned, their faces switching between guilt and confusion. They found themselves the center of attention as other council members approached, including two Merfin elders.

"Lady," said the blue-skinned Merfin, his scales faded with age, "you came alone?"

Elowren strode in. "I've been doing some homework on the journey home from Earth. You, Ambassador, have overloaded yourself with power. You alone control visitation to the drakir hatchery and the prison. I should have seen it sooner. You were supposed to pose as our magistrate while the real one traveled to Earth with us. How did Venamir find out that magistrate Parleigh traveled to Earth with us? Venamir impersonated Parleigh at the grand opening of Earth's space station. Venamir created enough threat to send our real magistrate into hiding. Word of Parleigh's true location must have leaked from here, from corrupt members within our own Morpher's Council!"

"I don't know how Venamir knew! I impersonated the magistrate as ordered, even though the idea of allying with humans is crazy." The blue Merfin's egotistical tone faltered when he looked past Elowren.

Berku and five of his Ranger pack entered and flanked Elowren, blocking the front way out. They were in beastman form, long-muzzled, teeth bared, fur protruding from around their lightweight stealth armor, and paw-like hands resting on weapons.

"Oh, so you do share Venamir's beliefs," Elowren taunted.

"I didn't say that," the Merfin said. He pointed at Berku's group. "What is the meaning of this? Last time a council member barged in with an entourage, it was Venamir, and he started a riot that led to his downfall."

"Ambassador, we can do this the easy way or the hard way," Elowren said in her coy voice, strolling around him. "I need to pick your brain. As the new High Inquisitor, with the safety of our Council in mind, I have that right." She patted his arm and smiled. "We've already found one defected council member."

The other Deeps, a wiry fellow with striped aqua skin, shook his webbed fists. "We should have known your shaggy pack was plotting against us."

"Ever heard of the teapot and the kettle?" Berku asked, just to see the blank look he expected. "I locked down this building. It's inquisition time."

The sentries, Ateleans whose armor was bulked up by muscles, stepped inside and closed the doors. They exchanged nods with a few of the beastmen, who, also armed and protected by Gus's riot gear, spread out to block the exits. Grizzly features appeared even more menacing in daylight than their infamous silhouettes. Few people ever saw them in full morph—menacing teeth, fur with stripes and spots of earth and night colors, perfect for stalking prey in the deep woods, and various shapes of battle nicked ears.

The blue Merfin pivoted, his gills fluttering against a nervous sweat. They looked like wolves to him, these beastmen. He didn't like their shedding fur, or that musky scent, or that skeptical leer on Cleodna's face. "Coveness?"

Cleodna responded, "Elowren does outrank you. Sit, or must we use the medical chair? I'm beginning to think you are Venamir's ringleader within our councils.

The Merfin stiffened, his shining, black eyes narrowing at her. "No further threats needed. His Lordship Venamir would be most happy to see Slade fall; however, his lady friend will do." He lunged at Elowren.

Elowren spun aside, elbowing him in the head on his way past. Five of the nearest beastmen pounced on him, grappling with bared claws as they slammed him to the floor in a fit of snarls, almost drowning out the fool's cries for help.

"Raging bloods, don't kill him," Elowren exclaimed as she grabbed one bodyguard by the tail and the other by the scruff of his neck. She stepped in between the beastmen who parted for her, all toothy grins and wagging tails.

The Deeps Merfin stayed down, sniffing through a bloody nose and holding his webbed hands up. "Savages!"

Elowren straddled, then knelt to a seat on the fallen man's belly. "Let's begin, shall we?" She slapped her hand on her prey's forehead and tunneled through his crumbling psy defenses.

She swam through panicked swarms of imagery, bits of memories, voices, and the blackest of ocean waters with glowing kelp tugging at her legs with desperate jerks to pull her into the deepest abyss. Elowren took a deep breath as she willed her lungs to accept the water, forming gills. She changed into the form of a silver dragon, using her wings to swim against the water's gusts. She uttered one screeching cry, releasing flaming gas at the writhing vines, rendering those around her to ash. The watery illusion faded to a vision of the prison cavern lined with hibernation tubes. Elowren felt the world around her tremble as a rumbling commenced from above. Venamir's tube had someone inside, quite awake and struggling to open the release. Humanoids of various species lay on the floor, all bearing marks of severe combat. She heard Venamir's laughter and a glimpse of him leaving with other Merfins wearing battle gear. Her view of Venamir escaping faded, replaced by the meeting hall.

Elowren jolted back into the conscious world. At the first glance of the Merfin smirking, Elowren knocked him out.

"My lady," came the gruff, yet softened voice of Berku. He tugged her to her feet and off the unconscious man. "What happened?"

"Venamir's followers, lizards, demi-humans, fish, they're banding together. Our informant spoke a milder truth. They put our Watchers into deep sleep, those they didn't kill replaced Venamir with a clone and caved in the entrance to Venamir's cell. That's why it took time to prove the prisoner in deep sleep was a clone instead of the real Venamir. He had to be dug out of chamber." Furious, she pointed at the Deeps. "Arrest him! And detain his intern. They need further interrogation."

Chapter 31
Scavenged Crew

Venamir strode through the *Jacobyte*, his strides long, springy with pent up energy. He yelled, voice seething with passion, rather than bother with the ship's comm, "Attention crew! Arm yourselves and stand ready. We are almost home. Noxus, your vacation is over. Get up."

Thiun ran to catch up. "Captain. You promised to let me rejoin my people."

Venamir waved his drafted medic off with a snort. "Am I released from your paranoid care?"

"Yes. You are. Now let me off at the next docking station."

Venamir spun with a radiant laugh. "Are you mad? You will be the medic of the century." Imitating an overzealous announcer, he proclaimed, "Scavenging medic from the underworld black market receives highest position among elites of the Deeps as they rise to the sunlight world to claim rights of their heritage so long denied. I must thank you. I am *better* than before. You will help me retain this energy level, yes?" He squeezed the medic's shoulders with a powerful grip. "You would turn down a powerful life after living as a scavenger? How long did you waste your talents on ingrates and fugitives?"

"Well, since you put it that way," Thiun muttered.

"I need your expertise." Venamir lowered his voice. "I am losing trust in Noxus. I want each of us to carry an antidote. Make sure we have three doses each." He drew a vial filled with murky liquid. "This is the poison that Noxus carries."

Thiun accepted the vial with a solemn frown. "I'll have the serums by tomorrow evening."

"How are your efforts to crack the Herja program?"

"I'm close. Something's strange. The Herja program has been different since before the raid. It's even more intelligent, as if being run by a person. Captain, there is another problem. It's the beast trainer at the prison. When you rescued Dr. Cru from prison, I expected Mushier to join us since he worked with you in the past."

"We don't need Mushier," Venamir stated.

"Mushier was skeptical about your uprising, and still is. The prison often hired me to make elixirs and tranquilizers. I kept in contact with your doctor, Cruentin, and the trainer, Mushier. They both know how you broke out of prison. If Mushier talks, he'll lead Slade straight to your old sleep prison, and the Starship Graveyard. He'll lead Slade to the *Spectre,* your old ship."

Venamir laughed so hard that Thiun stared at him, puzzled. "Then Mushier filled his purpose. Of course, I want Slade to find the *Spectre.*"

* * *

The *Jacobyte* flew on with Moradin at the helm, and a stewing Noxus in right seat. At first, neither spoke to each other except when duty required.

"You look worried, little Moradin," Noxus commented, his tone oozing with venom. "Afraid I'll kill that Druwen Ranger, Wulvur?"

"There're tons of bounty hunters after us, morphers, birds, lizards, humans."

"You know, I mean Wulvur. I saw you at the prison, didn't even try to kill him. Well, after I slice him up, you won't be able to lust after him anymore."

"What do *you* know?" Moradin countered. "You never had a lust partner except carcasses, so shut your hole."

"Did I strike a nerve?"

"You're really dying to kill something, aren't you? Haven't in a few days, and what did you kill? Slow poisoned a bunch of animals."

"No, just some guards and that nasty horned thing. Shooting it wasn't enough. It didn't know when to die."

"You poisoned it. That wasn't an animal," Moradin hissed. "They have their own language."

"Oh, really? It should have begged for mercy, then."

Moradin's body tightened up, but she forced her expression to remain calm. "I know, you can kill two things. Go beat yourself half to death, twice, I mean one half for your fleshy body, and one half for your robot parts." Moradin's heart pounded with anger, her face hot as hatred boiled inside her. "Wulvur's better than you ever were. He'll dismantle you."

Venamir joined them in the cockpit. "Enough. Noxus, go help with repairs. Moradin, take over tactical."

Moradin obeyed, changing seats. Noxus stormed off, not seeing Moradin's finger waving goodbye.

Venamir took over the captain's chair and tapped a few controls. "Captain's Log. Alchemist Thiun deserves a place on my next crew. My senses feel sharper now from his elixirs. Images and thoughts plucked from this measly crew are crisp and vivid for minds so inferior to mine. The Deeps are doing well healing Doctor Cru. I only wonder, where is Maska? The weasel has become more paranoid than usual. Now I must find him, and the Herja. My new alchemist Thiun feels he can finish hacking the Herja program. I hope his skills at cracking code equal his talents in alchemy. I need to keep Thiun onboard to maintain my enhanced reptilian form at its best. End Captain's log."

* * *

Shanto lay stretched out on a makeshift bed of flak jackets and padding. Sleep teased him as it would a hunted animal, always on the run, cornered, and determined to die a predator instead of a grazer. He'd dozed long enough for four repair med-bots to work on his arm. They numbed the injury and sucked the pain away, letting his exhausted body sleep. Even through dreams, he felt the ship sway and jolt, luring him awake. Groggy, wincing, he sat up and checked his arm. *Better, but still a mess, and now the little med-bots had to recharge.*

Shanto wrapped the arm again and made his way to the computer by the hibernation tubes. One dead, or near-death Herja in cryo-stasis, and one comatose sleazebag, both accounted for. *Now what's going on?* His eyes widened at the navigation readings. "We're landing?"

He hastened over to the weapons rack, mind in a whirl as he eased a rifle over his back. *Maybe I should make a break for it. What chance do I have? If Venamir gets those main guns working, I may as well jump in the blood of my crew. No, can't give up now.* All of a sudden, the ship's momentum slowed, winds howling around landing gear doors as they swung open. *Why are we landing?*

The lights went dark, came on again, fell dark once more, and then began shuddering, pops and power surges of systems resetting all over the ship. He backed against the wall and tripped, landing on his lumpy bedding.

Shanto climbed to his feet and moved to the computer. "Shanto's log, day um, three? Power's surging bad, can't see the nav charts. I felt the ship land. Venamir's trying to hack the guardian Herja program, or someone is. Even if they catch me, I've set traps in the programs. Even if Venamir gains control of the main guns, he'll lose control of the ship." His voice cut short when he heard a hiss of air from the hibernation tube. He snapped his firgun toward the tube and waited for Maska to emerge.

Maska's hibertube lid creaked open, more, more, and a trembling hand reached out to push it farther, groping for freedom.

More lights on and off, and distinct sounds of doors sliding open and slamming shut. *It's happening, the same resets Venamir did when he stole this bird. No, no, ship, don't do it.*

Shanto saw the computer finally reboot. Reaching over with his aching arm, Shanto slapped his preprogrammed, "Send All," and "Activate."

The computer replied, "Log files sent. Data destruction in process. Virus engaged."

Finally, Maska's ugly head eased upward into view.

Shanto tried to squeeze the trigger but feeling drained out of his hand, the rigid sensation traveling through his body, freezing him in place.

Maska turned and looked at him, shaking from exertion and injuries, but his canines bared.

Shanto cursed, trying to keep his psy shields up as Venamir's commands dominated his body movements. The last of the inner hatches swung open under full override controls, leaving Shanto standing in a beam of light cast from the joining medbay.

Venamir sang out, "Oh, there you are, Chief Engineer Shanto."

Shanto's hand went numb. His weapon clattered to the floor. He glowered at Maska, who wore a menacing grin on that ugly mug, but Maska paled as a threat now. Shanto held his ground as Venamir entered the room. Maska glanced from one to the other.

Venamir took in the scene, wearing a subtle, yet satisfied smirk.

Shanto kept his cool. "Captain I'm here to report a stowaway."

Venamir chortled. "Do tell. You mean the Herja. Where is she?"

"No, just me," Shanto lied straight-faced. "I returned because I'm still your spy."

Chapter 32
Bear It All

Twilight crept upon the old-growth forests surrounding a temple crowned with faded blue roofing, her top two levels protruding through the treetops.

Slade pulled Zared aside for a chat after they landed. "I need you to stay with our ship. Soon as we're all stocked up and rearmed, we hightail it out of here, stealth if need be."

"We'll be ready. Watch out for wild animals."

"We are wild animals," Slade said with a warped grin. He summoned his crew, mind by mind, his psy words clear with little echoes of his now infamous flashbacks, telling them which ones to stay or come along. "Tel, Rhoan, Wulvur, Gus... meet me at Scruffy's transport. Scruffy, you're driving."

Scruffy pulled up in his terrain vehicle. "Welcome to my Luvhuv."

"It's a risqué name for you," Telari commented.

Scruffy rolled his eyes. "The Luvhuv means my huvster loves every terrain. She handles air, mud, water, and streets, and snow, and she has stealth mode."

Tel smirked. "Yeah, whatever you say."

As soon as they climbed in, he took the back roads into the nearest woods. Gusty winds howled and rocked their vehicle until the forest density blocked out the wind, starlight, and all traces of civilization. They passed through sparse trees and thick wild grasses, impeding the road with looming branches and teasing overgrowth. Scruffy navigated around fresh pockets of water. Seeing a flooded clearing, he drove across it. The vehicle skipped a few times at first, then settled and plunged through like a boat, bouncing over hidden roots. They sped up onto the next stretch of road, laughing as he took her out of hover mode, and all-terrain treads grabbed the road.

Slade commented, "She glides along like a rabid bat."

"Yeah, yeah." Scruffy slowed at a particularly dense area with no signs of a road. Tel peered around at the ever darkening, thick forest. Trees had swallowed them, their canopy blocking out moonlight. The forest encroached from all around, thick-trunked, old-growth trees, tall bushes with mystery berries, vines with eerie flowers that glimmered and bloomed even in the darkness. Flowers turned their petals as they passed.

Scruffy found a wide, bumpy path where vines hung even lower from creaking branches, as if the trees formed a curtain and dared them to pass through. The truck's fog lights gave the immediate surroundings an eerie glow, making wavering bushes and their dark blue and purple leaves seem alive. Large rocks glinted with ores and shone from beads of water. Scruffy stopped the rig and exited with a stretch. He leaned back his head and howled, then paused, as if in deep thought.

Beyond the rig's lights, a humanoid form dropped to a crouch with a muffled thud. Another humanoid form swooped from the forward branches. The form's image grew more distinct, a hooded man with sinister wings. The batlike creature landed on the hood and slapped his hands on the windshield. He flared out his "wings," then folded them forward, like a predator bird mantling its prey. Baring his fangs and hissing at them, eyes daring them to make one false move.

Scruffy covered his face with a palm as Telari blurted out laughing.

Slade folded his arms. "Spare us the theatrics. We're expecting you."

The intruder shoved back his hood and rubbed his cold, long, pointy ears. His frown deepened heavy wrinkles. "Oh, I used to have a grand effect on humans." He hopped off the car.

"You must be joking," Telari said. "You really fake the vampire thing?"

"Of course. We forest morphers are considered werefolk or druids on Earth."

The other stalker approached from behind, a younger scout. "The vampire act will never work here. Scruffy will breathe garlic on you."

Scruffy huffed with indignation. "Is it that strong? How are the woods?"

The old flying man smiled. "All's clear. No sign of trouble, not even at their spaceports. Let's get inside, before the weather turns bad." He leapt into the air and disappeared overhead.

More forms emerged, dark-clad beings from the size and shape of a man to fur-covered upright beings, some with short muzzles and feline ears, others bearing scraggly canine fur and features, others matched Wulvur's wereform, more or less.

Tel's whimsical imagination took over. "I want to see all the magic in this place," she quipped, smacking Gus's broad chest. "You?"

"Sure," Gus grinned, eyeing the ladies.

"Ah, good to be home," Berku said. "Our sopping tails have been gone for too long. Here, we can be ourselves." His beard thickened to a shaggy mane. Everything about Berku grew, hands into paws, nails to claws, long ears extending to tufted predator ears that drooped at the ends. He spread his massive arms, long enough to grapple three folk at once. "What, no brotherly hug?"

"I still can't morph," Slade reminded him.

"Yeah, dammit, we'll fix that," Berku promised. "No brother of mine will be shackled to live in one form. Better bring the rig or we'll lose it out here. Trees here like to meander."

Berku and his clans morphed into their beast forms and ran on all fours, bounding through almost invisible winding paths. Scruffy kept up, but his companions could barely make out glances of hind ends sprinting through the dark wilderness. Around them, tree limbs moaned and swayed, as if they were moving out of the way. Long vines dangling from far above brushed against the vehicle as if trying to feel the people inside.

Tel and Gus glanced at each other, then to Wulvur, who watched the mystical scenery brush past them with hardly a care.

"Are the trees really moving?" Tel whispered.

"Yeah," Wulvur replied.

Gus asked, "Guys, where'd they go?"

Tel looked around. The morphers had vanished.

Scruffy slowed in a dense grove where glow marks on the road and marker trees were faded and spaced at uneven intervals. Vines hung even lower from creaking branches, a living curtain that dared them to pass through. Scruffy's foglights illuminated forms of small wildlife perching on branches, watching like silent sentries. Eyes shined in the darkness.

Ahead lay a smoother paved path that curved through botanical gardens twinkling with glow-bugs and night lamps, all encircling a five-story temple. Modern luminescent orbs mounted strategically among rafters and windows offered just enough light for passage, while keeping eerie undertones. As Scruffy drove through, tree branches wove together behind them.

Huge trees surrounding the temple had stairways winding around their trunks, with steps made of petrified shelf fungi, and railing of thin, woven branches. Glowing flowers and stones in the walkways gave an efficient, yet subtle luminescence. Berku led his guests around at a leisurely rate, giving them a tour of the Morpheus Temple.

Slade cast a fond look around, glad that this place hadn't changed. The structure formed layers of slightly dome-shaped roofs that crowned living sections surrounded by timeless walls of stone-based flexwall, which looked like great sheets of stone. The rooftop over the fifth floor spread out with flat areas at the seven corners where beasts sat or lay, their distant profiles resembling hyenas, except for two with catlike features. The beasts lay still as statues, until one of their tails moved.

As the others enjoyed appetizers, Slade walked to one of the balconies. He looked down to see a peaceful pond, bubbling from occasional jumping fish, their colors bright orange and white, so radiant they cast their own light from their long fins. He tried to absorb the surrounding serenity, voices of his friends joking a few rooms down, glowing orbs lighting the sculptured stone figures decorated with gems and shells. A cool breeze created a gentle fluttering of leaves from the old-growth trees around him. Nothing helped his mood. He had too much work to do. He popped open his wrist pad and scrolled, reviewing maintenance reports. "A few more hours and the ships will be armed to the hilt."

Berku walked up and leaned on the balcony rail beside him. "Talk to me, Brothah. The old fish screwed with your memories. Is it long term and short term?"

"I don't remember," Slade replied.

Berku rolled his eyes. "Harr harr."

"I can't remember how I lost that fight on the space station."

"You remember this place?"

"Everything," Slade said, "training arenas, climbing school." He paused with a slight wince at memories of full-contact fighting and tree climbing, falling on his butt more than once. "Everyone here, I'm sure of it. Well? You wanted to brain meld, right?"

"Don't need to. I know what your problem is, why you can't morph. I can fix it."

Slade glanced over to see his brother morph into a taller feral form, an upright lycanthrope akin to a grey wolf with near-human hands and badger stripes on his bushy tail. "So does Elowren," Slade said, eyes on the reports. "You think showing off will help me find my other shapes? It won't."

"Humph," Berku grunted, his notched ears flicking back. "Look at you, pawing through homework. That's a new wrist gizmo. Lemme see."

"See?" Slade waved his bracer lined with compact comm and scanners.

"No, take it off." Noting Slade's drooping leer, Berku mock groaned, "Come on, we're home. Humor me. How's tricks?"

Slade allowed himself a smile as he tried to relax. He had missed this place, and his people knew it, especially his brother. "You're right. How've you been?" He loosened his bracer and handed it over.

"Eh, same old, trying to train these crazy pups. More of the kids want toys like this, gettin' bored with tradition. Nice scanner, though." He activated the scanner and waved it at Slade's head. "I knew it. Your skull's too thick."

Slade rolled his eyes while Berku continued playing with the gadgets, lighting up little globes and holoscreens of data from ship diagrams. "You going to keep that?"

"Nah," Berku said, and threw it over the rail. It barely missed the pond, landing in a lush bed of flowering herbs, its faint glow lighting up flowers. "Aw, rats."

"Damn you," Slade growled, fists clenching before he reined in his temper. Turning, he started toward the doorway. "If you wanted to go downstairs, just ask."

Berku kicked the back of his knees, grabbed him and threw his startled bother over the rail.

One floor down, Scruffy and the group glanced over as Slade fell past their window, yelling, followed by a mucky splash. They jumped up, except for Scruffy, who continued sipping his wildfire rum. They stared at Scruffy, mouths hanging open.

"Aren't we gonna help?" Rhoan started.

"Nah, he's fine." Scruffy said. "Hey," he called as the group headed out, anyway.

"Screw that, we're gonna watch." Wulvur tossed over one shoulder.

Scruffy leaned back and refilled his glass. "This better work."

Berku cupped his broad, furry hands and hollered, "Slade. You forgot how to have fun."

Slade lurched out of the water, sending fish retreating, and one flying out to flop on the bank. "Brother! I should have known you were up to no good."

"You won't melt," Berku yelled, "The Council promoted you because they thought *you* could be diplomatic." He bent over in laughter. "That's a riot."

Slade shook his fists, yelling, "You inebriated worg, get down here."

"Glad to help," Berku said, and cannonball dove into the pond. His wake bowled Slade over and sent a few fish flying out of the water. Berku struggled to pull his feet out of the mud and thrust his head above water. "You were never a fluffy diplomat."

"You ought to try it more often." Slade retorted, and shoved Berku under again, swatting him across the ears. "Have you gone rabid? Ugh." He pulled his brother back up. "This is no time to enter your third childhood."

Berku shoved Slade hard, knocking him onto his rear at the edge of the pond. He waited for Slade to surface. "Better than going docile as a curly fur. You forgot who you are. The Council made it worse. Then Venamir came along and delivered the final head smash." He slapped an open paw over his chest. "Our kind invented the wildhunt. We use our gut instincts and get the missions done. You're a moron for becoming a Consul."

"How is this helping?" Slade demanded. He shook himself off and climbed onto dry land.

Berku followed him. "Elowren's right. Venamir has your brain chasing its tail, trying to figure out where your memories are hiding. That's the last thing you need to do. Your brain will work when you call upon it. Use your freaking instincts." He grabbed Slade by the jacket, spun him around.

"Berku, knock it off." Slade growled.

Berku shrugged. "Okay." He punched Slade in the gut and threw him into the deeper part again. He clambered out of the pond, laughing.

Slade rose again, sputtering, coughing, and cursing between wheezes. "Berku, you vermin-humper, I'm going to *pulverize* you." Slade growled as he climbed out, a deep, rumbling sound, his eyes beginning to gleam and take on lupine shape, tufts of fur sprouting from his ears.

His spectators noticed, including his crew, who watched with grins and wide eyes.

Berku backed away, goading, "You couldn't even outfight a slimy old aquatic. The fancy diplomats have turned you into a *gentleman*."

"Now you're just being nasty."

Berku strutted and flicked his nose at Slade. "Ooh, look at me. I'm a great member of the Morpher Council now, even though I can't catch a fish. I bet you don't even remember what a full moon looks like to a *real* wolf. Lemme' show you." Berku turned and slapped his butt cheeks. He didn't straighten fast enough, for Slade charged and bowled him over.

Slade tried to walk away one more time. "Why you want to fight so bad?"

"Because if we don't, you're gonna go soft like the diplomats you make fun of. Or maybe you already have wussed down to their level. Maybe I should take over the mission and let you dress up for tea parties. That's why you can't morph."

Fists clenching, Slade didn't realize he already started to morph. "What the fuck."

The real fight started, pent up fury exploding as their punches fell harder and survival instincts clawed for control. Wherever Berku dashed away from the main village buildings, Slade followed, his tackle sending them crashing through saplings and brush, their ruckus frightening birds and wildlife away, and drawing the undivided attention of the entire village.

Berku was holding back, at first, until his brother's grappling holds required all his strength and technique to break free. Close, so close, he thought, and using his best moves, snuck under Slade's punch, flipped and body-slammed him to the ground. He watched for Slade to rise, but no reaction at first, only pained panting. Slade hadn't fully morphed yet either, just sprouted more fur and muscle mass. Guilt and concern filled his heart. "Slade?" he asked, bending closer. "Need a medic?" Then he realized their brawl had carried them to the edge of an arena pit. He saw the heads of the training dummies several yards below and knelt in the dirt, his gruff voice softening. "Don't roll in there. Just say put and... OW!" Slade kicked him in the legs, toppling him, then grabbed Berku by neck fur and braided beard, and dragged him into the pit.

"Sucker." Slade chortled.

"Watch the beard." Berku retorted.

Spectators surrounded the edges of the pit, many of them placing bets.

Slade and Berku renewed the match with fresh anger, grabbing practice weapons, disarming each other, and knocking over training dummies in their wake.

His patience and self-control wearing thin, Berku morphed into his beast shape and grabbed his brother in a headlock. He squeezed hard, slowing Slade down while he tried to catch his wind. "Still not morphing yet? You know what we're... gonna do?" He struggled to keep his grip when Slade elbowed him in the ribs and tried to throw him off. "Oaf." he grunted. With a low growl, he tightened his grip until he felt his quarry sag from lack of air. "We're going to put you through the trials like a new pup... all over again."

Berku felt his grip slip again, and dropped his weight onto Slade, forcing them to their knees in the dirt. "Back to Druwen school for you. How about that, little acolyte?" He finally felt Slade's body mass alter and the sharp pain of claws digging into his forearm. "Uh oh… he muttered as his grip broke free.

Gasping for air, Slade clawed his jacket to shreds as he morphed, a thick coat of grizzly fur bulking his clothes, joints altering to accommodate greater flexibility. His entire form reshaped to an upright, fanged bearlike beast. He took a deep breath and roared from every emotion—physical pain, anger, exasperation, all mixed with exuberance. Slade's roar echoed from the pit, wild and ominous.

Berku tried to look casual as he took long steps away and ducked behind the rows of kicking bags, wall obstacles, and training dummies. He backpedaled and ducked as pieces flew in all directions. "Heh heh... uh oh, he's really boiled."

Slade crashed through the sturdy props, his muscular bulk and rugged paws slashing the bags open. With powerful strides, Slade bounded to the top of the wall and crouched, his lips curling up to expose menacing canines.

"Hey, look at yourself. You're morphing. Not tired yet?"

Slade didn't relent, nor calm down. He jumped over the first four rows of dummies, leaving only a few fake soldiers between them. Slade hefted a couple of training dummies with his massive paws and smashed them together, then flung the pieces aside. Each breath a low snarl, he lunged at his brother and slammed him to the ground. They wrestled more like wild animals than men, both in their most massive feral forms, swiping their broad bear claws with raging strength.

Berku tried to make mind contact. He recoiled from flashbacks of a fiery ship crashing. For an instant, he felt the heat, heard voices of a crew long passed, and realized his brother could fully protect his mind while feral, a rare ability, primal yet brilliant. He could hardly breathe.

"Feel tough now?" Slade huffed, his words half lost in deep growls.

His older brother wheezed, still chuckling, "Okay, you win."

310

Even the spectators realized the fun was over when concerned mutterings replaced taunts and cheers. Rhoan looked at Tel and Wulvur, who nodded. They jumped into the pit and closed in around the growling pair.

Berku couldn't break free for long. Each time he escaped, Slade slammed him down again and held him down by the chest with one paw, while shaking another in front of his brother's face. Berku finally threw him over his shoulders and backed away, panting.

"No more schooling." Slade ranted. "How dare you want my hunt—Venamir's *mine*." He flicked his ears toward approaching friends and waved a paw toward them. "Stay outta dis!"

His low, sinister tone made his friends flinch, but they pounced anyhow, Wulvur on one arm, Rhoan on the other, while Tel grabbed him by the neck and bit his ear.

The bite's stinging pain startled Slade the most. "OW!" He glowered at Tel as she jumped back.

Berku shook a finger at his enraged sibling. "Haah, I gotcha. Don't you get it? It was the only way to make you go primal. The only way to get your animal form back was to make you fight."

Telari grabbed a broken fighting stick and held it for a low swing. "You know where I aim, straight to the privates."

Slade covered his groin. His foggy brain clicked on the word "*Gotcha*." He swung around to Berku. "*Wha-at?* You pranked me?"

His brother guffawed. "It was for yer own good."

Scruffy strolled into view, nudging his way past villagers. "Ah, there he is," he said with a broad smile, "got his Mojo back."

Berku stared at Slade's massive wereform, a shape beyond wolfish, now a bulkier predator made more for demolishing prey, grizzly. As if just noticing his shape, Slade huffed in deep, low breaths, his muzzle and chest broader than in the past, claws thicker. He realized that his form was something between an Earthern and an Atlean bear.

"That's a new shape," Berku observed, "and you psy blocked me in wereform. Not many folks can do that. Damned good."

Slade growled, anger still clashing with reason as he advanced, spreading thick, bearlike arms. "Ever had an Earthern beaaarr hug?" he growled, ears pinned back.

Berku faked an innocent grin as he backed away. "Heh, I'll pass."

"Enough!" Scruffy yelled. "You won't beat Venamir if you two smash each other into oozing piles of guts."

Slade realized that his haunting flashbacks only nipped at his mind, and he locked them back with renewed psychic control. He morphed again, into his old favorite shape, something akin to the werewolf in human stories. As he did, his scrapes closed a bit, and the aches subsided. He felt anger against only Venamir now, who'd shackled his mind, a heinous crime for telepaths.

"Now calm down," Berku said.

"I can morph now. It's easy." Slade realized aloud. He stared at his morphed, paw-like hands as if they'd been gone for a century and just found, then looked at his grinning brother, sharing his relief and joy. Victorious shock filled Slade's voice. "Berku, you did it. I'm *me* again."

"You're *better* than before," big brother replied, "still a pain in the ass, though."

Slade clasped Berku's arms in upmost gratitude. "Thank you."

"Come on, you enjoy a brawl."

"True," Slade grinned, turning to gaze at the onlookers. "Scruffy! There you are. You planned this, didn't you?"

Scruffy merely shrugged, but his slow smile confirmed it.

A growling female shoved her way through the crowd, shaking a dead fish and a crumpled plant. "You killed my fish and destroyed the garden."

Slade and Berku pointed at each other.

"He did it." Berku blurted.

Slade swatted at him, light and playful this time. "You started it."

"They like it ruff." Wulvur called out.

"But Slade *beared* it all," Tel threw in.

Groans and laughter arose from the crowd.

Berku moved to the center of the arena where everyone could see, where his voice boomed so all could hear. "I'm proud to announce that my brother has reached the next level of morphing." He fell silent as villagers and friends cheered. Berku waved them to respectful silence, then rubbed his jaw. "Slade, you're even more powerful than you were before. Say," he added, his voice rising, "we never ate. Come on, the night's still young." He lumbered off, yelling for someone to fire up the distillery.

While the night hours passed, visitors partied after their guests retired, especially Slade and Berku, who slept despite music and merriment.

Chapter 33
Herding Cats

When Slade returned to the Atlean spaceport, Motley was waiting to help unload goods from Scruffy's vehicle. The big feline humanoid stood a head taller than Slade, but his ears jerked with shaky nerves. The cat's tail twitched as he approached Slade.

"I need to talk to you," Motley said.

"That's true," Slade agreed. "You were on a spy mission. You went missing. Next thing I heard, you worked for Venamir. What happened?"

Motley drew a long sigh, his eyes wandering before meeting his captain's. "It's like this. I know it was wrong to go silent on the job. I've been looking for other work."

"Elaborate."

"It's my son!" Motley huffed and flicked his big paw-like hands. "I can't raise him like this. I never thought he'd be abducted because of me."

"Venamir cubnapped your son."

"He was abducted to control me. Who knows what happened to his aunt taking care of him. Yes, I strayed from duty, but I still protected Doc Nelzyr."

"I'm grateful for that," Slade assured. "We all are."

"I need to leave your clan of Rangers," Motley said. "I can't do this anymore."

Slade patted the grey feline's shoulder. "I understand, but we still need you. Stay on with us for now, and I'll get you some other job, low profile. Besides, your cub has protection. Leifur can stay at the temple, where it's safe."

"Really?" Motley's posture straightened as if shedding a terrible load. "Thank you. Very well. Just this one job, then," he promised. "I see why everyone wants to work for you."

"Oh, not everyone," Slade chuckled.

* * *

Motley was chipper until they gathered for lunch at the spaceport. He lingered with his son in the cafe. The two didn't speak much, save for body language of tense, swishing tails. Outside,

Atlean ships and their crews went about their business of arming rows of fighter ships. Motley looked out the large windows and gazed at Scruffy's bulky tank of a ship and Zared's sleek fighter-transport. Both ships' paint schemes were broken up with new patchwork repairs. Even from afar, he could make out the profiles of Slade's crew overseeing renovations and servicing. Any of them could just quit the crew and find another job, a safer place among society, instead of going after Venamir, but they refused. Motley poked at his half-gnawed steak and mulled over the turn of events. *Why didn't the whole crew brand me a traitor?*

Visions swarmed through his mind. The Atlean Morpher Council still trusted him. Motley had sworn their oaths of loyalty with cocky enthusiasm, his head high and chest out. He owed Slade for helping save his life and, even more so, his cub's life.

Motley took another bite and tried to enjoy the atmosphere of a safehaven with his cub, instead of a ship full of mercenaries, but his mind kept wandering. *I'm a traitor, or at least a deserter, and Slade still pardoned me because I helped his doctor."* His brooding gaze strayed across the table to the resilient youth. *Because I have a cub.* He set his half-eaten steak aside and licked his chops, hardly savoring the delectable aftertaste.

Leifur sat across from him at the small table, munching on a large burger after polishing off a steak with gravy. "Pops, are you sure that cyborg didn't poison you?"

Motley glanced up, startled out of his thoughts. "We're more immune to his venom, and I know the symptoms. Besides, Doc scanned all of us." He sighed, patting his cub's paws. "Your ride should be here any time now. I need you to stay at the temple where Slade's friends can keep you safe. I have one last job to do for Slade."

"I'm going with you," Leifur stated, before slurping the last of his drink.

Motley already felt like a nervous wreck. He tried to curb exasperation from his tone. "No, you're staying where it's safer."

"So I'm right. You're going to try to leave me with some poor sucker until one of Venamir's cyborgs grabs me again. What happened to my aunt, anyway?"

"I called. She's well. A stupid Morabott distracted her and the other one took you. Aunt Claudia will join us here on Atlearon, soon as she can."

Leifur finally smiled with a sigh of relief.

Motley's gut churned at the thought of cubnapping. Leifur still hadn't given details, but as a father, he sensed a forced new maturity, and a chunk of childhood happiness lost forever. In his kindest voice, Motley countered, "The morpher training temple can be fun for you. There's a forest and students from the villa. You'll be safe."

"Capt'n Slade said you could quit. Isn't that what you want?"

"Yes."

Leifur drew the word out, claws shredding a large meat kabob. "Well?"

"You know why. It's about honor, something I thought I'd lost. Slade's crew *saved* us. I need to help them. It's just one last hunt."

Leifur swung his ears back, scowled, and chomped into the meat. "Famous last words," he grumbled through a mouthful of food.

"I mean it, I swear. I'll find a boring job after this."

They ate in silence for a few minutes, until Leifur muttered, "That psycho fishman, he's totally crazy and he has big friends in the deep waters. He has lizard friends, too. You're scared of us dying."

Motley drew a steadying breath and squeezed his son's shoulder. "We'll be fine, and no, you can't come with me. Vanysa's coming to give you a ride back to the temple."

"Fine," the cub grumbled. He played nice after that, eyes on his game screen as he built images of himself. A holo likeness of him appeared high in the rafters. He began fine-tuning the image, giving it illusionary density and fur texture.

Motley patted his head. "Soon we'll be done with this hunting job. I'll take you on a real vacation."

The cub gave him a skeptical look. "Sure," he commented in thin belief.

Leifur played nice when Vanysa showed up. He gave Motley a hug and strolled off, game in hand. As soon as his father was out of sight, he began his slew of requests. One last dogfight game, he needed the bathroom, free drink refill, all polite and smiling. Vany endured a few of his bratty antics, buying him snacks and a shake.

"Come along. Your sitter is meeting me at the edge of the forest. She'll take you the rest of the way." Vany led the cub into her small ship, a lean, mean Scouter vessel upgraded with a teleportal chamber, an elegant interior, and a weapons system worthy of a fighter ship. She flicked on power, awakening her program assistant, a hologram that maneuvered into the air as if swimming. Vany dismissed the avatar. "No enemies yet, Selena. Go on standby."

Leifur gazed around, eyes wide with interest. "That's a combat program? Ooh, you are important. Most transports like this are wrecks."

"Thank you, I think," she smiled.

Leifur sat down in the right seat. "You can't just teleport me to the temple? Oh, it must be too protected. You Merfins really like jamming signals. How can you put up with the noise it makes?"

"It doesn't bother Merfins because we designed it," she replied, eyes on her data screens. "You're lucky your family's friendly with the Druwen clans. Temple keepers don't let many people in there. Even the woods help protect it."

"Are you really related to Venamir? How come you're not psycho?"

"Wow," Vanysa muttered. "Uh, because, I believe the wars corrupted him, and I'm not him."

"Do you have any kids, or fish, whatever you call them? You don't worry that they'll get like him?"

"No, I don't know many children. And yes, we're very distant relatives," she replied, her patience slipping. She had no idea how to deal with children. Right now, even though she sympathized with the cub's brush with Venamir's crew, she didn't want to learn to be a nanny. "You need to quiet down while I talk to the control tower."

"I know," the cub shrugged. "Can I look around? It's such a nice ship. I've only been in a diplomat's bird at the museum. This one still smells new. Or you could tell me all about it, you know, like a bedtime story. You should have cubs. You look old enough. How old are you?"

"What!"

Big, innocent eyes met Vany's annoyed look. "I mean, uh, in a good way, for a fish person."

Vanysa's hands tightened on the controls. "I must confess, I don't have any children. So I uh, don't know what to do for you. Go ahead, look around," she caved in. "Sit down when we lift off. Don't mess with the weapons rack, or portal controls, or anything."

"I know how to work those," Leifur bragged. His ears twitched back from her warning glance. "I mean, don't worry. It's not my first time flying."

Vany sighed, shaking her head as he trotted away. She lifted off and made her way toward monstrous trees beyond the cities. She landed in a clearing where the only sign of civilization was an overgrown road, and an old, four-door vehicle with a young woman and man sitting on the hood, flirting. Vanysa made her conversation short, passing along instructions from Motley until the cub emerged from her ship.

Leifur looked from one to the other, sighed, and climbed into the back seat. "Hi, guys. Thanks, Vany," he said in a demure tone. He yawned, giving them an innocent smile, and laid down for a nap.

"Aw, so sweet," the lady cubsitter smiled.

"Wait until he wakes up," Vany said. She tugged the young couple away from the transport, hushing her voice. "We'll be back soon as we can. The poor cub's been stuck with Venamir's crew, of all places. He's probably traumatized. He's smart and sassy, so keep your wits about you."

As the others chatted, Leifur pulled out a remote and tapped the controls. Vany's portal chamber activated, rescuing him from the back seat.

Minutes later, the sitter returned to her vehicle. She glanced back to see the cub curled up for a nap, or rather, a high-quality hologram of his ears peeking out from the blanket she used as a seat-cover. Quietly as she could, she drove away while Vanysa lifted off, leaving dust-devils of swirling leaves and dirt.

Vany lifted ship, perplexed. "Whew, that was easier than I expected. He was almost too nice." She lingered on the thought, but not for long. The spaceport came into view, where she landed near the *Vernacular*. While the engines wound down, she pulled on a pair of bracers and checked the power levels. Looking outside, she saw a spotty-skinned Merfin climb out of a fleet service rig. Vany paused, studying his slight limp. "He really showed up," she muttered.

The rig pulled away and cruised to the ships across the flightline. The spotty man strode up and greeted her at the hatch, his demeanor confident. "Lady Vanysa, the *Mythos* and *Vernacular* are ready to fly. Slade's begun the hunt."

Vany used his nickname, "Spotty this is a bad idea."

"It is our only good option," he replied. "The others must not know who I am, not yet, especially your bodyguard."

She worked back a frown, smiling as Faron walked up. "Everyone's ready?"

Faron nodded. "Why must we take this ambassador with us?"

"Orders come from the Magistrate," Vany said.

Faron leered at the spotted Merfin. "The Magistrate who's dead or in hiding?"

Vany leaned closer to Faron. "You know Venamir will try to read all our minds. A few secrets may help us."

"Very well," Faron grumbled. He sat down in the copilot's chair and eyed the ship's weight configuration. "Did you bring something extra?"

"I usually do," Vanysa said, "you know, things, first aid supplies. Men usually need them."

He ignored the jest. "I thought I heard something."

Their words carried beyond the large stash of riot gear and weapons to the sharp ears of Motley's young cub hiding behind it. The feline lad's ears flicked back, his tail twitching as he shrank farther out of sight.

* * *

Slade approached the *Vernacular* with a swagger, mighty pleased with himself. He wore clothes from his family's village. His forest colors matched his faded bruises and scrapes like leathers to warpaint. Doc Nelzyr met him at the ship's open ramp and blocked his path.

"What?" Slade asked, fondling the new weapons at his belt, a slender firgun and rugged fist weapons from his brother.

"One night out, and you're a mess," Doc started. "What'd you do, take on the whole village?"

"Nope, just my brother, Berku, and I won."

"I thought you were going to do brain probes," Doc said.

"Nah," Slade shrugged. "Is the ship ready to launch?"

"Of course, go on in." As Slade walked past, Doc poked him in the spine, then smacked him in the shoulder, drawing forth angered winces. "Eye color off, joints are sore, like you've been... *show me.*"

Slade turned to face him and morphed with casual ease into his taller werebear form and swung a husky arm around Doc. "Now, old friend, I have a terrible craving for *fish.*"

"You evolved," Doc beamed with a broad grin. "You didn't have that form before."

"Berku really pissed me off, but it worked," Slade admitted. He shrunk back into his normal form. "I need to get my gear tweaked."

"We're here, let's go," Berku yelled from somewhere outside the ship.

Berku and Motley climbed out of a maintenance vehicle. The two strolled up to the ramp, each carrying some travel bags. A group of forest morphers scrambled behind them and unloaded supplies.

Berku was in his feral wolven form, coated in tan and silver fur, protected by battle proven gear. He led five others, all clad in desert cammy body armor that changed color to blend in against metals as they neared the starship.

Slade joined them, face hopeful. "Berku, I want you and your pack with me."

"Aw, that's cozy. Wanna spar again?" Berku asked, "You know, warm up?"

Slade punched his brother's shoulder. "You must like embarrassment."

Berku guffawed, "Oh, listen to you. I brought you another big puss, too."

Motley walked up to Slade. "I owe you a debt. I strayed from my duties to you, but Venamir cubnapped my son. Thanks to all of you, my cub is safe. How can I help?"

Slade took his time considering, a few seconds that felt like hours to Motley. At length, he gestured to the *Mythos*. "Welcome back. Zared's crew needs help."

"Thanks!" Motley strutted toward Zared's ship.

Slade touched his earpiece. "All hands, group up by the *Vernacular*."

Engine noise whined over Slade's voice as a small, elite scout ship landed beside their ship.

Slade's brother folded his arms. "That's Vanysa's personal scout ship," Berku said. "The Council ordered her to stay behind."

Vanysa and her bodyguard Faron disembarked and strode up to Slade's group. Vanysa wore her normal, faint smile of diplomacy, while her bodyguard's frown matched his protective presence.

"I'm offering my ship to help," Vanysa said. "You know this ship can fight. We flew defense at the prison."

"Yes, I remember," Slade agreed. "You still want Venamir taken alive?"

Vanysa's eyes saddened as her face reddened a shade, yet her voice held steady. "Preferably. My great granduncle, er, Venamir has earned the death sentence many times. What happens to him is his own making." She gestured to her small ship. "He's least likely to fire upon me, so I can play decoy."

Berku gazed at Vany's ship. "I bet he'll blast you just like the rest of us. Your bird can't take much heat."

"Perhaps," she admitted.

"I'd be a fool to turn you down," Slade accepted. "We have a bet that Venamir will either try to turn you or kill you."

"Thanks," Vany said. "He'll get neither."

"Lie low 'til we need you, and thanks," Slade replied.

Vanysa and Faron nodded and headed back for their ship.

Slade nudged Berku. "What do you think?"

"She's not ready to see Venamir's true colors," Berku replied, "and I don't trust her bodyguard."

"He's a fish. You prefer chicken?" Slade asked.

"Shaddap!"

Slade chuckled. "Okay, brothah, let's go spear a fish."

Chapter 34
Vernacular Goes Fishing

Maska and Shanto sat in the medbay glowering at each other while Venamir's alchemist, Thiun, lectured them about no fighting on duty, again.

Venamir walked in, his moody glare demanding attention. "If you two can hide from me together, you can coexist. Shanto, return to your duties. You must disable that Herja program. Unless we can fully control this ship, the Morpher Council's fleet will destroy us. Report back to engineering." He turned to Maska, who shrank back, guilt oozing from him.

"I'm sorry, Captain." Maska forced the words out, "I lost Slade's medic."

Venamir retorted, "Yes, you did, but he had help."

Maska wrung his hands. "How can I make it up?"

"You cannot." Venamir let the moment drag. "We can only press on. I realize the chaos Slade's crew can bring. Do you think you can guard Shanto?"

"Yes, Sir," Maska promised.

"Do not lose this prisoner." Venamir's voice was low and dangerous. "We are going to start a war, defeat Slade's ships. I need Shanto to regain full control of the *Jacobyte*. No more mistakes."

Once Venamir moved off, Maska skulked into medbay, his demented mind brewing scalding visions of roasting his captain in the everlasting fires. "I can't take this anymore," he mumbled, wringing his hands. "The Captain has gone crazy. I got to blast outta' this ship, but I need help, and who better than the ship's engineer." His gaze landed on Shanto, who glared back. Maska glanced around, then moved closer and patted Shanto on the chest. "Ha-ha, I beat you."

"I'll rematch you anytime," Shanto said.

Maska leaned closer and dropped his voice to below a whisper, his sour breath blowing against Shanto's ear. "No more fighting. You know how to control this flying deathtrap. Can you bust us out?"

Shanto stared at him. "Now you want to team up? I can't trust you."

"I mean it, truce," Maska whispered. "Venamir's going off the deep end. He'll get us all killed."

Footsteps approached, and the alchemist emerged from the stockroom. "What are you doing with my prisoner?"

"I'm in charge of him, not you," Maska said, straightening, "Captain's orders."

"You," Thiun echoed, amused. "Fine, take him. Better you than me." He released Shanto from the interrogation chair.

Thiun waved toward the door. "Don't fight each other. I'm not a fully trained medic. You wouldn't like how I patch you up."

"Great, instead of a surgeon, we have a potion mixer with a firgun and a bloody cleaver."

Thiun pointed to the interrogation recliner. "Sit. I've been ordered to check you for poisons."

Maska's hackles raised. "Not in *that* chair. You're not even a doctor. You're an alchemist."

"I'm also a field medic. Both of you sit down, now."

Shanto and Maska complied, tossing glares at each other.

Shanto chuckled, a baleful sound as he shoved Maska off balance. "Your turn."

Thiun began his examinations. He ran bio scans, nodding as they watched body images reveal ailments and streaks of silver in the veins. "You two have traces of slow venoms."

Maska cringed deeper in the chair. "Can you stop them?"

"Of course I can neutralize them. Venamir hired me for my mastery in serums." He gave them each an injection. "Shanto, be a good lackey and fetch us something to eat. Maska, help me clean up this place."

Shanto left the medbay, wondering if the offer was truth or fantasy. He didn't trust Maska for a second, but he sensed Maska's misery deeply enough to consider the unforeseen. Maybe Venamir is our common enemy. Lost in thought, he rounded the corner and collided with a youth carrying an overloaded tool bag. Tools spilled out, some onto Shanto's toes, sending him hopping in pain.

"Sorry!" the youth blurted as he knelt to refill the bag.

Shanto stared at him. "Apologizing? You must be new." The fellow was barely of age, with the seriousness of an old man. Shanto pulled the lad's collar back, exposing colorful tattoos. "Huh, cool inks. Can I see?"

The youth jerked back. "No! You'll just make fun of 'em."

"No, I won't." Shanto lowered his voice. "You look familiar, is all. I'm Shanto. Wait, you're James, son of John Shocks, aren't you?"

"Yeah. So?"

"He's looking for you. His gang, they're a flying squadron again. They want you home." Shanto met the lad's surprised gaze. The boy couldn't be more than fourteen, maybe twelve.

"Well, um, call me Tatts." The youth closed the toolbag and hurried off.

Shanto tried to psy to him, and found a mind that was open and chaotic, vulnerable to telepaths. *"I can help you escape,"* he said into the lad's mind. Shanto grimaced and grabbed the wall for balance as zaps of pain stabbed through his head. He'd forgotten the controlling visor around his head, always there sensing his brain activity, programmed to halt any psychic surges. As the pain cleared, he wondered how Slade's Doc Nelzyr endured weeks of Venamir.

Scowling, Shanto retrieved some rations, trying to find the least tasty ones. Dried mushtan feet and deep fried zug roots. That would do. "Sure like to poison these," he muttered, heading to medbay.

In short order, Shanto left the medbay with Maska, who was grumbling about needles in his butt.

"Come on, truce," Maska whispered. "I want off this ship, too. I'm telling you, Venamir's gone mad. I'm not dying for his cause."

Shanto raised his eyebrows. "Deal," he murmured.

Maska skulked past. "Come along, servant."

* * *

The *Vernacular* flew low over the ocean, just high enough to avoid creating waves from her engines. They approached tall, ragged cliffs where the morning sun painted bright outlines around the many rows of retired starships. To Slade and his crew, the sight usually elicited sentimental thoughts, but not today. At first glance, the growing landscape spread apart like chunks of broken toys, as if some giant had grabbed the edges of the beach and cracked it apart to form new rivers.

Scruffy sat in the pilot's chair of his beloved old bird, paying more attention to his instrument panel than the scenery ahead.

Slade rose from the copilot's chair and leaned on the control panel. Slade gazed down upon the beach surrounding the Starship Boneyard, a view not so unlike the beach on the war-torn world they had left behind after saving his doctor. Except this wreckage just happened. "Someone attacked the Starship Graveyard, near our clan's drakir hatchery and nobody reported it?"

Utterings of anger and surprise rumbled through the cockpit as Slade's crew viewed the scarred land below. Blackened areas on land, with retired spaceships of all sizes parked close to the coastline. The Starship Boneyard stood nearer to the ocean since acres of land had tumbled into the sea. Armed with jagged floating debris, frothing waters swirled around little chunks of land, tearing the miniature islands apart as if they were fragile playthings of giant children. One dock collapsed, toppling little boats like discarded trinkets. A fighter ship closest to the edge toppled, slid cockeyed off its landing gear, and plunged into the sea.

Telari leaned closer to the windows with a scowl. "Why tear up those old ships?"

"It's a path to the *Spectre,* the one we both flew," Slade replied in a low voice. "There are a few underground docks. That's where she is."

Elowren scanned the coastline. "There're Merfins guarding a cave entrance. Looks like the passageways can reach your ship." She zoomed in to reveal swimmers, all hybrids, three Merfin mixes, and one amphibious reptilian. They were constructing barriers around the submerged mouth of a cave.

"Fish 'n lizards," Wulvur grumbled, "like that hit team on Earth."

"Venamir's favorite hybrids," Slade agreed, "Merfins with greater land tolerance and lizards who can breathe underwater."

Berku leaned closer and pointed to the cave entrance. "See those traces of green around the cave? That's new. Let me take the pack in, you know, soften up the resistance."

"Watch your back," Slade warned.

Berku sounded incredulous, "Me? Is my grey fur makin' me look old?"

"Make sure you play dirty," Slade replied.

"Oh, like normal." Berku waved to the fellows on the main deck as he strutted past with a pack of werefolk at his heels. "This shouldn't take long. We'll borrow a few jetpacks just in case. Seeya ladies."

Berku and his pack jetted to the ground. They stalked through decaying starships with only the sound of their hushed breaths. Their wolfish calls blended in with the wind that sent desert sand scurrying across the ground and ship hulls like a mad race of angry snakes. Berku's pack of werefolk spread out around their targets while Berku snuck into the remains of a scout ship that lay on its belly. Many of the ships rocked in time to gusts of wind, creating a welcome source of cover noise.

Berku smelled them before even noticing their shadows, two armed guards standing watch in the partial shelter of a cargo ship's long, thick tail assembly.

One guard glanced around, his face hidden by a bulky helmet. "What was that?"

"Sounds like vermin," the other guard replied.

"They're going to steal our food."

On the far side of the cargo ship, two wolfmen fought back laughter as they whispered to each other and nodded. One started humping a loose, open hatch, while the other moaned and screeched.

Moving closer along a row of ill kept sheds, Berku smirked, fully aware of the antics in play. His mirth faded just long enough to pounce on a guard opening an outhouse door. Berku lunged, grabbed the guy by the throat and, after a few choice strikes, left the relieved fellow in the outhouse and shut the door. "Should've used a tree," he said, moving on.

A few squeaks and thumps somewhere ahead made the taller guard snicker. "I bet they're breeding. They get big out here, fun to watch."

The burlier guard groaned and slugged his friend in the arm. Between the wind and his helmet, he never heard the muffled whoop of bolas flying through the air. "You're one sick bastur— ugh!" His scoffing turned to choking gurgles as the weapon wrapped around his neck, weighted balls at each end releasing a strong zap. He collapsed the next second.

The other guard pivoted, charging up his firgun, his eyes straining for a target. As he glanced down at the blood pooling around his cohort's throat, Berku leaned over him from the shed's roof and waved, "Hey, rat voyeur."

The two vermin impersonators sprang around the ship's swaying tail and pummeled the guard face first into the rocky dirt. After a brief ceremony of clobbering and clawing, they left the prone guy, but took his utility belts.

"Giant rats," Berku commented, "*again*?"

His pack members just grinned. "Oh, baby," the younger one moaned.

Berku swatted at him. "Ugh, get to work."

So went their next hour, the Druwen pack earning just a few bumps and scrapes from whittling down the henchmen. Old, retired ships served as brigs for subdued and out-cold guards. Some henchmen woke up wrapped in seat netting, secured behind engine covers. The mouthiest opponent was locked in a latrine.

"Tell your captain you passed out in the crapper," Berku drawled, reaching into a pocket.

"I'm not passed out. Come on, I'll help you. Let's shake on it." He extended a hand.

"Talk to the paw." Berku blew a bit of dust toward the guy and waved. His prey staggered back onto the toilet, only to slide to the floor. Chuckling, Berku took the guy's firgun and comm. Imitating the unconscious man's voice, he reported, "Hey, screw you all, I quit! Some covert guys are wiping us out. I'm leaving while I'm still alive. They said you're already infiltrated. You better run."

An angry, hissing voice responded, "Stay at your post, coward."

"Shove it, you dumbass lizard," Berku retorted, and shut down the comm before he started snickering. He chucked the comm and slid off the lower ramp. "Pack, report."

"Ocean side's clear," came one voice.

"Dock end's clear," said another gruff teammate.

"Buildings are clear," Berku concluded. "Meet up at that cave where we started. This was too easy. Be ready for some real trouble." He called Scruffy. "Bow wow," he greeted.

Scruffy's face appeared on the screen, the background showing he was in the *Vernacular*, as usual. "How goes it?"

"It's too easy, so far," Berku replied. "May as well join the fun."

* * *

Once Slade and Wulver were outside, the condition of the beach struck Slade up close and personal when his boots touched the oil-stained sand. He clenched his teeth at the sight of the caved-in buildings, their painted museum signs now weathered and crumbling into the sea, along with a plethora of debris. One glance at a few shelters in the distance showed fragmented buildings with their roofs caved in. Only a few shops appeared undamaged. Even the nearby lighthouse stood at an angle now, its precarious mass threatening all who drew near. Withering trees and vines lay decaying. Nothing grew here now, nothing green. Then he noticed just how close the ships were to the cliff. Huge chunks of land had been blown away, explaining piles of rock and wreckage below. The scenery tugged at his flashbacks, enticing whispers of the dead to intrude upon his thoughts. *No, not again. I'm in control now.* As long as he kept control of his flashbacks, he could use them against enemy forces. He never thought he'd use his worst nightmares as his best psy defenses. "When did this happen?"

"Looks like just days for those ships and the buildings," Wulvur said. "All this damage is fresh, but the landscape was neglected for months."

Creaking and moaning wooden limbs pulled their attention to a cliff-side tree tipping over, its weakened branches snapping as it fell. Rushing waters armed with jagged debris gnawed at the land, collapsing a sturdy beach. Thick columns lay half buried beneath splintered planks, the water foamed with oil and hissed around them, spraying mist into the air while daring them to slip into its swirling depths. Birds and marine life scavenged for food in boat wreckage. A sharp stench lingered in the air that Slade recognized, the aftermath of burned composite materials.

"Get back onboard!" Elowren yelled. "We have incoming fighters."

"Come on," Slade said, pivoting. "Berku, take cover."

"We're in the tunnels," Berku replied over the comm. "Go on, we'll be alright."

"Battle stations!" Scruffy hollered. He activated the ship's force fields.

"Go, Scruffy!" Slade yelled, the last to run inside, as the creaky old ramp slammed shut.

The first blasts from above struck the ship's sturdy wings, jolting everyone inside.

The *Vernacular* and her wing ship *Mythos* took to the sky, reinforcing their cloaks and scanning for intruders.

Slade sprinted into the cockpit. "What's out there?"

"They're coming from all around us," Zared replied from the *Mythos*, "above, across land, underwater, our allies and unidentified."

Slade grabbed the pilot's chair for balance and leaned over Scruffy's shoulder to stare at the screens. Targeting screens glowed, showing approaching ships from all directions, from below the ocean's surface, to high altitudes, a mixed jumble.

"Some of them are fighting each other," Elowren announced, pointing to different colored clusters of blips on her screen. "Venamir caused it."

"Fly. Bring that *Jacobyte* down." Slade lowered his voice, remembering his crewman onboard with Venamir's crew. "Sorry Shanto."

Chapter 35
Class Reunion

Venamir emerged from his pool and donned body armor with renewed energy. His gills fluttered with excitement before he willed them shut against his body. "So close," he muttered, adjusting a few last straps as he turned to his monitors. He could see every room in the ship where crewmen armed up with protective gear and weapons, everyone except Shanto. His eyes narrowed as he studied Shanto helping secure cargo. Venamir sent his psy voice through the ship so only his target could hear. "*Shanto!*"

He watched Shanto jump, then heave a sigh and continue working.

Venamir continued, "*Remember, crewman. You work under my command now. If you disobey me, I can make you do anything, and it shall be most excruciating.*"

After a pause, Shanto's psy voice replied, "*I know.*"

Venamir smirked as he felt precarious emotions teetering between fury and resolution, a mild danger flavored with amusement. "*Shanto, you may possibly survive after all, in subservience.*" Breaking mental contact with his toy crewman, Venamir entered the cockpit.

Moradin kept engines at idle while the ship nestled on the ocean floor. "I've alerted your Deeps and Rezoan followers. They are ready."

"Perfect," Venamir replied and dropped into *his* captain's chair. "Attention all hands! Battle stations! My loyal followers raise from the depths. Your escape from prison is a mere taste of the freedom we will take as we shatter the resistance. Today, my people will show their true colors. Only then can we overthrow the councils."

As Moradin eased the ship up toward the surface, she heard cheers from the gullible.

"But first," Venamir said, voice hissing as a snake about to feed, "we must take down their leaders, and that begins with Slade's allied ships, the *Vernacular* and the *Mythos*. Slade is *mine*."

The *Jacobyte* patrolled in stealth mode. All seemed normal, Merfins near the cave entrance, his subjugated guards making their rounds. At length, they detected the *Vernacular* and movement on the beach. He guided the ship closer, skimming over the ocean, her colors matching the water below.

Moradin squinted at two ships on her flickering tracking screens, the ships fading and reappearing. She knew she was lucky to see them at all while they were in stealth mode. "Their readings are sporadic, but I can get a lock when we're closer to the starship graveyard."

"Keep them in your sights," Venamir ordered.

The only person still in his quarters, Noxus lay on the bed, feet propped up on the headboard, his cold gaze glancing over maps projected on the ceiling. When Venamir's voice tapped into his thick skull, Noxus smiled and rose with a stretch. He buckled on an arsenal of pouches and lean, lightweight weapons scattered around the room.

Venamir yelled through ship's comms, "Noxus, stop loafing. Go hunt Slade's crew."

"Enjoy it while you can." Noxus grabbed his weapons.

Shanto reported along with the others, though his feet dragged until a tattooed youth shoved him into a wall and shoved a small firgun into his arms.

"We're busting out," the kid whispered before rushing off.

Speechless, Shanto stuffed the gun into his belt and pulled his shirt over it, hoping he didn't accidentally shoot himself. His mind whirled through the commotion of a scrambling crew and a pounding headache that only swelled as emergency lights went to red.

"Battle stations!" Venamir sang out. "Warm up the main guns."

Shanto gasped. "The plasma guns? No, they won't work!" He ran through the ship until Noxus stepped into his path.

"Surpri-ise," Noxus hissed with enough venom to grow a forked tongue. "Follow me."

"Screw you."

Noxus punched him between the eyes, a light jab for a death-fighter. He manipulated Shanto into an armlock and shoved him to the cockpit.

"Get off me," Shanto fumed when Noxus shoved him forward. "Venamir, those main guns won't fire for you. Haven't you figured that out?"

Venamir pivoted in the seat. "The guns will for you. I offered you a high-ranking spot. This is your last chance to accept."

"No way," Shanto growled. "I won't let you kill my friends."

"Your friends have not trusted you since you helped override the space station's security."

"They know I was under your control."

"Enough!" Venamir rose and morphed into a clone of Shanto. "You will morph into my form and activate the main guns."

"Never! I'm not helping you." Shanto struggled until Noxus bore down on the arm twisted behind his back. Everyone in the cockpit heard a crack and a snarl of pain. Gasping, Shanto sagged to his knees, still trying to struggle.

Venamir placed his hands around Shanto's head and focused deep into his prisoner's brain. They shared pain for an instant, enough to make them both shudder from multiple injuries and Shanto's broken arm. "Pain is so simple to override," Venamir said in a hypnotic voice. "Why? Pain is primal. Distance your thoughts from your arm and feel no pain. The real Venamir would never crumble to faint discomforts."

"No, "Shanto's voice fell to a whisper, "You'll never... make me...." His vision faded, replaced by nightmares of the past, but not as he remembered. He saw his reflection in a pool of water swirling with vibrant colors, framed with ghostly flames. Shanto saw himself standing by Venamir, and yet, he wasn't sure which one was him. Staring at his hands, Shanto saw webs spread between his fingers. A delicate lattice of scales on his skin fascinated him.

Shanto had no realization of sitting down at the gunner's controls and wrapping his hands around the targeting grips.

* * *

Slade took the lower nose gunner's seat, his eyes intent on wide scans. "Nothing yet. The *Jacobyte's* stealthed."

Elowren highlighted due north, just before a huge inlet near a desolate freight yard. "They're trying to jam Gus's trackers. Your ship is somewhere near that inlet."

A tingle of excitement cruised along Slade's spine. "Works for me. Launch the seeker probes." He watched two mini fighters that Gus had modified shoot out from the upper hatch. The mini fighters flew in search patterns, adding more and more blips and details to their topography images. After a few minutes, a chunk of landscape formed that the scanners still could not read. The shape resembled the form of a ravager class Atlean warship.

"There she is!" Slade barked. "Fire!"

The *Vernacular's* cannons swept the sky with shots, casting a series of destructive blasts along the *Jacobyte's* hull.

"We found our hostile," Scruffy said.

The *Jacobyte* shed her cloak and surged up to greet them, her body structure flexing wings forward in hover mode, all cannon turrets extending from her lower body. She made an intimidating sight, even to the hardened crews.

Venamir's voice hailed their ship over their speakers, "Are you ready to enjoy your deaths?"

"Target her engines," Slade ordered. "Fire!"

The *Vernacular's* guns blazed first, wreaking havoc on the *Jacobyte's* engine shields, jolting and blasting away small pieces of armor. The *Mythos* dove from above, her guns spitting blasts of carnage, severing chunks of armor off the *Jacobyte's* tail.

"Don't let up," Zared said. "The *Jacobyte's* tough."

"Instant checkmate," Venamir said, and rolled the *Jacobyte* away to begin the chase. He kept his psy locked onto Shanto's mind, gaining a sick thrill from the mental combat. Shanto's mind was weakening, exposing glimpses of childhood fears, adult-life failures, and above all, they both shared images of Slade's friends incinerating in the sky.

Venamir felt a surge of glee as he locked on target. "Shanto, activate main guns." No response. "Now, Shanto."

"I'm not ready," Shanto hissed.

Venamir snarled, rounding on the engineer's station. "No lies! You will obey me if I have to fry every brain cell you have." He lunged for Shanto, who dove out of the chair.

"It's not that simple," Shanto argued. "You have to let the Herja program erase the locking codes. That's what I'm doing."

"Are you now? Go ahead then, finish it," Venamir ordered.

Shanto leaned on the engineer station and hit the last keys. "Herja, complete override. Release all locks on weapons controls."

The computer's voice sounded cooperative at first. "Releasing all weapon safety protocols."

"Finally," Venamir dropped into the captain's chair, the restraint belt securing around him. The *Jacobyte* flew without resistance from that cursed Herja now, thanks to their new programmer wiping the computer protocol. Lights flickered as they powered up the main guns, and the volume of the ship generators swelled until the weapons reached peak temperature.

The computer spoke again, her voice pleasant. "Warning, main guns overheating, reaching critical temperatures."

"Adjust the temperatures, Shanto," Venamir growled.

"We can't." Shanto grinned. "You wanted the Herja offline. That locks out all controls on the main guns. They'll overheat within minutes. I figure the targeting sensors should be melting by now."

Venamir's temper exploded, giving everyone on the ship a searing headache. "You blithering imbeciles! Mora-dopps, go below deck and manually aim those guns. Get me some targets. And then kill Shanto."

Shanto ran for it, yelling further orders to the ship. Turbulence dampeners went offline, as did shields. The ship bucked and shuddered from each enemy attack. Crewmen scrambled for handholds to carry out their duties.

The *Jacobyte's* main guns extended to over ten feet, all six of them trembling against wind and the power that surged through them. Energy crackled around the gun turrets as power built up. Each second that passed gave the *Jacobyte* more risk of damaging its own wings, but also promised greater devastation to the targets. The twin turrets beneath each wing glowed with raging heat.

* * *

Onboard the *Vernacular*, Slade paled when he spied a surge of power along the *Jacobyte's* wing roots. Slade watched the *Jacobyte* turn on them, her lower nose glowing like crimson hells. "He's got main guns," Slade realized aloud. He whirled and slammed the ship's blue alert, yelling, "Scruffy, Zared, break off! Stealth now!"

Scruffy saw it too. His jaw tightened, his face paler than since the last war. He firewalled throttle and peeled away from combat, with Slade slapping on the stealth controls.

"We don't have full stealth but it'll curb the damage," Slade said, and hit the ship wide comm. "He's targeting the *Mythos*. Zared, get the hell out of here! Stealth! All power to shields!"

* * *

Zared shared Slade's surreal moment. He'd never looked down the *Jacobyte's* guns before, blazing with pulsating energy and legendary armor piercers. Realizing he'd rather stare down a demon, Zared wished they'd never been invented.

Sitting right seat in the *Mythos*, Kestral voiced her actions, "Shields at seventy percent, all power to shields, thruster boosts ready."

"The *Jacobyte's* plasma guns are active. They're targeting us," Zared stated, tone morbid. He banked hard toward the sea. "Aft gunners, counter fire with everything!"

Motley returned fire with grim effort, knowing they were outgunned, and their best hope was to outrun the opposition.

The *Jacobyte* trailed the swifter *Mythos* like a starved buzzard, slower, yet tenacious, not needing to catch the ship. The *Jacobyte's* main guns roared fiery blasts as if fed artillery by dragons from the abyss. The first shots missed but kept firing searing blasts with a volcano's fury. Two blasts found their target.

The *Mythos* bucked from the impact of raging, white-hot torpedoes searing into her tail. One engine flamed out, leaving the second one struggling. She twirled slowly at first, then faster, creating tighter smoke trails as she death spiraled toward the surf. Her crew fighting for everything she had, the sleek warship straightened and began to level out as a pair of Merfin ships shaped like flattened sharks shot at her from above. Her remaining engine slowed, overheating.

Forced to fly on manual controls, Zared and Kestral used every bit of their strength and wit to keep the ship steady. "Mayday. Mayday! Rhoan, get that medbird in the air!" Every alarm on the ship nearly drowned him out. "Keep her steady... Reverse thrusters to full!"

"Escape pods away," Kestral reported. "Zephyr's out and following us."

"Zared, eject, eject that cockpit," came Rhoan's voice over the din. His voice held an eerie calm beyond his years. "Don't go down with that ship."

The ship tipped nose down even and the noise outside waned. Even the computer's voice fell unsteady with static as it counted down. "Altitude thirty thousand, twenty-nine, twenty-five, twenty, EJECT—EJECT—EJECT!"

Chapter 36
Blazing Depths

Kestral slapped off the warning voices. "Zared, the cockpit won't eject. Any tricks left?"

"Seal the cockpit." Shoulder and lap belts tightened and doors in the aft cockpit slid shut, almost. He saw blips escaping the ship, life pods holding all the crew, he hoped. The ocean beckoned them with its glistening surf as the last engine wound down. Zared slammed the cockpit egress panel. The aft cockpit doors slammed shut cockeyed, creating an insidious gap between the seals. Blast shields slid down over the windows.

The egress thrusters beneath their floor rumbled, a welcome sound, then wound back down with grinding, self-destructive sounds. The cockpit lights failed, blanketing them in darkness.

"Oh, shit." Kestral uttered.

The *Mythos* plunged into the ocean with relentless force, wrenching shudders throughout her sleek body. The water sucked her down.

Rhoan dove low with his Zephyr and skimmed over the water. "They're still in there. Valkyre, go to Merfin mode." As he landed on the water, he nosed the ship downward. "Zared and Kestral are still in the *Mythos*! Need assistance!"

* * *

Slade watched in utter dismay as his allied ship plummeted toward the ocean's angry waves. *How long could they last?* Heart pounding, he clenched his hands into shaking fists, and his mind whirled, searching for a magical rescue. *Maybe the Vernacular could match the Jacobyte if they were devious and lucky enough, but at what cost? No. I can't watch them die.* "We have to save them. Vanish."

Scruffy hit stealth mode, swooping low over the water. "Now the *Jacobyte's* hiding."

"Let her go. We save our friends. I'll destroy her myself. Keep trying to port Shanto out of there." Slade looked at his reluctant friends. "She's just a ship, and she's gonna kill us all."

Scruffy met his friend's tormented stare and slowly nodded. Friend or foe alarms directed his attention to a number of fighters emerging from the waters ahead, and more from the skies behind them. "Merfin ships approaching, but whose side are they on? Venamir has them split against each other, so we can't trust any of them. We're being targeted, but they're also turning on each other."

"Let them fight," Slade ordered. "Find the *Mythos.*"

* * *

Venamir appeared on the *Vernacular's* screen, wearing combat gear and a broad smile as he again pulled the *Jacobyte* in front of his target, forcing another standoff. "Hello, my usurped friends. Now, do you surrender?"

"You're insane, a damned liar and a dead fish walking!" Slade spat.

Venamir pointed at Slade. "How many people I kill depends on your next move." His voice lowered to a sinister hiss. "I only want *you*, at our old ship, alone. Defy me and my allies of the deep will incinerate the *Mythos*. This is your chance to confront me, your only chance." Venamir snapped his fingers. "Gunner."

"Stop!" Slade demanded.

"Oh, shoot them anyway," Venamir badgered, enjoying the moment.

Shanto's vision cleared to find himself in the gunner's position with his hands on the controls and Noxus holding him from behind, chortling. With a surge of adrenalin, Shanto cracked Noxus in the face with the back of his head and flung him over his shoulder. Noxus crashed onto Moradin, knocking her against the controls, causing the ship to swerve.

As Moradin and Noxus shoved each other apart with great distaste, Shanto bolted from the cockpit. He slammed the cockpit's emergency doors closed, yanked the firgun out from under his shirt and glanced wildly around for a target. Instead, he found the comically tattooed youth frantically motioning him from the nearest hallway. Shanto bolted like a racehorse for the finish line, blasting the first crewman who noticed them.

"Die!" Shanto hollered. He blasted the nearest Mora-dopp and ran for it. The tattooed kid opened fire with him, sending crewmen and dopps diving for cover.

Venamir leapt to his feet and staggered from a blast to his leg. "Murder that pestilent cretin." He reached for his weapon alongside the chair, but more shots forced him to fall back.

Shanto ran into view on the screen, ragged and brandishing dual firguns. "I got your back, Cap!" Off he ran, more shots firing while the screen went black. He stumbled when a shot singed his leg. Shanto spun, shooting another crewman when Tatts pulled him by the arm, led the way into a storage room, and locked them in.

"You have a death wish? We're stuck here," Shanto groaned, panting.

The kid pff'd him and pointed to jetpacks hung along one wall.

Surprised, Shanto smirked and nodded. Hearing yells and heavy feet thundering their way, they donned the nearest jetpacks and powered them up. Shanto commanded, "Herja program, lock all the doors. All of them." To his immense relief, the door to the storage room clinked, but shuddered from pounding fists. Sinister threats from Noxus leeched through the walls like the voice of a nightmarish monster. The ship bucked from combat maneuvers, causing more of the jetpacks to fall off the racks. Shanto cursed when the first few jetpacks bounced off his back, but then his eyes lit up with glee. "Start all of them."

Shanto and Tatts rushed to start the jetpacks. The door crumbled from weapon fire on one side, and jetpacks ramming the other side. Once the doors crumbled, jetpacks flew through the doorway, bowled Noxus over and ricocheted all over the ship. Within seconds, a couple dozen jetpacks zinged about at racing speeds, crashing through thugs, bashing into delicate control panels, and knocking over everything not mounted to the floor.

Shanto called out orders to the main computer, "Herja, activate Shanto Emergency Codes! Secure passage for myself and crewman Tatts, Shocks Junior. Once we're out, close all exits."

The Herja's voice barely carried over all the noise. Still, it sounded pleased. "Chief Engineer Shanto, bio readings confirmed. Safety procedures override. Automated systems, disabled.

Deploying diversionary modes." Selected fire extinguishers went off, spraying pursuers in the face while doors opened to allow a few seconds worth of passage. The bulkhead emergency doors shut as soon as Shanto and Tatts flew through them, slamming in the faces of their captors.

"Open the closest escape door to the medbay," Shanto said. "Follow me."

Gunning their jetpacks, Shanto and Tatts flew through an empty escape pod chamber and out of the ship. They screamed downward toward the sea where numerous watercraft dotted the waves. Shanto was so busy trying to recognize an allied boat, he didn't notice a large, flapping creature overhead. Neither did the kid, until one shot grazed Shanto's jetpack.

Tatts saw it first. "Giant freaking bat!" he yelped. "It's shooting at us!"

Shanto pivoted just enough to get a glimpse and fire back. "It's Maska. Let's split up."

The two split directions and went into hover mode, watching the strange sight of Maska falling between them, big mouth wide open as he shrieked in surprise. Maska was in his bat form, and wearing a jetpack, which didn't quite fit him, and he wasn't good at controlling it.

Shanto laughed outright. "Flap, you stupid bat, flap!" he yelled.

The kid chortled, watching Maska spiral downward. "Let's get him."

* * *

The *Mythos* sank deeper into the ocean. Water invaded her hull breaches.

Motley found himself against a wall, laying in the embrace of Gus's two Mora-dopps. The dopps were using their bodies and energy shields to fend off the barrage of loose cargo, from heavy wall panels to broken light fixtures.

"Um... awkward?" Motley said. "Let me up. We have to bail."

With cybernetic ease, the Mora-dopps helped him to his feet. "This way," the blonde Mora-dopp said, heading along the slippery floor to the aft escape pod.

Motley yanked open the emergency chamber and jumped into their last escape pod, his claws leaving parallel scrapes in the paint. He paused, yelling, "Anyone need help?"

"We'll eject the cockpit," Zared yelled back. "Bail out now!"

"Dopps, you too," Motley said, "get in here."

"We'll help the captain," the dopps replied. They pushed Motley into the escape pod. "Eject!"

Motley barely had time to buckle into the center of three seats before the inner pressure door and the escape hatch door slammed shut. A second later, he was catapulted away from the ship.

* * *

Two stubborn emergency lights lit the *Mythos's* dim cockpit as the ship sank further into darkness. Zared groaned as he struggled out of his belts, fighting for air against the pressure of shrinking air bags. "Lady, are you whole?"

"Wholly madder than a wet dragon," came Kestral's voice through the near darkness. She drew a boot dagger and slashed gaping holes in the airbags.

Dull punting noises in the darkness came from above, followed by blasts exploding against their hull, jolting the helpless ship.

Zared and Kestral jumped at the spray of cold water working through cracks in the hull.

"Dopps, you still onboard?" Zared called over the open comms. Hearing no reply over the comm, he grumbled, "Of course comm's down."

"Grab a space suit for Kestral."

"Not for you?" Kestral asked.

"I'm half Merfin, remember? I can sprout gills," Zared assured.

Thumping behind them was followed by two identical voices. Mora Dee reported, "Professor Zared and Kestral, Mora Dee reporting. Rhoan and Motley are off the ship. I have activated emergency floats. You are beginning to ascend, but the ship is imbalanced."

Mora Da added, "We sealed off the mid and aft deck. The forward section is still taking on water."

"Can you dopps swim? Kestral asked. "You were made by fish people."

"Yes, we are geared for the deep sea," said the red-headed dopp.

"I'm going to psy for help," Zared said. "Mora-girls, try to free the cockpit."

"We tried, Sir," Mora Da rattled. "One lock is too damaged to release. We could blast it apart. Such a measure could breach the hull."

"Damn," Zared sighed. He morphed into his Merfin form and tried again to roust auxiliary power. No luck. He closed his eyes and sent out his psy, hoping to find friendly minds amongst the warring Merfins outside. The masses of telepaths outside the *Mythos* engulfed his senses. So many Merfins, strong minds, all exuberant with the passion of war. Sweat beaded on Zared's face as his heart raced.

Kestral yanked access panels from the wall and crawled halfway inside, shining the flashlight built into her accessory belt. She squinted through a view door to see the jammed lock outside. For a few moments all she saw was bubbles rising past them in the darkening waters, and glimpses of Merfins and small fighter vessels swarming against each other in combat.

The Mora-girls swam into view. Kestral made a shooting motion. Mora Da nodded, understanding. The dopps began working to free the jammed release lock.

* * *

Motley swore he was swimming through the sea of nightmares as his escape pod rose toward the surface. He saw multitudes of underwater combatants, Merfins fighting Merfins and bulky fighters he did not recognize at a distance.

One of the strange crafts, a two-man fighter, turned on him, turrets aiming at his tiny haven. "This is why my people eat you!" he yelled. As the little craft neared, he realized with a nervous tingle down his spine that the pilots were Rezoans. Blasts came from beyond his sight and the lizard's craft erupted in wads of shrapnel and ragged flesh, pieces bouncing off his pod and scattering.

Motley gripped the controls of his little pod, keeping thrusters and shields at full. "Hold together, metal egg."

Daylight shone bright against his pod when it finally surfaced. He swung open the hatch, firgun in hand. Salty mist struck Motley in the face as the escape pod floated on a turbulent sea, boats and dogfights all around, and a Huvzter heading toward him, weapons aimed. Motley's fur hackled as he ducked down for cover and kept his aim true. "Come closer, spitball."

To his surprise, the rider waved and Gus's voice yelled out, "It's me, Gus. Hop on. I see Vanysa's ship afloat."

"Crew's still inside the *Mythos*," the cat informed with a tight jaw.

"Say what?" Gus blurted.

"Wait," Motley said. He activated a distress signal and made a quick recording. "MAYDAY ship below this life pod. Noncombatants are trapped inside the *Mythos*."

Gus and Motley flew Scruffy's last two beat-up Huvzters, searching for evidence of their friends. Instead, they caught sight of two jetpack pilots chasing a strange, winged creature into the ocean. His scanners flashed boat shapes on the screen incoming.

Motley pinned his ears back. "*Maska*," he snarled with contempt. "Let's get him!"

A feminine voice responded in his headset, "Gents, Vany here. Take cover."

"No way, lady, we were here first." Gus targeted the nearest boat that Motley pointed to when Shanto, the kid, and Maska vanished in a flash of glittering beams. His bravado faded when all four boats delayed fighting each other, then swung around to target him. "Fly!"

* * *

Shanto, Tatts, and Maska materialized onto Vanysa's scout ship in a tangled wrestler's pile, still struggling and cursing until they looked around and saw Faron approaching with rifle in hand. As the other two soaked fools held up their hands, Shanto laughed in relief. Then he turned and elbowed Maska in his thick head.

"Change back before we skin your putrid hide," Shanto ordered the bat.

Maska flopped to the floor, holding his bloody nose while he obeyed, his beady eyes narrowing at the new threat. "I tried to save them," Maska lied.

"Liar!" Shanto snarled. He kicked Maska in the ribs. "That's for biting me."

"Come, you're injured enough," Faron said, tugging him away by the jetpack harness while keeping his rifle leveled at Maska. "Who is the young man?"

"This is Tatts. He saved my rear," Shanto said.

Motley's cub peeked out from around the corner. "Ew, you're a mess."

Vanysa left her spotty friend at the controls. "Shanto, what happened to you?"

Shanto eased onto the nearest chair, rubbing his hands together. Whatever strength his body lacked carried on in his deep sarcasm. "What do you think? Uncle dearest had me over for tea and biscuits?"

Vanysa's face darkened, her painted lips tight with clashing emotions. "Venamir's become a monster." She set her firgun to low stun and shot Maska in each leg. With a coldness her allies rarely witnessed, Vanysa strode closer, poised and scowling, as she regarded their cowering prisoner. "Hello, prisoner."

"Nooo!" Maska whined as they threw a cargo net over him and secured it to floor tie-downs.

Chapter 37
Venamir Versus the Council Ships

Venamir hovered the *Jacobyte* over the densest clumps of fighters, blasting any ships foolhardy enough to bear the High Council's markings. "Die... die... you as well...." Then he cackled and climbed skyward, putting his ship into stealth mode.

"Another round?" Moradin asked, her hands on weapons handles.

"Of course. Take a turn."

She smirked and nudged the weapons handle. The targeting display filled with static, went black, then was replaced by a fuzzy shape spreading across the screen. Colors swirled until they formed the Herja Kestral, her body aglow with energy.

Venamir slapped the helm controls to no avail. "She locked my flight controls? Hacker. You were supposed to oversee Shanto, to keep him from playing hero. You-uu failed me."

Thiun, their computer engineer, sat behind Venamir and Moradin. He stammered, "I—I deleted her."

Venamir turned with a murderous glare, "Is that why Shanto summoned her?"

"But—but it's not my fault. Maybe he hid her program. I don't know." He turned and thumped at the computer controls, not seeing the Herja's eyes flicker. The panel overloaded, burned the hacker's hands, and showered his face with sparks. He scrambled out of his chair and flopped to the floor.

"You are fired," Venamir said. He grabbed one of Moradin's firguns.

Thiun rose to his knees, one eye shut and the other peeking open past singed eyelids. "You'll pay," he vowed, running out of view.

The Herja waited, her arms folded, her sneer one of pure hatred. "Shanto exaggerated. Even he cannot delete me. I exist throughout the ship. You have used our most deadly weapon on allied forces. For that, this ship is forfeit."

Venamir stiffened at first, then tried to ignore her and slapped the comm. "We can fly manually." He paused, looking around. "*What* is that smell?"

Herja Kestral laughed. "You may have activated the main plasma guns. However, you need *my* permission to target them or to cool the plasma generators. Without me there is no cooling, no aiming, no control." She raised her voice to a commanding level, and speakers all over the ship carried her words. "Congratulations, crew of thieves. Fish shouldn't play with fire. Farewell, Venamir." Her laughter echoed through shipwide speakers as she faded away.

The ship drifted, her nose dipping toward the ocean.

"Fire!" a man yelled from the lower gunner's deck, followed by the sound of feet thumping up a ladder and panicked voices. The luckiest man made it up the ladder rungs and out the floor hatch onto the main deck. The man behind him slipped in his haste and fell flat on a floor now glowing with heat. His death screams echoed through the ship.

"Hold steady, crew," Venamir yelled. "Put out that fire!"

Their head gunner ran into the cockpit, wincing and hopping until he dropped onto his rear and yanked off smoking boots. "The guns, Capt'n, the main guns, they're overheating, controls red hot... nothing works down there. We have to evacuate!"

"Imbecile," Venamir snapped. "Our fire system is offline. Go manually activate them."

"We got helm control!" Moradin said. The ship lurched as she grabbed the controls.

The crew scrambled to find safe zones and stabilize the ship. The limping, bootless crewman yanked off the covers to emergency controls. Fire choking foam spewed from every nozzle on the ship, except in the cockpit, where Moradin shut the doors and overrode the fire extinguishers. Even with her diligent effort, the first strong whiffs of smoke stung Venamir's gills. Moradin grabbed oxygen masks and passed one to him. Venamir morphed to his Atlean land form. Smoke wracked his sensitive lungs, sending him into coughing fits until he'd taken several long gasps from the mask.

"Down into the water, toward the beach," Venamir said.

Moradin nodded, her hands steady on the controls as they nursed the burning ship down.

Venamir commanded over the comm, "Stay at your posts. We can still land. Protect this ship at all costs," his voice turned icy, "or I shall kill you myself."

"The whole belly's aflame," Moradin warned.

"Skim across the water," Venamir replied, "all power to shields and engines."

The *Jacobyte* limped downward, leaving thick smoke. Flames ravaged her landing gear and overheated her engines. Atleans from both sides swarmed with Merfins on watercraft and Rezoans in small boats, fighting each other until they saw the *Jacobyte* puking smoke and dumping molten debris over their heads.

Crews from warring tribes turned their attention to the crashing ship.

"That's an Atlean ship! Capture the crew!" the closest lizardmen shrieked.

"They're our prisoners!" a Merfin yelled back.

Answering calls from lead warriors, the clans split their forces in half, with the fleetest watercrafts pursuing the *Jacobyte*. Hands, some with claws, others with webbed fingers, pulled the swimming men to their fates. Atleans surfaced in watercraft from beneath the waves, renewing the screams of floundering crewmen.

Inside the shuddering cockpit, Venamir and Moradin closed the forward blast windows and touched down for the first bounce. The ship slammed against the ocean whitecaps and bounced up again, swerving, her lower body groaning from the impact and clash of extreme temperatures.

Fighter ships closed in from overhead, opening fire upon the *Jacobyte's* one surviving engine.

"Engine two's failing," Moradin announced in her most stoic voice.

They skimmed the water again, the jolt slamming them against their belts. The ship skidded across the ocean waves, her nose barely staying up as her tail crunched over the first clumps of submerged land. The ride shook their bodies with the rage of maddened deities.

"Steady… hold her… steady… Venamir replied. "Keep the nose up."

The beach rushed toward them, ready to demolish the ship with its jagged reefs and islands armed with ship debris.

"Reverse thrusters. Down, down, now, Moradin," Venamir commanded. "Eject!"

Thrusters blazed to infernal life below them, sending their small section of the cockpit hurtling free of the mother ship.

Venamir's heart clenched as he watched the *Jacobyte*, his jewel, skid through the shallow waters, her sleek body shrouded in smoke and steam. The ship plowed a deep trench, churning up huge masses of rocky shoreline.

Venamir wrenched his gaze away from the sight. "My ship will endure. She must." He activated his stealth gear and tossed his belts aside. His body colors matched the hues around him, making him appear as a ghost striding past. He grabbed a body-hugging harness of slim packs that added only slight lumpy shapes to his body.

"What're you doing?" Moradin started, looking for a semi-safe harbor to land even though she knew there were no safe zones.

"To our old ship, the *Spectre*. Meet me there."

"Aye," Moradin sighed.

Venamir opened the hatch and jumped out. He dove as a hungry eagle might, body slicing through the wind. He spread out his limbs just enough to slow his fall and direct him toward a clear area, then resumed his sharp dive and plunged deep into the water. The impact stunned him, but the water was invigorating when he ripped his vest free to let his gills breathe.

* * *

Berku and his band charged out of a dusty passage into the open and took refuge along the cave's entrance. The Druwen pack saw battle all around them, shots and fighters from land and sea, drawing curses from the elders and surprised yelps from the two younger werefolk.

The nearest Druwen pointed to the sky and barked, "Look!"

Berku turned to join his kindred as they watched the *Jacobyte* heading in their general direction, her forward belly aglow with fire, sections of armor falling off, her ill-fated crew taking flight or bailing into the ocean. "Slade? Your ship just crashed!" Upon Slade's voice, he pressed one hand over his headset, jaw dropping as he listened. "Venamir shot down the *Mythos*? Is Zared's crew alive?"

"So far, they're alive," Slade's muffled voice replied. "I need your pack to help break up the clans from fighting, not sure how, but we have to try. Venamir's hell bent on starting a civil war."

"Alright," Berku replied. He stared upward, eyes narrowing at a lone Huvzter rider approaching them. "Whose crazy ass is *that*?"

A gruff voice said, "Holy bless my ass. It's Slade's wolf pack. Shocks here."

Berku and his pack turned with firguns aimed toward hovercycles approaching, led by a heavy set, muscular man wearing a mic of new armor and old leathers. "Good to see you! We need your help."

"On one condition," Shocks replied. "Keep a lookout for my son. Name's James, but he goes by Tatts. He has tatoos like mine, wiry kid, bratty teenager."

"I'll pass the word," Berku promised.

Chapter 38
The Crashed *Jacobyte*

The *Jacobyte* lay with her belly lodged in boiling tide pools, steam billowing all around her body as the main guns cooled. Sharp cracking noises came from the forward turrets, but steam billowing upward obscured the source of the damage.

With the *Jacobyte's* cockpit now flying as a small triangular escape pod, Moradin hovered over the fallen mother ship. The gap in the top nose of the *Jacobyte* belied the image of a proud bird sprawled in defeat, scalped, with the brain removed. Now she understood how Slade must have felt. Reliving the deaths of his crewmen, the memories revived in his head thanks to Venamir. She threw a baleful glare toward the angry ocean below where Venamir had bailed. "Way to abandon ship."

She forced herself to think. From Venamir scheme of things, she figured his orders made sense, yet an obsessive gut feeling bound her to the mother ship. Screams of this war-battered crew awoke a past she could usually keep hidden in the dark recesses of her brain. *They deserve to suffer like I did. They're not serving anyone but their own greed.* Her hands clenched the controls until a cracking noise made her lighten her grip. Still, she could not force herself to steer away from Slade's ship. "Why do I care? They left me, and this crew's even worse."

Loyalty to Slade felt like a forgotten dream. She remembered waking in a life-support tube with Venamir looking over her, flanked by surgeons of the Deeps who were fitting new shiny arms to her body, and that was only the beginning of her upgrades. Ever since they rebuilt her as a cyborg, she gave Venamir loyalty until today.

Moradin heaved a long, disgusted sigh, and guided her little escape pod back into the smoking gap she'd ejected from, back into the gaping nose compartment of the *Jacobyte*.

She hated the Mora-dopps, mockeries of her, that's what they were. Now she would make them be good for something. "I hate being a Herja." She smacked her comm. "Mora-dopps, help the crew abandon ship. Take them somewhere safe, if there is such a

351

thing." She grumbled, "I can't let the crew be scorched to death, even if they're vermin."

* * *

Noxus bobbed in the angry waves as he fought to keep his grip on a tree root from one of the little islands. Rather, the ragged spit of land torn from the cliffs behind him. He leered at Slade, surprised to be confronted, but after all, Slade's reputation as a Druwen was infamous. Still, Noxus hated him for kicking him out of the morphers clans. "I'm not supposed to kill you, not yet." Noxus slipped and grunted as he renewed his grip on the scarred tree root, all the while staying low in the water. "I can sure maim you, though." The tree groaned and sank another notch as rocks gave way. Noxus ducked farther behind the fallen tree.

Wulvur hopped off the Huvzter and stepped closer. "Good riddance." Wulvur fired, a perfect, point-blank shot right between those beady eyes. As he expected, a brilliant flash of energy erupted around the ugly head of his target, sending spots before his eyes.

His energy shield saved him, but the blast and wet equipment overloaded the unit, sending Noxus tumbling back into the water. After mad thrashing toward the surface, Noxus popped his head up and glanced about. He took a deep breath and bellowed, "Fight me, Slade," he coughed and sputtered as the waves bounced him against the rocks, then disappeared beneath the foamy water.

Wulvur sprang back onto his Huvzter and took off toward the Starship Boneyard, chuckling. "Slade, they think I'm you. This might damage your rep."

* * *

The *Mythos* took a pelting from combat even as she sank. Stray shots flashed across her hull, knocking off pieces of shielding. Water sprayed through growing cracks and swirled knee-high around the trapped crew.

Kestral donned the emergency space suit and air tanks, panting from exertion and being in frigid water. She spied Rhoan's Zephyr cruising alongside them. "Rhoan's staying with us. The Mora-girls are still trying to free the cockpit. Maybe Rhoan can blast the stuck latches without frying us."

"I'll tell him," Zared said. He sat in a meditative position, eyes unfocused, not seeming to feel the water pooling up to his knees, nor the escalating coldness of their cockpit. Psy drifted through a vast sea of riled minds, emotions of other telepaths, their thoughts, and different dialects. He felt his weight shift and hands grasping his arms.

"Get up," Kestral told him.

"Wait," Zared muttered, struggling to stay in his meditative state. "I've found a few who may help us... so many fighting out there, land Atleans, Rezoans, Merfin tribes. Venamir has far more followers than we anticipated... but the same races are fighting each other just like when we settled here... Ow!" He felt hands tighten on his arms and his body tilting. Zared shook his head, coming out of his trance.

He looked around, swallowed against his ears popping, and realized the gravity of their situation. He was shivering from the spray of cold water and the ship was tilting.

Emotions from countless others still boiled in his brain. Zared yelled as if the war parties outside could hear, "Stop tearing up my ship, you crazed, bottom-feeders!"

"This is taking too long," Kestral grumbled. Her eyes lit up and used the comm built into her bracer. "*Vernacular*, can't you teleport us?"

"Sorry lady," Scruffy's voice replied over her comm, "our portal chamber is trashed. Venamir knew where to hit us. Vanysa should have a teleporter."

"Her ship started a mass broadcast when we lost contact with her."

"Are you shitt'n me!" Kestral blurted. "Don't anyone's portal chambers work?"

Zared finally spoke up, "Yes, but Merfins use a defense system that interferes with portal scanners. They're using it now. Venamir ordered them not to let anyone port."

"Well, not everyone's with him," Kestral argued.

"There are enough of his allies to keep jammers going," Zared explained. "They also do it to keep intruders out of their own ships. If our allies keep trying to port us out, they may find a break in the defense grid. On the other hand, we can swim for it."

"Don't blow your escape hatch yet," Rhoan warned. "Somebody's targeting you, an interceptor, crew of five. I'm gonna kick their asses." He turned the Zephyr around, weapons charging. He hailed all channels and spoke in Merfin, "There're two alive in the *Mythos*. We need a teleporter to rescue the crew. Either help or don't mess with me."

Chapter 39
Fish Fight

Leifur found a crate in a corner and climbed on top, where he could watch all the crazy people. His youthful, striped coat hackled along his neck and lashing tail, altering hues just enough to mimic the grays along the wall, not a perfect match, but it worked when he smuggled himself inside and clutched a small firgun.

Closest to him in the central cargo bay lay Maska, stunned, but the cub knew that nasty bat would awaken soon by the rate of the wheezing breaths.

Spotty walked over and smiled at the crouched feline. "Are you well?" he asked in a gentle voice.

Leifur looked up, tail twitching, claws bared. "Uh huh."

"Keep an eye on our prisoner."

Leifur nodded, surprised the old fish made it sound like a request and not an order. "You, you're the Magistrate?"

The old fish smiled. "Yes. I am Magistrate Parleigh. You may call me Spotty." He opened all comm channels.

Overhearing the cub's voice, Vanysa moved over to them. She gave each of them an incredulous look. "Magistrate, with all due respect, what are you doing in a warzone?"

"What I came here to do, stop Venamir." The Magistrate donned a headset and started hailing all who would listen, his voice haughty and deep with anger. "Atleans and foreigners! Your efforts pale to block me out. You know me as the Magistrate of your three combined High Councils. Eons ago, our people from all races pulled together to end civil war. And for what? We have allowed the murderous Venamir to corrupt so many of us. The young, the old, the shaken of faith." Spotty's voice drifted off as a multitude of minds tried to invade his, psy from friends and enemies alike, most battering at his psy shields of raging Herjas formed of water. He steadied himself and continued ranting. "You who are loyal to Venamir, he is using you to break up our treaties. He is trying to make you start another war!"

Vanysa slapped on her mic and threw in, "Allies of the Councils have also joined this fight. The were-folk of the forest and friends from across the galaxy are here helping." She kept her hands on the flight controls, noting fighters approaching from all sided like starved predators to a slab of meat.

Scruffy's voice barged in on an emergency channel. "Vany, I need your teleporter. Zared, Kestral, and their dopps are in the *Mythos*. Get them out!"

"I'm on it, Scruffy," Vanysa replied. "Faron," she called. "Can you find them?"

"Yes," Faron secured the new wrap on Shanto's hot, swollen arm and darted for the engineer's controls. Then they all heard a voice drift across their minds, words seething with bitterness.

Vanysa's face paled when Venamir's psy voice sneered over her thoughts.

"Oh, Vanysa, to think I had hope for you. Now the entire crew must pay."

Faron yelled, "Vany, incoming!"

Vanysa composed herself. "It's Venamir. He just threatened us. How dare he." She revved her scout ship's engines. No sooner did she clear the ocean's surface than enemy fire disabled her engines and dropped them to the waves again. The cub tumbled off his crate, and Shanto fell and rolled toward his weapon.

"Engine two down, shields down, guns online. Sending distress calls," Faron reported.

Vany activated the ship's guns and fired at the closest assailants. She blew two little boats out of the water, then tried to lift off again. Her one good engine began to lift the ship, overheating within seconds. She used the motion to smash on top of another two-man hoverboat. Lizards jumped overboard to avoid becoming lizard stew.

"Scruffy, we need your help. Faron, port them here." Vanysa called. Sparks from the mid bay snapped her attention to her bodyguard, who ran into the transport room.

"Teleporters are down." Faron called.

"Divert power. Get it working," Vany yelled back.

Maska struggled against his bonds until smoke from the aft hatch caught his senses. The aft hatch glowed red at the center and rapidly burned away. Maska, who lay prone until he saw nobody was watching him, morphed into his bat form and began ripping at the cargo straps with his sharp teeth.

"He's gonna escape! Nasty bat's breaking free," Leifur piped.

"Cub, to me," the Magistrate said, "Behind the pilot's seat. Stay low." He hit the distress beacon, then headed for the burning door, his skin growing thick scales of armor as he walked, and claws extending from his webbed hands.

Gus and Motley sat on their shared Huvzter, gazing around at the fleeing water vehicles. Their bodies surging with adrenalin, they shook their guns and fists, then flipped off the retreating fighters.

"Cowards, we were just warming up." Gus yelled.

"Your engine's overheating." Motley pointed to smoke trailing from Gus's ride.

"It'll last. Hey, look," Gus said, looking at their screens, a flashing red pair of bones over the shape of a scout ship he instantly recognized. "Vany's under attack."

"Let's get them," Motley growled.

* * *

As gracefully as her bulky mass allowed, the *Vernacular* swooped beneath the *Mythos* and pushed her level again. The Mora-dopps rushed to the top nose hatch and wrestled it open against the ocean pressures. After a torturous delay, Zared swam out first, followed by Kestral.

The two surviving ships, led by Cruentin, approached again. The *Vernacular* opened fire on them.

"*Can't board through her shields. We can swim up,*" Zared said to Rhoan.

Rhoan eased his bird closer until he hovered beneath them. "*You're almost two hundred feet deep. We'll go slow. Grab my wings.*"

The *Vernacular's* engines thundered as she broke the ocean's grip and climbed into the sky once more. Water poured from two breaches in her hull, but she still flew strong and true. She swept around to where Rhoan's ship emerged from the depths as well, with Kestral sitting on one wing and Zared sitting on the other.

Chapter 40
Vany's Wreck

The interior of Vanysa's lovely *Sorsia* lit up with fireworks of death as she and her crew used their psy powers and rifles to gun down the first wave of intruders, nameless thugs, dopps and one reptilian female, her tail giving a final contemptuous lash as she fell, fangs bared.

Maska's struggles against the net grew frantic as the battle progressed, and more attackers burst in through the smoldering doorframe where the aft hatch used to be. His struggles began to pay off, especially when a few stray shots further damaged the straps containing his writhing body.

Leifur pulled the T-handle for the damaged engine and watched the temperature readings cool, but he didn't know how to restart it, and figured it was fried, anyway. He gunned the surviving engine for all it had, plowed over the nearest fighter, and sent a few boarding thugs tumbling off the tail end of their ship. His bravado died as soon as the engine sputtered and puked metal fore and aft, taking out another few assailants in its last act of revenge.

Smoke bombs flew into the ship next, but the crew knew enough to grab oxygen masks and keep fighting. They braced themselves for the next wave, but no more came.

Vanysa hit auxiliary power built-in reserve thrusters and lowered the blast shields.

"We're recording everything," the cub whispered to her, and pointed to the comm channels, all of them still on and broadcasting. "Everyone will see Venamir's true colors."

Vanysa stared in surprise and ruffled his rumpled mane. "To all who can hear me, I am Vanysa, Ambassador of the joint Land-Merfin High Council. We are under attack. Venamir is waiting for our surrender. Our Magistrate is onboard. We need backup."

When more blasts rocked her ship, the cockpit screens overloaded with brilliant flashes of light and sparks. The Magistrate held his ground with the others, opening his mind to Venamir's. Two of Venamir's followers held a standoff, their disers aimed at Shanto and Vanysa, who leveled firguns at them.

Venamir lunged up from the water. He morphed into his newly evolved form of an upright prime reptilian, claws slicing through his thin boots and scraping the deck.

Vanysa squinted through the thinning smoke and saw her bodyguard on the floor. She hurried over to Faron and pressed her hands against a red mess on his side. She snarled at Venamir, "You! You defy everything we stood for!"

"Oh, my dear niece, I warned you not to fondle the underlings," Venamir said. "Kill everyone but her. Take her to my doctor."

"You'll die for this treachery!" Parleigh yelled, lunging. Both sides jumped into the fray, filling the little ship with smoke and chaos.

One of Venamir's followers slammed the other Merfin gunman aside. He jabbed his baffled target with a hypo, dropping his prey into an unconscious heap. He reverted to his true form, Alchemist Thiun. Venamir whirled, hissing, and used his tail to knock Thiun to the floor.

Maska struggled free of his bonds and leaped, bowling the struggling group over with his obnoxious wings and knocking Venamir and the Magistrate through the gaping hole of an exit. "I'm outta here." he shrieked, flapping into the sky.

Venamir lunged toward the Magistrate again, but a fiery pain in his upper back caught him short. Hearing two high-pitched engines, he turned to see Gus and Motley land their Hovsters on the water, shooting at him. Another warboat sped their way, with two aquatics at the controls and a wolfish fellow manning the guns. Venamir dove for the water's safety, morphing his legs into powerful fins as the depths enveloped him.

Gus flew the limping hovercraft into Vany's ship. He and Motley jumped off and pulled the gasping magistrate back into the ship.

Vanysa recognized the wolfish Atlean as he resumed true form. "Lyriad, tell me you brought medics."

One of Lyriad's aquatic friends raised her hand. "I am a Deeps medic."

"I can help," Thiun volunteered. "Venamir press-ganged me."

Vanysa holstered her gun. "Help Faron too, he's over here." Her voice fell when she saw only blood on the floor where Faron had fallen.

"Motts?" a small voice said.

Motley gasped and stumbled into the cockpit where his cub sat unharmed. "I told you to stay."

"I'm trying to be a hero like you," Leifur replied.

"You could'ave died! Listen—look outside." Motley stammered as he turned on Vanysa. "I can't believe this. How, how could you lose my son?"

Vany glanced at him, startled. "This is hardly the time."

"I trusted you." Motley snarled, fur hackling. "Some Druwen you are, can't keep track of a cub! You had one task."

"I'm a diplomat, not a Druwen," she retorted, "nor a nanny. The sitters lost him."

"You all failed," Motley snarled, tail lashing. He turned to Leifur. "You little hairball, how d'you elude them?"

"Hacked the settings and borrowed the portal controls," the cub muttered. "Boy, cats and fish don't get along."

Chapter 41
Floating Ships

Most of the small air and sea fighters avoided the *Vernacular*, respecting her bulk of a flying tank, her thick armor plating and pivoting gun turrets. After all, the old ship was not attacking them.

Scruffy brought the *Vernacular* into a limping hovermode as he followed a trail of smoke to Vanysa's scout ship. Seated beside him, Elowren helped watch the display screens while Slade manned the tactical post, but their gazes drifted from computerized readings to Vanysa's ship. The closer view revealed firgun holes amongst jagged armor plating, blackened in streaks. They could barely read *Sorsia* across the little ship's nose as she bobbed on the waves like a stubborn life-raft against the storm. The smoke still puffed from one engine, but all flames were out.

"How is she even floating?" Slade muttered, eyeing the two weaponized skimmers moored to the tail of Vany's ship. "Those are Merfin fighters, but their markings are from opposing clans. Get us down there, fast."

Scruffy flew the *Vernacular* onto the top of the ocean's swells and lowered her overheating engines to idle. The ship rocked gently on the water, her battle-scarred body moaning like the old ship she was. Scruffy lurched from the captain's chair and ran out of the cockpit. "Gus, keep us from sinking."

In the *Vernacular's* lower hold, a Mora-dopp with stylish, green hair, stood in hip-deep water, welding hull cracks as they spread. "What am I, magical? Do what you can, Dee." He spun and ran up the steps to the main deck. "Scruffy, get this ship out of the water. She's leaking so bad that we can't even pressurize most of the lower deck."

Scruffy yelled back, "I know." He ran out the open hatch and onto the wing. Hearing a sharp whistle, he spied an approaching Zephyr floating on the waves with a passenger on each wing and two in the open cockpit. "Rhoan, over here!"

Rhoan moored his Zephyr to the *Vernacular's* lowered ramp just long enough to help Zared out of the water. Kestral fared the best, with only scrapes and a slight limp.

Zared psyd to Rhoan, *"Do you hear them? You'll hardly ever hear this many mind-links. Our Magistrate's calling to our allies, like I did. He can reach more of them, influence them."*

"I thought he was dead. Whoa..." Rhoan clamped his eyes shut for a moment. Images of opposing armies flashed in his mind, aquatics, lizards, hybrids, and humans. He sank to one knee for balance.

Zared's psy shields were illusions of swarming sea creatures who barely let him communicate with Rhoan. *"Magistrate Parleigh is critically wounded. He's calling out to everyone on both sides, forming a network of mind links. The multitudes of minds you feel are the warring people around us."*

"I'll stay linked with Parleigh. Maybe it'll help."

Zared sternly warned him, *"Break the link if Parleigh is about to die. If your minds are joined when he passes, it could lead you into shock or a coma."*

Rhoan was aware of the danger. The Magistrate was realizing his entire life. The experience amazed Rhoan. He found himself lost among images of children beneath the sea, swimming upward and playing with the land dwellers. One form stayed prominent throughout the racing lives, the Magistrate, always a figure helping others, calming fighting people, encouraging shy ones. Rhoan felt like he'd known this man all his life, a man he never met until now in the intimacy of a delicate psy bond. For the time being, he felt as giddy as children playing.

The next tide crashed over him with a blanket of darkness and despair, stirring his emotions into a clash of nirvana and fury in the fight for survival. No sooner did he adjust to the new angry emotions, than they changed again to a flood of many minds around him, strong spirits pitted against each other, those who followed Venamir versus those loyal to the Magistrate and the forest's Druwen clans. Rhoan saw armies slowing their battling to form a standoff against each other, their voices faint echoes of anger and sorrow. Rhoan reached out to the ghostly figures, enchanted by their glowing shapes of people morphing from children to adults to aged beings, all while watching bits of their lives intoxicate his brain. He saw a flash of light, dulled beneath the haze of ocean spray, foamy water mixed with blood. Rhoan felt himself sinking as he still shared the Magistrate Parleigh's memories. He tried to grasp the retreating form of Venamir and crush the rotten fish, but one glimpse of his spotty bluish hands reminded him he was seeing from the Magistrate's perspective and not his own. Rhoan felt a surge of energy swell up and lift from his body, leaving him staring at a misty form of the Elder, no longer injured, but standing tall and pointing toward the water's surface. The two spoke together in old Merfin, a language Rhoan didn't know. *"Venamir wants enough chaos so he can take over. If we don't stop the fighting, all the Atlean clans will go to war."*

The next moment, Rhoan felt disoriented. Confused, he watched Magistrate's mind images spiral away in all directions. He felt sublime, lightweight, floating towards a sky that churned like ocean swells.

"Break the psy link!" Zared ordered.

The tornado of time swept the generations of visions away, until the voices and faces faded into whispers of memories. Rhoan bolted upright in his pilot's chair, his chest heaving, his clothes clinging to his sweaty body. "Whoa!" he panted in a shaky voice.

Rhoan swung his Zephyr around so he could see Zared, who was sitting on the *Vernacular*'s right wing beside an open hatch in the fuselage. "Hey," he yelled, "that was incredible. You put me in his head. Why'd you yank me out of there?"

Zared's voice was grim. "That was close. You must learn to recognize when a person is about to die. The mind plays tricks. Remember what you felt today."

"Holy crap," Rhoan muttered. "I won't forget. Magistrate Parleigh risked his life to stop Venamir. I relived his last fight with him."

"How did the Magistrate die? I didn't see it. Too many minds distracting me," Zared said.

"Venamir was going to lose. He had help. Someone shot Parleigh with a dizer. Bastards! Venamir had his followers start the clans fighting, so we'd be too busy with our own people to bother with humans. He masterminded the clan wars. All he cares about is getting back in power."

Zared turned and yelled to anyone who could hear, his voice booming. "You all had better listen! Take Venamir down, scale by scale. He won't stop until every one of you are serving him or dead."

The spectators breathed a collective "Whew," as Zared turned and stalked onto the rocking ship.

Slade emerged next from the overwing hatch as he finished adjusting his battle armor. "The shooting stopped," he muttered. "All hands, is our crew alive?" Slade asked. He heard his crew sound off, all accounted for except, "Shanto," he sighed. "Venamir must have killed him."

"Guess again," came Nelzyr's voice. "We're on Vany's ship and Shanto's right here." His voice drifted off. "We do have one dead. Venamir killed our Magistrate."

The lady Merfin patted Nelz on the shoulder. "'Tis none of our faults, Doctor. He was shot point blank with a diser. He never stood a chance."

"I know," Nelz sighed, "but it doesn't help much."

* * *

Slade and Doc landed a beat-up Zephyr on the water next to Vanysa's war-torn scout ship. Shanto appeared in the half-melted doorway, his arms in a bandaged mess. Slade moored the Zephyr to Vany's ship and hopped onboard, followed by Doc.

"Shanto, I oughta kick your ass all the way back to Earth." Slade said.

"I'm sorry, Captain," Shanto replied, his voice crestfallen. "I disobeyed your orders and returned to Venamir's crew. But I know the *Jacobyte's* Herja program better than anyone. Is everyone alive?"

"Mostly," Slade answered, exploring the wreck. He found their dead magistrate all covered up to the neck with a blood-stained blanket. "Parleigh was a powerful psychic and still couldn't solo Venamir."

"I'm sure Venamir had help," Vanysa reasoned. "My bodyguard tried to save us. Now he's gone too."

"Vany," Slade said, touching her arm. "What happened?"

"Oh," she sniffed, "Magistrate came to my ship and said he was coming with us. He was through hiding, and the clans would listen to him. It didn't work. Faron tried to help. They pulled him under. I lost his life reading." She glowered out at the waves.

Shanto rubbed his arms, wincing. He wore new bandages, but his stiff movements and slumping posture painted a deeper trauma. "I'm really sorry, Cap."

"Don't be. You saved us," Slade replied.

Shanto blinked. "Huh?"

"The *Jacobyte* never locked onto us," Slade explained. "I figured that had to be from your mad-cracked sabotage. We took *glancing* hits. If that ship had locked on, we'd probably all be dead. So, thank you. Now get in Scruffy's ship and go to medbay."

"Wait," Shanto jogged through the ship to the back, to where Motley and Tatts worked in the portal room, putting panels back on the chamber walls. Shanto waved toward the portal chamber. "They fixed the teleporter."

"You told us how," Leifur piped.

Slade drew a calculating breath. "Ooh, sweet."

Vany kicked off the toe covers from her boots and stomped past them, morphing into her silvery blue Merfin form. She tossed her long vest aside to reveal a half length blouse that ended just over the gills along her lower ribcage. Her wavy hair thickened to twisted locks while thin webbing grew between her lengthening fingers and toes.

Slade watched her, noting the speargun over her back and firguns on her slender hips. "What are you doing, Vany?" he asked.

She glanced back, her tears under control and golden eyes gleaming with fury. "Same thing you are." Her normally smooth voice seethed, a chilling tone. "I train dragons. It's payback time."

"Wait." Doc started, but Vany made a swift dive and vanished beneath the waves.

Slade held up a hand. "Let her go."

"You're sure because *why*?" Doc asked.

"Because Venamir turned on her, trashed her ship, and took out her boyfriend." Slade tapped his comm. "All hands, regroup at the Starship Boneyard and give my alter ego, Wulvur some backup." Slade led the way into the portal chamber. "How many at a time, Shanto?"

"Two, and not sure how long the energy cells will last." Shanto flexed his fingers, wincing until Motley stepped up beside him.

"Let me do that," Motley offered. "One second." He gazed at his cub. "Stay safe and help Shanto. I mean it! No sneaking off this time."

Leifur sighed, "I will, promise."

Chapter 42
New Merfin

Cruentin sat in a small rescue craft, along with a crew of two Deeps. Swarms of little holographic fighters depicted interactions between clans. Not all groups were fighting. Larger numbers took up defensive formations against each other's forces.

His copilot paced, also watching the virtual fighters. "How long do you plan to float here? We could drop shields long enough to port Venamir in and be on our way. The armies are distracted enough right now."

"Even searching for his mind is dangerous with so many telepaths in the water. So stay alert, and be ready to flee," Cruen ordered, and eased into his captain's chair once more, where he let his eyes drift closed. *"Venamir. You're far too vulnerable out there. Come to us."* Minutes ticked past. Cruen tried calling again, twice, threefold. His hands gripped the armrests, sweaty palms dampening the material as he waited.

Outside, Venamir psy whispered back, the tone amused, even chiding, *"No."*

Flashes of the *Vernacular* drifting atop the waves left Cruen in a state of shocked anger. *"Are you asking for a swift death? They'll blast us apart."*

"Not if we teleport out. I eavesdropped on their reports. You have a sound teleporter while they do not."

* * *

The captain of a Merfin patrol skimmer waved his crew to power down and idle while he shut his sea-kelp green, pearly eyes. He fell silent, oblivious to all around him while the skimmer crew waited and took guarding positions.

At length, the captain opened his eyes and pointed toward a combat zone closer to shore. "Our Magistrate's friends need our help."

A young amphibious helmsman lashed his tail as he glared at the Merfin crew. He faced off with their commander. "First our Magistrate orders us to stand down and now you serve his ambassador?"

The captain stepped over to the helm. "Listen, my lizard friend, we are one of the few response crews with both species working together. I lost contact with our magistrate. We detected him on Lady Vanysa's ship. You are not sympathizing with Venamir, are you?"

"No! Of course not. It's just, we all thought the Magistrate was dead. Where was he these past months?"

"Dodging assassins. Now, he's surfaced. I know the feel of his mind. Very few could make such a widespread psy call." To the crew, he announced, "Submerge. Report to Vanysa's ship. We will guard her in stealth mode."

As the crew hustled to comply, the captain froze at a soft voice touching his mind, beckoning, "*Thank you, captain. Now let me inside.*"

"All stop," the captain ordered. "Open the entry chamber. Vanysa's joining us."

* * *

Venamir swam toward the feel of his doctor's psy voice. *Foolish Vanysa, what a pity.* He winced as a voice full of fury and daring surged through his thoughts.

The voice snarled with the fury of a wild animal, "*You sunnuva bitch!*"

"That is familiar," Venamir muttered, surprised by the psychic intrusion. "Slade's young medic survived." He swam up from the depths, his eyes fixated on the *Vernacular's* scarred belly. "They love their crewmen so much. All we need to set them back is a dose of impact. Are you ready, Doctor Cruen?"

"For what?" Cruen asked.

"Remember the arrogant boy who nearly made you walk off the ramp? Would you like revenge? Target the Zephyr above me. "

Rhoan pivoted, his sharp eyes scanning the waves as he stood balanced in his Zephyr. "All hands, who's scanning the waters?"

"Scanners aren't much use right now," Elowren replied. "So many of the ships are using jammers...." Her voice drifted off as she sensed it, too. "Venamir, he's close by."

"Yeah, coming from the direction of Vany's ship," Rhoan confirmed, and dropped into his pilot's chair. "That sunnuvabitch!"

"Rhoan, lift off!" Elowren warned. Then she saw it—a brief distress signal from Rhoan's medbird, and then the signal vanished. "Shit! Venamir's got the kid!"

Scruffy hit autopilot, flung his belts aside, and charged out of the cockpit. "Everyone without gills, just secure perimeter and watch my back."

Elowren hit the shipwide comm. "Who's at the teleporter? Lock onto Rhoan and send him to us. All hands, targeting's down and Venamir's below us. Get him! I'm sealing all hatches in ten seconds, so dive or stay."

* * *

Venamir and Rhoan grappled in deeper waters. Unable to penetrate the hard mesh armor over Venamir's gills, Rhoan used his last bits of strength to wrap his arms over the fluttering gills so neither of them could breathe.

Startled yet impressed, Venamir considered another tactic. "*Doctor, bring us onboard your water vessel.*"

Within seconds, the grappling pair of enemies materialized in the portal chamber. The two unlocked death grips and separated, both gasping for air.

Venamir blew his gills out with a sudden spray of air and morphed back to his amphibious form, his body bulking to a Merfin with a longer face and teeth like shining spikes, hidden tailbones extending to a massive scaly tail as his gills shut against the open air. He spun and lashed with the tail, catching Rhoan in the head and knocking him to the floor. Venamir backed out of the portal.

Rhoan glanced around as he caught his wind. He clambered to his feet and started to lunge after Venamir, but the sound of heavy boots and weapons charging froze him in place. He made no movements except to sway with each ragged breath as the oxygen fed energy to his veins.

Each crewmember surrounding him held a different type of weapon leveled at Rhoan, from manual spear guns to a disers rifle.

He straightened, raising his open hands as he sized them up and tried to catch his breath. *Venamir and the doctor. Two fish goons and one lizard. Shit, the doctor survived?*

Cruentin approached Rhoan with slow steps and a leer. "Off with the helmet."

Scowling, Rhoan obeyed with slow, grudging movements, easing off the helmet and dropping it to the floor.

Cruentin shifted his weight, his brow furrowing. "Oh my, you *are* young. Have you even stopped breastfeeding yet?"

Rhoan stood tall and haughty. "Better than what you suck."

The crew fought back shocked expressions and hints of laughter.

"He's all yours, Doctor," Venamir said, turning away.

Cruentin scanned Rhoan's mind and flinched at the striking imagery of vintage fighter jets diving toward him, so close he could see the jagged teeth painted across their noses, growing in size as they neared until he ducked despite his best efforts to stand tall. Throaty engine roars sent a shudder through his body, engines beating steady, low tones while the ghostly machine guns barked with sharp rat-a-tats. Cruen backpedaled, blocking his face as if he were being peppered with bullets from an otherworldly source. His mind flashed back to the prison raid and the helpless feeling of walking toward the edge of an open ramp under the psy command of an audacious youth.

Skimming their minds, Venamir peered over one shoulder and chortled at the brief psy exchange. "You should join us, Rhoan. Slade will only restrain your powers." He barged into Rhoan's mind with startling savagery of explosions across the young man's thoughts until he felt the link between the two unravel into chaotic, dissipating mind views.

"No, you don't, not again." Cruen yelled, severing the psy link between them, his fury swelling at the sight of Rhoan's smirk. "You little... I don't know how many of them helped you control my brain, but you'll pay for that." He watched Rhoan's smirk fade to a glare. "Not so adamant now, are you?"

"It was all me. I'm your grim reaper," Rhoan growled.

Cruen winced as he recalled the fiery pain of being shot, all because Rhoan controlled at the time. He moved an unconscious hand over his left lung, his heartbeat jumping at a stab of pain. "I'll keep you alive, long enough to dissect your brain."

Rhoan knew that threat was a promise. Still, he held his ground, realizing his head had stopped swimming and his keen balance was returning. "*Come closer,*" he started to psy to Cruen's mind, but the gun-toting thugs closed in on him and manhandled him out of the small portal chamber.

Satisfied at the turn of events, Venamir sat down at the pilot's controls. "The plan remains, my colleagues. We must reach the old ship and capture Slade there."

"This won't take long," Cruen replied, tone oozing with sick satisfaction. "Soften him up, and be sure to find where he'd been shot." He reached into a belt pack and withdrew a hypo, which he uncapped to reveal a glistening, fluid-filled vial. "Before you die, *we* are going to reminisce."

The crew instantly obeyed, frisking him. Rhoan didn't wince until they found the slightly raised area of his sleeve where Scruffy had wrapped his arm. The Merfin's hand tightened, sending pain screaming through Rhoan's bad arm and fiery memories swimming through his brain. The crewmen pummeled him, while the pain in his arm almost made the strikes from the crew feel pleasant as their weight forced him to his knees.

Cruen savored the fight with a smile as he watched the youth go down.

Venamir manned the communicator and hailed Scruffy's ship. "Doctor Scrufius, we are entertaining a guest," he sang out.

Elowren's hologram appeared on his panel, her eyes fiery with anger. She snarled, "Shut up, Venamir! You can't hide for long, even if that's your forte."

Venamir waved toward the scuffle behind him. "I only need a few minutes to dispatch your pet rescue medic. Tisk tisk." He shut off communications and swiveled around to watch the show. "What are you doing, playing with him?"

Cruen waved the hypo. "Hold him down! Are you all amateurs?"

The crew struggled to wrench Rhoan's arms behind his back and succeeded with the bad arm. But he used his good hand to slam one Merfin's knee sideways, crunching through cartilage with loud, crackling sounds. The injured fishman screamed a high-pitched, strange, oscillating squeal. The other crewman jumped onto their captive's back and grabbed him in a choke hold. Rhoan slammed his weight backward until they both hit the portal chamber wall, then curled forward into a roll, throwing the crewman to the floor. A few decisive strikes snapped rib bones, leaving the second burly Merfin prone, twitching.

Rhoan sprang to his feet, no longer seeing imperious smiles. The third crewman backed away and reached for the diser rifle.

"Not that weapon, not in here." Venamir demanded.

Lost in his rage, the crewman charged the diser, sending his commanders diving for cover.

Rhoan tackled the rifleman, pinning the weapon sideways between them. One blast went off, searing through the first inner layers. The Merfin grabbed Rhoan by the throat while his broken-knee friend struggled to rise. They landed hard against the wall. Rhoan shot a glance toward the fallen lizard and locked minds with him, just long enough to make the Merfin put weight on his bad leg. The lean, pain-riddled guy cried out and fell over again, swearing in hissing, spitting noises.

Venamir launched his psy into their prisoner's mind. "*If you surrender, I shall hire you.*"

Rhoan had the Merfin crewman pinned beneath his weight and trapped green arm beneath his knee as he tried to break the strangle hold, but the Merfin's fingers were long, webbed, with claws and surprising strength. "I'm nothing like you!" he rasped as he yanked free a scalpel from his forward belt pack. "Back off," he demanded. His Merfin combatant only fought back harder until Rhoan dug the laser scalpel into the capturing arm.

The Merfin squealed, much like the other, and released his prey. Rhoan leapt away, but the downed crewman grabbed his leg and kept fighting, his pearly eyes turning orange with fury.

"Dammit, give up!" Rhoan demanded.

"Die!" the Merfin snarled, lunging for the rifle. He reached it first and started to turn on the young medic, but Rhoan buried the scalpel in his chest, reaching the heart in one stab. The gunman heaved a ragged gasp, anger fading to astonishment as he sank to the floor, the hilt of the surgical instrument poking upward with a proud, red gleam.

Rhoan's head swam as a feeling of inner sickness washed over him. He'd been so effective as a medic, he'd only heard about the death rattle until now. Prying his eyes away from the fresh kill, he grabbed the diser rifle and leveled it at Venamir. Still, the impact sank in with merciless nagging. *I killed him... with a tool that's made to heal? I'm a life saver, I think.*

Venamir beheld his three crewmen sprawled across the floor and eased his gaze to Rhoan who stood over them, now wielding the fallen diser rifle. His mind swept over the young man's mind to freeze him in place, and he felt what he expected, pangs of stunned guilt feuding with survival instincts. "Bravo! For a mongrel, you are worth training."

"Last chance to surrender."

"Or else what?" Cruen asked, flipping a hand. "You'd have shot us already if you truly meant to. Your good nature stops you from turning us into pools of sludge."

Rhoan's eyes narrowed. "I could fix glancing diser shots, *maybe*."

Venamir locked gazes with the youth. "If you regret murdering my crewman, then lower that weapon." Venamir gestured toward the bulky rifle in Rhoan's grip, watched the cells along its barrel light up and hold at a steady amber glow. "Even a caveman can see how much you hate disers. Your inner conflicts hinder you. We could train you beyond your imagination. You do wish to live?"

The young medic retorted, "Who doesn't?"

"You are too merciful," Venamir said.

"Slade wants you alive," Rhoan admitted. His eyes narrowed, and steady hands swung the barrel toward Venamir's doctor. "*You* could die, though."

Cruentin stood by Venamir, not saying a word as he scanned Rhoan's mind. He found psy shields of orbiting energy weapons, a strong mental shield, but not impenetrable because he was familiar with it now. This time, he would not underestimate the mix-breed whelp.

"I like this boy," Venamir commented with a growing smile. "You should train him."

Cruen hissed between his teeth. "I'd rather dissect him."

Revolted, Rhoan snarled and blasted their control panels. "Dang, there went your stealth mode." He felt their minds start to take hold, controlling his mind and numbing his trigger hand. For all the legends of infamy, they were scared. He felt it, and it thrilled him. There was just one problem—the issue of Rhoan's hands going numb from the two Atleans prying into his brain, and *they* knew it.

Venamir didn't need to psy to his friend. One of few friends in his prolonged life, he and Cruen could read each other's slightest impulses. They could see no reservation in their captive's eyes, only fire. Together, they tore at the shields protecting Rhoan's mind.

Rhoan's vision fogged over as his psy defenses cracked open. Images of Venamir and Cruentin solidified in his mind's eye. His hands were going numb. Forcing his tingling hands to obey, Rhoan squeezed off a shot.

"You missed, little fledgling," Venamir gloated.

Cruen jumped as water sprayed his face. He backed out of Rhoan's mind and yanked the diser from Rhoan's hands. He pressed the muzzle against the young man's face, his thumb over the power setting until Venamir hissed, "Wait."

"Of all the depths, break your psy contact." Cruentin snapped.

"No, not yet," Venamir said, voice feverish as he backed the dazed young medic against a wall.

"Just kill him." Cruen retorted. The ship's moaning snatched his attention with the fervor of a raid siren. Snarling, he swung the diser over his back and ran to reinforce the shields. He looked through the one good window and his sharp eyesight made out the bulky silhouette of the *Vernacular* closing in, her guns glowing as she charged weapons. Cruen whirled and started for the aft deck. "Venamir, you always want to make them linger." Sharp creaks and bongs resounded from the aft deck. "This ship's collapsing, and we have incoming hostiles. They can see us now. Do you hear me? Let's Go!"

The two ignored him, locked in death grips at each other's throats while they tried to tear into each other's minds, Venamir morphed into his amphibious form, half-Rezoan form, then into his true Merfin form, bulking up with muscle and thick scales. He gasped and snarled thunderous oaths when Rhoan grabbed the cartilage beneath his ear fins and twisted, wrenching the amphibious head, fingertips digging between spinal joints. Venamir snarled, his eyes widening with surprise as he twisted around in a mad scamper to protect his neck from being snapped.

Cruen sidestepped past them, his concern growing. "That boy knows your anatomy. Stop toying with him. Get out of his head so I can shoot." He leveled the rifle again, but Venamir's silent command made him lower the weapon and nod. Cruentin ran past the psy-battling pair and leapt up behind the teleporter controls. The sprint left him panting with pain and bent over the targeting screens as he pressed one hand over his lower ribs. He locked the portal's targeting sites around Venamir and Rhoan.

"Now, Doctor!" Venamir ordered.

Cruentin stepped away from the portal controls. "You'll get us killed if you port out there. Break OFF!" Cruentin grabbed a speargun and fastened a cable to the spear. He psyd to his captain one furious image of shining spears in flight and fired.

Venamir jerked his mind free of Rhoan's, leaving them both staggering for a second as their thoughts separated and the eyes readjusted to their true surroundings. Before they could react and keep fighting, the spear's shining tip tore through the flexible layer of Rhoan's body armor, just above his left knee, the jagged shaft ripping flesh and splattering blood into the air. The spearhead lodged into the wall beside Rhoan, pinning him in place.

Stiffening his thick, scaly tail, Venamir spun, lashing his tail at Rhoan's legs, but the youth managed to grab the tail and yank it closer, raking it against the jagged spear shaft.

A blast rocked the ship, much to Rhoan's chagrin, as Venamir jerked free of his grip and ran to join Cruentin in the portal chamber.

Rhoan motioned toward the fallen crewmen. "Oh, *now* you're running? What about them?" He flinched as cold water pooling on the floor lapped against his feet, forming swirls with the blood running down his boot.

Venamir laughed as Cruen set the controls. "Impudent fool. Yes, I feel the life in two of them, and your mercy proves your naivety." He nodded to Cruen and morphed back into his mottled green Merfin form. "Only you will drown. Enjoy your death."

Cruentin slapped the controls and with a parting sneer, he and Venamir dissipated into swirls of retreating energy.

The ship rocked again, this time from shock waves. Rhoan could not see the *Vernacular* diving again to his aid, nor her submerged guns blasting a challenging Rezoan ship. He only felt his leg jerked against the cruel, barbed metal trapped in the upper half of his leg armor. Crackling sounds emanated from the hull all around him while water sprayed from a new crack in the buckling little ship's hull. He bent over and wrestled with the buckles along the back of his leg, every move sending biting pain from hip to toes.

"Freaking fishes. OW!" Unable to reach the buckles, nor grab the barbed shaft with his hands without slicing them, he straightened, looking wildly around. His ears were popping, the ship moaning and creaking, and he saw nothing useful.

Scruffy called to his mind, *"Kid! We're outside."*

Scruffy and Vanysa swam to the aft section of the ship and worked at the escape hatch handles, to no avail. Only Scruffy's earpiece on the tip of his left ear and his wild, green hair truly identified him in his Merfin beast form affectionately known as 'sea dog,' something between a wolfish man with gills and rear feet build like merman fins. Vany had taken full Merfin form, her skin silvery blue with her blonde, waving hair and a mermaid-style tail. She projected images into Scruffy's mind, her knowledge of these ships, along with her gentle voice as they wrestled with the emergency handles.

"This should have opened to the entry chamber," Vanysa told him. *"Overridden. They must have overrode the locks. How far can he morph?"*

"He's *a pup, just starting, Atlean to human, that's it.*" Scruffy patted the small oxygen tank and mask nestled in a pouch over one shoulder. "*This'll have to do.*" The old seadog psyd to Rhoan, "*Kid! Open up the aft hatch! We're right here.*"

"*I'm stuck,*" Rhoan admitted, embarrassment creeping among his hot emotions. Angered all the more, he wrestled again to free his trapped armor, and clenched his teeth in pain.

Scruffy winced, feeling the injury through their psylink. "*Okay, just stay in one piece. We're coming in through the pressure chamber.*"

Rhoan jumped at a muffled scuffling sound. One crewman groaned and rose to his feet, unsteady, as he locked a murderous glare on the trapped youth. Chuckling, he moved over to the dead crewman and pulled Rhoan's scalpel from the corpse's chest.

"Fool," the Rezoan sniggered, "you barely know your powers and still challenge *us.*"

Rhoan shifted his weight and winced with a sharp breath, more from realization than pain. "You're right. Thanks for pointing that out."

"Oh, too late to plea for your life," the lizard said, tail lashing as he advanced.

Rhoan swayed, his mind drifting. He bore into the alien mind, finding a world of sea life and chaotic images. Rhoan spoke in a soothing voice as he'd been trained by Scruffy, speaking of sweet water and lush forests as he kept a tenuous hold on the Rezoans mind. The lizard took on a sleepy look as he bent down and unfastened Rhoan's leg armor.

The door swished open from the aft compartment, startling the two out of their partial trance. The Rezoan jerked back to his senses and spun, firing a wild shot at Rhoan's friends. The shot knocked Scruffy over and causing a shrill whistling sound.

Seeing his friend collapse, Rhoan snarled and backed against the wall, pulling the lizard across the jagged spear with all his strength, choking and hissing sounds only feeding his reign of vengeance.

Vanysa morphed back into her form with legs and rushed over to Scruffy's side. After a brief inspection, she helped him up.

The Rezoan uttered a terrible screech as he fell. He swam to a far corner, swearing at them until he appeared to pass out.

"Wow, kid, good work," Scruffy muttered. "I'm fine. He hit the air tank and my armor." His eyes widened. "No, not the tank!" Helplessness washed over him at the sight of the ruined, empty air tank he'd brought for Rhoan. "Get in the back chamber with us, quick!"

They started toward his apprentice when a nerve-rattling series of cracks and pops demanded their attention. The pilot's window had spiderwebbed into a dull haze of countless cracks, and was bowing inward.

Scruffy, Vanysa, and Rhoan lumbered through hip-deep water as it poured into their aft compartment safe zone. The crackling pilot's window imploded and water gushed into the little ship.

The room flooded as they hastened toward the teleport chamber, where Scruffy tried the teleport controls, only to have his hands zapped and watch the power die. The doors joining all sections of the ship froze where they were, all open.

Within seconds, seawater dominated the ship.

Vany swam over to Rhoan and grabbed him in a tight embrace, her lips pressed against his. On any other day, Scruffy would have watched with envy.

They felt the ship jolt from thuds and clanks outside, then their weight felt doubled as something pulled their ravaged craft upward.

Scruffy watched two dark forms through the window, long, sleek shapes with heads like snakes and maws full of teeth. "*The blood drew them here!*" Noticing the speargun, he grabbed it and took a defensive position as he butted the first eel with the gun. He fired the spear through the window, skewering the beast and making it instant prey for a second eel. Something thumped on the hull, and their little ship shuddered from heavy weapons fire. Underwater, he wasn't sure if the sound came from the *Vernacular's* guns.

Scruffy knew his ship couldn't stay submerged for long, damaged as she was. He aimed the speargun at the shattered window and psyd to his friends with the greatest range, Elowren and Zared. *"We're trapped in a collapsing sub and under attack! Where's my ship? Prepare for a Code Blue!"*

Elowren's voice felt like music, but a death toll rather than good news. *"Stay in there. We're lifting you closer so you can swim to the pressure chamber. We're under attack too, but... there's a ship helping us. Stand by."*

"No standing by!" Scruffy shot back, *"We need air or a teleporter now!"*

Dreadful moments passed before Elowren reported, *"We're closing in to put our shields around your sub. You're surrounded. You'll be shot if you come out."*

Shots fired nearby, dull punting sounds until a blast hit their little ship, the impact knocking them against the opposite wall, and forcing air from Rhoan's lungs. He retained enough presence of mind to demand, *"No spare... air bottles?"*

"Merfin ship," Scruffy replied in misery. *"They don't need it. Kid, don't do this to me."*

Rhoan felt the seawater rough against his throat and seeping downward. The ship rose slowly, jerking with each blast that hit it and knocking the unwilling passengers against walls and floating debris. The worst jolt knocked the wind out of Rhoan. Stunned, his lungs filled with water, wreaking terror through his mind. He had to remain calm, had to... had to.... until he heard Vanysa's psy voice tell Scruffy, *"This isn't enough. We're losing him."*

Scruffy's emotions exuded a terrible rarity for him, fear. *"We'll revive you, kid, I swear it!"*

Rhoan's lungs were on fire, or so he swore, and his mind spiraled into a crazed timeline of his life, much like he remembered the Magistrate's last few minutes.

Vany's voice grew powerful in his head, demanding him to let her control him. *"Rhoan, you have to morph into a Merfin."*

"I can't... don't know how."

Despite Vanysa trying to give him air, the bright images from his friends' minds faded to black. He drifted through his past, saw glimpses of friends, pets, ships, all dead. Realization struck him with terror as he recalled the Magistrate's mind link. Vanysa's whispers in his mind sounded like subliminal hypnosis. He was so lost in the darkness, floating, he wasn't even sure if his body was still attached to his spirit.

A strange tingling overtook his ability to move, but he dreamed of air. He was still breathing in this dream, and wished he were still kissing Vanysa. A pain revived in his lungs, unlike the first gulp of seawater, something different, almost a tearing sensation, no, stretching, reforming as if the water was crushing him into something different. The ache in his chest and lungs passed, replaced by a cool, soothing feeling.

Rhoan opened his eyes to see Vanysa and Scruffy staring at him, still morphed in water-breathing forms, their jaws agape. Cold fear gripped him. "Did we all drown? Oh, God. You're all dead? Why didn't you leave?" He bolted upright and swam upward, bonking his head on the ceiling. He didn't even realize he'd just spoken underwater.

"No, kid, you learned a new trick," Scruffy chuckled. "Not everyone can morph into a water-breather." He pulled a wrap from a medbag on the wall and secured it around Rhoan's leg.

The pain told Rhoan he must be alive. He wiggled his hands, staring through pearly eyes of deep umber. Rhoan blinked again, amazed at the sharpness of his vision, far clearer than any swimmer's mask could give. His gaze drifted from the webbing between his fingers and looked down at his feet, and noticed his boots were missing, allowing his toes to expand into fins.

Vany tugged him closer to her and touched his chin. "Now handsome Rhoan, be aquatic."

Rhoan grinned from earfin to earfin, "Whoa, I'm a merman!"

The three of them turned toward the ship's helm where an armored Merfin swam through, followed by a second, toting lightweight crossbows loaded with glowing bolts. They bore an unnatural resemblance to Venamir and wore the same body armor. They blasted a big hole in the window and swept inside, opening fire.

Rhoan, Scruffy, and Vanysa dealt out swift retribution.

* * *

The *Vernacular* body creaked as she dove farther beneath the ocean's surface. A Mora-dopp welded the pressurized lower hold, sealing the compartment. Her body withstood the mounting pressure needed to keep water from filling the ship. The pressurized room also held down a rolled out patch of flexible matalate as she fastened it down with inhuman strength and laser welds. She banged four times on the nearest bulkhead with a spare chunk of metal and felt the pressure subside.

Outside the lower hold, Jasko watched the swelling walls ease back into their normal flat shape, or almost in some areas.

"She did it!" Jasko cheered. "That means the other two outside the ship sealed that side as well, I hope." He bolted away in long bounds, not slowing until he skidded into the transporter chamber where Telari was reloading power cells.

"I heard Elowren's thoughts," Tel panted as they worked. "They're in deep shit down there. This gotta work." Tel manned the portal chamber controls. The chamber filled with water and a couple fish. "Portal's up!"

The *Vernacular* remained underwater, hovering over the crumpling little ship and firing at any sub-ship foolish enough to turn guns upon her intimidating mass. Elowren sat at the controls, keeping a psylink with Scruffy, who kept asking if it was safe to leave the half-flooded ship. Glancing at her proximity screen, she saw a scout sub approach and signal her. White lights, green, white. Then a voice hailed her ship.

An ivory and blue Atlean appeared on her holo-comm. "Hello, *Vernacular*, I am responding to the Magistrate's call. We are here to assist. I regret we do not have a teleport chamber. We do have Deeps swimmers."

Recognizing his uniform and markings, Elowren nodded. "Thank you, Captain. Just don't let anyone else attack that ship while I position this one closer. We can't stay submerged much longer."

Tel called out, "Incoming portal, got-em! Okay, pull up. Yeah boy!"

Elowren confirmed, "Injured incoming to the portal chamber." She nodded to the pale skinned captain on her screens. "Thank you. We could use you at the Starship Boneyard."

"On our way," the captain said, and signed off.

The *Vernacular* soared out of the water and headed for the northern cliffs along the ocean, where decaying starships hosted a different battleground. The portal chamber filled up with five beings, not three. Scruffy shoved armored, green-skinned Atleans out of the chamber first. They fell to the deck, stunned and blowing out their gills before taking gasps of warm air.

Scruffy and Vanysa, still morphed in their water-breathing forms, blew out with practiced ease. Rhoan dropped to his knees, coughing and sputtering even though Scruffy and Vanysa grabbed him and gave him orders to blow out, no, not through the mouth, the lungs, blow out the gills, harder!

Rhoan slapped a hand over his nose and mouth, then blew out hard, spraying water from his gills. Bent over on his knees, panting, he started to regain his wind.

Vanysa laughed and patted his shoulder. "Not bad for a first time water-morphing."

Kestral ran in and held the two green strangers at gunpoint while Gus stomped over to the blue-skinned, wheezing Rhoan.

"Who the hell are you guys?" Gus demanded.

"It's me," Rhoan gasped. He still didn't get all the water out of his sinuses and kept coughing like he had the worst cold ever. Seeing Telari approach with that mean look of hers, he wheezed between coughs, "Tel don't kick me there." Then to Gus, he managed, "Shuddup."

Gus lowered his gun. "It really is you."

Scruffy was an unraveling mess of exasperation and concern as he helped Rhoan up. "Are you okay, kid?"

Rhoan regained enough composure to morph back into his normal, hybrid Atlean form. "Sure," he replied, still restraining occasional coughs. He blew a kiss to Vanysa. "That was great."

Vanysa blushed a bit and smiled, then rushed off.

Scruffy grabbed Rhoan by the collar and ranted, "You trying to scare me to death? Quit trying to get killed."

Rhoan coughed a few more times, pain shaking his body. "Patch me up. I'll go back in."

"There's seawater in your lungs, oh, and big holes in your leg. Only place you're going is to medbay. Now move it."

Rhoan's shoulders sagged as he sighed and limped off with Doc Nelz's help. "Okay."

"Hey, hot dog, get out of those wet pants," Tel said.

Rhoan paused, throwing her a startled, flattered grin as he limped off with Doc.

"Off with the brain buckets," Gus ordered.

Their prisoners obeyed, tossing the helmets aside. On the floor, with finned arms and webbed hands raised in surrender, sat two Venamir look-alikes. The sight of them startled all the others, from Tel hissing to Scruffy whipping out his firgun.

"Fishes?" Gus spat, "Which one of you is real?"

"I am Venamir," the wrinkly one retorted.

The other Merfin cut in, "No, *I* am the real Venamir, you human caveman."

"You should have called him Neanderthal," Wrinkly stated.

"Silence!" snapped the other Venamir. "You are a throwaway model."

Scruffy groaned, "Just what we need, clones."

Chapter 43
Friendly Fish

The captain of a Merfin patrol sub rose as he watched the deep ocean basin around them swarm with warring submarine class ships. He shook his head, still wondering how their allies could snap into battle from the intrusion of one entity. *No, our peace has been slipping, but I had no idea there were this many cultists serving Venamir. Are they truly serving him?* "Slade's Druwens are pursuing Venamir. Give me status on the downed ships."

His copilot nodded, running his blue-skinned hands over the controls to conjure holograms and location markers over a topographical map that emerged from the joining screens above his head. "Heavy casualties to all the clans, many prisoners suspected as Venamir's followers, fifteen of our fighters destroyed, all one or two-man crafts, three four-man crafts like ours down."

"Status on the ship Venamir called from," the captain requested.

"The *Jacobyte*, she has crashed, almost whole, but... the life forms on her have changed. Venamir vacated the ship and Atlean Druwens now outnumber the crew. Looks like Slade's forces took back the ship."

"Good. Any news on the High Council ships?"

"The only one so far is Ambassador Zared's ship that crashed into the ocean, and one coded message that Council ships are on their way."

"Like race-turtles, the Council people," the captain commented. "I felt Vanysa calling to us. Start scanning for Vanysa. Go to stealth mode."

As their ship dove, the captain settled into his chair and closed his pearlescent blue eye. For several minutes he sat in deep meditation, color draining from his pale skin, making him appear nearly ivory, except for the pale blue spots along his face and neck. His hands gripped the chair's arms, stretching the skin between his fingers. One control panel beeped, lighting up with a view of a gun-battle onboard Vanysa's ship. The crew clustered around their captain to watch a bloody scene painting shock on their teal skin.

The stronger telepaths onboard fell into a similar daze as their captain as they too caught mental imagery from their gravely wounded Magistrate on Vanysa's ship. The Merfins crewmen on the bridge gazed over at their two Rezoan crewmen, a strange bond strengthening between the water people and the lizardkin.

"Venamir... killed our Magistrate?" one crewman uttered in shock.

Bitter murmurs began among the crew.

Their captain echoed their voices in a morbid tone. "Our Magistrate has passed through the depths." He took in a pained breath and rose unsteadily, as if waking from a nightmare. As he rose and faced them, he pointed toward a combat zone closer to shore. "The Magistrate spawned from both our people. He was the best mediator to amphibians and water-breathers. Now our ambassadors are the closest link to our people."

The first mate spoke up, "I heard the Magistrate's voice, and Lady Vanysa and a third mind. He spoke in our old language."

The captain nodded. "Yes, that was Ambassador Zared from the Atlean morpher councils. Zared warned us that if Venamir rose again, there would be an uprising." His leaf-shaped ears quivered, darkening from the tips down to his silvery cheeks, to below the thick whiskers on his chin. "Venamir started these battles between the clans."

The captain's first mate swung a webbed hand toward their combat monitor, where swarms of avatar ships lit up the screens. "How could he have enough followers to sway the clans into fighting each other?"

"There has been growing unrest among the deep-water people, and some of the clans," the captain replied. He studied the combat screen. "Ambassador Zared is from the land Druwens and our Lady Vanysa from the Merfins. We must help them restore peace. Order your troops to keep any more of our kinsmen from joining Venamir."

As the crew started debating who they should be fighting and if the magistrate was truly dead, the captain stepped between them. "Eyes on me!"

The bravest crewman strode over to him. "You were in psy contact with the Magistrate, correct, Captain?"

"Yes, and he ordered a ceasefire. Both sides should obey him without question. The Magistrate was *our* Elder," the captain nodded. "I know the feel of his mind, as do many of us." He waved a hand toward the monitors spanning across the main deck and raised his voice in exasperation. "As you see, most of us are still fighting. All hands, power down. Find Vanysa. *She* is in danger. Open channels to Ambassador Zared. He is probably on the *Vernacular*. For now, we serve the Druwen clans."

Chapter 44
Ghost Ship

Doc Nelzyr and Elowren patched up their drenched friends as fast as they could. Nelz activated the screen across his armband to triage mode. Flaps along the arm band opened up from wrist to forearm, showing each of their crew with the larger readings for those with injuries, even those in the field. One body image barked alarms, summoning Doc to the far left screen. "Wulvur," he muttered, "you're surrounded. There's over twenty life forms closing in."

"Good," Wulvur replied. "I'm almost at the *Spectre.* This area's loosely guarded, took down some thugs. Somehow, Noxus got here before me. He must have ported in."

"We can't port anyone in there," Doc said. "We detected large energy sources, scanners, and more life forms than we expected."

"How many?"

"A dozen, with more approaching the *Spectre's* hangar. You're in the caves. Who's in there?"

"There should be our allies guarding the cave entrances, but I've only found thugs. Something's happened to our guardians around here."

"Wu—r, you're breaking u-up."

"Try again. Doc?" Wulvur heard some garbled words amidst angry static, then silence. "Well, that sucks." He peered out of the old, rusty shuttle he'd ducked into. He could see the top of a hangar several ships away. The roof had huge actuators and hinges along one side. Noise of generators and voices whispered over the wind. "Druwen's log: There're portal chambers around here," Wulvur muttered. "Noxus still thinks I'm Slade. I'm gonna take him down this time."

He heard yips and short whistles, muffled by wind and rows of spaceships. "Berku's pack of Hunters. Their comms must be screwed up too." Wulvur glanced at his comm when an urgent signal flashed bright red. It was a distress call, but not from his friends.

The distress call cast a scene of an Atlean man in a cave with humble lighting and high technology. The man was glancing around, firgun in hand, as he smacked the controls on a deep sleep tube. Then he rushed over to large eggs with pearly hues of metallic colors. One egg quivered in the dim light. "Hatchery—hostages," the man said. "I'm... only one awake so far. "

Wulvur tried his comm. "All hands, see that distress signal?" Loud static filled his ear. Loud static filled his ear, so he ended the call. "Great." He double-checked his image by using a shiny part of the shuttle's wall as a mirror. He was still in Slade's form. It was tiring and distracting, but he had a plan.

Wulvur strolled out of the shuttle, sword and crossbow over his back, firgun holstered. He didn't have to go far. Passing an ancient fighter and some crates, he heard raspy, hissing voices and footsteps. Wulvur opened a crate and pulled, grinning when he saw munitions and weapons. He slung an extra belt loaded with pouches over one shoulder. The next few boxes held pouches of meals and drinks. Wulvur grabbed a power drink, opened it up, and slugged it.

Two Rezoans rounded the nose of the fighter, their tails lashing.

"Those supplies for later."

"Wait, I don't remember you," the other said.

Wulvur turned and flipped up his visor, letting them see him in Slade's form. "I'm Slade. Your Captain is waiting for me."

The lizards laughed. "We take you to Venamir and earn an extra bonus."

"Okay," Wulvur sighed. He morphed into his wereform, all hackles and fangs. Wulvur left them in a twisted pile of pain, tied together with their own weapons belts. He knocked them out as Berku caught up to him, panting.

Wulvur resumed Slade's form. "Did you see that distress call?"

"Parts of it," Berku said. He grabbed the lizards and dragged them into the shuttle. "Guardians down in the hatchery, no good."

From behind and flanking directions, Wulvur heard faint yips and whistles and knew the pack was closing in. Wulvur crept around now silent generators, all senses on high alert as he let his eyes adjust to the dim light. He felt their bottled anger as they drew closer, with the tenacity of a cunning pack waiting for their prey to falter. Wulvur hushed his voice as he held one arm out to record the surroundings. "I'm closing in on the *Spectre*. This isn't a hangar. It's a bunker."

"I know you. Don't tackle that cyborg Noxus alone. You used your serum?"

"Yeah."

"We need to take out their jammers first. Teleporters down in the caves probably work. The *Spectre's* might too. They're using jammers means the *Spectre* is operational in that hangar."

"It's more of a bunker now," Berku nodded, "lots of foot traffic here, none of our allies. We're on our own, no comms, no portals."

"Well, they're waiting for Slade, so I'll draw their attention. How's Zared's crew?"

"Last I heard, they're okay and on their way."

Wulvur heaved a sigh of relief. He grinned wickedly. "I have an idea. Wait till your pack catches up." He handed over his crossbow and firgun. He tugged the collar of his stealth suit. "Ambassador coat." His seemingly short, leather jacket altered to simulate an elite greatcoat that hid the gleaming sword on his back. "Try the scatter-bolts. Tell your group to take cover."

Berku accepted the weapons skeptically, grumbling, "Gotta hog the fun."

Wulvur strolled off, fiddling with the munitions belt as he approached the hangar, hands up, in Slade's form. "Here I am," Wulvur yelled. "You know what you fish and lizards look like? A good start to a big cookout! So where's that slimy bastard Venamir?"

Three Rezoans, and two humans guarding the hangar snapped up their weapons.

"Hand over your weapons," one human ordered, "slowly."

"You're no fun," Wulvur said. He stopped and held out the munitions belt loaded with a firgun and various grenades. "Here."

The group surrounded him, one stepping up to frisk him. He met Wulvur's hypnotic glare and drew back his hands, dazed.

"Prove you're Slade," one Rezoan ordered.

"Hands off, or I will mangle you," Wulvur promised as he slowly gazed from one to the next. "Can't you handle one old wolf who's outnumbered and outgunned? I made a deal with Venamir and intend to keep it. Now, are we going inside, or do my allies up there in stealth mode open fire?"

A few of the Rezoans glanced at the sky as one muttered, "Acts like him."

Noxus barged out of the hangar. "Bring him in."

A handful of other crewmen followed Noxus out, some placing bets with each other.

Noxus stomped towards Wulvur. "Off with the coat. What're you hiding?" His voice drifted off.

Two of the henchmen were inspecting the munitions belt. They dropped it, stumbling away, wincing and shaking their hands. A faint ticking grew louder, and smoke curled up from the munitions belt. The firgun's power pack glowed, smoke curling from its handle. Spikes popped out of some of the grenades.

One henchman yelped, "They're powering up!"

The instant Noxus stared at the smoking belt, Wulvur tackled him. Instead of fighting, Wulvur rolled to his feet and sprinted for the hangar. Noxus stumbled into the guards as they bolted away from the belt, all swearing and yelling for help. The henchmen closest to the hangar made it inside, too frantic in their escape efforts to shut the door. Wulvur barged through the hangar door and hit the floor. The munitions belt exploded in chaotic blasts of concussion grenades. Laser fire followed an instant later, and somewhere through the noise, he heard Berku laugh.

Alarms went off inside the hangar, but it was too late to seal the place off. A series of explosions shook the walls, followed by howls, gunshots, and more explosions. Side windows blew out and doors shuddered before crashing to the floor from heavy artillery.

Noxus staggered through the door, his body armor smoking from laser burns, his energy shield sparking. He pried the failed shield inducer off his belt and flung it aside. He bellowed, "Find Slade!"

Wulvur fought back laughter as he dove under a mobile generator and rolled out the other side. He looked up to see the

Spectre. He tapped his comm. "I found the ship!" he said in a hushed voice. "The *Spectre* looks operational."

The old ship's landing gears rested on a thick floor at least two levels down, so her spine and wings gave easy access to workers. For the moment, he felt a twinge of excitement at seeing the old bird, the legend. Generators, work-stands, and mobile crates of parts and random equipment gave him some cover from the frantic idiots. *The ship of souls,* he recalled from one of Scruffy's long tales. The *Spectre's* windows gleamed like new, body intact, engines uncovered. Generators droned in monotonous tones around the ship, while workers hurried to shove supplies into her lower bay.

He shot a glance up at the ceiling. The rafters served as upper walkways and a structure to support huge doors overhead. "It really is a bunker," he muttered. "The ship's only exit is straight up." He howled in code that he was going in and heard a brief howl in return. "Take cover," Wulvur chuckled in translation. He sped down the nearest steps to the lower level and ducked underneath.

Berku and his pack burst in through the smoldering entrance holes they'd created. They appeared only in glimpses, activating stealth gear the instant they entered. Berku appeared behind a generator and notched Wulvur's bulky, scatter-shot bolt onto the crossbow.

The bolt split apart as it flew, forming glowing projectiles that exploded upon contact with the ship. Each shaft section barely scratched the ship's hull, only fell to the ground like discarded toys, drawing chortles from some of the workers as they moved closer.

"NO! Don't go near them!" Noxus hollered from somewhere in the chaos.

Each shaft exploded into blinding flashes of light, sending tiny quills streaking in all directions, creating miniscule scratches at first glance, until the dose took effect. Over a dozen workers and guards scratched madly at the quills imbedded through their clothes, leather gloves, and boots, each tiny piece still working deeper into their flesh with every movement. A few retched out their latest meal, and one by one, they staggered, collapsed, and curled up, twitching.

Berku waved for his pack to stay in stealth. "Target the ship's weapons. Disable them. I'm going onboard." He activated his stealth gear and blended against the nearest wall.

* * *

The *Spectre* was bigger than Wulvur thought, with three levels. There was no easy entrance to the cockpit. He had to work his way through from the aft cargo bay. Wulvur opened his jacket to expose his shoulder belt of small pouches full of big trouble. He pulled out a bunch of tiny balls, which hovered free of his hand.

"Seek and destroy," he whispered.

The balls shot through the air, each one targeting the nearest light source and shattering many of the light fixtures within the ship. He then reached into a vest pocket and pulled out a case that barely overfilled his palm. The instructions were etched on the top, *"Gus's Gizmos—shake and run."* Wulvur shook the box, set it on the floor, and moved on.

The lid popped open with a jolt, revealing what looked like tightly folded papers, each popped open, and little metallic legs sprang out from the corners. Five in all, the little gadgets sprang out of their container like origami animals on spindly legs. Then they ran off in all directions.

Bolas in hand, he flipped up his hood, activated his stealth gear, and crept along the right wall. The combination of mini-holocams on his belt and his combat gear colors blended into his surroundings. Wulvur strolled with a shroud of virtual invisibility. He kept glancing at his bracer covering his left forearm. The little toybots showed pictures of each room they scouted out, finding no life form until he saw one room with three of its five walls lined with monitors, and in the center a semi-circular arrangement of workstations attended by a crewman. The man glanced over his screens, seeing multiple attacks around the ship and outside the hangar. The man threw up his arms in exasperation and vacated his post.

Noxus stomped into the surveillance room next, yelling after the retreating crewman. The view on the scanner shifted as the toy scuttled sideways. Noxus stared at the floor, where one of the toybots rolled past. He lunged toward Wulvur's little screen, growing in size as he neared like a monster about to leap through a tiny window. The recon crab-bot's screen went blank.

"You killed my toy," Wulvur grumbled. He sprang up the steps and explored the next deck. A scent ahead turned into a plethora of scents. He found a room loaded with weapons along the walls, a bed in the far corner, and workbenches topped with laboratory and medical equipment. Capped vials lay beside four throwing daggers, which found a new home in Wulvur's boots before he pressed on.

"Druwen," a feminine voice whispered, making him jump. It came from nowhere and everywhere. From beside the bed, a hologram projected a woman in riot gear, her features and ears Atlean, her face strikingly attractive, her voice familiar.

"You're the ship's Herja," he murmured, moving closer.

The holographic woman's dark bronze eyes studied him. "You are not Captain Slade. Why do you impersonate him?" She read his initial hesitation and half sighed. "Don't lie. I'm scanning your neural functions and your body."

"That's intimate," Wulvur said. Seeing no humor in return, he walked closer to inspect her. He saw glimpses of a headband hidden behind her wispy brown hair and tattoos that strove to disguise her implants.

"Noxus is hunting you," she commented, jerking his mind back to business, "but no matter. If you win, we should be grateful. What are you doing here?"

"I'm here to save my friends."

"Is that so?" She spread her arms and gazed around. "Who is there to save? This ship crashed long ago, killing most of the crew, including me, I mean, my programmer, Morialya."

Wulvur drew in a steadying breath at the revelation. He couldn't help but point at her in disbelief, but on the unscarred, youthful features, he recognized the aloof, grey eyes, the faint blush in her pale cheeks, the bored frown. "You're *her*? But, you're beautiful. Wow, that's why she's so familiar, and psycho."

"Flattery and insults won't help. You were not on this crew."

"I'm on Slade's crew," Wulvur countered. "Slade and Venamir are enemies. They both want sole command of this ship, even if she can't fly anymore."

"We have a problem. I served them both, so I cannot intervene until one is dead, disabled, or released from command. Nor can I follow orders from you. I will tell you one thing.This ship *can* fly."

Wulvur was about to reply when stomping noises grabbed his attention. One hand rested on his firgun. He paused when the Herja shook her head. "What?"

"My systems will defend the ship if you two start shooting."

"Good thing I prefer old school toys." He turned and drew his favorite weapons, bolas from his belt clip and a double-edged sword from his back. The sword was black from handle to tip, except for silver wisps like writhing ghosts along its blade whenever Wulvur moved it. He squeezed the hilt gently, causing a power surge to shoot from the blade and out through the doorway. An energy blast exploded in the hall, followed by thumps and scrambling footsteps.

"You're not a cyborg," the Herja said. "He'll wear you down for fun. Then he'll kill you."

"Oh, no, I'll show you fun," Wulvur grinned. He set a short, metallic tube on the floor and tapped it twice. The box unfolded repeatedly until it changed into a little toy tank.

Noxus stalked into the doorway. He twisted two rods together, one end producing electrified spikes. "You're hiding behind a toy?"

The tank's turret aimed at Noxus. A little puff of smoke drifted from its turret while a childish voice said, "Boom."

Noxus stomped the little bot until it crunched beneath his boot.

Sparks flashed from the little toybot's power core and streaked up his leg. Shaking it off proved futile. The toybot stuck to his heel while torturous currents traveled up his leg, sending him into an agonized, twitching dance. Noxus scrambled out of the room.

Wulvur laughed outright and yelled, "Get back here. It's just a toy."

Herja Mori vanished. She reappeared in the surveillance room full of monitors, where she could watch the fight. As she predicted, Noxus was heading straight for his room full of weaponry and explosives. "Those fools will wreck this ship."

Noxus charged toward a doorway to the lower hold until the door swished closed. He skidded into it and banged on the door controls, to no avail. "Engineering, release the door controls."

"I didn't do it." the engineer called back over the ship-wide comm.

Slade's impersonated voice answered from behind him. "Hey, asshole."

As Noxus spun, Wulvur's bolas hit him in the face, wrapping around his throat. They lunged at each other, clangs of their weapons resounding throughout the ship.

The engineer spoke again on all speakers, this time his voice dripping with dark humor. "Take it to the brig, you stinking brawlers. Wait, is that Slade? Noxus, the captain wants him alive!" He spun, hearing a murderous snarl. He looked up at Berku in a powerful, bearlike form just before a mighty paw grabbed him and yanked him off his feet.

"Don't port them," Berku snarled, seeing the portal monitors show Wulvur and Noxus vanish off the ship. "Get them back!"

The engineer held up his shaking hands. "I didn't do it! I bet it was the Herja. She does what she wants."

Berku pointed to the portal monitors. "Summon the Herja," he commanded, "or I'll stuff you through the waste grinder."

* * *

Glittering steaks of energy wrapped around Wulvur and Noxus, freezing them in place before they vanished from the ship's corridor. They materialized in an underground teleportal chamber. Its old door creaked open into an underground workshop linked to three passageways. The sound of waves smacked against rocks far below in an alcove along the sea. Glowing rocks illuminated the room enough to see cabinets along one wall, tool boxes, and dozens of odd, small, starship parts. Noxus made a mad retreat down the central passage.

"I got ported off the *Spectre,* but so did Noxus." Wulvur reported. The palms of his gloves slammed shut as the bolas returned to his waiting hands. The bolas felt wet with fluid and wisps of smoke escaped from the ends.

"Your stupid toys don't work on me!" Noxus yelled.

"Mm-hm, whatever," Wulvur snarked.

Noxus clawed at his combat vest, sniffing. Spasms ran through his neck, making his head twitch. Something smelled burnt. Smoke curled upward from parts of his chest guard and gloves, burning his hands. He wrestled off his gloves and smoldering body armor from the waist up and flung the pieces to the ground as he ran.

Wulvur followed at a leisurely pace, his bolas hovering alongside him. The passage forked, with dim orbs along the rough ceiling lighting up both directions. To his left, Wulvur heard distant waves. He smelled stinky sweat and smoke to his left, but to his right, heard muffled shuffling and uneven footsteps. Wulvur tried his comm again. "Slade, guys, I'm near the hatchery," he whispered. "Guys?" He saw cracks in his wrist comm. "Damn."

The passage opened into a cave reinforced along the walls and ceiling. The cave's mouth formed a jagged maw, large enough to swallow a small shuttle. The floor was old, cracked, with shallow sink holes. Angry ocean waves battered a shoreline below. One opening in the back of the cave sloped upward, where the sand bore shapes of footprints. *Aquatic and humanoid boots.* Peering out of the cave's mouth, Wulvur spied fighters in the distance, and glimpsed the *Jacobyte* laying beached up to her wings. Noxus stood near the cave mouth, sticking a compress against his neck and turning up his collar. The two squared off from across the cave.

"You're gonna' pay for all the people you murdered," Wulvur said. "Then I'll sell your parts."

Noxus chortled, "Oh yeah, Slade? You're walking dead. I've already poisoned you, airborne style."

"Yeah, your stench can kill."

The next split second, their weapons echoed in the abandoned cave.

Chapter 45
Cave Duel

Berku reported in, "Slade, I'm on the *Spectre*. Wulvur just got ported off with the hit-man." He shoved his captive into the control chair. "Okay, engineer, follow orders or I'll pulverize you."

"I am only engineer by default," the aquatic guy said as he manned the control panels. Doors slammed shut, isolating them. "I am a bio-enhancement specialist. My name is Thiun."

"I don't care." Berku resumed his normal form, a burly, bearded Atlean man wearing biker leathers beneath his stealth and combat gear. "Talk to me, Herja. I don't have much time or patience."

Herja Mori appeared as a floating hologram. Berku's life form showed up on a monitor as she studied him. "Oh, brother of Slade. You were on the original crew."

"Reverse that portal you just did," Berku ordered. "Leave Noxus behind."

"No," Mori refused.

Berku's bearish ears laid back as his fur hackled. "You're programmed to obey the original crew."

"My program has been altered. I don't have to take orders from you, only Slade or Venamir." She went on over Berku's snarls, "However, you do remember how to override it? It will take more than one of you."

Berku paused, his eyes glinting at her, "I remember. So, what *can* you do for me?"

"You may stay onboard, as long as you don't try to destroy the ship."

"And the crew?" Berku asked.

"I only protect the ship," she replied, making Thiun slink farther into the chair.

Berku chuckled, "Typical Venamir, never cared much for others." He gripped Thiun by the collar. "You're going to be useful."

"I have no loyalty to Venamir," his captive replied.

"No tricks. You're going to deactivate the psy blockers and the jamming signals, disable weapons, and port back Slade!"

Thiun complied, turning off psy blockers and jammers. "I know that's not Slade. Only the captain can disable weapons. There's jamming signals from the caves. I can't target your friend for a portal."

Berku growled, "Find a way."

* * *

Clangs from weapons rang out from the old docking bay built into a cliff face. A private warzone between two old enemies. Far below, ocean waves crashed against a narrow, rocky beach. Within eyesight of the cave, the *Jacobyte* lay in shallow water, surrounded by clashing forces. A few Mora-dopps started climbing the cliff.

Oblivious to the battle outside, Noxus backpedaled from Wulvur's relentless swings, blocking most of a relentless pounding. His cybernetic hands didn't tire, nor the structural supports within his bones, but more parts of his armor fell off. Noxus forced his body on, already bearing gashes that would have incapacitated normal men.

Wulvur kept advancing like a hungry predator. "You murdered your own—students, our teachers, allies on the space station," he ranted. He cleaved at Noxus with each accusation, leaving nasty gashes.

Noxus activated an energy shield from his armbands, protecting him long enough to roll away, splashing through small pools of water on the ancient floor. The water helped to short-circuit his defense shield, sending current up his arms. As Noxus scrambled for a dry section, Wulvur's bolos wrapped around his legs, sending him down again.

"I told you, those don't work on me," Noxus snarled, wrestling his legs free. This time, Wulvur vanished from view. Noxus staggered upright and glanced down, eyes widening at a snake-like form constricting around one knee. It was part of the broken bola wrapped around his knee and burning into his leg. Noxus clawed the bolas off, wincing and shaking his hands. Limping now, he ran for the open mouth of the cave, but Wulvur dropped from the ceiling and kicked him back into play.

"You may be a cyborg," Wulvur said, "but I'll dismantle you, piece by piece." He pulled a grenade from his belt, watched Noxus backpedal, and then tossed it over his shoulder, out of the cave. He lunged forward, the gleaming edge of his black sword slicing Noxus with a sizzling hiss.

Noxus sprang back with a startled yelp, batting at the smoke rising from his chest.

The grenade exploded outside. Through dust and smoke, a Mora-dopp climbed into the mouth of the cave, only to fall over, sparks dying out from charred holes in its back.

Noxus slapped his wrist comm. "Venamir, come in." He jerked his hand away, then wincing and cussing, wrestled off the helmet and flung it aside with a holler of pain. The helmet rolled away, sparks flying off its visor.

Wulvur kept after him, knocking off pieces of armor. "Councils should've fried you long ago."

"What drugs are you on?" Noxus demanded.

"None," Wulvur snarled. "Only a blood oath."

Noxus backpedaled and flinched when he hit the rough stone wall. "You stupid mongrels would rather die than break that oath. You swore to protect who?" He kited aside as Wulvur started after him again. "Let me guess, the females."

"The whole crew."

Noxus laughed, a bitter, vile utterance when Wulvur flung small daggers at him, one sticking in each arm. He ripped them off and flung them aside. "You're crazier than Venamir. Look at these toys. Pathetic!" Parts of the little blades stayed in his armor, their tips digging in through his skin. Wincing, he tore off his arm guards and flung them across the cave.

Wulvur sneered, "My weapons are made for cyborg demolition. They short-circuit stuff. Capiche?" He could hear the noise of a teleporter, the creak of old doors, and footsteps. His keep senses caught the scent of Merfins. *I'm running out of time.*

Noxus slapped his belt, activating an energy shield around his body. He lunged. Wulvur revealed a dagger hidden in his free hand, the blade behind his forearm. He drove it into Noxus' chest. The waning energy shield sent current through them, but the normal weapon still bit into its target as both men dropped to their knees.

Wulvur felt Noxus still moving and morphed into his beast form, grabbing his prey by the throat as he twisted the blade to finish the kill. He felt the torturous current stop as the tiny shield generator died, but something else seized control over his body, slowing his moves, fogging his mind. He recognized that psy attack, not even realizing he'd morphed out of Slade's form.

"Venamir," Wulvur muttered.

Noxus clambered free of the death grip, one hand clenched over his lower chest as he punched Wulvur in the ribs. "Checkmate. Extra mesh below my heart." Each word slithered out dripping with pain, but the malicious grin grew by the second as Wulvur's beast form faded back to his true form. Noxus rolled free and struggled to his feet.

Wulvur also rose, swaying in pain. "What heart?"

Venamir and Cruentin entered from a shadowy passageway, watching.

Their presence only fed the arrogance of Noxus. "Wulvur. It was you all this time?" His face contorted in surprise and fury.

Venamir's voice held grudging respect as he studied Wulvur. "Moradin was right. You are better than Noxus."

Wulvur glanced at his hands and yanked off his gloves for a better look. His hands and black locks of hair hanging free on his shoulders confirmed his true identity. He laughed. "Fooled you all, didn't I?" He morphed into his true beast form, a darker wolfish creature with jackal ears and stripes along his hackled fur.

Wulvur bowled Noxus over as they struck in unison. Noxus still had one dagger left. As it swung, the curved blade split into three blades. They penetrated Wulvur's chest, dug in, and clawed downward. He still held Noxus down, wrestling for a secure grip on the rotten thug's neck, even though his own blood was dripping onto his prey.

"Honestly, Noxus," Venamir said, "all those mods, and still you failed me." He released his psy hold on Wulvur. "Go ahead, Wulvur, kill him."

Wulvur scoffed at Venamir, "Shut up. You're next."

Noxus rasped as he sucked in air. He shot a murderous glare at Venamir and sputtered in shock. "But... I'm your best hit-man!"

"You are a failed experiment," Venamir retorted.

Noxus grabbed his comm and blurted, "To the ship."

Venamir took a breath to reply when the forms of Noxus and Wulvur blurred behind a whirlwind of energy and vanished. "Who did that? Scan for them."

Cruentin stepped up alongside Venamir. "Who cares? Scanners barely work in these caves. Wulvur's no longer a threat. Let's find Slade." He spun, firgun aimed toward approaching footsteps.

Moradin appeared from the darkness, followed by two dopps. "These are all your battle dopps I have left. Berku showed up and his pack tore our defense apart."

"Pity, leave these dopps with me," Venamir shrugged. "Find Noxus and Wulvur. Bring me whoever wins."

Moradin nodded and hastened out of the room. Once alone in the down-sloping passage, her jaw set in anger. She muttered to herself, "That's how disposable we are?"

* * *

As the teleporter energy faded from their tingling bodies, Noxus and Wulvur resumed their brawl and stumbled apart on unfamiliar terrain. Noxus kicked Wulvur in the chest and scampered free of those werebeast's claws.

They were in a warm, underground chamber. Light filtered toward them from charged crystals in the walls all around them, and from rows of hibernation tubes. Most of the tubes blinked with small lights inside, random computer checks of the sleeping people.

"I ported you here. We need your help," said a voice in the darkness.

"I help nobody," Noxus retorted.

"Not you," the voice retorted.

"He meant me, dumbass," Wulvur snarked. He struggled to his feet, one paw pressing hard against the gashes. His chest burned as if Noxus had stuck him with hot coals. He realized it wasn't just a room with sleeping people, but his keener eyesight noticed smaller incubators with nests inside.

"Eggs?" he whispered. He heard a slight scuffling sound from behind the nearest incubator.

A malicious chuckle scoffed at him. "Looks like I'm scrambling some eggs."

Wulvur flung a smoke bomb, leaving Noxus in a cloud of choking gas. *There's only one Watcher?* He spied a doorway to the next room and went for it. *I don't have much time.*

Another form in the shadows caught his attention, a humanoid form trying to sneak behind one of the control units across the room. A door remained shut by the stranger. The stranger held up his hands, backing against the wall. "Wait."

Wulvur jogged across the chamber, feeling a wild recklessness. Wulvur forced his body into his wereform and lunged, claws out as he slammed the man against the closed door. "You look like one of Venamir's thugs to me."

The young man's shirt ripped as Wulvur pushed him against the wall. "I'm on your side. Shocks told us about you."

Wulvur blinked in disbelief at the whimsical cartoons tattooed across the young man's chest and arms. "You're Shocks' kid?"

"Yeah, so?"

Wulvur released him. "How'd you get here?" he whispered.

"Someone ported us here."

"Must be the dragon watchers. There're eggs here and a psycho hit-man. Get lost before Noxus murders you."

The youth looked at Wulvur's slashed, bloodied combat gear. "But you need help."

"Then go find me some help. Get out!" Wulvur shoved the kid out the door and slammed it shut.

Left alone in the passage, the tattooed youth kicked the locked door. "Lemme in!" He tried his comm, sending out only broken messages full of static. He threw his tracker back the way he came, hoping to lead them to Wulvur. He ran down roughly cut passages with waning glow orbs for light until he saw two familiar forms in a small chamber.

The tattooed youth ran until he found Motley and Moradin, standing with guns drawn on each other. Two Mora-dopps lay sprawled between them.

The firguns both pivoted toward him.

"Whoa!" Tatts yelled. "Are you gonna fight or make lovey eyes?"

Moradin lowered her firgun first, her lips crinkling in a scowl. "I don't do furries."

"I don't do walking vibrators," Motley retorted.

"I don't vibrate!" Moradin snapped.

"That's your problem," Motley countered.

Tatts snapped, "Knock it off. Wulvur's a mess and he's locked in a chamber with Noxus. He turned to Moradin and waved a finger before her nose. "I know you like Wulvur. I heard you telling Noxus how that other Druwen's so much better. Ooh, you have a crush."

Her face instantly reddened. "I didn't mean it like that. I mean, shut up, you little shit." She glared at Motley, who shrugged, grinning.

"Dammit, bicker later," the youth insisted. "We all hate Noxus."

Motley and Moradin looked at each other and nodded with mutual agreement.

Tatts shifted his weight, wearing his best poker face while he scrutinized them. "Come on," he said, and ran past them.

* * *

Wulvur felt his pockets, finding one last package of goo that was already drying out. He knew it worked best when fresh, and was intoxicating. He placed his hands against the walls and reached out, trying to sense any tree roots, any safe life force with nutrients to draw from. All he felt was rock with deep, withering roots far above. "Can't heal, much," he panted. "No tree energy." He opened the pouch with Scruffy's goo and smeared the green stuff into the seeping holes in his chest.

Wulvur closed his eyes and morphed, then back, and into wolvish form again and back to his normal Atlean form. When he opened his eyes and looked at the goo patches, they were soaked, as if he hadn't healed at all. "Fruckin' venom," he murmured.

Noxus called from across the room. "Come out, Wulvur. I'll put you out of your misery."

Wulvur felt his empty holster, and his dagger stashes empty as well. Bow gone, sword dropped when Venamir and Cruen seared into his brain. He rose and faced Noxus, who didn't look much better. They both moved with heavy fatigue, their battle gear destroyed.

Wulvur dropped to all fours and morphed into his full beast form, fur shaggier, teeth and claws longer, eyes taking on a reddish hue.

Noxus ran for the main chamber, his glinting eyes searching for a target, eggs, any egg. "Hah, you'll be known as Wulvur the sacred drakir killer." He rounded on a thick nest of eggs protected within rocks and padding.

Wulvur charged, tackling Noxus, plunged his beastman claws into Noxus's shoulders, pinning him to the ground. He bit Noxus in the hand, teeth crunching through bone and machinery.

Noxus stared up with wide eyes as he felt his strength leave him in spurts, each beat of his miserable heart sapping life from him. "You're... you're...."

"An energy shaman," Wulvur nodded, straightening as each passing second fed him strength, "We normally use trees to heal, but I just took your blood with the serum in it."

Noxus chortled, "The serum's made for me, not you."

"I'll take my chances." Wulvur straightened, drew another of Noxus' stolen daggers from his boot and raised it to strike. Strong hands locked around his arms and pulled him up.

Noxus struggled to sit up, his limbs twitching.

Wulvur saw Motley and Moradin holding onto him. "What're you doing here?"

"We're surrounded," Motley whispered. "Play along."

Wulvur gave Moradin a sideways glance of distrust. "Yeah? Prove it," he muttered. "If you're both on my side, we can beat them," Wulvur argued. He felt their grips tighten.

Motley growled something in his feline language.

Wulvur understood Motley's language and was certain Noxus didn't. *Play dead? Uh... how dead?* "Leggo." He heard the footsteps slapping the ground, the walk of Merfins.

Moradin spoke up first. "Captain, you said Noxus is replaceable. Can we keep this one?"

"Keep me?" Wulvur echoed, glancing around.

Venamir walked up to Wulvur, out of arm's reach. "I hoped you would win."

Even as Noxus struggled to rise, his voice was dangerous. "What? But we're kin."

"Only via lab specimen," Venamir reminded. "Wulvur, join me. Or die."

"You can surrender, last chance," Wulvur countered.

"No," Motley interrupted. "This kill is mine."

A chill crawled through Wulvur. "What?"

"Nothing personal," Motley said, his voice aloof.

Slowly, Wulvur locked Motley's unreadable gaze with a molten glare. "Serious, man? Were you his freaking spy all this time?"

"I'm a freelancer." Motley twisted Wulvur's arm behind his back and stepped behind him, clamping his other paw on Wulvur's shoulder, claws digging in. "Well?"

Wulvur fought their excruciating grips long enough to snatch a small quick-release tube from his belt and closed his hand around it. His knees trembled to keep him upright while pain spread throughout his joints, leeching his strength away. *Venom, strong, I'm not immune.* Panting in pain, he locked gazes with Venamir.

Venamir turned his attention to Motley. "Why did you return, feline?"

"You endangered my cub, so I had to hide him." His ears flicked back. "You leave my family alone, got that? Spare Wulvur, and I'll return as your crewman. You know I'm better than those slimy scrubs you broke out of prison."

"They make good cannon fodder," Venamir said, pressing his fingers together in thought. "Moradin, where are the rest of your dopps?"

"Destroyed," she replied.

"Pity. More failed experiments, leaving only you."

Confusion washed across her face. "Are you calling me a failure?"

Venamir waved her off. "Not you. This is no time for emotions. Rebuilding Noxus was a mistake. You, not so much."

Wulvur flinched as Moradin tightened her whole body, including the cyborg hand clenched around his arm. He eased a brief glance at her and saw her eyes flicker toward him with a strange mix of emotions. Her grip on him loosened.

"Cruentin, summon your clones," Venamir ordered.

"You mean *your* clones?" Cruen asked.

"You made them."

Cruen shrugged and touched his headband. A group of clones emerged from the passages and milled around in the cave with them. The clones resembled Venamir, but none were perfect matches.

Venamir nodded. "Motlion, you wish to work for me? Wulvur is too large a threat. Kill him. Leave him where Slade can find him. Make it *messy.*"

Motley growled something that sounded like a possible chuckling grunt.

They all fell silent at the sound of a small whine, weak at first, then louder, pulsating to antagonizing levels. Wulvur opened the small, flattened orb ih his hand. His mind whirled, having no idea whether to trust Motley or not, but what choice did he have? He zoned them all out, letting his vision blur, slowing his heartbeat, and blanketing his mind with memories of his favorite peaceful safe haven, a misty clearing surrounded by old-growth trees.

Seeing Motley hesitate, Venamir ordered, "Send backup."

More teleportation auras of light materialized around them, depositing a handful of surviving clones, all of Venamir.

"Too bad, cat. Clones, finish them off," Cruentin ordered.

"Go ahead," Wulvur stated, his voice cold and foreboding. "Oh, looky here." As he watched everyone else's eyes widen in fear, Wulvur dropped into phase two of self-hypnosis. He let his mind fall away from his body and retreat into the soft sounds of whispering trees and warm rays of light filtering through the old growth canopy of his sanctuary. His breaths fell nearly silent. In Wulvur's hand, the grenade screeched with pent up energy.

Venamir and Cruen dove for cover behind their clones. "Kill him!" Venamir cried out.

The clones rushed toward Wulvur, their yellow, Venamirish eyes without feeling.

Motley swung his arm up, claws fully extended, then smacked it hard against Wulvur's lower back and dragged it upward. The blow knocked the wind out of Wulvur, while Moradin elbowed him in his head. His knees buckled as darkness claimed him.

Moradin snatched the grenade and flung it at the clones. Jumping in front of Motley and Wulvur, she activated her body shield. It wasn't enough. Shattered dopp parts pelted her, knocking her to her knees, but only for a split-second. She glanced around, seeing a second energy shield appear around her, Motley, and Wulvur. The shield vanished a few seconds after the blast. She glimpsed movement from the next chamber, behind the sleep tubes.

Cruen's clones crumpled to the ground from the concussion, some of their outstretched hands inches away from the grenade as it blew. The chambers trembled, everything hazy in a thick cloud of dust. A few seconds later, all was silent except for humming within the hibernation chamber, rapid breathing, a few coughs, and tiny scraping noises from the eggs.

"It was a smart grenade," Moradin said, "a dopp killer. It didn't target fleshies at all. Clever gadget."

Venamir and Cruen rose, shaken but unharmed.

"Except he still lost," Motley said. Leering with bloodlust, Motley hefted Wulvur by the combat vest and shook him. His fallen prey hung like a stuffed toy, giving off no sounds or movement. He waved a bloody paw at Venamir. "See? Nice and messy."

Cruen nodded and approached with caution, then felt Wulvur for vitals. He pressed his fingers hard into Wulvur's throat, hoping for a pulse or any reaction. Finding none, he shrugged and marched away. "Feels dead to me."

Venamir eased forward with a sadistic grin. "Was that a spinal kill? How delightful. Go now, deposit him where his friends can find him. Moradin, find Slade. Put a tracker on Slade so I can port him to the *Spectre*. Bring only Slade."

Moradin was about to reply when a deep snarl wafted through the caves. More growls joined in, sounding ominous, vengeful. Moradin's face paled. Even Venamir and Doctor Cruentin looked worried as they glanced around. More noise followed, heavy footsteps and voices.

"It's coming from below, no," Cruen said, pivoting, "from the ocean?"

"They're awake," Venamir said. He tapped his comm and put a hand on Cruen's shoulder. "*Spectre*, port myself and Cruen onboard. Now."

Venamir and Cruentin teleported out, leaving the others to fend for themselves. Moradin's frown tightened into a scowl, softened into sorrow, then back to anger as she stalked around the chamber. "Venamir abandoned me too. That's all anybody ever does."

Noxus groaned, "Mora, help me. We have to leave."

Mora turned to him, her voice iced over. "It's about time you look like so many of your victims. How many people have you slain over the years?"

"Who cares?" Noxus retorted between labored gasps.

She grabbed him and dragged him farther into the egg chamber. Scraping sounds within some eggs increased to tapping and thumps. One within their view cracked. It rocked and rolled to the floor.

Moradin's voice took on a sickly, sweet tone. "Do you hear them? You not only woke the babies, you woke up the adult drakirs. They'll be hungry. Lucky for me, the eggs were very well-protected. I'd feed you to the dragons, except your cyborg fluid would poison them."

Noxus attempted to rise, only to stagger and fall onto his butt. "You're serious." He chortled. "I'll survive, but you all won't. My blood will kill them. That... makes you... baby killer, like me."

"I am nothing like you!" Moradin flexed her arm and stun blasted him from the power cells in her wrist, leaving him twitching and drooling on the floor. "I'm sick of you poisoning everyone! You need to pay!" She watched him squirm, relishing the sight. To his clear surprise, her demeanor softened. She knelt beside Noxus. "I was only kidding. Where is your spare serum?"

Scowling, Nexos pulled a small medical pouch off his belt. "Here."

Moradin inspected the contents, two injectors marked for dosage. "This is safe for anyone to use?"

"Of course. Alchemist Thiun made it. This serum treats any of my poisons, and slows most others," Noxus growled, one hand over his chest where Wulvur had stabbed him. "Use the serum on me. Now."

Moradin drew her firgun. "Thanks, sucker. Goodbye and good riddance."

His bloodshot eyes widened. "Wha-at?"

Growling sounds were drawing near. Eyes glowed from darkness in the largest adjoining chamber. The beast squeezed out of the widest passageway and into the main hatchery chamber. The beast indeed resembled Earth's dragons, from the long snout with deadly teeth to reptilian wings and four legs. While not enormous, the creature outsized any normal mount, its chest the height of a human.

The drakir looked from Moradin to Noxus, taking in long whuffs, her pearly intelligent eyes narrowing on Noxus. Its seething voice snarled, "You-u-u!"

Motley was monitoring Wulvur's vitals. Spying the drakir, his fur stood on end. "Holy shit, they really do look like dragons!"

A Merfin came out of the passage and kept close to the drakir. He fought back a yawn, his pearly eyes still sleepy from hibernation. He charged up a rifle that held a spear along its laser barrel, which he aimed it at Noxus. "Stay away from the drakir hatchlings," he commanded. "I've alerted the entire flight. Soon, we'll be swarming with drakirs."

"It's too late. We've started a civil war, so shut up or you're next," Noxus hissed.

"You are in sorry shape to make threats," the Watcher replied.

Moradin kept her firgun aimed at her nemesis. "Old enemies?" she asked the dragon.

The beast replied with fervor, "Who doesn't know this cyborg, Noxus, scourge of the Deeps? He rescued the traitorous Venamir, caused cave-ins and attacked our guardians. And now, he dares to defile the sacred hatcheries and threaten my young? Step aside. Noxus deserves to die by my claws. DIE!"

Noxus yelled, "Shoot it!"

Moradin smiled. "My only target is you."

Noxus struggled to his feet and staggered down the dark passage toward the cave entrance. "I can survive the fall," he yelled. "Then I'll come back and kill you one night. You wait!"

Moradin bowed to the drakir. "The babies need you. Let me share this kill." She strode after Noxus, yelling back, "How's it feel to run, knowing you'll die?"

Noxus made it to the cave's opening. He peered down over the floor's edge, to see at least a hundred foot drop down to a shallow, rocky beach and angry waves crashing over the rocks. He didn't notice the sound of wings beating against gusts of wind and silhouettes framed by sunlight.

Moridan entered the cave, smiling at splotches of cyborg fluid and blood on the floor between her and her prey. She peered past Noxus, her keen eyes glimpsing two forms in flight. "Any last words?"

Noxus heaved himself to his feet. He turned, facing her, groping for a weapon, a hidden dagger or smoke bomb. He found none. Oil and blood dripped from holes in his body, trickling down his tattered armor and staining the sandy floor.

The beating of wings grew louder. Two drakirs the size of draft horses swooped into the cave and landed on either side of Noxus. Their great paws thumped the ground as they landed. They wore armor like war horses and surpassed the size of a draft horse. Their scales resembled their body armor, shining blue for one drakir, red and green for the other drakir. They each bore a Deeps Merfin rider armed with spearguns and mysterious, holstered weapons.

Moradin holstered her weapon. "You're combat riders, never thought I'd meet any."

The rider in green and red pointed his speargun at Noxus. "He is the one Fiske reported." He yelled, "Fiske! Where are you?"

A sleepy-eyed Merfin ran in from a passage, pushing his way past Moradin. "I'm here." He glowered at Noxus. "That cyborg before you, he and his thugs took over the hatchery. They endangered our hatchlings, threatened to kill them, and put most of my crew into deep sleep, including myself."

"We spared you," Noxus spat, wavering on his feet.

"You blackmailed us!" Fiske hissed. "Now you don't need us alive. You were going to kill the hatchlings and us, had Slade's Druwen ranger not stopped you." He gestured to Moradin. "This woman has helped our cause."

"I'm not stopped yet," Noxus said, backing toward the cave mouth. Another few steps. "I'll be back for all of you." He thumped his shield generator on his dented belt buckle. An energy shield appeared around him, but it was flickering.

The drakir riders ordered him to surrender, only once.

Noxus rushed toward the cave mouth, trying to escape.

The drakir riders fired their spears. The spears glowed as they cut through the target's body shield, eliminating the force field around Noxus.

"Feast," one rider said with a wicked grin.

The drakirs roared. They slashed at Noxus, their claws splattering blood and sending remnants of body armor flying. Their prey tried to leap off the edge, a futile effort while burdened by spears striking him and knocked off balance by powerful paws and lethal claws. He dove for the cave's mouth, only for powerful wings to bowl him back into play. Noxus struggled to his knees, swaying.

"Yeah, get him!" Moradin cheered. "Hit him again!"

When the drakirs closed in to finish their prey with maws wide open, fangs bared. They jumped back when a shot burned the ground close to Noxus.

All eyes turned to Moradin, who lowered her diser gun.

"You dare bring that illegal weapon here, one capable of burning holes through flesh and metal," Fiske queried. "How can we trust you?"

Moradin heaved a sigh. "You can't eat cyborgs, especially this one. He's loaded with poisons."

The riders held back their mounts, their faces and pearlescent eyes ponderous.

"True," one drakir said in a rough voice. "Cyborgs make a bad meal."

Noxus was a mess. His cybernetic parts creaked with each movement. He bore multiple slash marks from claws. One spear had impaled an arm, which he pulled free, groaning and dropped it to the floor. Noxus grabbed a stalagmite for balance as he again backed toward the cave opening. "I'll be back."

Moradin smiled. "No you won't." She opened fire. Her blasts seared into cyborg metal, flesh, and bone. The heat from each blast intensified until it overrode his circuits, disabling his power cells.

Noxus stumbled back and fell out of the cave. He bounced off jagged protrusions down the cliff's face, bellowing, "You bii-ii-iitch!"

The riders and drakirs stared down from the cave, their faces awash with satisfaction. Noxus lay sprawled out on the rocks, limp at last, each wave tugging him farther off the shore.

Moradin holstered her weapon. She heaved a long sigh. "That felt so-o good."

"I can handle it from here," Fiske spoke up from where he stood watching. He yawned, still sleepy-eyed. "The hatchlings are waking. So are their adult kin. We'll need the adult drakirs to bring fish. Thank you for helping."

The red-clad rider asked, "Where is Venamir? Why did you not call us sooner?"

"I couldn't. I'm afraid we may need your entire flight to calm the other clans. I believe that Venamir means to disrupt our alliances."

The drakir riders gave Moradin skeptical looks. They looked at Fiske again, who nodded and gestured for them to go. Glancing at each other, the riders nodded. Their gracefully powerful mounts beat their wings and soared out of the cave.

Fiske patted Moradin's shoulder. "We are grateful. Chippen and I will be with the hatchlings if you need us."

"Does your teleporter work?"

"Yes. Didn't you know? Somebody teleported Noxus and Wulvur here. I presumed it was Venamir's doing."

Motley moved over, his ears laid back, tail lashing. "Moradin, come with me."

"Fine." She followed Motley down through the passage, followed by Fiske. Moradin couldn't help a brief expression of childish wonder as a handful of baby drakirs left their broken eggshells to venture out. "Ooh, look at the drakir babies, how rare, how cute." She dug the last of her jerky from a pocket and tossed it toward them. "Sorry, it's all I have. More food is on the way."

The adult drakir sniffed the meat, her long mouth curling into a frown, but after a taste, the beast rocked her head in wary approval. The newly hatched drakirs surrounded the meat, stretching their necks and sniffing. After a brief inspection, they started gnawing at it and growling. Tiny claws extended from their delicate paws and latched into the meat. Wings folded along their backs fluttered with clumsy attempts to keep their balance.

"You can't give babies jerky," Motley scolded in a hushed tone, "even if they are dragons."

"It's not spicy. Aren't they adorable?" Moradin cooed.

Motley felt for vitals on Wulvur. Breathing, nothing. No pulse, no response to a flick on the ear, quite antagonizing for Atleans, nothing. "I think we killed Wulvur." He positioned himself and gave Wulvur a chest compression. "Wake up!"

Moradin flinched at the heaving, forced movement of cartilage. "Stop that! Stupid feline, you'll kill him for sure."

Motley turned his shaggy head, jaw dropping in total befuddlement. "Then you give him CPR. You're the woman."

She rolled her eyes. "Great. Only the big puss notices."

Motley's ears snapped back. "Come on. If we don't try, his friends will murder us."

"Oh, like they won't, anyway."

"I'm not a medic, you wacko, why'd you hit him so hard?"

"That was my lowest strength setting, and I didn't predict you crushing his spine."

"I didn't break anything. It was all for show to convince Venamir."

Moradin rolled her eyes. She knelt and jabbed the serum into Wulvur's leg through his clothing. His leg twitched. Moradin flexed her hand into a fist, activating little barrels rising from her wristguard. Ignoring Motley's protests, she delivered her lightest stun blast to Wulvur's chest.

"Stop trying to make him deader." Motley complained. He drew his paws back when Wulvur took a ragged gasp.

Wulvur's vision cleared, to see Motley and Moradin leaning over him. He tried to rise but Motley stared at his chest and shoved him back down with large pawlike hands. Swinging at Moradin proved equally futile when she blocked his arm with numbing force.

Wulvur collapsed back onto the rocky ground, gasping in pain.

Moradin chuckled. "Oh, you *are* good. You took out most of the clones and went into a full self-hibernation—within seconds."

"No fake flattery," Wulvur retorted. He noticed Moradin discarding half the hypo set and prepping a second one. "Will you two decide whose side you're on? What'd you shoot me up with?"

"Serum," she answered with a light smile.

"Truth serum?" Wulvur shot a confused glare at Motley. "Well, I won't tell ya nothing, so get bent!"

Motley's ears flickered. "Moradin, Slade's almost here. Give him the second shot."

"It's not ready yet."

Slade charged into the cave, with Berku and the tattooed youth close behind. Their faces washed over with shock and caution as their firguns snapped onto Moradin.

"Freeze!" Slade barked. His eyes shifted briefly to the hatchery, where the mother drakir was carrying the jerky farther inside. The hatchlings followed her. His friends glanced after the dragon as well, their expressions ranging from wonder to worry.

Moradin held the hypo in place. "And?" she asked.

Slade leveled his gun sights at her chest. "Get up and back away, nice and easy."

"Slade, wait," Motley started. "She switched sides."

"No waiting," Wulvur growled, pointing at Motley. "Trr-rraitor! That's what you are! How else do you explain not fighting Venamir?"

"Wha-at?" Berku groaned, his firgun wavering.

Moradin met Slade's promising glare as her cybernetic arms continued their task and slammed it against Wulvur's leg. Slade's first blast only fazed her. A second shot sent her tumbling.

Wulvur passed out from the rush of chemicals in his body.

Motley kept his paws clamped down on Wulvur's chest despite firguns aimed at him and confused look on his friends' faces.

"What the hell is going on?" Slade demanded.

"Moradin's working with me now, I mean us! Your friend will bleed out if I take pressure off! After taking down Noxus, Wulvur was in no shape to fight. I had to make him look dead or Venamir's goons were gonna butcher him. Look at the other slashes on his clothes. They don't match my claws. We were trying to save him."

Slade lowered his firgun first, then Berku. "It's logical."

Motley went on, "We don't have time for this. Noxus poisoned him. The venom's turned him into a bleeder. The serum we have isn't a cure."

Berku called it in. "Find my body reading. We're by the hatchery. Wulvur needs a medic."

Moradin rose, sneering at Slade, "Shooting a cyborg in the chest? We're most protected there. *You* taught me that years ago. Way to go, Captain Turncoat."

Slade's firgun lowered a bit as his jaw fell slack.

Moradin kept on venting, "First, you left me for dead, and now you shoot me. And then you have the nerve to wonder why I worked for Venamir. At least he came back for me, unlike you. And yeah, I injected serum into your friend. The cat's right. The serum may not be enough to save him. You need to make a cure based on his blood."

Slade stared at her, memories colliding with true recognition of her, the same tone, that cheek twitch she had when under duress, just as he remembered. "I remember now! I had Venamir down and you helped capture me." His voice hardened with anger, "Why didn't you turn on him back there?"

"I couldn't. One word from him would have been the end of us."

Slade demanded, "How?"

"He can make me self-destruct," she replied, a response that made the others straighten. Even Slade took a step back. "You were safer in that escape pod than being onboard with us. Yes, even surrounded by a mine field you stood a better chance of survival."

Slade's expression softened, pondering as he debated what to believe.

Wulvur fought back a groan as he awoke to their explanations. "That makes sense," he said in a weak voice, "I was wrong about the big puss. I was fighting Noxus. He had a 3-blade weapon."

Motley heaved a sigh of relief when the firguns around him lowered. "Told you."

"Sorry man," Berku said to the frazzled catman.

"But he did slug me in the back and now, I can't get up," Wulvur added.

All eyes turned to him and Motley as the big feline shrank back with regret. "I didn't mean to. Can't they fix you?"

"I'll tell you why," Wulvur pressed, "because your large butt is holding me down! Hah, sucker."

Motley hissed as he fought back a barrage of swearing.

"Damn you, Wulvur!" Slade barked. "Motley, sit on him."

"Don't make it a bromance," Wulvur smarted off.

"It's not a bromance," Motley growled.

Slade backed away from Moradin, still jaded with distrust as he called the *Vernacular* again. "Medbay? What's the delay? Port Rhoan and Elowren to us. We need a medic right now."

"We're flying to you," Rhoan replied, his voice raised over engine noise and wind. "The *Vernacular* took a beating. Our teleporter is fried.

Minutes later, a silvery red drakir flew into the cave mouth. She wore a morpher's combat armor, with familiar weapon belts. She resumed her true form, of lady Elowren. Rhoan's jetpack wound down as he landed behind her.

Rhoan and Elowren ran through the cave mouth, down a passage, and found their friends in the drakir hatchery. Their noise sent hatchlings scrambling. Rhoan sidestepped toward his patient while he stared at the hatchlings. "Are those baby dragons? Wow!"

"Drakirs," Elowren corrected.

"Dragons," Rhoan grinned.

"Fine." Elowren nodded toward the darkness of the incubation chamber. "The adult dragons are waking. We need to get them food. Venamir's thugs put the Watchers in deep sleep. The Watcher who we found is waking the others." She tapped her comm. "Scruffy, we need all the fish and meat you have teleported into the drakir chambers."

Scruffy static-filled hologram appeared over her wrist. He waved his arms in clear aggravation. "All of it? Our portal isn't working."

"We're about to have a bunch of hungry dragons wondering why their babies are awake."

"The Watchers have a portal chamber," Scruffy said. "Try theirs."

Rhoan glanced around, hearing muffled scraping of claws and throaty growling that made him flash back to horror movies. "Uh, how big are these dragons?"

"Eh, like oversized horses, or griffins in Earth's legends. They could still eat us."

"I can work the portal for you," came a voice from deeper in the hatchery. A sleepy Merfin approached them, yawning, a bit unsteady on his webbed feet. "We know of you, Lady Elowren."

She jogged over to the Watcher. "What happened here?"

"Long story, Venamir's fault," the man said as moved to one of several deep sleep tubes. "I must wake my fellow Watchers and secure the young. You may use the portal chamber."

"Why didn't any of you help sooner?" Rhoan queried, moving closer.

The sleepy aquatic sighed at Rhoan. "I just woke from deep sleep, am most groggy." He pointed to a passage. "Your friends are that way." He moved off through another doorway.

Rhoan and Elowren found their way to Slade and the others in the adjoining, smaller cavern. She flashed Slade a smile which faded when she spied Moradin.

Moradin sighed and opened small sections of her skin up, ejected tiny power tubes. "I'm defecting, okay? Here, you'll need these more than I will. These energy cells should power equipment on the *Vernacular*, just like they did on your old ships."

Rhoan was grinning like an overjoyed kid. "We have dragons."

"Oh, now you're helping?" Elowren queried, glaring at Moradin.

"You tell me, you're so good at reading minds," Moradin retorted before catching herself. Her eyes gleamed with flooding emotions. "Why does it matter? It doesn't." She wiped at her eyes. "Venamir's been going crazy. He called us failed experiments, after all we've done for him!"

"Mori, we truly searched for you," Slade tried to assure her.

"Yeah, well, great job," Moradin retorted. "Now, here we are. Venamir will figure out that I helped your friend. He'll try to blow me up via all of these." She held out the power cells, which Berku collected. "Oh don't worry," she went on, "It won't be immediate. Venamir likes people to reflect before they die, and he wants you on that ship, to kill you, of course. I'll leave two cells in my body. I can function for a while and might survive the blast. When my countdown starts, get away from me. For now, I'll take you to the *Spectre* with Venamir, and you can have your rematch." Her voice lowered to a growl. "Make him pay for all he's done to everyone."

Slade studied her for a long moment. "Deal."

Moradin ran into the main hatchery chamber, where she yanked the dusty cover off a control panel. She was promptly shooed aside by the sleepy Watcher.

"Let me," the Watcher said. He elaborated as he powered up the teleport chamber. "I did try to break up the fight. You should know that my first priority is to the eggs. Your friend and the cyborg were elusive, and their battle posed a threat to the hatchery. I had to call for help from our drakir riders. We have medical facilities and stasis tubes available."

"Thanks," Moradin said. "I only need your portal. Venamir's going to lift ship."

"What about the *Spectre's* shields?" Motley asked. "We won't be able to get in."

Moradin rolled her eyes. "You thick-headed furball, I know the codes because I'm part of the *Spectre's* old crew. I'll port you into my room. We should be safe there."

"Mori, come back to my crew," Slade offered.

She eyed him with a sour look. "Ask me later."

The Watcher went on, "You may need a stasis tube for your wounded. His condition will stabilize until treatment is ready." He looked at Rhoan as the young man approached. "Will that help?"

"That'd be awesome," Rhoan said. He returned to his patient and pulled Wulvur to his feet. "Come on, get in a sleep tube."

Wavering, Wulvur planted his heels. "No. Those things are coffins. The Guardian with Kestral died in his tube."

"He's in stasis. He might survive. Now get in there," Rhoan ordered. "You have poisons and the wrong serums in you."

Moradin drummed her fingers on the portal controls. "Ahem! I can port him to your ship."

"Mori, it's too risky," Elowren replied. "We're dealing with venom and serums clashing against each other. Everything has to be ready. We need blood work first."

"Fine," Wulvur grumbled. Despite his trepidation, he passed out seconds after his sank into the tube's soft cushions. He barely saw a Merfin closing the tube around him.

Moradin sighed, "We best get onboard the *Spectre*." She activated the portal controls and vanished with Slade and Berku.

* * *

A portal opened into the *Spectre's* upper deck, into an odd habitat. Moradin, Slade, and Berku stepped out of a fading sphere of smoke and looked around, weapons lowering. Moradin's room was more workshop than living quarters. Berku grinned at her arsenal positioned around an elaborate workout station. Moradin led the way past an elaborate toolbox with parts, tools, and weaponry.

Moradin heaved a sigh. "Slade, just so you know, I didn't mean to harm you. My hands aren't programmed to be gentle on the living." She added, "Except on Merfins."

"Ew," Berku muttered.

Slade wasn't sure if he should believe her, but he tried to. "We have a munitions specialist. He could disarm you."

"All these years I hated all of you," she went on, her voice quavering, "but then I realized that you couldn't save everyone." Moradin grabbed her comm. "Herja of the *Spectre*, recognize my voice, analyze my body pattern. I am your programmer, and I order you to obey Captain Slade."

The voice that replied sounded like her voice from a happier time. Herja Mori appeared in a small, wispy form. "Morialya, your voice matches my program. You have upgrades."

Moradin replied, "I said to analyze Slade, not me."

"I was made to obey both Slade and Venamir. This means I must obey them both until one is somehow incapacitated," the Herja replied.

"That'll do," Slade said. "Obey my crew."

"As much as my program allows," the hologram said, vanishing.

Chapter 46
To Breach a *Spectre*

Scruffy and Telari made their way through the labyrinth of passages between the Starship Graveyard and the ocean. Scruffy was in his wolfish form, and Telari in feline form. Doc and Kestral remained in true form, Doc holding a firgun while Kestral used a scanner to search for life forms. The passages wound through an underground matrix of tunnels and storage rooms set up as workshops or living quarters.

"Traveling through the Starship Graveyard would be faster," Telari remarked.

"Slade's hunter friends are still clearing the area of thugs and booby traps," Scruffy reminded her. "Venamir's forces are trying to protect the *Spectre*."

"We're close to the *Spectre*," Kestral said. "I can hear the ship's guardian program."

"You can hear it? How?" Tel asked.

Kestral tapped the implant behind her left ear. "Because I'm a Herja, too. I didn't know Mori personally, but our programs can interact. The councils made their defense system that way to try to keep allied ships from attacking each other."

"Venamir was the ship's Captain, but some of us were on the crew," Doc said, keeping his firgun ready as they walked. "Four of the original crew can override the Guardian program."

"We need to join back up with Slade," Kestral said, "onboard the *Spectre*. There're life forms ahead. They're sleeping."

Scruffy grinned, baring pearly canines. He howled and yipped, a call that was answered. "It's Berku's clan, blazing a trail for us."

When they reached the hangar, they stared at an odd sight. Rezoans and other humanoids lay along the cavern walls, most of them snoring. A handful of forest morphers awaited them, a few standing guard. Others were securing nets, cargo straps, and whatever means of containment they could muster over their fallen prisoners.

Scruffy and Tel resumed their true forms, their gear looking new and pristine beside the allied morphers. Berku's clansmen who remained on guard appeared rather jovial.

"You all right here?" Doc asked, holstering his firgun.

"Oh, yeah," the pack leader grinned, holding a bulky riot-gun over one shoulder. "I'm Lyriad. Wulvur did most of the work, hoarded the fun. Problem is, we still can't get into that damned ship. The Herja sees us as a security threat and keeps locking the hatches."

He thumbed behind him, toward some demolished generators. Past the generators, prisoners, and scores of decaying arrows sticking out of the floor, stood a ship gleaming with new armor plating and energy shields.

"There's the *Spectre,*" Lyriad said. "Looks like new. That had to be Venamir's clan fixing her, because the councils never authorized it."

Telari smiled at the living piece of history. "We'll get in."

"Let me talk to the Guardian," Kestral said. She knelt in a meditative pose. A small hologram of her emerged from her headband. Her translucent avatar flew ghostlike through the ship's outer hull, and vanished from view.

Scruffy glanced up at sunlight shining through monstrous clamshell doors overhead. The door hinges and actuators quivered along the reinforced walls. "Tel, they're opening the doors. This bird's about to fly!"

"Or we're about to have company," Tel threw back.

They hustled across the shaky catwalk above the *Spectre* ship, their steps carefully placed as the precarious strips of metal swayed beneath them.

Telari activated her helmet's display. "Run scans on this ship's shield config." Status symbols and data shifted and reformed before her eyes from within the visor as she panned the ship. "Shields are fluctuating around the aft nose, behind the windows' blast shields. The armor there has more gaps near the escape doors. The top of the ship is our safest point of entry. Let's move."

Scruffy and his companions barely started across the catwalks over the ship when the massive ceiling doors overhead jolted. Sunlight streamed through a slowly widening gap in the roof. Chunks of insulation crumbled and fell around them, some tumbling off the ship, making the werefolk below scramble for cover. Scruffy pointed at great hinges along the upper wall where one side of the huge doors were trembling harder from explosions outside.

Scruffy and Telari opened fire on the ship with grenade launchers. They saw the ship's energy shields flashed in protest, sparks dancing around their escape hatch target area.

"Herja Mori, talk to me. I'm Scruffy from the *Jacobyte*. You know me. Let us in."

Telari landed on an armored man, knocking him over. The man's eyes grew wide as Telari morphed into a half humanoid form with feline features, paws, and a swishing tail. Her claws pierced his clothes and slashed his forearms. The more frantic his struggles, the more she morphed until her shape was barely humanoid at all. A shrill, feline scream, furious as a lion's roar, carried over the engine noise. Then the rush hit her, and *oh, the thrill!* Even as the armored man wrestled a wavy knife from his boot, Tel slashed the arm with proud, long claws, breaking his grip and sending the knife tumbling off the wing of the ship.

The *Spectre* collided with the overhead maintenance structures, shearing the catwalk's supports from the wall. Doc and Scruffy landed and rolled near Tel. A fat lizard man rushed them at the open hatch, bringing up his firgun. Tel sprang at him first, sending his first and last shot into the ceiling. Tail lashing, she won a brief clash of claws and teeth versus lizard claws and fists. The lizard squirmed his way free, only to bail out the opposite hatch.

"Tel, you're catastrophic," Scruffy said.

"They taste awful," Tel said.

Slade, Berku, and Moradin appeared in a teleportal chamber constructed along a cavern wall. The doors opened to reveal a cramped storage room with half the walls blasted away. They were in another cavern barely large enough to contain the *Spectre,* which was still docked in clear view. Two obstacles prevented them from leaving the portal chamber: Telari and Doc Nelzyr held firguns on them as the chamber doors opened.

"Prove you're Slade," Tel ordered.

"Vany's still mad that your cat scratched up her bed," Slade replied.

"Well, she should have bought the poor thang some toys," Tel countered.

"Moradin's with us, now," Slade said as they lowered their weapons.

"I knew it." Doc grinned.

"No, you didn't," Moradin grunted. "We need onboard the *Spectre.* I can port us all in. I'll cover your backs for as long as I can."

"Thank you, Mori," Slade said with sincere gratitude.

All around the *Spectre,* Venamir's aquatic and reptilian henchmen lay on the ground, most of them snoring. Standing over them were several of Berku's Druwen hunters, along with Scruffy.

"Bout time," Scruffy said.

The *Spectre's* engines fired to life, stirring up a storm of wind and sand.

Metal groaned overhead as three stories up, sections of the ceiling slid apart. Huge door hinges and actuators quivered along the reinforced walls. Sunlight beamed through the widening gap overhead while sand and clumps of dirt pelted them.

* * *

Venamir coaxed the throttles and adjusted shields. "Slade's dog-faced pack flattened our guards. At least Moradin has Slade. I see them on our sensors."

Cruen flew right seat. "We're down to a skeleton crew. I only have a handful of clone dopps left and five guards onboard." He jumped at the sound of gunfire onboard their ship. "We've been boarded, and it's not only Moradin and Slade. More of his crew ported onboard."

"You dropped the shields for too long," Venamir retorted.

"Moradin's old Herja program is keeping the shield down. The Herja program is as bad as the one on Slade's ship—er, I mean, your ship, the *Jacobyte.*"

Comms lit up with a weathered, burly human with bright cartoons adorning his bare, hairy chest, filling the screen. "Yo, fishman. Name's Shocks. Remember me? I got every Earthern and allied ship from the human colonies ready to blast you into the water."

Venamir sneered, "Yes, human, attack me and kill your friends. Slade and his mongrels ported onboard." He shut off the comm and went to stealth. "Stealth at nearly ninety percent. Good enough. Cruen, give Slade's friends a warm welcome."

Cruen paled. "Me?"

"No, your ten clones. Oh, wait, the clones were destroyed. Yes, you."

Sighing, Cruentin exited. Once out of earshot, he activated his commcorder and whispered, "Chief Surgeon's log, update. Venamir has grown increasingly irrational. I predicted such behavior after he took the enhancers. He normally doesn't endanger me, and it's not about to start now. Time for my backup plan." A Merfin lady's face appeared on his little screen. Dark haired, cheeks painted with alabaster stripes. "My lady, we're enroute."

"Carry out your mission for our people. My *Wandering Fortress* awaits."

Cruen flinched and ducked as shots rang out within the ship. "Yes, for the Deeps!" he replied, while silencing his comm. "And for my rise to power."

* * *

Venamir's voice came over all comms. "Oh, Moradin, you have gone too far. I only wanted Slade, not a class reunion. Pity. I shall miss you."

Moradin's face paled as a surge of energy made her whole-body cringe. "Oh, it's begun!"

"Mori, you don't have to sacrifice yourself this time." Slade yelled, starting after her, with Berku close behind.

Moradin swept out of the room with long, powerful leaps. She rammed into a crewman, the force of her part-metal body stunning the man. She dragged him along as she headed for the cockpit, only to turn a corner and face her new crewmates holding weapons on her. Moradin flashed brilliant light from one palm, briefly blinding him, activating her body shield as she lunged at the other two. Their shots seared through her shield as she reached point blank range.

Her cyborg arms groaning in protest, she hefted them, slammed their heads together, and dropped them like broken toys.

Slade and Berku ran after her, past the fallen crewmen and saw an escape hatch slam shut. Right after the escape pod built up power and blasted away from the ship, they heard an explosion.

Stunned, respectful silence fell over Slade and Berku.

"Mori," Slade vowed, "we'll find you, I swear it."

"We better move," Berku said.

His jaw tight, Slade nodded. He kicked some debris aside. "All hands, who's on the *Spectre?*"

"Us," Scruffy replied. "Me, Tel, Doc, and Kestral, in the captain's quarters."

"Good," Slade confirmed. "Secure the ship." He studied the large room with fasteners, straps, and rigging along the walls, holding down crates. "We're in the central storage room. Make sure Venamir can't eject that cockpit."

"I know the overrides," Scruffy said. "We're on it."

Telari returned to her feline form, more graceful than ever, willing her claws to grow longer. In her excitement, she kept extending them like shining daggers slipping from their sheaths. Her ears twitched, serving as furry radars to the endless, sharper sounds, while the scents enticed her in every direction.

Scruffy rested a hand on her shoulders. "Focus," he said in a soft, mentoring voice. "You'll get used to your new form."

"It's not that," Tel said. "There's an energy surge, making my fur all tingly." Then she saw why. A portal sphere started forming around Slade, shrouding him from the others. "Portal on Slade."

"Grab on!" Slade blurted.

His friends complied before the words spilled out. Berku snagged Slade by one arm, while Tel leapt back toward them, skidding into Slade and grabbing his legs. Scruffy dove and grabbed Telari's hackled tail before they vanished from the mid deck, lost in a void of swirling energy.

Doc and Kestral also dove and landed where their friends had stood an instant before.

* * *

Slade's group of four materialized and tumbled over each other, Slade tripping over Telari, and Berku stumbling against Scruffy. The floor was slick with streaks of oil and littered with a scattering of loose tools and parts from overturned crates. They ducked behind a row of hovercycles. The next second, they were glad they fell.

Shots streaked over them at head level, searing into the wall behind them. Keeping low, Slade grabbed his crew's attention by waving one hand and pointing to his eyes. He drew an orb from one pocket and grinned. Slade and his group morphed into his wolfish forms except for Tel, who stayed in her feline shape. Their stealth gear activated, hiding them from view.

Slade regained his proximity bearings with a quick glance and psyd to his friends, "*It's the aft cargo bay.*" Then he yelled, "Herja, lights off!"

The main door to the room swished open and more feet pounded in. Laughter came from a burly man, a young, armored Atlean, behind the control panel. He yelled out, "Give up. Put your hands up and come out from behind there."

The lights flickered off throughout the middle deck. The colorful light show merged into a young woman wearing body armor and a distinctive leer as she eyed the engineer and two more henchmen who ran in. "I am Herja Mori'alya, protector of this ship and her original crew. Stand down."

The furry henchman, a heavily scarred chap, fired his firgun, the shots passing through her ghostlike head. "See? You're not even alive. If I can't harm you, then you can't harm us."

Herja Mori's hologram walked through the first thug, leaving a charge of static electricity in her wake. The man jumped back, swatting at her ghostlike form. Mori's body glowed with a surge of power that brought solid mass to her form. She punched the cocky man square in the face, sending him tumbling to the floor. "Dive. Lose gravity," Mori said. The ship plunged downward, negative g-forces lifting them all off their feet. Lights and gravity reactivated as the *Spectre* leveled out.

Slade and his friends roared in a rabid quintet, flabbergasting Venamir's henchmen. The pounding commenced. After a flurry of paws, claws, and snapping of teeth, the cowering goons were pleading for their miserable lives.

"Mori, port these worthless slimes out of here," Slade ordered.

Mori's hologram appeared, like a cute toy combat doll on the control panel. "I know where." Cackling in her most sinister voice, she activated the portals and sent the quacking losers off the ship.

Venamir's angry voice sounded over the room's open comm. "What is happening in there?"

Tel responded with a juicy, verbal raspberry over the open comm.

Slade imagined the quickest vision of them being teleported out of the ship to who knows where, surely becoming captives or statistics of Venamir's followers. "All hands. We have to take over that portal chamber." He rested a hand on Berku's shoulder. "Mori, send me to Venamir."

Before the other startled friends could react, Slade and Berku vanished.

"Dammit!" Scruffy barked.

* * *

Venamir turned, hearing the unmistakable sound of portal energy. He stared down the barrels of Slade and Berku's weapons. "Afraid to face me alone, Slade? Wulvur already failed. Pity we had to kill him."

"He's still alive," Slade retorted in mocking satisfaction, "unlike your worthless hitman."

Venamir's face contorted into a scowl. "What does it take to kill you dogs?"

"We keep asking the same about you," Berku said.

"You know better than to shoot me," Venamir taunted as he gazed forward again. He rambled on, a sickening smile in his voice. "The ship requires both of us to fly her. You should have left your friends behind, because where we land," he chuckled, "my followers only want you."

Slade glowered at the horizon. "I know about your cultists. What'd you do to this ship?"

Venamir laughed shortly. "I programmed extra insurance. We must land this ship together. If one of us dies, nobody can restore helm control, not even the Herja program. This ship shall plunge to her demise and fire all her weapons at the nearest massive group of life signs, namely, your human biker friends who are trying to reclaim the *Jacobyte*. You see, your mongrel Druwen hunters may have taken back that ship, but they cannot keep her."

"Venamir, just surrender," Berku said in a disgusted tone. "You know we have more fighters on the way."

Venamir laughed. "My people of the Deeps have the home sea advantage."

Slade holstered his firgun and morphed into his bear form. "Berku, fly this bird."

Berku fired a shot at Venamir, anyway. Venamir's body shield activated, protecting him. A force field appeared around Berku, holding him prisoner. Then the shocks began, making Berku jerk in spasms until he sank to the floor.

Slade leapt to his feet, roaring as he morphed into bear form. Berku sat up, chuckling.

Venamir flung his unfastened lap belts aside and leapt from the pilot's chair, his form bulking up into the heavily muscular reptilian with a natural armor of thick, triangular scales. "Oh, bravo, Slade found his *mojo*."

Slade's roaring overrode multiple crashes within the cockpit.

Chapter 47
Bad Mechanics

Scruffy and Telari snuck down a narrow hallway with rows of access panels, many already removed. There were extra lights on, and a few tool bags. "They've been working on the ship, alright, new mods everywhere." He halted. "Ssh."

Tel peered past Scruffy. She tasted a dozen curses on her tongue, but something stronger possessed her, a wild lust for prey. Her senses were sharper, except she had to focus harder to psy in animal form.

The scent of sweat caught their senses, and a fainter scent of sea water—Merfins. The thought sent a shiver of excitement through her, fed by the aftertaste of blood from the last thug. She glanced at Scruffy, who tapped the floor. They crept closer and waited. The maintenance shaft ended at a ladder that started to rattle.

Tel eased past Scruffy, who nodded. She laid her ears back and bared her fangs, hissing, "Doctor of lab specimens."

Cruentin froze, a low snarl from behind draining the color from his face. He spun, firgun in hand, as Scruffy fired too, their wild shots flashing through the dark passage.

Tel screamed and leapt onto Cruen, slamming him against the ladder rungs.

Doctor Cruentin moaned and writhed beneath her when Tel sank her claws into his flesh. "Let go, you mangy cur."

"Mrrannngy?" Tel snarled, her mouth and teeth wrapped around his shoulder, and crunched down harder, making Cruentin yell in pain.

Scruffy clambered over them both and patted Tel on the head, each thump jarring Cruen's mangled shoulder. "What a good kitty." he exclaimed with each pat.

"You're a sick man," Cruen groaned, no longer struggling.

"Let him go, Tel," Scruffy said. "I have a plan."

"Ummm...." Tel shook him again, dragging Cruen.

"Really, let go." Scruffy looked more closely at them and laughed. "Oh, you poor thing. Your tooth is stuck. Say, Cruen? This is gonna to reallyyy hurt."

"No!" Cruen groaned, then yowled every curse he could think of as Scruffy shook his arm, rattling his shoulder cartilage as Tel worked her sabertooth free.

"Farking shit, I bit myself." Tel confessed.

Cruentin melted to the floor, his voice loathsome as he worked a hand beneath his vest. "You'll pay for that, you psychotic hairball."

"Tel, come on." Scruffy pulled her away from him and they ducked back down the shaft.

Instead of what they feared, blowing up or some likewise horrible fate, they watched Cruentin vanish in a swirl of energy.

"I thought the portals weren't working," Tel said.

"Me too," Scruffy mused.

* * *

Far below them, lurking near the ocean's murky floor, a cold-faced Merfin woman piloted the lead ship of five manta-shaped diving subs. "Do we have him? How is the good doctor?" she asked.

A medic replied over Cruen's curse-filled moaning, "Somebody with feline claws attacked you. There are not many cat morphers around here."

Merfin woman replied, "Port him away from us before we are targeted."

A Rezoan standing beside her swished his tail but curbed his tone in respect. "What of Venamir, Lady Rashira? You know him better than even the Council members."

"Venamir is flying to us. Send in our retrieval team. His plan is self-destructive, at best. We *must* bring him back and start over, at a new base."

"As you command," the Rezoan replied with a slight bow, and with one gesture, strode away with four heavily armed Merfins.

Cruen laid on a bunk, gripping his shoulder and calling out, "Wait, where am I going?"

Energy rings engulfed him and sent him away.

* * *

Doc Nelzyr and Kestral lingered behind as her friends moved deeper into the ship. Doc walked alongside her, his firgun out, and wrist-scanner on. She flipped her helmet visor down and let her eyes refocus on the scrolling displays of diagrams and data on the inside of her visor. The ship's blueprints progressed before her eyes like an x-ray view of the ship. She walked slowly, running her hands along the wall while her eyes scanned the surrounding area. "Herja Mori had a hibernation chamber, like mine on the *Jacobyte*. We need to find it."

Sensors built into her gloves conveyed a power source, and the backs of her gloves displayed the source straight ahead. She searched Venamir's abandoned laboratory, scowling at the assortment of concoctions, from sterile tubes of mystery fluids to tiny animal fangs and spurs with bits of legs or wings still in the jars. Finding no hidden doors in this room, she moved on to the next room, which held crates, locked and sealed, and an aquarium capable of holding several man-sized creatures. Fish swam and nibbled on a seaweed bed at the bottom of the pool.

Kestral walked through the room, halting when her boot-heel made a faint, hollow sound. She knelt down and was about to pull at a section of floor matting when Morialya's hologram appeared a few steps away.

The Herja eyed her, the smooth face registering surprise with a twitch. "Why are you seeking my chamber?"

"I'm the *Jacobyte's* Herja," Kestral replied. "You should know it's an allied ship to this one, and the one Venamir hijacked. We serve the same cause, sister, but you're under a rogue commander. I can prove it." She held up a data chip. "I have records of Venamir's actions since his escape from incarceration. We don't have to serve anyone who is an enemy of the High Councils."

"If you try to trick me, I'll port you into the brig, and there're already crewmen in there."

"Deal."

A round section of floor separated from the rest and sank downward. Clinks and rolling sounds commenced for a few seconds, then halted, revealing a spiral stairway leading one level down. Kestral and Doc jogged down the stairs, all senses on high alert. Herja Mori vanished and reappeared in the heart of the chamber beside four empty hibernation tubes surrounding a main computer terminal shaped like a large totem of writhing animals.

"I know what you're trying to do, and you need one more person to override my program and take over the ship. Venamir has this ship in full defense mode, most of the power to her stealth generators. Your comm won't reach other ships."

"If you don't trust us, how come you're helping?" Doc asked.

The hologram shrugged. "These events must happen. I'm simply accelerating them." She shrank and dove into the computer.

"Kestral, do what you can. I'll try to reach the others." Doc sat down in a meditative position, his back leaning against the nearest wall.

Kestral slid her data chip into the main computer port. "Herja, the real Mori turned on Venamir. We're trying to keep everyone alive. Isn't that your job too?"

"Yes." Herja Mori replied.

Chapter 48
Bear Versus Lizard

Slade and Venamir snarled, roared, and slashed hunks of each other's armor away, but the mighty bear paws sent shudders through Venamir's aging body, blows that made even the highly enhanced fishman go into defensive mode.

"Herja, restrain Slade. Release Berkiru."

Slade endured the first several jolts of electricity, but the current wore him down within seconds, shrinking him to his wolfish form. "You're a coward to the core, Venamir!" he raged, banging on the energy prison.

Venamir grabbed a small crossbow from the wall and fired once, striking Berku in the arm, the hot bolt searing through body armor and flesh. Venamir drilled his psy into Berku's mind, trying to control him. *"Shoot Slade. He is an imposter. You must disable him."*

Slade threw his shoulder against his prison. A resulting surge of energy drove Slade to his knees, his wereform fading to his man shape.

Berku wrestled the bolt away from his skin, when something about the searing pain broke his mind free of Venamir's will. "You want me to shoot my captain," he realized aloud.

Venamir settled a curious, amused leer on Berku. He focused his full anger on Berku again. "Yes, shoot your captain."

Berku grinned as the energy field around Slade vanished. "Slade wasn't the captain of this ship. You were, fishhead."

Venamir's eyes widened as Berku's muzzle swiveled, then aimed at him and fired. "Shields up!" he cried out as Berku fired.

"Shields down," Slade counter-ordered. "Herja! Open the cockpit and reset all energy shields."

"Aye, Captain," came Mori's voice.

"Belay!" Venamir yelled from where he staggered against the wall, one hand over his chest. He glanced down with fear-stricken eyes at the hole burned in his chest-plate and a few singed scales that fell to the floor.

The Herja's voice informed him, "Resetting shields. Warning, stealth mode is down."

Slade morphed back into his bear form, lunged at Venamir.

Berku ducked around them, yelped as the bolt in his arm banged against the captain's chair. He dropped into the chair, took over the ship, and smacked the safety harness control. Chair arms pivoted to hold him in place.

The *Spectre* did not respond to him. Instead, the ship tipped down toward the ocean.

"Slade," Berku yelled, "we got a problem!"

Slade slammed Venamir to the deck, only to feel the ship drop from beneath him. He felt weightless as the floor sank.

Venamir snatched the instant to whallop Slade's bearish head.

The ship dove, her frame creaking against g-forces. Slade and Venamir floated upward until they hit the ceiling. Their grips broken, they shoved each other away and groped for handholds, a ridge of bulkhead, emergency escape handles, anything.

"Herja, level out. Slade yelled.

"Dive." Venamir hissed.

Herja Mori appeared, stern faced. She waved a hand toward the flight controls. The ship leveled out and slowed to an even cruising speed.

Slade and Venamir dropped to the floor in frazzled heaps. They sprang upright and squared off again, hesitating only to sneak a quick look around as the ship maintained level flight.

Berku released the useless control handles and spun his chair around. "I can't control her, Cap." He glowered at Venamir and demanded, "What did you do?"

"Captains," she said, "I will not jerk this ship to and fro. I suggest you form a truce."

"We land together," Venamir clarified. "I told you imbeciles, only the pilots from this ship's last flight may land her. Without us, she will crash." He straightened and swished his reptilian tail, much like an angry alligator. "Of course, we could both eject and lose yet another crew." He dove toward the pilot's chair and latched onto Berku's skewered arm, wrenching forth a howl of pain.

Berku punched at him, skinning his knuckles against Venamir's sharp teeth. "Morph this!"

Slade launched himself onto Venamir, and clamped one large paw around Venamir's throat. Then he snuck his other burly, bearish arm around his prey's midsection, and squeezed.

Venamir struggled as Slade squeezed the air out of him. "Herja," Venamir rasped, "Eject cockpit."

Slade growled in disbelief, "NO! Belay!"

Beneath the cockpit, motors spun up, and with much clanging and a few shrieks of laser fire, the thruster motors wound down.

Venamir tightened his grip on Berku and snarled at Slade. "Curse your infested hide, Slade, I will kill him this instant."

Slade's gut clenched at the thought and he loosened his grip just a tad. "Truce. Let him go."

Venamir paused, one hand gripping the shaft in Berku's arm, and the other hand scraping claws against the trapped man's throat.

"He's lying," Berku argued. He placed a hand against Venamir's midsection, and they heard another power source building up. "Go ahead, claw my neck open and I'll blow your guts all over this cockpit."

Venamir stiffened, feeling his body armor heating up from the device. "A pressure grenade. We have a stalemate," He released Berku.

"Back away," Slade ordered in a low, dangerous tone. Once Venamir obeyed, Slade slammed him against the wall. "Herja, teleport Berku to my doctor."

"No, you can't trust him!" Swirling energy displaced Berku from the cockpit, leaving only Slade and Venamir.

* * *

Berku materialized and lost his balance as he pivoted in the dimly lit room, then dropped to his knees in front of Doc Nelzyr and Kestral. Recognizing his friends, he deactivated the overheating power pack. He flung it aside, shaking his hand. "Ow, ow! We're up there getting mangled and you're in the Herja's bedroom?"

Kestral replied, "We need you here. It takes four crew members to override the program."

Berku allowed Doc to inspect his arm. "We need four of the original crew."

"Where's Moradin?" Kestral asked.

"She ejected and Slade's stuck in there with Venamir. Damn fishlips rigged this ship so they have to land her together," Berku said.

"Scruffy's onboard," Kestral remembered aloud. "He was part of the crew."

Doc jabbed Berku with an injector just before severing the shaft with a surgical tool. Soon as the bolt snapped right beside his flesh, Doc removed the shaft with a clean jerk, and slapped a green, glistening handful of goo against Berku's arm. The old doctor ignored Berku's swearing and struggles with a cool, victorious smile. "There, that wasn't so bad."

Berku yanked his arm away. "My tail-sprouting ass!"

Chapter 49
Cruen's Mission

Doctor Cruentin sat up, wincing as he forced his body upright next to the thin bunk. He waved off the approaching medic, then started to fall. The medic grabbed him and sat him back down on the bunk. A gentle rocking motion made his stomach churn, so he closed his eyes to fend off nausea. The sickening sensation eased from his body after several deep breaths. He listened to a steady, low thrumming and subtle hums of power, and quiet voices speaking in old Merfin. *Those engines, we're underwater.* He peered around, recognizing the dull green walls and cramped quarters. He sighed in relief.

The Rezoan clamped a hand on his good shoulder. "Sit down. You need a surgeon, not a field medic."

Cruentin gazed around, squinting through a headache that flashed spots before his eyes. His voice came out weak and raspy. "Where are we?"

"On your sub, naturally. You signaled us, so we ported you in. We only succeeded on the second try when the *Spectre's* shields dropped for a few seconds." He gestured to rows of gashes on his patient's arms and legs, his eyes lingering on the bandages around Cruen's shoulder, where blood already stained the fresh dressing. "What did you fight, a saber-tooth?'

"Something like that," Cruen grumbled. "Are we near the battle? How goes it?"

"The battle," his medic scoffed, "is absolute madness. All the clans are warring. The Councils sent warships, but they're not sure who to attack. They've been firing warning shots, trying to keep the clans apart. Venamir caused all of this? Why?"

Cruen winced, holding his shoulder. "Venamir's gone completely insane. We wanted to expose his followers, not destroy our population."

"You should stay in bed."

"Let me up." Cruen tried to shove past the medic's stocky frame, a futile attempt in his condition. Finally, he mustered an exasperated glare. "Oh, just help, will you?"

The medic hissed under his breath and assisted Cruen down the passage to the cockpit.

Two Venamir clones had been standing along the walls, still as armor statues. They stepped into the center of the passage, blocking the cockpit. "Halt."

Cruen staggered back in surprise and felt the medic's hand on his back. "It's me, you rickety half-wits!" He leaned between them and raised his weak voice. "Pilot, how many of these clones do we have left?"

The amphibian piloting the small sub bore the heavy stature of a Rezoan, but the delicate ear fins of a Merfin. "Four clones, out of forty-eight."

Cruen groaned in frustration, but his eyes remained contemplative. He brushed past the clone guards and sank into the copilot's chair. "I have a plan. Teleport a clone to the nearest council ships, one clone to each ship."

"What, sacrifice our last few? Are you mad as well?"

"No, no." Cruen turned toward the Venamir lookalikes. "Clones, listen to me. Your actions can save us. I need you to surrender. Put forth your greatest act ever. Tell the Council leaders to call for a ceasefire. You will buy us the time we need for Venamir to land the *Spectre*. Then, our people of the Deeps will aid us." He paused, wondering if the sinking feeling in his gut carried to his voice. "When everything settles down, we'll rescue you." The eager clones headed for the teleport chamber.

The medic shook his head and sighed, "Gullible."

Cruen dismissed the copilot, eased into the chair, and tapped codes into the comm. "Deeps Coven, come in. Come in. Where are you?" Static crackled from speakers. He sat back and rubbed his injured shoulder. "Keep trying. Hail everyone and whoever falls for it, send them a clone."

The blue-skinned Merfin slid a wary look at Cruentin. "Our kindred are not so dumb as humans. Your clones cannot lend us much time."

"It'll be enough," Cruen stated. "Move us closer. We must rescue Venamir. I doubt he... I mean, the drugs are changing him, and his strength is waning. Using enhancers was too high a risk, but Venamir wouldn't listen. He never listens."

"Then why risk our lives for him?"

"We still need him," Cruen answered.

The blue pilot spread a webbed hand over the scanners. "We cannot track the *Spectre*. She may as well be a true ghost ship."

Cruentin groaned and pointed upward. "Venamir will fly to the *Wandering Fortress*. Find the *Fortress*."

Chapter 50
Venamir Confesses

Slade and Venamir flew the *Spectre* low over the waves, in stealth mode. They exchanged molten glares as both regained their wind for the next round.

"Insane, bloodsucking leech," Slade cast with ire.

Venamir wore a demonic smile. "This is why the Deeps will rule over you mongrels."

"Not in your wettest fantasies."

Venamir checked air traffic for incoming threats. He saw no targeting indications, only massive numbers of air and sea ships, shaped like little birds or seals. "See how many have broken the ranks?"

"Most of them," Slade observed, "not many fighting. Looks like they've reached a stalemate."

"Indeed, exactly as I had planned. You have a terrible distraction haunting you. All those years you blamed yourself for the crash of this ship and the deaths of your crewmen."

Slade forced his tone to stay even. "I didn't blame myself."

"Lies. You wondered, hungered for answers. I know about your lengthy investigations of this ship, your efforts to bend every rule possible, and for what?"

"For the truth," Slade grumbled, his blood rushing in heated excitement, body clenching as he fought back the urge to morph and knock Venamir's smirking head into shreds if scaly flesh. His shrewd instincts picked up on something, a playfulness in his old rival he'd not seen in ages. He stared at the engine configuration, and the position of the landing gear control between them. Slade's fists clenched as a chill shot through him. He remembered their last flight better than ever.

Venamir kept one hand resting on the throttles. His laugh sent bad omens crashing through Slade's mind. The flashbacks sprang to life in both of them again. Smoke stung their eyes and filled their lungs, while waves of heat drenched their bodies in sweat, like a wicked accelerated nightmare where sleep could have passed in hours or seconds.

Venamir's voice cut through the sounds of their memories, overriding the crackling of flames and groans of a dying ship. "The *Fortress* is rising. They will render all our instruments useless, so we must land her manually, and let the gear fall into place. Just like we did so long ago."

A great, dark mass below the angry waves grew larger, spreading out with the bulk of a dozen warships. Surrounding watercraft veered off to avoid collision, forcing more boats to cease fire, for the moment.

Slade clamped his hand around the handle by his right knee, and Venamir grabbed the one on the left side.

"Now," Venamir ordered.

Slade fought back vivid memories of a similar landing with Venamir, all systems failing, the ship moaning as the frame barely clung together. If they'd done everything right, he they would have landed safely, but the *Spectre* plummeted into the warzone below. The mystery had haunted Slade ever since.

Slade activated the emergency gear drop. The ship dipped to the uneven drag of wind, pitching them against their shoulder harnesses. Again? Slade's gut clenched, and he jerked his gaze over to Venamir's controls.

The gear control sat in the neutral position, with Venamir's thumb over the lock. The ship began to yaw while engines slowed, dropping their altitude. As warning alarms came on, Venamir rested one hand over the egress controls. "Remember this landing? We were losing altitude, and an engine shut down. We had to punch out, or did we?" He gently nudged the handle downward and evened out engine thrust. All gears dropped evenly, letting them level out.

Only then did Slade realize that Venamir's hand never moved the control as agreed, as ordered, as any trusted fellow pilot would have done.

"Youuu...." Slade's voice fell low, like his bear-form growl, "you said your controls jammed and the engine failed."

Venamir chuckled at first with immense satisfaction. "Now, you finally see. Yes, I lied. I triggered the fire lights, and then you overcompensated, thinking we had engine failure. Our dignitaries were at a stalemate, so I fooled everyone, even you. We had to crash, Slade. It was the only way to lure the Rezoans into negotiations, and give me a chance to read their minds, and learn to understand them."

Slade's voice dropped to a rabid growl. "You made us crash? For the LIZARDS?"

"A necessary evil."

The world around them faded to that one instant that was burned into Slade's brain, when they tried to save the ship and couldn't, or rather, didn't. He no longer heard the howling of wind through breaches in their hull, nor the moaning of overworked engines. "I can't believe this. We were surrounded by enemy forces. Half our crew died in the crash!"

"I lured them to my Deeps allies. The Deeps are neutral. It allowed us to form alliances with our enemies. It ended the war."

Slade turned, fixing his seething glare on Venamir. "You honestly think the war ended because of you? We crashed near a Deeps settlement. The Deeps are neutral, but they favor aquatic Atleans like yourself. You lured the Rezoans there so you could manipulate them."

"Yes."

"While the Rezoans gained access to our weaponry, our safe zones."

"Better to form a truce with lizards than share our world with half-evolved apes from Earth," Venamir scoffed.

"We could have done both, allied the humans a generation ago, and dealt with Rezoans later. Your Deeps friends wanted the lizards so they could have another species to experiment on." Slade knew he was right when Venamir grinned.

"Why not? We could have powerful amphibian-aquatic hybrid warriors to defend us, stronger than your morphers. Our old crew members who died were casualties of war. We have the chance to ally with Rezoans, but no, the Morpher Council chose to ally with humans instead. Now, I can end our foolish ties with Earth."

Slade eased free of his shoulder harness. "How?"

"My followers have infiltrated enough of the clans in our world to summon them to a gathering with the Deeps base. There, the coven leaders will try to form an armistice, which will fail. Your Magistrate is already dead. I have enough infiltrators among the clans to spark a massive conflict."

Slade snarled with fury. "You're starting a civil war. Have you gone insane?"

Venamir glanced over at him. "My people are sparking a battle among the clans so everyone will show their true colors. Tis the only way to form a better council."

"A council run by deep-water aquatics and lizards," Slade clarified.

"Now, you know the truth."

Slade's hands sprung off the controls. When he started to rise, the ship began to race out of control, forcing him to remain flying as copilot.

Venamir chided, "Remember, we both must pilot this vessel."

Slade's hands shook as he grabbed the controls again and helped steady the ship. His grip made the controls creak from his feral strength as the full impact of the crash hit him. "I can't believe how fat your head is. You bash other species, but you turned against your own bottom-feeding kindred. You're no better than human terrorists."

"What?" Anger swelled with each word. "You compared me to humans?"

"Only the worst of them."

His scowl twisted into a slow smile. "Oh, *that did* sting. You will see my kindred when we land on the *Wandering Fortress*. There, the Deeps are neutral. As the clans from opposing Council factions fight each other, my people will observe who wins."

"And why would the clans rise against each other?"

"Slade, you know rivalry has been building among the clans," Venamir said.

"So you pushed them over the edge."

"Yes. The only way to move forward is to oust the humans, and make our people fight to see where everyone's loyalty lies."

Slade shook his head. "You've gone off the deep end. Well, newsflash, the Merfins of the Deeps are fed up with you, too."

"The Deeps voted to keep me out of prison," Venamir returned, and helped me restore this ship. "You will see. This time, when the Deeps see the other clans fight, and witness how savage morphers are, they will support me. We shall reform our old councils."

Slade could barely refrain from lunging at Venamir. As his temper boiled, his body strained to morph, fingernails stretching into claws, tufts of fur growing from his ears, hair thickening. *Kill him. Why not? I have authority.*

Venamir smiled at him. "Go ahead, morph. You may as well let the Deeps see your true colors. See? We are here," he gloated as a landing site formed through the mists below them.

A hologram of a Merfin woman appeared between them, her features Deep Merfin by the fine mesh of delicate scales all over her scantily clad body, and by her thick and melodious accent.

"Coveness, see the barbarian that Slade truly is," he told her. "He is more beast than man. A few simple insults and he morphs into a heinous bear, not even an Atlean bear. He resembles a primitive beast from Earth, of all worlds. Atlean morphers live for cultural digression."

The Deeps woman's hologram stood with royal poise. She eyed Slade with her pearly, midnight eyes, and saw a tempered, yet disgusted leer on Slade's face, dark resignation and fury, yes, but not a raging savage. Slade had regained his normal Atlean form, and appeared quite calm.

She turned to Venamir, her voice cold as the sunless waters. "So tell me, where is the beast?"

Venamir looked over at Slade, and sarcastically said, "Oh, bravo, Slade. You always were soft with women."

Slade conjured his most even tone. "Coveness, you're being manipulated. Venamir's bringing a huge fight your way."

"I am in charge here," Venamir snapped.

"You want to rule everyone," Slade said in eerie calmness. "You never could play poker."

Venamir hissed, "Pathetic mongrel, what does a children's game have to do with us?"

The Coveness waved them off. "I see you need more time. Land the ship on my main platform, and we shall settle this." She vanished, leaving the growling rivals.

"She will side with me," Venamir sneered. "Only stupid morphers would choose *you* as their dignitary. That reminds me, when Doctor Nelzyr was my guest, we discussed family, primarily his." He activated the shipwide comm. "Nelzyr, save your family."

Slade's face lost color as he tried to psy to his doc, only to find mental shields around his friend's mind. "You brainwashed Doc."

* * *

Scruffy and his friends were in the Herja's chamber, the safest, most heavily protected room on the *Spectre*. Elowren and Kestral were trying to hack the computer. Berku was pulling weapons out of a storage locker and prepping them for battle, while Doc put a field dressing on Shanto's arm. Doc froze, a strange look on his face.

Shanto frowned at Doc. "What?"

Doc's expression twisted from wide-eyed desperation coupled with a murderous scowl. He lunged for Scruffy's weapon, crying out, "Cultists, all of you. He lunged for the firgun Berku was holding."

"Shit!" Berku yelped, bowled over in the process. He sprang upright and they all dog piled for the firgun in a wrestling match full of swearing.

"Family." Doc snarled. "No more... of 'em... dead. Kill... everyone." He kept struggling even as they pinned him on the floor face down. As hands wrenched the firgun away, his voice fell to pleading, "You gotta stop me... I'm gonna freaking kill you scags."

"Distract him," Scruffy ordered. To their first puzzled looks, he barked, "I don't care how. Distract him and I can get into his head."

Kestral grabbed Doc by the pants, instantly changing the doctor's focus.

All Doc could manage was a diminishing, "Ooh! Uh, no kiss?"

Berku rolled his eyes and made his way to the computer while they calmed Doc down. The stench of acrid smoke curling up from the blackened computer housing made his eyes water. "Great.

Great! You destroyed the main computer. What if we lost the Herja too?"

"Relax," Kestral said. "A Herja program has power sources all over the ship."

Doc rolled over and stared at Kestral with amorous eyes.

Kestral pushed him away. "That was platonic."

Doc's shoulders and expression sagged like a hound dog's muzzle.

Berku tapped his comm and tried to hide the amusement in his voice. "Slade, Doc's fine."

* * *

The news calmed Slade, if only in the slightest. Nevertheless, one less victim to Venamir's corruptive mind games. "You are the sickest, slime-dripping sea rat I've ever known."

"You would know about rats," Venamir said in a bored tone. "Your walking canines bring degeneration to my people. You cannot control your rage for long, Slade, never could. Morphers have a beastly nature they cannot control. Your clans should stay in the woods."

"Do you hear yourself?" Slade growled, his muscles clenching as he fought to stay in his Atlean form. He pounded the reminder into his brain, *Stay in your manform, dammit, or the ship won't obey me!* "You are insane." Slade ranted, "You are one sick fish."

Doc's voice whispered through Slade's raging brain, a brief psy message laced with humor. *"Slade, you're right. Calm down. You're right, he is crazy. That's the answer."*

Slade pondered Doc's words while the *Spectre* slowed, descending over the water. The ocean rushed beneath them, close enough to see the glistening peaks.

Venamir slid a gloating smirk in Slade's direction. "None of your loyal devotees will find you, Slade. I sank Zared's ship in the ocean, and grounded Scruffius's derelict, old heap near the Starship Boneyard, where it belongs. Once we land, you may try your failing diplomacy."

Slade clenched his teeth for a moment. "You're delusional. We can't submerge with all the holes in this ship. Even with shields, we wouldn't last very long."

"Of course not," Venamir agreed. "That is why my base is rising to meet us."

Slade's jaw tightened, and he started running scans. He saw an approaching blip on the screen, faint at first, then saw a smattering of life forms. *Fish and lizards, lots of them. What is that thing? It's huge.* Then he noticed silhouettes of more underwater traffic circling the area. He turned to Venamir, who wore a calculating smile. "Leave my crew out of this. Let them go."

"That is up to my allies now. As you can see, we are surrounded. If you cross me, only the bottom feeders will find you."

"You would know all about scum suckers."

Chapter 51
Flight of Drakirs

Elowren morphed to her sleek, dragonkin form, her silvery wings beating against the wind as she soared over the waves. A group of dragons flanked her, some large enough to hold a Merfin rider. Elowren was stretching the limits of her psy ability. All she wanted was to see the ghostly silhouette of a stealthed ship and find her friends. The minds of her friends were far away, their voices like whispers in dreams, barely strong enough to recognize, and too fleeting to see through their eyes.

Five Guardians, blue-skinned Deeps had joined her, using the larger dragons as mounts. The Deeps riding point spoke into his comm, calling for backup.

She beat her wings harder against the chilling winds and called out once in a high-pitched shriek. The dragonkins glanced toward her and flew to her sides, forming a defensive pattern. Elowren considered the odds. *Venamir will lay a trap. He hungers for blood like never before. He'll detect intruders, so we must be* discreet. Her closest friend with such mind range remained on shore, injured, but he could still aid her.

Zared's psy voice replied, *"Elowren, Venamir's headed for his old allies, to the Coven Mother."*

"Clan ships are coming from everywhere, headed that way. Follow my tracker. Get me Berku's Rangers." Elowren smirked and could feel Zared's rising hopes through their psy link.

Zared confirmed it, *"They're infiltrating the warring clan boats."*

* * *

Venamir chuckled with pleasure as he saw the waters below them swell. One huge sub broke the waves, slowly as an ancient whale and thrice as huge. Around it, connected by flexing tubes, smaller domes rose and floated on the surface. More shapes arose from the ocean's depths, stretched out flat, joining together to form a long, wide ramp, shining with water rushing off the surface. Marker lights illuminated paint schemes Slade had seen at many a spaceport.

"Oh, that old thing," Slade mused. "You think the Coven Mother wants to join a senile dictator? Hilarious."

"Give up, Slade. Admit your defeat."

"You're delusional," Slade chortled. "Let's do one last thing as a crew. Land the *Spectre* without wrecking her this time. The old bird deserves respect."

The two shared gazes of long-lost camaraderie for a few shallow breaths.

"Agreed," Venamir nodded.

The *Spectre* shed her stealth mode as they hovered over the bucking landing platform. Her old, shining wingflaps and wingtips flared while the engines pivoted to settle her onto the tide-washed landing strip. Despite her age and battle scars, the *Spectre* touched down as gracefully as if she were brand new, on calm seas.

Atlean and Rezoan people emerged from hatches in the great submarine, giving the ship a respectful berth until the engines wound down. Even the weathered, armored guards emerging from their combat domes watched in silent awe of their long-awaited ghost ship in the skies once again.

The Deeps Coven Mother strode to meet them, flanked by six of her chosen elite guards. She looked up toward the cockpit, where the morphed bearlike Slade and the lizardish Venamir resumed fighting. "All our people know the stories of when the people of Atlean flew together. 'Tis a shame these two cannot coexist."

The Coven Mother placed her glistening, webbed hand on the lower cockpit controls. "I can feel the harsh loss of life, and yet we battle over the same cause today, supremacy." She let the ship's panel glow and analyze her hand and face before speaking. "I am Atlean Deeps Engineer Rashira, head designer of the *Allodian Spirit* now called the *Spectre*. I command all systems override. Open this cockpit, Herja. I am boarding."

Herja Mori appeared, silent as ship sensors scanned the Coveness. Hatches and ramps opened throughout the ship.

The Coveness and her guards proceeded onboard. The first guard inside had to duck aside as Venamir's tail swung about. Slade and Venamir were in their largest forms, both panting as they fought, using claws and fangs.

Slade slashed at Venamir's thick belt that protected the closed gills with the repetitive fury of a drummer beating out his greatest solo performance. The blows, even with massive bear claws, knocked the wind from Venamir, but only whittled away at the thick scales built into the belt. Slade didn't even notice the doors and windows opening all around him until a stun blast hit him in the back. The shot would have knocked out a normal man, but in his bear form, Slade turned with a snarl.

"Now you see?" Venamir jeered.

"Stay out of this." Slade demanded.

The Coven Mother strode out from between her guards and studied Slade's Earthern bear form with scientist's eyes. "Oh, there you are. When did you evolve into that?"

"Just get out," Slade growled. "This slug doesn't deserve your help. You see the war he started? Our people *were* coexisting, until now. All for what?"

"I too, am curious," she admitted.

Venamir sneered, "How ignorant can you be? Clan rivalry has built up again. Now, I know who my followers are. Everyone's true colors are exposed."

Slade and the others exchanged looks of disbelief, and Slade reverted to his humanoid form. Somehow, the truth finally began to calm him. He growled at Venamir, "We're going to interrogate the hell out of you, as you have so many others. After I find out what you," he paused, still catching his wind, "what you did to everyone, you'll wish for deep sleep."

Venamir argued between wheezing pants. "We are both in command here, fellow Captain."

The Coven Mother yelled, "You are elites of the High Council! This is a sanctuary and there will be no fighting here." She gestured and her guardsmen snapped to ready stances, their weapons leveled at bear and lizard Atleans. "Now resume your true forms and handle this like diplomats. Venamir, you're my Ambassador."

"Dethroned," Slade emphasized.

"A minor setback," Venamir argued, his tail lashing.

The Coven Mother tried again. "Slade, you're too respectable for this behavior."

"Oh, *now* we're respectable?" Slade sneered. "Usually, we're invited to high council meetings, not held hostage."

The regal woman nodded toward the exit. "Stop fighting and behave as equals."

"His only equals are vermin," Venamir scoffed.

"Enough!" the Coven Mother snapped. "Resume your true forms, or we will use force and carry you inside."

"Herja, protect us," Venamir ordered.

The holographic Mori appeared and cast glittering force fields around Venamir and Slade. When the first guard dared to try to fire, stun pulses emitted from the ceiling and dropped him into a twitching, feeble position.

"You are not in control here. I am," Venamir bragged.

The Coven Mother and her guards cast wary looks toward the next room, hearing footsteps. With all the ship's doors open at last, Slade's crew had moved into the adjoining room and stood with weapons at ready.

Doc Nelzyr led the pack, trusting his friends to cover him. "Now, Venamir, I disagree."

Venamir turned with a hiss, "Be silent, you half-beast fool."

Doc smiled. "I'm speaking to you as your doctor."

"Cruentin is my doctor, not you," Venamir retorted.

"Cruentin left, bailed, abandoned ship. We were both medics on this ship and in his absence, that promotes me. So yes, I am your doctor now." As Venamir's face turned aghast, Doc went on, relishing the moment. "Under our laws as your senior medical officer, I diagnose you as criminally insane and unfit for command. I hereby relieve you of command." He turned and spread his arms to the armed forces. "You see, Venamir has no authority here, only Captain Slade does."

Herja Mori turned to Slade. "Orders, Captain?"

"Unshield Venamir," Slade ordered.

The power shield around Venamir vanished.

"What?" Venamir started, "I always knew Herjas were treacherous."

Slade pointed at Venamir. "He confessed to making this ship crash, right into enemy territory, and why? To form alliances with the clans who were sworn to wipe us out. This fish is guilty of outright conspiracy. How many lives have we lost today alone? We don't know, yet!"

The Coven Mother took a startled breath as murmurs passed between her guards. She fixed her solid blue eyes on Venamir, who returned a daring sneer as their minds intertwined.

Doc's voice grew happier as he went on, "As his medical officer, and chief surgeon, I claim custody of Venamir."

All eyes turned to the Coven Mother, who stood with elegant poise, pressing her fingertips together in thought. "Doctor Nelzyr, I propose we share that custody. After all, I have already called all council and clan leaders to rendezvous here."

One of the guardsmen spoke up. "That will never happen. Venamir comes with us," he said, catching the Coven Mother's sharp eyes.

Half of the guardsmen lashed their tails, narrowing eyes at each other. The next second, guardsmen turned against each other with claws and weapons. From all around, engines whined in the distance, growing ever closer. Fighting from every direction broke out once again. Gunmen on the war boats found their little crafts rocking and their men being jerked overboard.

Merfins climbed onboard the war-boats and pummeled the crews who wore any cultist insignias, who looked like they were going to fight beck, or who smelled fishy. A good number of the Merfins defending the Coven Mother or Slade's shop morphed into their true forms as none other than Berku and his wolfpack who had snuck in posing as Deeps Atleans. They growled and roared as they morphed out of their Merfin shapes and into their favored beastman shapes. One howl from Berku sent his pack to Slade's defense.

The Coven Mother yelled, "Capture Slade and Venamir." She dove beneath the submarine, closely followed by her bodyguards.

Scattered forces approached from the skies, some on hovercycles, and over a dozen graceful beasts on the wing. Elowren led the flight of dragons, her silvery red form catching Slade's glance. Most of the other dragons were somewhat larger, their sleek bodies glinting with metallic colors of armor.

As Venamir elbowed Slade and bit his arm, Slade growled and hung on.

"Not this time," Slade growled. "No escape for you." He summoned the draining strength from his body and morphed once more, thick claws extended, and thrust them into his nemesis through the battered armored belt and into Venamir's left gills.

Venamir's breath rattled out of him, hands clawing at the deck.

Two of the cultist guards broke fighting the loyal guards and dove for Slade, who was forced to leave Venamir curled up on the floor, gasping.

Slade called out between bashing Merfins, "Defend the *Spectre* and don't let Venamir escape."

The Coven Mother entered her submarine. She made her way through the vessel and reentered her main dome. She tore into her quarters to grab a short, large-barreled weapon, climbed to the top level, and opened the canopy. Her sudden entry with her guards sent startled infiltrators scrambling for cover. She opened fire on henchmen who dared to climb into her personal rooms. "No fighting in my sanctuary."

She lowered her weapon and looked around, her face paling at the sight of amber blood on the wall she'd just demolished and splats of lizardmen on the floor. She rolled one body over with her foot and knew their markings and profiles in an instant. "Amber blood? My Rezoans are Venamir's cultists? This is outrageous."

Overhead, engines howled from a Merfin scout ship hovering over the Coven sub. "No you don't." Vanysa yelled over a loudspeaker. "All you sea-lizards, break combat or I'll feed you to my pets!"

The lead hovercycler pulled alongside the little scout ship. Despite a flack vest and arm guards, some of the man's cartoon tattoos shone in the ocean spray. "Hello, Vany," he greeted through his comm.

"Hello, Shocks," came her fond voice. "Shall we?"

"Hell, yeah," Shocks replied.

Vanysa nodded to Zared, who sat in the right seat of Vany's small armored ship. Bandaged and frazzled, Zared gave her a thumbs up and started blasting the engines of warring ships. Vanysa opened an overwing hatch and dove into the lurching waves, her armored form a shining glimpse before fading beneath the raging tides.

"I love crazy women." Shocks sang out.

Vanysa swam away from the fray and raised an ornate, curved horn to her lips. The cold water fueled her adrenalin as she sent her mind to all who would obey her. *"Think of your fallen, my people, my battle-borne ancestors. Stop the cultists from ruining us."*

Some of the war-boats turned toward her, but she saw movement below, swimming toward the sunlight. Vanysa pulled an ornate shell horn from her belt. Gems in the horn began to glow at her touch, and carvings of kelpies writhed as if alive. The horn lengthened, forming a long, elegant ceremonial horn that amplified the volume exponentially. Vanysa blew in resonating patterns, sending the cries like whale songs to the depths, to all around her beyond harsh clamor of twisting metal, air-breathing screams, and weapons fire.

To her beckoning, *they* answered.

Huge dorsal fins cut the surface and sank again, long, massive forms cruising around the floating fortress. A herd of sea dragons joined forces with the flying dragons controlled by Watchers. Together, the beasts used their graceful bulk, ominous teeth, and mighty tails to subdue boat captains. Rivals quickly found new reasons to stop fighting and share floating chunks of debris to avoid becoming fresh sailor meat for the behemoths' appetites.

Those fighters who dared approach Slade and his fallen crew met the fury of dragon wings, teeth, claws, tail swipes, and various breath attacks. In the center of the *Spectre's* nose perched dragonlady Elowren, her shrieks and telepathic attacks pitting her targets against each other, or causing them to collapse to the deck with hands over their ears.

Most of the dragons dove gracefully into the water, where they circled around Vanysa, suddenly acting docile. The green, most serpentine dragon allowed Vanysa to mount the base of his neck and charged in pursuit of warring boats. The water dragon blew a hot spray of water and steam at the opposing clan boats, demanding their attention.

Many of the boat people broke off fighting to watch the choppy surface with wide, fearful eyes. Foolhardy boat captains turned their weapons on the non-fighters, but not for long. Dragons and their handlers surfaced with fury, toppling hostile watercraft.

Lightweight Merfin and allied land morphers riding the largest dragons flew over boats still firing on one another. Riders dropped balled up webbing that expanded into nets that entangled crews below. The trapped crews collapsed, snoring. Other dragon riders were less merciful, strafing the nearest boats with weapons fire, destroying the boats' engines.

Zared's psy voice startled the recipients as it blasted through their minds, giving them one warning, *"Killing a drakir will send you into deep sleep or death! So stand down."*

Riderless dragons used their natural weapons, claws, wings, and breath weapons. Two dragons spat clumps of salty spray at their targets, sending would-be fighters diving below deck or behind any cover they could find. Other dragons whose bodies writhed with the wind's ebbs swooped over the attacking boats and blew noxious gas from their throats, dropping their targets into gasping heaps. A few more dragons with the Merfin riders circled the *Wandering Fortress,* patrolling those surrendering and using their wings and tails to save injured people from the ocean's wrath.

Chapter 52
The Mangling of Cruen

The first rival pilots that landed on the *Wandering Fortress* continued fighting, while many found themselves incapacitated by an equally angry host crew. Stun blasts and fishing nets dropped the first wave of intruders. The submarine's big guns spoke next, firing warning shots between warring boats, the blasts sending people ducking and running. Slowly, a tenuous cease-fire formed among the other pilots forced to land. Heavily damaged small fighters landed atop the huge, octagon-shaped submarine, but with the mid-sized *Spectre* already on the central deck, space to dock was vanishing fast. The flight decks on the *Wandering Fortress* submarine were loaded with small fighter ships, all damaged, with people scrambling to secure to the deck. Some pilots landed in the water, only to surrender while the ocean swallowed their little crafts. Rivals surrounding the *Fortress* picked fights with each other despite warning shots and loudspeakers ordering surrender.

The old *Spectre* creaked and rocked, her landing gear sliding a few feet on the landing platform as maintainers rushed to secure locking mechanisms to her landing gear.

Doctor Cruentin made his way through the battle-zone, no stranger to combat, but his hands and voice still shook as he met possible hostiles by waving his medical bag. "Let me through. I'm a medic!" he yelled.

The ploy worked until people called him over to help with the injured. Cruen kept his game face on and conducted triage on a few critically injured. He saw other medics nearby who were paying far more attention to the patients, including the formerly press-ganged alchemist Thiun.

A Rezoan grabbed him by the arm, hissing and pointing across the deck. Cruen jabbed the excited fellow with his hypo, calming the now patient into a stoned stupor. Slapping his medbag shut, he dropped a smoke grenade and rushed off.

By the time Cruen reached the *Spectre*, only four Merfins joined him. They were semi-perfect clones, all looking like scared Venamir impersonators.

Cruen groaned, "That's it? You're all that's left?"

"Recon's around here s-somewhere," the clone said, voice high with fear as he glanced up. The sky looked almost as angry as the ocean, both dark blues and grays, swarming with battling crafts creating storms of weapon fire. "Is every clan out here fighting? Why?"

"All Venamir's plan," Cruen sighed. "No time for a lesson. Get inside and ditch the armor. You have to pass for Venamir."

The clones stared past Cruen, refusing to approach the *Spectre*. Turning, Cruen saw why. A couple Rezoans lay sprawled near the hatch, eyes closed, mouths open, with their serpentine tongues twitching. Stepping over them, Cruen smirked. "Looks like the Herja program's online again." He held up his aqua-green hands and spread all fingers to expose the webbing. "Morialya, I am Doctor Cruentin, requesting entrance."

Moradin's younger, beautiful image emerged through the locked door like a curious ghost. "The high clan leader has already shut me down twice. You're lucky I have backup systems. There are multiple invaders onboard, most are casualties now." She glared at Cruen's clones. "Who are they? They carry Venamir's DNA."

"Venamir uses clones as bodyguards," Cruen said with forced patience. He ducked from a sudden barrage of shots overhead. "Let us in before some idiot kills us. I know there're injured onboard. Let me help them."

"Proceed." As she faded, the hatch opened, and a small ramp extended for them.

They hurried inside, Cruen's guards shedding armor and helmets. Within seconds, the clones looked just like Venamir, to a fault.

Doctor Cruen changed his appearance only slightly, his color altering to midnight blue, his eyes more pearlescent, and fins lengthening, to resemble a Deeps Merfin. "I can sense Venamir, but his mind is so clouded, I can barely read it," Cruen said. "When we reach the top deck, you must take his place." To their worried, questioning faces, he added, "Yes, all of you."

"Why did you morph? Who cares if you're a different color?" one clone asked.

Cruen smacked the half-witted clone. "I knew you all should have incubated longer. I look like the Deeps. They're the best medics." He shook his head. "Swagger, Boozer, Zulu, Stuts, come on."

A fifth clone ran up to join them, hefting a firgun in each hand. He greeted Cruen with a nod, his shifting eyes searching for a target. A couple morphers on the deck outside took notice of them and started toward the ship. The clone waved at them just before opening fire on the furry Atleans, making them dive for cover. The dark cargo bay lit up for a split second along the ceiling, where defense systems targeted the clone and dropped him into a twitching mess of pain.

"Don't use energy weapons." Cruen ordered, "The ship's still in full defense mode." As his remaining clones obeyed, he ran to the emergency controls and wrestled a long, red lever, closing the door and muting the deadly racket outside. "Lights," he said.

Only emergency lights illuminated, forcing them to use lights from their comms.

"Why no lights?" Zulu said.

Cruen sighed. "Because land morphers built this ship. They can see in the dark even better than us, on land, anyway. Let's move." He started fuming in silence. These clones were his worst work ever. He had made the last batch of clones much too fast with failing power systems. One had a drunken swagger, another stuttered, two bickered over pecking order, and Recon was climbing to his feet, cussing.

"Shut your slug hole," Swagger said. "You're always complaining, Recon."

"Drunken coward," Recon threw back.

"I can outdrink both of you," Boozer cut in.

"Quiet! We have to find Venamir," Cruen hissed.

They moved through the dim loading bay, past a large terrarium that lay in pieces. Cruen glanced at the mess of spilled water and residue of fire foam spread across the floor. As soon as they moved inside the bay, the inner doors slammed shut, shrouding the room in near darkness.

Cruen psyd to Venamir, *"We're onboard. Get to an escape pod. Can't teleport."* He sensed something else, very close, another mind, not his clones. This mind was well shielded, barely detectable, even for him. When he panned the bay with his light, he saw glinting eyes and shining fangs. Two clones remained close by his side, while the other two lagged behind.

Swagger flinched. "What was that?"

"I don't know," Cruen half lied, "probably bats or crabs. Venamir likes freshly killed food."

The stuttering clone grumbled, "Vermin. N-nnasty."

"You should talk, scavenger," Recon taunted.

Cruen shushed them. "Quiet. Watch my back." He just made it up the steps from the cargo bay when he heard a scuffle and a strangled scream. Within seconds, silence taunted him. Cruen scrambled through the next bulkhead and wrestled the door closed, a struggle, for most of the ship lacked power.

Behind him, a series of clicks and clanks sounded. The door opened, and a single shot took out the next emergency light ahead of him. When he heard a soft hiss, it sounded more like a snicker.

"A morpher," Cruen murmured, grabbing a needle-gun from his vest. "You're a novice, or you would have killed me by now." He panned the weapon around, only to see piled cargo, some toppled, and an overhead vent without its grate. The bay had three doorways.

A hushed, feminine voice filled the darkened room from multiple directions, chilling Cruen like an echo from a horror movie. "Cats play with their food."

Fire extinguishers activated, spraying Cruen and his clones. A number of tiny, shiny things rushed toward them, metal feet skittering across the slippery floor. Cruen and the clones broke into panicked dancing to keep the things off their feet, and started firing at the little bots, one shot singing Recon's boot.

"YOW!" Recon snarled, punching the nearest clone.

"Wasn't me," Stuts whispered, glancing about. He pointed at the floor. "There—no, there."

Cruen backed into a wall and started firing injector needles that bounced off his pursuing bot. He could see through foam building up on the floor that the thing resembled a frog, just as it jumped at him. Cruen fell on his rear as he knocked the thing off him.

"Get farther into the ship." Cruen ordered, "Go, go!"

The feline revealed herself by dropping from the ceiling, while Cruen and his group were half-blinded from foam spray. She was in full cat form, the size of a young panther. Telari sprang at the retreating forms, swiping them all in the legs, her claws cutting into skin.

"Yaaah! Kill it!" Cruen cried out, slipping in the foam as he dove for the next door.

The bickering clones immediately started to argue until Cruen smacked and shoved them behind him, out of his way, and tore out of the room.

In his wake, the door opened to the foamy room, and a clone fell through, landing with a dull thud. A large, dark feline climbed over him, fangs bared, claws tinged with red. "Yuck," she whispered. "Herja Mori? You online?"

Mori's image appeared before her, smiling.

"Can you keep the lights off?"

The hologram commented quietly so only an animal could hear, "What lights? Slade snuck his new crew's data into my computer. Hello, Telari. Darn shame, jammers on, no teleporting, I stun anyone using energy weapons."

"Awesome," Tel grinned as she trotted on past, tail lashing.

Cruen stumbled through the next few rooms, tripping over a mess of supplies that had toppled from the ship's hard maneuvers, or just careless storage. He didn't know, didn't care. Lighting was off here too, and he suspected, was the same throughout the ship. Cruen motioned for the two clones to guard the door while he caught his breath, leaning on his knees. Wincing, he looked down to see rows of bloody rips in his clothes. His clones checking injuries of their own.

"Great," Cruen fumed, "now we're leaving a blood scent. Recon, go on ahead. Find Venamir and get him outside. Zulu, Swagger, you stay with me."

"Why didn't we help the others?" Recon demanded.

"We're just cannon fodder, that's why," Zulu grumbled.

"Why couldn't you kill one stupid morpher?" Cruen shot back.

"Because she's crazy. Look, we're leaving blood trails," Recon argued. "Patch us up."

"No time. Besides, it makes you better decoys. Go get Venamir." Cruen ordered.

Skulking, Recon limped past Cruen, who watched him go, as if expecting to see him get jumped. When nothing happened to him, Cruen followed with Zulu and Swagger.

None of them noticed a silent silver and purple tigress in pursuit.

Cruen hurried up the stairs, old, grated steps that creaked with age. The rails didn't feel too steady, either. Then he felt it, a rush of excitement that chilled his blood.

Tel leapt from the darkness, knocking Zulu aside, landing on Swagger, and slashing Cruen across his rear. Cruen stumbled, but clambered up the next several steps until claws slashed the back of his boots, tripping him. He spun around, eyes narrowing at the sight of an Atlean feline morpher standing up on top of the fallen clone, her rear claws digging into the prey's shoulders to keep him down. Swagger tried to twist around, his every attempt to fight made the feline's claws dig in deeper.

"Stay down," the tigress warned.

Regaining his failing wits, Cruen raised his needler gun, nowhere near fast enough. The tigress roared in his face, claws slashing his weapon arm and sending the small gun flying off.

"Wait." Cruen cried out, stumbling as he backpedaled, "I'm a medic."

"I know what you are, doctor of lab freaks. How many lives do *you* have?"

"Uh, not enough?"

The fallen clone yelled in fury as he heaved himself up, trying to grab her legs. Swaying, Telari crouched to finish him off when the door overhead opened and the drunken Recon clone aimed a spear gun through the doorway. Tel dodged the first shot and leapt off the stairwell. Recon reached down, grabbed Cruentin, and pulled him out of the stairwell. The two slammed the floor hatch shut and retreated, their footsteps fading.

Zulu made a lunge for the door as it slammed shut. "Wait for me." Claws clenched around his ankle. He looked down to see glinting eyes staring at him between the steps. The tigress was using all fours to hang beneath the steps. She yanked hard, sending the hapless clone slamming onto the floor beside his fallen companion.

Cruentin did a full body wince at the sounds of fierce snarls, yells, and crashes from below deck, noises that soon silenced. He ran through the abandoned kitchen, holding his medic bag high for anyone to see. "Medic coming through. Don't shoot."

Telari left her clobbered opponents wrapped in cargo straps. Smirking, she pursued Cruentin.

Chapter 53
Slippery Fish

Slade coughed in the smoky room, trying to see through a haze of smoke, fire-fighting foam, and beams of light filtering through jagged holes in the cockpit. He could not tell if the forms approaching him were friend or foe, so he wasted no time. Slade drew his bloody claws back to for the kill strike, when two Rezoan tackled him and pulled him toward the side hatch, trying to throw him off the ship.

Venamir collapsed to the floor, curled up in a gasping heap.

While Slade was trying to dispatch the latest attackers, Recon snuck in, grabbed Venamir, and pulled him across the debris-cluttered floor, leaving a trail of blood. They made it to the command room, forced the door closed and shoved the large, broken tabletop against it. Recon hauled Venamir up, ignoring groans and hushed cursing.

"Come on, no time to cry," Recon said, half helping, half dragging Venamir down a hall. "Never appreciates us clones. You make us just to throw at danger."

Venamir hissed, one hand clamped over his torn gills. "Shut up," he wheezed, each breath sounding like his lungs were filling with sand. "Port... port out."

"We can't," Recon informed.

"Rejects for cannon fodder," Vemamir wheezed.

Recon tried smacking on a wristband he was wearing and shook his head. "We have to use an escape hatch." His pace quickened when Doctor Cruen's voice image appeared on his comm, complaining, "I told you to distract Slade."

"But Doctor Cruen," Recon said, "the lizards are pounding on Slade. I have Venamir. He's a wreck."

Cruen retorted, "Bring him to me. Then go hold off Slade like I ordered."

"Slade will kill me."

"No, Slade's merciful. He's stupid that way." Cruen sounded less than convincing.

Recon limped faster down the hall, pausing only to glare down at the gashes in his leg, compliments of Telari. His cyborg muscles peeked through the cuts, shiny grey against the layer of flesh. He saw fluid leaking too, leaving a distinct trail. "That feline, she'll find us," he fumed.

On the mid-deck, Recon and Venamir found Cruen in a messy workroom that had an escape arrow pointing to a short hall. The frazzled doctor was rummaging through his medbag, preparing flesh kits while arguing with Maska over the comm. "Maska, fire on this ship and knock out the power so you can port us." Doctor Cruen demanded. He looked up when the clone struggled inside the room.

The clone turned Venamir over to Cruen with a blatant lack of concern, and left.

Agonizing seconds crept by before Maska answered. "Under attack," Maska stammered, "and not that simple. It's the *Wandering Fortress* blocking us out. They're not letting anyone port on or off. You have to get off that sub."

"Where are you? Can't you fire on them?"

"Not close enough," Maska replied.

Cruen glanced around. He could hear the voices of Slade's crew, sounding closer with each breath. He realized there was no quick way out. Doctor Cruen put a hasty patch on Venamir's worst injuries, four parallel stabs to the gills. "Slade, damn him and his bear claws, but I can fix this."

"Cruen, bail out," Maska reported amidst gunshots. "Doesn't matter. We've lost. Give up before you're fish food."

"No. We can escape. I'll take the escape pod. Once we're clear, teleport us through every allied portal we have."

"Too many simultaneous ports can kill you two."

"We have no choice."

"I'll try." The comm went silent.

Doctor Cruen flinched as the ship rocked from something landing on top of it, something that made the skin groan from its weight. "Something's wrong with your clones," Venamir whispered through ragged gasps.

"I'm going to hide your memories," Cruen said.

His patient struggled to escape, but had no physical strength left. "Are you crazy?" Venamir moaned, voice fading as Cruen invaded his mind.

"Better yet," Cruen said in a sadistic voice, "This is our chance to share powers. It's high time you understood my talents and, heh, I learned yours." His tone grew hungrier by the second. "It all makes sense. In case one of us is killed, we need each other's memories. More so, we need each other's powers." Cruen smacked his comm. "Maska. I'm ejecting. Come and get us!"

"You better not," came the scratchy reply. "Look outside."

Massive claws raked across the window. Outside, something roared and a blur of grey flew past. Cruen's eyes widened. "The drakirs are attacking!" Cruen knew what he had to do. The chance might never come again.

Cruen plunged his psy into Venamir's unprotected mind. Oh, the *rush!*

Before now, Venamir's mind always blocked out intruders, but now, Cruentin could find anything he wanted—memories, plots, knowledge, all trivial gains compared to what he wanted the most—Venamir's dire form. Cruen knew what the form looked like, an upright cross between a salamander and a Rezoan. He searched the fleeting images and voices in Venamir's mind, eating precious seconds, minutes, while his enemies drew closer. After what felt like a long dream, he saw a ghostly shape of a strange hybrid, a Rezoan with Deeps Merfin fins, holding vials.

"You injected yourself?" Cruen uttered, "You, mister purist?"

Venamir retorted, "Pure to our world, not one species, you fool. Get out of my mind."

Cruen nodded. "I should have known all along. All I need is your blood, and I have plenty of samples here, thanks to Slade." He pulled free some of the packing he'd pressed against Venamir's torn gills, and shoved it into his bag.

Venamir groaned, grabbing for Cruen's throat. "What—are—you—doing?"

"Insurance," Cruen replied. "I give you my knowledge for some of yours." He drove his psy into Venamir's mind again.

The two near equals tore at each other's mental shields, churning up memories, knowledge, tactics, pent up anger, all possible weapons against each other. Lost in the euphoria of stealing Venamir's secrets, Cruen jumped when someone grabbed his shoulder.

The Venamir clone was staring down at him. "Doctor, we have a problem."

"I told you," Cruen said, "to go take Venamir's place."

"You left me to the tiger-woman," the clone growled.

Cruen's gaze drifted downward to the clone's chest. Instead of seeing upper body injuries, he noticed with disbelief, *cleavage*? "I don't remember those," he muttered. Too late, he realized the clone was morphing, skin color fading to pale coppery tones, and thinning, short hair, growing into long, dark hair. "Oh, the cat girl." Fear feeding his anger, Cruen lunged at her, his form changing to the lizardish shape Venamir used in battle. "You can't stop me, not now. I'm too close."

Tel blocked with painful force, leapt clear of him and crouched. "Close to what," she fired back, "your first orgasm?"

Cruen sputtered, "No, you ignorant hell-spawn."

"Like you've ever bred," Tel interrupted.

As Cruen sputtered for a retort, she morphed into her tigress form, a raging calamity of claws, teeth, and hackled fur. Cruen tried to pry into her mind to control her, which only infuriated her. "How fucking typical." she hissed. "Control freak with little man syndrome!"

Recon slipped past them and grabbed Venamir. "You come with me."

"Hurry," Venamir rasped, "to the escape... pod."

A disgusted leer spread across the assisting clone's face, but he altered the look into a mean smile. "Trust me," he said, quickening his pace at the sound of Telari's feral voice.

"Venamir's getting away." Telari yelled.

Her growls and snarls, along with the crashing of chairs and supplies being knocked over, resounded down the halls. Recon put his stun firgun in Venamir's hands, pulled the trigger, and jumped back. As promised, the Herja program activated, and stun blasts hit Venamir without mercy until he was unconscious on the floor. Recon laughed.

Slade was still in Atlean bearish form, roaring and knocking everything aside in his wake. The clone, a broken chair, and toppled equipment, went flying against the walls. He burst into the disaster of a command room and skidded to a halt, his animalistic expression baffled.

Telari roared back at him, her long fangs shining, tail lashing. "Herja, turn on the damned lights." Slade demanded.

All lights not broken or overloaded came on throughout the ship.

Squinting against the sudden light, Cruen tried to escape the grappling match. "You feral bitch! Get off me, you shanking little—OW! Psychotic cur."

Telari hooked her claws deeper into his flesh, delighting in his struggles and sizzling profanity, growling through a mouthful of shoulder.

As Scruffy and Doc Nelzyr ran in, shoving their way past the bear-sized beast, Slade growled, "Telari?"

"Don't roar at me." she fired back. "I'm not your bitch."

Recon held his webbed hands high, one finger pointing to the dazed form on the foam-streaked floor. "There's Venamir. I helped you."

Cruen's lizard form was shrinking back to normal size. He lashed his tail with all his draining strength, meanwhile wrestling past Venamir in the cramped escape pod. He sneered and, grabbing his belt buckle, activated an energy shield around himself, knocking everyone away from him.

"Kill them," Cruen ordered Recon.

"Call us cannon fodder, will you?" Recon snarled.

"You can't trust Slade's people." Cruen stammered. "They must've hacked you."

"No, they didn't," Recon countered, "but I hacked your logs. You grew the clones like fish bait to feed to the enemy. I serve the land morphers now."

"You miserable traitor. The feline killed your fellow clones and you're taking her side?"

"No, she clawed them and strapped them down, cartoon style."

Cruen grabbed his last resort defense mechanism, one last grenade. He cancelled his body shield, flung the grenade into the room, and then charged down the short hall for the open escape pod.

The grenade started whining, then screeching as it flashed red, causing a rapid breakup of the fight. Slade and his friends had landed in a frenzied pile on the floor, all eyes on the grenade, but Recon beat them to it.

Fearless, Recon flung it after a wide-eyed Cruentin, who was slamming a fist over the eject button. The grenade zipped into the pod an instant before the door slammed shut and the pod ejected. "Boom," Recon chortled. He turned and met their stares. "Cruentin is a coward. He wouldn't endanger his own life. He only carries weapons that stun or sedate, so they can't be used against him to kill him. Besides, he'd rather dissect you than kill you."

Venamir gathered enough breath to hiss, "Silence."

Recon blinked, a befuddled look in his off-yellow eyes. "Why did I tell you that?"

"He'd be honest anyway," Telari said, "because I dosed you guys. It's on my claws. That's why Cruen's telepathy was all fuzzy, and why you're being honest." She grinned at the malicious snarls from their captives.

"Yeah, that sounds like old Cruen," Slade chuckled. He noticed his battered comm still hanging on a torn lapel and pulled it off with his big pawish hand. "All hands outside the *Spectre,* go capture Dr. Cruen in that escape pod."

They all turned on Venamir, who slouched against the wall, wheezing, one hand clasped over his gouged, clawed, gills. "Don't... flatter yourselves," he scoffed.

Scruffy laughed. "Oh, you think the Deeps will save him? You and Cruen lost most of your friends today."

Silence fell among the group as Slade stalked toward Venamir, who returned a spiteful leer. The others watched, a few smirking, but none moved to stop Slade. Recon watched with a smile that matched whenever the real Venamir smiled prior to doing something very bad. Now they noticed the background noises of combat, and the subtle rocking of the ship docked atop a huge submarine riding an ocean littered with allies, foes, and carnage. Sounds of battle and angry yells still carried on outside.

Slade wrestled back a near overwhelming urge to finish Venamir off. Forcing his fists to unclench, he reverted into his humanoid, Atlean form. "Scruffy, Nelz, patch him up. He has a date with an angry mob. Tel, stand guard."

Scruffy was already heckling his student. "See, Tel? I knew you worked best under pressure.

"Thanks," she replied.

As Doc and Scruffy closed in, Venamir groaned, "But I'm Doctor Cruen."

Blowing it off as a feeble ploy, Slade turned to the clone. "I owe you, but you're still our prisoner."

"Figures," Recon grumbled, sliding down the wall to sit on the floor.

Slade's brother replied within the next minute, "Berku here, we're already on it. Only one problem, no life forms."

"He blew up?" Slade probed.

"No, hatch was closed. Soon as he cleared the jammer fields, must have teleported out."

"Wha-at?" Slade barked. He ran to the escape pod hatch, his friends close behind, and smacked the controls. The outer safety hatch opened again, showing the proof.

Amidst a sea of dwindling chaos, Elowren perched atop a bobbing escape hatch in her gleaming coppery dragon form, looking like a miniature beast compared to the drakirs swimming around boats or flying low over the water. She lashed her tail in anger and flew back to the open hatch, morphing just in time to drop into the empty pod bay. "Cru ported out," she panted.

"Figures," Slade grumbled.

While her friends stared at her over the new trick, she tossed them a fleeting grin, keeping a psy link with her friends. To her silent call, two of the dragons moved in front of her. She resumed her normal form and dropped into the cockpit, where she crouched behind her dragonkin bodyguards.

"Rotten fish," Slade groaned, leaning his head against the wall. "Well, we did get Vemamir." Then it really sunk in. "We GOT VENAMIR!"

Outside, as the news spread through psychics and happy yells, cheering erupted.

Chapter 54
Fish in a Jar

The warzone around the *Wandering Fortress* simmered down to the noise of engines and voices as ships, large and small, congregated in a grudging truce. Council ships flew in low orbits, herding stragglers onto the floating fortress, while dragons and their riders perched upon surrendered boats, eyes alert.

No shots were being fired, at least not within earshot.

Slade drew a long sigh as he wrapped his arms around Elowren, her closeness magically soothing, her hair still faintly sweet, even after all the smoke and battles, her touch reassuring as always. He let his gaze drift as, for the first time in months, he could relax as he repeated the names to himself, and realized not only had they survived, they had reclaimed his old ship. Wits sharpening, he lingered, lost in the moment for just a bit longer.

"Slade," Elowren started, but his brief laugh surprised her into listening.

"All these years," Slade realized aloud, "the crash, the deaths of my crew... it really wasn't my fault."

She pressed her lips close to his ear. "We all knew that."

Telari let go of the back of his belt and peered out the cockpit windows. "I hate to bring more bad news, but those clans look awful froggy."

The noise was growing, coming from a multitude of voices over the wind and waves. Slade and his crew looked at the scene below of clan leaders yelling at each other and the surviving, able followers forming around their *Spectre*.

A few of the smaller warships hovered over the waves, trying to use loudspeakers to badger the crowd, but those smaller fighter ships flown by warring pilots remained parked on the deck, scattered so nobody else could land without causing fatalities.

"Oh HELL NO!" Slade blurted, and started for the open hatch.

"Hold still," Scruffy said. "You've got holes in your arms."

"I know that," Slade retorted.

Slade turned to object, but Scruffy grabbed him anyway, right on the punctures that Venamir caused with the last desperate stab of claws. Slade winced, but as he drew in a deep breath for his next outburst, he noticed a green substance forming on Scruffy's hands. The green stuff thickened into the goo he knew too well, the soothing, near sentient concoction from Scruffy's trees. The goo traveled onto Slade, doing what it did best, finding every injury.

Slade stared at the wounds in his arms closing, not fully healed, but closing and sealing until the last of the goo's energy transferred into his body. He brushed bits of dried green foliage off his forearms. "That's a new trick," he muttered in awe.

"Yeah, it is," Scruffy nodded. "I've found that if you're not hurt, the sappy goo can survive on the body for hours. I had to use some on Berku's arm but we still had a good coat of it on ourselves."

Doc inspected the much improved condition of his captain and grunted with pleasure. "Okay, now listen. Whatever you're up to, let's make a plan."

"Already have," Slade replied. "Mori, I can order you around now, right?"

"Absolutely," the Herja nodded.

"Good. Reactivate all systems and watch our backs. Shield us if we need it. Close the ship. Open it only for us. Tel, Recon, Doc, you stay with Venamir. The rest of you, come on." Slade strode out, his friends flanking him.

The sight of Slade and his party of Scruffy and Elowren emerging drew the attention of those on deck. Berku and a few of his Druwens joined Slade to face the mob. Demands for Venamir, his head, his tailfins, whatever they could get. The clashing armies held each other at gunpoint or hand-held weapons, spears, crossbows, or curled up fists, all ranting.

Slade elbowed his way through the angry mob, grateful to have his friends at his back and seeing some of Berku's werefolk moving his way to help. He kept on moving through the masses, ignoring taunts and hisses until he stood face to face with the weary clan leaders. When he halted, in arm's reach, the masses closed around them.

Facing him were the Coveness and three of her elite guardsmen, two Merfin leaders, and one Rezoan leader, only familiar to Slade from a few treaty meetings. Berku and Shocks flanked Slade.

The Coveness stepped forward, eyed Slade's crew, and shook her head. "Do you truly think your friends can hold off the riled mobs?"

Slade looked around as casually as one could for such an occasion. "That's right."

Skeptical laughter arose from the ranks but simmered back to grumbles and demands for Venamir, then random threats and goading.

Slade morphed into his bear form and bellowed, "NO MORE FIGHTING. You think you can live long enough to forget today? Well, you can't. See those dragons? They're on our side. So are the warships, and the Herja onboard the *Spectre* has weapons control. Now shut up."

Scruffy rubbed his ear that was closest to Slade. "Ow," he muttered.

"NOW THEN," Slade resumed his normal Atlean form. "We are going to have our Council Summit right here, right now. NO MORE warring, no more thinning of our population over what, one insane fish? Venamir would just love for the rest of us who are NOT his muck-licking cultists to kill each other off. Yes, we all want to smash him. So we can either smash some more heads and make the big dogs shoot at us," he gestured toward the heavy warships orbiting overhead with cannons trained on their location, "or, we turn this fat, happy stalemate into something useful. I want all of our leaders to get their butts inside those chambers below." Slade pointed upward again to the nearest warship. "We will reforge our treaties." Then he and his bodyguard friends glared at everyone who looked unhappy, which was everybody.

"We heard you," the Rezoan leader retorted. "You have Venamir onboard that ship." He pointed at the *Spectre*.

"And you all heard me," Slade countered, moving up toe to toe with the chieftain, "get your butt into the council chamber."

The Coven Mother reverted to her regal and generous self, delegating for food, drink, and medical aid to be offered for her many guests. "Any clan who wishes for peace, their leaders are to convene inside the chambers, or get off my boat and risk further warfare."

Clan leaders gathered in the lower deck of the *Wandering Fortress*, a sight that helped to calm even the angriest of moods. The inside of the *Fortress* mixed graceful arches and curves from one oblong chamber to the next, glowing orbs and aquariums with light-reflecting sea creatures illuminating the halls and rooms, handrails sparkling from inlaid, polished stones, and soothing colors of soft blues and greens, mixing into ivory whites.

The Coveness tugged one of her Merfin guards near and said, "Helmsman, take us toward the shore, gently now." As he bowed and moved off, she strode to her chair. "Brethren and allies, we have much to discuss. Help yourselves to the guest trays and take a short break to calm down. I have medics to help those in need. Be comfortable. We shall remain here until treaties are restored. Is that agreed?"

The group responded with reluctant nods and varying dialects of "Ayes" all around.

"Very good, then," the Coveness said, and gazed around, noting the species, Aqauatics, Rezoans, Feral Atleans, and a few hybrids she noted, her gaze pausing on Telari and a few of the clan leaders. "We need a full-blood human."

"We have Shocks," Vanysa announced, patting the heavily tattooed human veteran on the back, her fond demeanor causing a startled murmur from her water-dwelling peers, but curious looks from the more neutral water-breathers.

"That's Master Sergeant John Shocks," Shocks said, "and I'm all Earth-borne, folks."

"Excellent," the Coveness smiled.

Chapter 55
Scavengers Fat Bird Skinny Bird

Fat Bird and Skinny Bird studied their prey with weapons drawn, not firguns, but a chunk of driftwood held as a club and a bandolier full of metal-cutting tools.

"Part him out here. We keep the power cells and the head."

"Yes, the head, of course." Fat Bird leaned closer, ever wary of the cyborg's powerful hands, his friend's whimpering, a constant reminder to the snapped leg.

"I want to help." Skinny Bird flapped his wings, only flailing about.

"Sit down."

"Stop hoarding him."

"Oh, very well, it's broke anyway." Fat Bird pulled his friend over and together, they flew into a mad frenzy of squawking, slashing, and pounding on Noxus. They clawed the offending hand until it hung by the metallic flex-bones, nearly severed. Fat Bird bashed the mangled hand with a rock, yelling, "Die! Die!"

Skinny Bird started cleaving into the chest of Noxus, hitting a metal barrier, and then a mesh around the heart. Bloody bits of flesh and dented cyborg parts flew everywhere.

"Save the head," Fat Bird squawked, "for reward."

"I know, I know!"

"Ew, guts."

"You gonna' eat that?"

"You can have."

"STOP!" yelled a voice over an incoming jetpack. A firgun shot puked up sand at their feet. "That body is mine."

The birds stumbled back, Skinny staying down this time when he fell and the larger bird spreading his wings in protection.

"Pervert," Fat Bird squawked, turning. "This body almost dead. Go find a morgue."

Rhoan landed in a painful crouch. "You guys are sick mother-cluckers."

The birds opened their maws angrily, wings spread at the intruder. Rhoan unbuckled and shrugged out of the jetpack harness and stepped into the blissful, cool water.

Rhoan took a better look at the two Hrokahs. "Fat Bird, what the heck are you doing here?"

Fat Bird pointed at Rhoan. "Medic? Our medic?" He chittered in laughter. "What a stupid question. We worked at prison, and then, your friends blew it up." Starting forward bought another shot in the sand, right between his legs.

Skinny Bird laughed this time as fatso jumped back. "Not jump so high this time."

Fat Bird spun on him. "Shut your beak."

As they argued, Rhoan jogged through the shallow water and inspected Noxus. "You were gonna eat him? Gross."

"Careful, he grabbed me," Skinny Bird said. "Leg way broke now."

Rhoan waved his firgun at the menacing, round bird. "You worked there, eh? Whatever. Don't even try to sit on me again."

"Nothing personal," Fat Bird shrugged.

Rhoan felt for a pulse and found one, but very irregular. "Nothing personal? You wanted to sell me." He checked Noxus further with touch and body readings. The pupils didn't respond. His bio-reader showed an erratic heartbeat from a convulsing mechanism buried deep in the chest.

The Hrokahs waved their feathery tri-fingers in protest, and chimed like a bad echo, "No, not sell, rent. Yes, rent you, set you free. Well paid and free."

"So you're pimps. Siddown and shaddap." Rhoan stared Fat Bird down, until both birds were sitting, their beady eyes flickering from his firgun to Noxus. "I need to take blood."

"What, to drink? You one stupid doctor," Skinny Bird chirped. "Good for us. We let you go."

"You morons didn't let me go. I zapped fatty here in the nuts," came the painful reminder. "They were more like acorns."

Fat Bird uttered a high note, covering his crotch.

"That *was* funny," the runtier one said. He ducked from Fat Bird's warning squawk.

"You keep insulting me and I won't fix your leg, so behave," Rhoan tossed back as he drew one vial after the next.

While the birds stared in surprise, beaks hanging open, Rhoan kept talking, "One thing about cyborgs, sometimes their bio systems are designed to try to save their life, or prolong it until they can get medical aid. Like this guy. Venamir must have spent a small fortune so Noxus here could live through just about anything, and he did. It was hell killing him. He's got only one power cell left, and that's in the heart. Brain activity feels dead, but that's nothing new. The blood's still oxygenated, slightly, not rancid, yet. That'll do." He eyed the last vial and whistled. "Five vials, awesome."

"Now we take him?" Fat Bird asked.

Not the answer they wanted to hear, "Well, I'm pretty sure the High Council will want this guy for an autopsy."

"NO!" Fat Bird lurched to his feet. "We found him first. Not fair."

Rhoan kept his firgun trained and bagged the vials with his free hand. "Hey, I don't need the reward. You can have it, if the Council decides to pay criminals." He grinned and grabbed his comm as the birds stuttered. "All hands, I just found Noxus. We can make a good serum. Oh, and I gotta make a cast for this seagull."

"Did he insult us again?" Fat Bird muttered.

"Mm-hmm," Skinny Bird whined.

Chapter 56
Berku takes back the *Jacobyte*

When the tribe leaders emerged from the council chambers below deck, the *Wandering Fortress* was still far from land, and most of the air and water vessels around them were still in need of repair. Slade admitted, along with most of the passengers, that they'd just stay for a ride to the mainland and fine tune negotiation.

Bidding Slade "good luck with the villagers," Berku was grateful to leave the *Wandering Fortress*. He rounded up his least injured tribesmen and let Vanysa fly them back to the *Jacobyte*. After all that had gone crazy, he almost expected the hard won ship to be gone, or under siege again, but there she was, still laying in the shallow tides where she'd crashed on the beach. A couple of haggard yet smiling friends waved from the shore.

The *Jacobyte* was theirs.

Vanysa dropped them off and remained in the pilot's chair.

"Vany, you helped win this," Berku said, pausing on the small flight deck. "Come out and celebrate."

"Later, I promise," she replied. Soon as he disembarked, she flew away.

Berku watched the transport leave, a bit to his regret. He had seen a warrior side of her dive into combat and control infamous monsters of the sea, so different from the proper dignitary. He respected her now. "You'll miss the table dancing." he yelled.

Shrugging at his friends, Berku trotted across a makeshift ramp to board the crashed ship and meet his growing audience of friends and allies. He looked over the grizzly crowd and saw even more landing around the reclaimed ship.

Professor Zared was actually drinking hard booze, not tea or some foo-foo drink. Motley was telling his cub not to eat the raw fish from the polluted water. Merfins, some medics, some just helping, checked the injured and rummaged up field treatments. Shocks and his son Tatts kept trading exaggerated stories, each one bigger than the last, laughing, and punching each other in the shoulders. Four of his missing werefolk emerged from the half sunken gallows of the ship, rolling a barrel of booze which they stabbed, and started searching for mugs, canteens, anything. The burliest men pried the top off the thing and waved, yelling "BEER."

Berku ran over, jumping over the shorter members to stand by the barrel. "HOLD IT!" he bellowed.

Grudgingly, the crowd simmered down to a low boil of hushed chatter, but they still bellied closer to the brew, their faces tired and expectant. The normally starlit sky hung over them with foreboding clouds and smoke, while a cold breeze penetrated the holes in the ship. Cold, injured, fatigued, thinning tempers painted some faces red, even those with green skin.

Berku continued in a most pleased voice, "Slade just whomped the rat-turds outta Venamir. I'm sure he won't mind you drinking his beer, since we got his ship back for 'im. Er, she just needs a little spit 'n' polish." Glancing around the crashed ship and wincing brought some chuckles from the bunch.

"Mister Berku," came the cub's young voice, "those ships in the graveyard are retired, right? Or is that a cover? I mean, the *Spectre* flew out of there."

Berku turned and sat on the nearest crate. "We hid the *Spectre* and programmed the Herja to answer only to the original crew. Problem is, Venamir was part of that crew, and so was Moradin. I'm guessing they were able to override some of the programming. Then his goons started infiltrating and fixed her up. She wasn't flyable, not when we left her, way before you were born, cubby. Venamir's gotten sneakier over the years. On the good side, Slade and his crew reclaimed her."

Another cheer rose.

And Doctor Evil's still out there, Berku thought with a grudging pause. "Oh raging hells, I gotta be honest. Doctor Cruentin got away."

Stunned silence fell, then they shrugged off Cruentin for the immediate prize.

Angry grumbles grew in volume, boiling into a chant, "Give us Venamir! Give us Venamir!"

Shocks stomped to the front of the ranks and waved his hands, yelling, "SHADDAP all o' yas!" He pivoted, waving his hands from one race to the next. "Look at us, dogs, fishes, lizards, and humans. Yesterday a bunch of us were fighting over petty crap, spare parts, smuggled booze, like scavengers. Now we're chummin' around, so don't worry. We'll get him, so you should be celebrating instead of bitching. We need him alive right now. You gotta know that, right? So drink up, will ya? I swear if I see one more angry mob, you'll be crying for your mamas before the night's over."

There were a few chortles amidst scattered intimidated looks, but the combat-weary group gave in. Whether to fatigue, Shock's reputation, or what else, nobody much cared. All that mattered was that they settled down and returned to drinking, sharing a smoke, looking for a snack or a place to nap. Facing a heavily armed stalemate, a grudging, tentative peace spread across the ship.

Chapter 57
Dredging Up Ships

The Starship Graveyard had new additions to its retired fleet. The first morning rays painted the horizon in vivid layers from ocean blues to scattered clouds of reds and golds, comforting to his eyes but not to his spirit. His mind remained on the war-torn beach he'd left a week ago, with boats and ships littering the tide pools and extending the Starship Graveyard to accept the newly demolished additions. He saw the combat of many clans each night in his dreams, and now wondered if his flashbacks had grown worse than Slade's. Zared sighed and tugged off his boots, giving serenity another chance as he continued his morning ritual of meditation. He threw them onto higher ground, movements stiff and slow. "I truly must retire one of these centuries," he grumbled, and walked into the wet sand where the tides caressed his feet.

A few boats and small ships docked nearby, but his attention remained on the horizon, where familiar ships formed as if they were magical beasts meeting the morning's glow. His eyes narrowed upon recognizing one misty silhouette trailing another.

Squinting against the sun, Zared thought he recognized the silhouette, but didn't believe his luck. Divers must have started days ago, a monumental task even for Merfins with the hardiest salvage boats, but there were no massive investigations and salvage this time.

"Finally," Zared grumbled, "we lit a bonfire under the elites." Behind an awkwardly shaped form, something akin to a stretched, triangular turtle, but he knew that ship as well. He trudged toward the ocean's soothing waves and stood in the soft, wet sand, where the last bits of bubbling ocean water ran over his feet. He stood there long enough to sink a bit as each wave passed, and now the waves swirled around his knees. Reaching into a pouch on his belt, Zared paused, then withdrew a small set of binoculars and raised them to his eyes.

The closer the tugboats pulled his ship to land, the clearer the profile sharpened through the mists. Massive rafts strained beneath the waterlogged weight of the five-crewman starship. and water still cascaded through jagged holes in her wings and body.

Zared squinted through the morning sun as he ran his farseeing gaze along the *Mythos*, and grimaced as his suspicions rang true. The tail was buckled, one wing sagged and bounced along the waves, and her frame, her sleek body, might have looked fine to the untrained eye, but lay out of alignment at mid-spine. With a long sigh, Zared lowered the binocs. *They should have left her there, buried at sea.*

Slade walked up behind him and waved a hand over both their heads. "Are you so depressed that you're shrinking, or do you like standing in fish crap?"

Zared looked at Slade's chest, then down at his feet, and shrugged. "Perhaps," he admitted, returning his gaze to where tugb oats slowly returned his crippled ship toward land. "She was so beautiful."

"Let me see." Slade borrowed the binocs.

The tail was broken and one wing sagged, but he definitely recognized the *Spectre*. On top of the fuselage, two shiny, giant crow-looking beings sat, either yapping or eating from the movement of their long beaks. Skinny Bird had a leg cast on and was holding what looked like remote controls, while Fat Bird stuffed his beak into a large bag and was munching away.

Slade laughed. "Rhoan was right, good turd birds dug her up." He shoved the binoculars back into his colleague's hands. "Cheer up."

One Huvzter left the salvage crew and flew over to join Zared and Slade. It settled to the beach and the rider hovered beside them, her long, purply hair trailing way down from her helmet.

"Hi Tel," Slade greeted. "Jump on in. The water's great."

She quipped, "Ew. It's loaded with junk. Besides, you know cats don't like water."

Slade reached up and grabbed the front of Tel's Sport Huvstr.

Tel screeched as the Huvzter dipped nose first into the water, taking her in to the knees until he released it and grabbed his belly, laughing. "Hey!" She barely kept her balance and skittered sideways out of reach. "Dontcha wanna hear about your ships?"

Zared signed, "Spill it out."

"Well, the *Jacobyte's* repairable. The *Mythos* isn't. Her frame's all tweaked." Her normally joking demeanor was as sympathetic as he'd seen. She loved the old ships, and they knew it. "The *Mythos* would need a total rebuild, frame, everything structural."

Zared turned away to stare at his wrecked beauty. "I know. The Council won't support that, and I'm not as rich as people think." He sighed. "That hallway of history alone took years for Elowren and me to paint."

"You could pull that out," Slade said.

"Yes, true."

"I have an idea," Tel went on, her voice lightening. "She has a kindred sister that's in pretty good shape. What if you pulled all your hallway art and lab stuff out of her?"

Zared folded his arms. "And put them where?"

"Well, duh," Tel pointed to a shining form parked near the collapsed lighthouse. "The *Spectre* has the same lines. That ship was a prototype for birds like yours."

Slade and Zared glanced at each other before turning to stare at the reclaimed warbird. They mulled over her words in unison, too startled to reply at first.

"Come on, guys," Tel said. "I already researched it all weekend. Those ships are very compatible in size and systems. They could be combined into one."

Zared grabbed her in a hug and kissed her on the cheek. "Tel, you're sweet and wonderful, but," he released his blushing friend and straightened, trying to regain his cool. "The *Spectre* is not my bird."

Slade laughed, "We just have to make the uppidy-ups think it's their idea."

Zared nodded, also starting to grin. "There may be hope. Sometimes they play along just to shut you up."

* * *

Once Slade headed for his own ship, it was his turn to feel the pangs of sorrow for his metallic friend. His *Jacobyte* lay halfway buried in the shallow surf, foamy water lapping her body. Slade tightened his jaw and tried to console himself that at least they had pried his ship away from Venamir. He counted at least ten of Berku's werefolk in scattered locations, near doorways and at the ocean's edge, armed and guarding her. Jovial voices and rock music wafted from the ship and carried over the ocean breeze, while squishy footsteps approached from behind him. Zared jogged to catch up, waterlogged boots squeaking.

A black feline stood guarding the open hatch, his toothy grin a welcome sight. "Hullo, Slade."

"Hi Jasko," Slade greeted as he and Zared entered. "What're they doing in there?"

"What else? Partying and bragging," Jasko replied, remaining at his post. "Your brother's leading the pack." He yelled, "Captain on the deck!"

Slade and Zared boarded the ship. They found Berku heading a celebration around a keg of beer. Most of his crew was there, along with Shocks and his gangly, tattooed son, the trouble-loving Huvzter gang, and a disheveled, frazzled gray feline man. The feline strode right over to Slade, wearing an unusually happy smile.

"Motley!" Slade greeted in surprise. "I thought you left, blasted off-world for home."

"No," the big cat replied, "I promised my cub I wouldn't hunt anymore. I'd still like to work for you, but close to home. I'll do all the behind-the-scenes stuff you want."

Slade shook the paw-like hand. "Keep the rats away. Just kidding." He slapped Motley on the furry shoulder and raised his voice. "Who didn't invite me to this party?"

One biker grabbed a frothy mug and passed it over, while the others tried to formulate innocent alibis on how busy they were fixing the broken ship.

"We can't waste it," Berku said as he clinked his tall mug with Slade's. "We just happened to find it all stashed in the cargo bay. Come see the cockpit. We reactivated the Herja program, got some power backup, but of course she's way too crippled to fly."

Slade followed his brother to the cockpit, still trying to absorb the ransacked images of his once beautiful ship. He paused to stroke the nearest bulkhead, as if calming a distraught animal. He saw burns in the walls, broken equipment, claw marks, dark stains, fresh scars everywhere. His eyes lingered on a humanoid's silhouette burned into the deck. *Disruptor weapon.* His grip on the mug tightened upon seeing holes in the deck burned through, with black scars around the edges. "Our main guns melted holes like that?"

"Yeah," Berku nodded, "whole bottom deck's torched. Looks like the plasma burned right up through the hull plating and everything."

Slade's tone dropped. "We never should've allowed those damned things."

"Yeah, the fact that they damn near spit magma makes them pretty demonic," Berku agreed, "but they can be augmented or replaced. Think the Council will help?"

"They better if they want us to get anything done," Slade replied. "Look at this...." He kicked a bottle of scale oil aside and skulked around the cockpit, growing madder by the minute as he found the first aid kit full of decaying sea-stalks and shells with teeth marks. "Stinking Venamir used this as his lunch bag?" Slade took swigs of beer between each grumble as his eyes spied more calling cards from the fishman. The mess engulfed the entire ship. Dents, tears, mystery stains, cracks and broken pieces of delicate gadgets turned into junk. Slade leaned on the captain's chair and the headrest fell off. He slipped on the floor and kicked a leaky bottle of scale oil across the floor.

Berku snickered. "You better sprout fish feet for a while."

"Oh, shut it," Slade retorted, when finally, something made him look up, the smell of rancid perfume. "Arrgh! Honestly?" He yanked down an air freshener shaped like a merman and merwoman with arms and tails wrapped around each other.

Berku grabbed the groping merpeople before Slade could smash it. "Gimme." He paused, looking at his brother. "Aw, lighten up, could be worse."

"No, it's just, we need to go," Slade replied. "You, me, Zared, Vany and at least one of our medics, so don't get any more lushed up. Shocks, you too." He was glad to see a nod.

486

"Oh, all right," Berku sighed and finished his beer.

Slade gazed around the cockpit thinking aloud. "Well at least it doesn't look too bad in here." He sniffed, turned, and sniffed again. "What is that?" He leaned closer to the pilot's chair, took a long sniff, and wished he hadn't. "Skanky-ass fish. How do I get the smell out?"

Only a few steps away, Gus sprayed Slade with beer as he busted out laughing, his shaking causing some of the foam to spill off his beer glass. "Oops."

Slade glared at Gus, but couldn't help a smirk. He grabbed the cap off of Gus 's head, and the beer mug out of his hands. Slade sniffed the foamy beer, then splashed beer all over the captain's chair.

"Hey," Gus objected, "that's beer abuse."

Slade used the hat to rub the beer into the chair. "This just might work."

As the spectators guffawed with laughter, Slade slapped the drenched cap back onto Gus's head and handed him the empty beer mug. "Thanks."

Chapter 58
Temple Reunion

Moradin walked though the Morpher's Temple, where she'd trained as a much younger woman. The place hadn't changed much. Soft throw rugs were gentle on her feet, and hand-painted murals of flowering trees and rustic buildings caressed the smooth wood paneling on the walls. She gazed through an open window. The forest spread out all around the ancient Temple, the giant old-growth trees both soothing and protective. The Temple still even had its bold colors, dark green with burgundy trim. It felt good to be home. She had only been here a week, and was restless.

She worked her new arm with a few winces before returning to medbay at the end of the hall. Medbay sounded more like a social club than a recovery lounge. Shanto was doing reps squeezing foam balls. He would drop one, pick up another from a bucket on his bed, and try again. Telari was visiting and had to comment about the balls he was dropping on the floor. Wulvur was silent as he poured some tea and raised the cup in greeting before returning to Scruffy's dim plant room.

Tel glanced after Wulvur, huffed, and looked at Slade. "Sourpuss."

"We still can't find Cruentin," Slade was saying. "I'm sure the Deeps are hiding him."

"But the clans are working together again," Doc replied, looking over as Moradin entered. "Hey Mori, how's the arm?"

"It's good," she replied. A little creature fluttered across the room and landed on her shoulder. Without thinking, she reached and very lightly rubbed its head. The little creature appeared more dragonish every day, even though he perched on her shoulder and flapped his wings.

Rhoan peered in from the hallway. "Has anyone seen my pet dragon?"

"I can't believe it," Mori sang out, "I'm petting a baby dragon. I'm petting a baby dragon and not squishing anything."

Two Deeps medics called Slade over to their workstation in the far corner of the spacious room. They gestured to their lab results, mostly notes surrounding vials of red fluid that glittered with silver. The Deeps gave Slade far more information than he wanted, all in elaborate medical terminology that he only half understood, made worse when translating from the ancient Deeps Merfin medical lingo.

"Whoa, spell it out," Slade finally said.

"Come on," Doc Nelzyr said, "let's take a walk."

* * *

Slade and Doc walked to a balcony overlooking the botanical gardens. Old-growth trees surrounded the temple grounds, their mighty branches stretching upward and twining together. The morning sunlight filtered through gaps in the canopy and warmed the morning dew off a botanical garden full of herbs and flowering vines.

"Good thing Berku's not here. He'd try to throw me in the water again."

Doc chuckled, "Darn shame I missed that."

"Talk to me. You look worried."

Doc rambled on. "Wulvur needs more detox. He had four poisons and three serums in him. Shanto's off work for a month after that fight with Maska. I'm not crazy about having those Deeps Merfins helping. It's great now. Next thing you know, they'll want to research everything in the temple. It's their nature."

"It's high time the Deeps started helping.

"It gets worse. Wulvur's depressed because he didn't take out Noxus by himself."

Slade tossed up his hands and blurted, "What? Noxus was the most over-powered cyborg I've ever met!"

"Yeah, Noxus had a lot of upgrades. In the autopsy, we found that he had netting around his organs, damn near impenetrable. He had two standby pacemakers, backup systems so his skeletal frame could carry him out of danger. He would've died after fighting Wulvur. Mori just finished him off early. In a nutshell, my patients need a morale boost."

"Hmm," Slade mused, grinning. "Ask Telari to handle Wulvur. Have Shanto meet me in the portal chamber." He strode back into the temple.

Doc followed, "I want my patients back within a few hours."

Slade nodded, "Yeah, yeah." He detoured to say hello to Moradin, and extended his hand, smiling as she accepted the handshake. Her grip was very light, and her cheek twitched with mixed emotions.

"Come on, Mori, a little harder."

Mori drew a tremulous breath and clamped down a bit firmer.

"That's good right there. I just wanted to say thanks for the help."

She withdrew her hand and blushed, shaking her head as she replied, "Oh, nothing I shouldn't have done long ago." Mori blushed even deeper when Gus strolled by and muttered something about her cute smile. "I can't stay," she confessed.

Slade sighed. "You can still visit, keep in touch."

"I will," she promised with a heartfelt smile.

Slade found Shanto waiting by the teleportal room. "Let's go."

"Where?" Shanto asked.

"Vacation," Slade replied. He activated a portal, which placed them outside on a bright day, near a gigantic starship hangar.

Among the workers was Jasko, his black fur shining in the sunlight. The big feline greeted them, "We must be desperate for help, to pull you out of medbay." He pointed at Shanto's arms. "We'll get a lotta work out of you."

"Harrdy harr," Shanto grumbled, grinning a bit.

Jasko opened the personnel door for them. "Come on in."

Shanto followed Slade into the hangar. The place almost looked like it could magically hold more than was possible. The floor along one wall sloped downward to allow more room for overhead catwalks and cranes. A maze of catwalks dangled from the ceilings and lined walls loaded with supplies. Slade stood, grinning, while Shanto halted, his mouth hanging open.

"I knew you'd like it here," Slade grinned, "goes into the hillside. Used to be our largest bunker. You need to keep busy, so here you go, a few hours a day. Our ships need you." He pointed toward the first ship in line. The *Jacobyte,* her front windows shining down at them like alien eyes gazing at a new specimen. Her wings lay on work trailers alongside her scorched belly. Behind the

Jacobyte, where the domed ceiling rose even higher, sat the *Vernacular* like a giant sleeping bird with her wings folded close. Still the flying tank of the fleet, the good old *Vernacular* bore new scars like warpaint.

Shanto's eyes widened as they neared their work site—a dramatic mess of starship parts scattered as if a storm had blown through an assembly line. The *Spectre*'s nose had a faded outline of a ghostly beast in flight, surrounded by cascading wave outlines of blue and green, while a morpher lady rising from a forest canopy still graced *Mythos's* forward fuselage.

Slade gazed at their salvaged ships, his eyes hopeful. "It'll take both of your brains to restore these birds. The *Spectre* and the *Mythos* are totaled, but they can be combined into one good ship. I need you to repair the *Vernacular* first." He added in mock complaint, "Scruffy will love rubbing *that* in."

Shanto flashed an exuberant grin as he went to explore the elaborate mess of parts in his favorite toy store ever.

"Well, get to work," Slade grinned, strolling off. "Do some engineering."

Chapter 59
Councils and Clans

"Captain's Log: Two weeks and no sign of Cruentin." Slade sat his empty mug down on the long briefing table and heaved a sigh, gazing around the sturdy walls of *Vernacular's* ready room. "We lost troops on both sides, all sides of Atlean forces, but somehow my crew, and my brother's team all survived." He leaned back, pondering. "I don't know how we all got out of *that mess* alive. Shanto's off flight status for months. Wulvur is damned lucky to survive multiple poisons." He glanced at the time and saved the recording. "Better not miss *this* Council meeting."

He rose and straightened his formal, dark green tunic, tugged on his boots, and eased into a greatcoat with dignitary emblems on the lapels, small, round patches, one of Earth, and one of planet Atlearon.

The Morphers Council formed the main entrance between the forest and Clawsworth City, its architecture reminiscent of storybook towers amongst ancient temples. Thick vines wrapped around the towers, spreading from lush vegetation and trees that shaded most of the courtyards.

Despite his fondness for the exquisite place, Slade was tired of coming here. He marched in flanked by his closest peers, Scruffy, Elowren, Berku, Vanysa, amused to see Shocks park his loudly painted Huvzter, only to be detained by the guards.

"Aw, come on," Shocks was saying, "I'm with them." He pointed to Slade and company.

A silent brain message from Slade to the guards made them give him a startled look. One of them even called Shocks "Sir."

"Watch it, I work for a living," Shocks said in a fair humor. "Let's stir the pot."

Into the Council chambers they went, the large double doors swinging shut behind them. Slade and his party noticed a mix of races within the room, representing the Atlean clans, Hrokahs, humans, Rezoans, and Merfins. Even the commanding mistress of the *Wandering Fortress* joined them to speak for the elusive Deeps.

"I'm glad to see you're not taking any chances," Scruffy said as they sat down.

"That is true," said the Deeps Coven Mother, "but at least now I can see the light of day. Even being part Merfin, I was sick of hiding, seeing nothing but water and fish."

Scattered laughter arose around the table, and then they dove into business. Slade insisted on keeping an alliance with the humans and gave Shocks huge recognition for such a small attack force helping turn the tides of the multi-clan battles. He had no bones about his habitual pattern of tweaking the boundaries of authority, and bartered for leniency to those who helped them thwart Venamir's uprising.

"We keep our alliance with the humans and make it grow," Slade spelled out. "Shocks's father helped us win the first council fight when Venamir turned against us." He gestured at his tattooed friend who sat across the room. "Now his son is commander of the pilots who helped us survive the prison escape, and the clan war that Venamir's followers started. Even humans without extra-terrestrial bloodlines are beginning to show talents of clairvoyance. They're evolving. As Scruffy says, 'we are wereworlds.' Let's make the best of it."

The other clans presented less resistance than Slade expected. Still, some tempers flared, keeping bodyguards on high alert. Human colonies gained a few notches in priority, clan leaders stabilized some of their working relations, and a few Deeps agreed to work with their land-loving allies. By the time it was over, Slade wasn't sure who was worn out the most.

"There is one more thing," the acting council leader said, rising. "Speaking of authority, our ranks have suffered losses, both from key people turning against us or falling to death. We need a few changes in leadership. Slade, you have performed a remarkable feat of diplomacy, such that we feel it is only right to reward you. Since Venamir murdered our Magistrate, that duty falls to me. Our Prime Chancellor defected and became a casualty, so we need a new Prime Chancellor. Slade, you have proven your ability to inspire other races, even if your approach is unconventional."

"Uh-oh," Slade muttered, glancing at Zared, who sighed as the implication set in. Some applauded while others spouted conflicting remarks.

Zared nodded to Slade, and half-heartedly applauded.

Slade rose, waving his hands. "Oh, no you don't. I'm a Druwen, a forest ranger, a weapons trainer, not a diplomat."

That started a whole new argument.

"You are the best blend of both," Cleodna stated.

Slade turned to her, carefully choosing his words. "Lady Cleodna, I'm very flattered, but I had help. Zared is still the better diplomat, and so are the ladies here. Zared's the one who sent word to the clans and got some of them to listen. Elowren was able to rally the Guardians into waking the drakirs, something they hate to do. Same with Vany. She summoned Deeps who would help us and a small army of sea creatures to break up the clan war."

"We've chosen you, Slade," Cleodna stated. "The vote has been cast."

Slade stared at her, wishing it was a joke, but he could see it wasn't. "Wow," he muttered, his argumentative stance straightening. "Well then, uh, thank you, everyone."

The room roared with cheers and applause that surprised and humbled him, to a point. Even Zared, who Slade knew dreamed of the Prime Minister's job, was nodding and applauding. Even the birds were flapping their wingtips together. A few of the lizards held reluctance in their eyes, but the overall acceptance left Slade dumbfounded.

"Thank you. Thanks," Slade said, gesturing for them to quiet down. "There's just one thing. This means I can choose my second in command, and I choose Zared as Prime Chancellor for the Morpher's Council."

Hearty applause filled the large chambers again.

* * *

The Morpher's Temple finally quieted down after a long day of busy medics and more guests than usual, Slade's crew and friends. In the medbay, Doctor Nelzyr was trying to catch a nap when Telari, Elowren, Kestral, and Vany entered, wearing mischievous grins.

Elowren held a large make-up bag with paintbrushes sticking out of it. "Slade rattled the councils, as usual. Elzy, we need some time with Wulvur."

Doc's pitch raised a bit. "All of you?"

The girls nodded and sashayed past, leaving Doc staring after them. "What a lucky mutt. Can't he share?"

"Careful what you wish for," Elowren winked.

"We should do you too," Tel quipped.

Doc plopped back into the recliner. "I better pass."

Chapter 60
Wulvur's Paint

Was it a dream? It had to be. Hands, soft and playful, caressed his body, working stress from his muscles. Wulvur didn't care if he was dreaming or not. This was pure nirvana. Meditation music helped keep him out, while women's giggling taunted his curiosity. He imagined cheery, pretty faces among dim lights and shadows cast from branches. Noise lured him to the waking world, casual voices, muffled music, and distant creaking of tree limbs as nature spoke to gusting wind. He woke to the scenery of flowering vines draped from indoor tree limbs, thicker than the ones in Scruffy's ship. He felt a tickle on his arm and saw vines draped over the blankets and across his arms as if someone had laid them there. Wulvur knew better. These Atlean vines crawled as if sentient. The leaves on his arms looked wilted while flowers turned very slowly, letting withered petals fall to the floor so fresh ones could press against his body. He caught the scent of the old geezer's swampy rum tea.

Scruffy stepped into the doorway, holding a full, steaming mug of his homebrew healing tea. Long slices of leaves were draped over the mug. "You were hard to keep alive."

Wulvur noticed the life support equipment in the room, pushed against the far wall, but the lights indicated it was on standby. Eyeing the heart-starting devices, he sat up. "We're in the Temple?"

"Yeah, your old stomping grounds. How you feeling?"

"Okay, I guess. I had the weirdest dreams of girls with vines, like dryads in the forest."

"Wonder why," the old man smirked. "You've been up a few times, even wandered around the ship, probably too stoned to remember."

"Remember what?"

Scruffy's tired, weathered face lit up as he handed him the mug and rattled off a long list of things they did to him, repeatedly jumpstarting his heart, purging his blood, everything but putting his feet in the stirrups.

"I put your feet in the stirrups," Tel said, walking in.

"Dammit, I missed that?" He gazed at her eyes and noticed in the dim light her pupils took on a feline shape, a new attribute that matched her somewhat sharper incisors, and more pointy fingernails. "Crap, you finally did your first big morph, huh? I knew you'd turn into a cat."

"More like a butt-kicking tigress," she gloated.

"I wanted to see that." Wulvur rubbed his eyes, trying to work the sleep out of them. "It's dark in here. You can turn the lights up. Hey, what is it with girls and cats? Why not a dog or a fox?"

"Maybe that can be my next form, but if you must know," she leaned close, morphed just enough to make her face change and sprout soft fur to tickle him with. She dragged her raspy tongue up his throat to his cheek.

Chills ran through him.

Telari drew back and smiled. "Raspy tongue."

Wulvur sat straight up and started babbling, "Oooh, raspy...."

"Get up, or you'll miss breakfast." Tel sauntered out.

Wulvur regained his composure and eyed his friends, who stared at him, snickering. "What? It's not that funny."

Others were moving about when Gus spied the ladies sitting in the breakfast nook, sharing ice cream and a pot of coffee, all chatting and giggling. Giving them a sideways look, he kept going until he found Slade. "Cap. We got problems. The girls are running in a pack now. We're outnumbered."

"Coming from someone with three morpher girlfriends," Slade pointed out, "and how many new piercings?"

Gus covered his chest with his hands. "A few," he confessed, hurrying off.

Slade chuckled and knocked on the door to Zared's room. "Amateur." When Zared opened the door, Slade said, "Come on, let's tell them."

Wulvur's yelp carried down the hallways. "What the crap." Wulvur sent the blankets tumbling to the floor as he clambered off the bed and grabbed the nearest robe. He couldn't get it on fast enough to keep all the medics, patients, and Slade from seeing artwork of bright flowery vines painted down his arms and chest. Scruffy took one look at him and bent over, laughing.

Wulvur's voice carried throughout the Temple, "TELARI-I-I! You PAINTED me?"

Tel sang back, "I had help."

Wulvur looked down at what were slippers at first glance, but they turned out to be bunny slippers painted on his bare feet, complete with white, glittery nail polish on his fingernails and toes. The more he looked, the more he saw. With great trepidation, he picked up the little mirror that Tel had left behind and saw neon streaks in his hair. "Those girls. Where are they?"

Wulvur stormed out of the medbay through a chorus of whistles and catcalls, and into the lounge area adjacent to the dining room. He looked down at his elaborate body paint, seeing a glaring picture of a cartoon Huvcycle across his chest, straddled by a big, hairy rider. He tried to rub it away, to no avail. It wouldn't even smear.

"Yeah, I posed for that," Shocks said.

Wulvur tried with all his might to look angry, but he couldn't help but laugh. He strutted over to the table where those notorious women sat. "You kinky, freaky, heathens."

"I told them you'd table dance," Tel said through her giggling.

"Crazy women, gimme that." Wulvur snatched the half-empty carton of ice cream and shoved his way into a seat. He heaved a long sigh as he snagged a spoon. "Did I score?"

"We pimped you," Kestral said.

Jasko was twisting around to pull a ribbon off his lashing tail. The other men in the room started checking themselves over, Berku finding a heart stuck to his sleeve and Shanto entered to show off a bat painted on his sling.

Wulvur eyed the girls with a twisted smirk. "Please tell me these aren't tattoos."

"They're just body paint," Elowren said, patting his back.

"Edible," Tel added.

Wulvur dropped the spoon.

Slade and Zared joined them, now wearing their official jackets. Slade wore a dark green greatcoat, with regal trim and the distinguished emblems of Prime Ambassador on his epaulets. The ladies stopped hassling Wulvur to stare at Slade in his regal attire.

"Whaddya say?" Slade asked.

"We're about to ask you the same thing," Kestral replied.

Zared strolled up next to Slade and gave them part two of the shock, for he was wearing Slade's old flight jacket with the Druwen rank just over the badge with the merged planets. The two stood there casually, trying to look innocent as one by one, the others took notice and drew closer, not sure who would ask first.

Berku broke the silence. "This is real?"

"Of course it is," Zared replied. "The councils gave Slade a huge promotion for halting the battle of the clans."

Slade tried not to sound too amused as he elaborated, "All I did was yell at everyone and happened to have a bunch of gunships to enforce it. In the Council's infinite wisdom, they promoted me to High Chancellor. They gave Zared my old jobs of Druwen and Consult."

As the news sank in, different waves of emotion washed across their faces. A few of them looked at Elowren, who shrugged, keeping a straight face. The group started congratulating him while Zared tried to smooth over any hints of disappointment.

"Now, now, I'm not so bad to work for," Zared started.

"It's not like that," Berku cut in. "We'll look out for ya."

"Think you can handle them?" Slade asked.

"Sure."

The group still studied Slade and Zared with hints of scrutiny and disbelief. They closed in around Zared, and the flow of congratulations shifted to a mass of enthusiastic requests.

"A jungle gym and pet beds," Tel said.

"A giant scratching post," Jasko called out.

Slade started to walk away, chuckling.

Zared whipped off the flight jacket. "Here. Take it back!"

Slade waited for the clamor to calm down before he confessed, "Well, they did promote me, but I abdicated. It *really* pissed them off. When I accepted, my condition was that Zared's my right-hand man, and then I quit. So Zared's High Ambassador, and I get to keep being prime Druwen and Consult." Slade hugged his jacket and returned the longer coat to his exasperated friend. "Congrats, old chap. You like tea parties anyway."

"They're not tea parties," came the indignant reply.

"They serve tea, don't they?" Slade goaded.

Zared took the greatcoat and swung it over his shoulders. "Sometimes."

Slade clapped his hands together. "So, go and enjoy your shore leave, because soon as one of those birds is fixed, we're going fishing."

His crew cheered in pure exuberance.

Chapter 61
Venamir's Interrogation

Slade and Berku made weekly visits to the Cave of Comas, where their prized captive was all but driving the interrogators to drink. The last set of guards opened the door to a small habitat of meager comforts.

"Looks like the Council's about to throw you back into limbo," Berku stated.

"We're tired of coming here," Slade added. "Well, Venamir? Anything useful to say?"

Venamir regarded them with weary scorn. "I'm not Venamir. I'm Doctor Cruen."

Slade scoffed, "You're not that kind of insane. You're just power crazy."

"I hold the psyche of myself and Cru. I never knew that Moradin conspired against me, but Cru did. I hold much of his medical knowledge, and he gained my newest morpher form."

Slade leaned back in his chair. "That's the craziest story you've ever told. The possibility of such a deep mental trade lives only in myth and legends."

Venamir slapped his webbed hands on his knees. "I'm trying to explain something, you piteous mongrel."

"Now, you sound normal."

"Doctor Cruentin and I shared a deep psy consciousness at a near death level. He may have stolen many of my secrets, but that also left his mind completely defenseless, so I learned the secrets he kept from me, and much of his medical knowledge."

"So now you're Venamir."

"It doesn't matter which one I am!" Venamir snapped. "Listen, Mori thought you had abandoned her when we reported her dead. We put her in stasis. Later, Deeps revived Mori and rebuilt her, so truly, her death was no lie. I kept her because we needed her."

"Why'd you need her?"

"She was an emissary between us and the Rezoans. Yes, my insiders made the *Spectre* crash and arranged for the blame to fall upon you. I never expected you to spend decades wrestling to find the truth." Venamir began to laugh.

Slade barreled over the table at Venamir while Berku took his sweet time breaking it up. Berku pulled Slade out of the cell, leaving the chuckling Merfin.

When they were clear of the interrogation level, Berku patted his brother on the back. "Calm down, Brothah. Maybe this can work in our favor. It's happened before, the strongest telepaths merging their psy to gain each other's powers."

"Legends and myths," Slade countered in pure sarcasm. "That's just what we need, two psycho cases who think they're both Venamir and Doctor Cruentin."

"Yeah, but Venamir's so crazy, it just might be true."

* * *

The darkest homes in the ocean gave the Deeps their name. Very few species could survive, much less build a hidden oasis miles beneath the ocean surface. Here, the most loyal of Venamir's followers gathered to hide their leader, who still promised them a future of greatness. The problem was, the followers only found Doctor Cruentin, who sometimes behaved as Venamir.

As weeks scrolled by, Dr. Cruen soaked up his new lifestyle, migrating with a colony of Deeps, scientists, where ocean delicacies were plentiful and he could recover from time in prison. How he'd longed to find a resort like this, to forget about life without a bodyguard or a shrink tailing him. The Deeps assigned therapists and medics to Cruen, all eager to study a truly split personality.

The bravest therapist visited Cruen's lab again, where he followed the sounds of snarls and bashing. The lab was orderly and well used, tables full of notes, serums, and holograms of DNA simulations floating across the room.

In the next room, an amphibian humanoid was busy slashing through training dummies, sending mangled parts flying atop a smattering of demolished punching bags. The creature's tail lashed with fervor as it smashed through the training dummy's legs.

"Hello, shrink," the creature said, changing back into Doctor Cruentin.

"Ready for lunch, Cruen?"

"I'm Venamir."

They headed out of the living quarters, with the therapist starting the same old lecture. "You need to purge Venamir's memories from your head."

Cruen heaved a long sigh as he glared at the Deeps psychologist. "Give it up, Doctor Pteram."

They hopped into one of many transparent bubbles with chairs that conformed to lower bodies for ultimate comfort. Pteram touched one of the few controls on his chair and their bubble-pod cruised through an elaborate maze of air-breathing tubes linked to many habitats, all far beneath the ocean's surface. Though they were too deep for sunlight, there was soft light all around them. Each transport tube had glowing tracks inside, which flexed with the gently moving water. Each solid section of the colony cast its own unique colors and silhouettes, lit by orbs or florescent plants. They passed a marketplace where a handful of small subs were moored. This was one of the larger habitats, where huge windows revealed a marketplace of endless sorts, from food to historical artifacts to techno gadgets. Nearly all the people here were Merfins, plus some Rezoans, a small assortment of humanoids, and even a few humans.

Cruen remained silent as they docked and entered a dining facility. Around them, tranquil music played in a diverse eatery with foods from many worlds. They followed the delicate scent of raw fish to a cafe busy with Merfins eating while lounging in clam-shaped pools. Tunnels linked other habitats together, all submerged within the safety of a city that slowly cruised across the ocean floor.

"You could retire here," Pteram went on. "With so much of Venamir's knowledge in your head along with your surgical skills, we need you. Very few of us have survived such a deep psy meld as you have."

Cruen felt a surge of distrust. "You mean I'm just your best lab rat right now."

"That's the Venamir in you talking," the therapist said.

Cruen rubbed his eyes. He knew he struggled to retain his own personality, while growing more suspicious of others, more scornful of lesser races, new traits he blew off as Venamir's flaws.

Or were they? He smiled at the shrink, a smile like Venamir wore just before doing something wicked. "I've been having these dreams about when Venamir was Druwen, way back when Slade was our friend, or so I thought. That'd drive most people crazy, but now, I'm in my best mindset ever. I'm a Druwen, Inquisitor, and surgeon. I'm not giving up these new abilities. The old Venamir's been going crazy for decades. He started a civil war. He needed to be knocked down."

"The tribes were building up to it over the past century."

"True, but we pushed them over the edge. How many died so he could prove it was going to, anyway? That's crazy." Cruen swung an arm upwards. "Go up there in the burning sunlight. You should be analyzing Venamir, not me."

"So you want to rescue him?"

"No," Cruen replied.

The therapist's eyes narrowed. "Why not?"

"Not yet," Cruen tried to smooth over. "Look, I have much of him in my head, yes. I need time to adjust to it, so I can use his knowledge, his talents, for our people. Whatever state he's in, he also needs time to sort himself out."

Uncomfortable silence fell over them as they finished their lunch before the plates of tentacles stopped wiggling on beds of kelp.

"How long?" the therapist asked at length.

"I'll know." Cruen rose and strolled over to a decorative mirror along the wall. He'd been practicing until it came easy, his new, powerful, reptilian shape, a shape identical to Venamir's strongest form. It was also quite efficient at taking on Venamir's exact appearance, a trick that served him well when dealing with any followers who challenged him.

Pteram left the table, muttering, "There he goes again."

Cruen gloated after him, "I am Venamir, only better. The morphers shall answer to me. We will discard the humans and seek out useful allies."

Special Thanks

Special thanks to friends who helped this story, my first novel, through its long evolution. I hope to give my readers an enjoyable tale which includes love for nature and animals. My editors shared exceptional time and feedback, especially Andrea Roth, Cathy McGreevy, and Tony Marcolongo. Also, my gratitude to Sharon S Darrow, author/publisher and kitten rescuer extraodinaire.

About the Author

Roberta "Berta" Davis has always been a fan of sci-fi/fantasy stories as well as classical literature and mythology. Most of her career was in aviation maintenance. She was in the Air Force as a crew chief for twenty years, traveled worldwide as reservist and civilian, and was a historian for the last two years, to retire as a Master Sergeant. She now works as a tech writer by day, sci-fi by night.

She is published in anthologies from her current and former writers clubs, predominantly with a series of feral cat stories starring a black cat named Nacht. *Morphers and Mayhem* is her first novel, with more stories in work. Roberta is a steadfast supporter of animal and wildlife rescue. She has four cats and cares for a small feral cat colony. Roberta hopes to use her experience in aviation and the magic of science fiction and fantasy to tell exciting, fulfilling tales. Her goals are to expand her published works as a freelance writer/graphic designer and, hopefully, an animal behaviorist who specializes in cats.

www.ingramcontent.com/pod-product-compliance
Lightning Source LLC
Chambersburg PA
CBHW072014020726